D0051136

Seduction Becomes Her

Also by Shirlee Busbee

Scandal Becomes Her

Seduction Becomes Her

SHIRLEE BUSBEE

CARLSBAD CITY LIBRARY
CARLSBAD, CA 92011
DISCARD

ZEBRA BOOKS
KENSINGTON PUBLISHING CORP.
http://www.kensingtonbooks.com

BUSBEE, S.

ZEBRA BOOKS are published by

Kensington Publishing Corp.
850 Third Avenue
New York, NY 10022

Copyright © 2008 by Shirlee Busbee

All rights reserved. No part of this book may be reproduced in any form or by any means without the prior written consent of the Publisher, excepting brief quotes used in reviews.

All Kensington titles, imprints and distributed lines are available at special quantity discounts for bulk purchases for sales promotion, premiums, fund-raising, educational or institutional use.

Special book excerpts or customized printings can also be created to fit specific needs. For details, write or phone the office of the Kensington Special Sales Manager: Kensington Publishing Corp., 850 Third Avenue, New York, NY 10022. Attn. Special Sales Department. Phone: 1-800-221-2647.

Zebra and the Z logo Reg. U.S. Pat. & TM Off.

ISBN-13: 978-0-8217-8026-8
ISBN-10: 0-8217-8026-3

First Zebra Trade Paperback Printing: July 2008
10 9 8 7 6 5 4 3 2 1

Printed in the United States of America

DEC - 3 2008

*Craig Egan, my youngest brother, who shares with me a
trait we both inherited from our mom—
the love of animals, especially* dogs.

And

*Heidi Edwards, for being instrumental in seeing to it that
the last book actually got to the publisher and
for being ever ready to hold my hand in connection with
all things computerized! Thank you.
And of course!
Howard, the love of my life . . . still.*

Chapter 1

"Do you think that he's alive?" Charles asked, staring down at the leaping flames on the hearth.

At Charles's question, his cousin Julian, Lord Wyndham, looked up sharply from the snifters of brandy he had been pouring for them. He knew immediately the identity of the 'he.' Raoul Weston, Charles's younger half brother. The Monster. Dead now for nearly two and a half years.

Handing Charles one of the snifters, Julian said, "We both fired our pistols at him, and our aim was true. He took two bullets in the chest. We both saw them strike, and we both saw the blood as it gushed from him. I do not believe that he could have lived, as grievously wounded as he was."

Charles flashed him a twisted smile. "But we found no body, did we?"

Julian made a face. "That's true, and I'll grant you that he may have lived for a short while—long enough to crawl away and hide from us, but I'm convinced that he's dead." He seated himself in a chair covered in fine Spanish leather not far from the fire. Quietly, he said, "Since that night, Nell has had no more nightmares of him, and that more than anything else convinces me that he is dead."

Charles nodded more to himself than to Julian, his thoughts on that terrible spring night over two years ago. Much had happened since then, and little of it had been pleasant. Not only had he discovered that night that his brother hated him and had planned to kill him in order to inherit Stonegate, but also that Raoul was a vicious killer of innocent women. My own brother! A monster! He took a breath. *Half* brother, he reminded himself painfully, remembering the way Raoul had flung those words at him. But Raoul's had not been the only blood spilt that night, Charles thought wearily. No. Raoul's mother, my stepmother, Sofia, had died, too. By my hand, Charles admitted, taking a long swallow of the brandy. I shot Sofia where she stood, and may God forgive me, in the same circumstances, I would do it again. For a moment, the ugly memories crowded close, and despite the warmth of the fire, he shivered.

Outside in the darkness of a November night, the wind whistled and shrieked around the stout walls of the house. The wind was brutal, knifing like a blade through any man or beast unlucky enough to be abroad at this hour, but inside the elegant library of Wyndham Manor, there was only warmth and welcome, and Charles was glad of it. Memories of that night would not let him rest, and they cut as fiercely through him as the wind outside sliced through any living creature. He tried to shrug the memories aside, gazing around the room, appreciative of the soft yellow light from dozens of candles that spilled through the handsome space, their bright glow driving away, for a brief moment, the darkness in his soul.

"Do you doubt that he is dead?" Julian asked with a lifted brow.

"I would have liked to find his body," Charles replied, taking another swallow of brandy.

"I repeat, we both saw his wounds. He could not have lived."

"Then why, when we looked in that cavern beneath the dungeon, did we not find his body?"

"Because he was bloody clever and found a crevice to hide in and die," Julian snapped, not liking to be reminded of that horrifying night—a night that he had nearly lost his wife, Nell, and their unborn child. Tiredly, Julian ran his hand through his thick black hair. "I would have preferred to have found his corpse, I cannot deny it, but we did not, despite an extensive search by half the men in the area. There were any number of fissures and cracks where his body could have lodged. We did not find him, but that does not mean that he is not dead."

Charles nodded. Logic told him that this was so, but like the pain of a wound, doubt ached within him. With an effort, he shook off his bleak mood. Flashing that particularly charming smile of his, he murmured, "We brushed through the whole affair rather well, didn't we?"

Julian nodded. "Lord, yes. Nell was safe, the baby unharmed, and that story you concocted about a madman kidnapping her and Sofia was brilliant. I was, I'll confess, left breathless by your idea of having our mythical villain kill both Raoul and his mother before slipping away down the sluice hole. Very clever of you. Raoul died a hero, supposedly helping us rescue Nell and Sofia, and it was a tragedy that Raoul and his mother died in the ensuing fight. The whole tale answered every question and allowed us to enlist the help of others to look for Raoul's body and, ah, the madman."

Charles took another swallow of his brandy. "And allowed me to inherit both my stepmother's fortune and Raoul's." His voice was bitter and full of disgust.

Julian looked at him. "Does it bother you? To have gained through their deaths?"

Charles shrugged. "Sometimes. Often." His jaw clenched, and he stared at the amber liquid in his snifter. "I loathed her . . . I dreamed often of the day that I would finally be free of her, and Stonegate would, not just in name, be well and truly mine and yet . . . ."

"A case of 'be careful what you wish for?' " Julian asked gently.

"Exactly! I got what I wanted, and more besides when you consider their fortunes, hers mainly, and yet I find that what I once longed for gives me little, if any, pleasure."

"Not even Stonegate? It was yours, though she ruled it. Sofia may have lavished her money on it and imposed her will over the place, but after your brother's death and that of his son, Stonegate was always your birthright."

"So it was," Charles muttered. "But by the manner of her death, Sofia has managed, even from the grave, to taint it for me. I can never quite forget that it was my bullet that killed her."

"And thank God you did kill her—there's no telling what she would have done if you had not fired. Never forget—she *knew* what her cursed son did down there, and if she could have killed all three of us, she would have. Never, *ever* forget that or that she knew of the innocents Raoul tortured and murdered down there for *years*, and yet she kept silent." Julian's voice hardened. "She helped him kidnap Nell, and do not doubt for a moment that she would have helped him kill her . . . and my unborn child. Only your bullet saved us all."

Walking over to the mahogany sideboard, Charles helped himself to another snifter of brandy. Glancing over his shoulder, he quirked an eyebrow at Julian. Julian shook his head.

His snifter refilled, Charles came back to stand by the fire, one arm resting carelessly along the marble mantle as he stared once more down at the fire.

Julian studied him, this cousin to whom once he had been so close before a nearly impassable chasm had opened between them. But that, thank God, Julian thought gratefully, had been mended at last.

Like Julian, Charles was tall and muscular with the same unruly black hair and green eyes so prevalent amongst the Weston family. Both men had the same harsh features, though Charles might have been considered the more handsome of the two. The resemblance between the two cousins was even more striking than usual—their fathers had been twins, and while physically, they could almost have been twins themselves, their personalities were very different. Charles had always been the more reckless of the two, and there was a coldness, a hardness within him that Julian lacked.

Of course, Julian admitted to himself, if he had been raised by a witch of a stepmother like Sofia Weston, who knew how he would have turned out. Nor had it helped that Charles's father had nearly bankrupted the family with his gambling and wild ways. Only his marriage to Sofia and her great fortune had prevented Harlan Weston from bringing his family to utter ruin. And after Harlan had died, Sofia had never let Charles forget for even a moment that it was *her* money that kept Stonegate running so impeccably. There was no denying that Charles's life under Sofia's thumb had been grim, Julian conceded, or that the last few years had not been difficult for him.

Even with the careful version that they had fed the neighborhood and the members of the ton, there had still been a few whispers and raised eyebrows. Charles's feelings about his stepmother had not been a secret, although he seldom said anything, and as was murmured by the most spiteful, her death and Raoul's was so very *convenient* for Charles.

Before the silence between the two men became uncomfortable, Julian said briskly, "Enough of this wallowing in the past. It is over and done with, and we both have much to be grateful for. Tell me, have you given up traipsing from one end of the British Isles to the other for the time being? Will you be spending the winter at Stonegate?"

"Perhaps. Not to dwell on unpleasant memories, but Stonegate is full of ghosts for me, and I do not think that I would enjoy being locked inside those walls with the wraiths of Sofia and Raoul for company."

"What you need," Julian said with a smile in his eyes, "is a wife. And children. They would drive out any spirits unwise enough to linger in your hallways—believe me, I speak from experience."

To give credence to his words, the door to the library opened, and a toddler with a mop of black hair and the Weston family features scampered inside the room. The child, a boy of perhaps two, was garbed for bed, and from his furtive manner, it was clear he had escaped from the watchful eye of his nursemaid. Spying Julian, he shrieked with joy and his white nightshirt flapping behind him, flung himself across the room in his direction.

"Papa! Papa!" cried the child. "I looked and looked for you!"

Julian had barely enough time to deposit his snifter on a nearby table before his lap was full of squirming child. "And you, my boy, have completely forgotten your manners. Come now, Adam, will you not say hello to your cousin?"

There was no real censure in Julian's voice, in fact just the opposite, the love and pride he felt in his son obvious. It was obvious, too, that Julian's household was absurdly informal for someone of his rank and stature. Charles could not think of another member of society who would allow even the heir such freedom. He grinned, liking the picture of the fashionable Earl of Wyndham as an indulgent father.

At Julian's words, Adam rested his head confidingly on his father's chest and glanced over at Charles. "Hullo," he said with a smile.

"Hello, brat," Charles returned equitably, smiling. "You've grown since the last time I saw you."

"Mama says I shall be taller than papa," Adam replied with simple pride.

"If you live that long," said a laughing female voice from the doorway. Tall and slender, her tawny hair caught up in a chignon at the back of her neck and her high-waisted gown of dark green bombazine flaring gently about her ankles as she moved forward, the Countess of Wyndham walked into the room. Smiling at Charles, she came up to him and kissed him on the cheek. "It is good to see you," she said, her sea green eyes full of affection. "Will you remain for dinner?"

Charles shook his head. "No, I only wanted to call to let you know that I was at Stonegate . . . at least for a week or two."

Nell's smile faltered. She searched his face. "Stonegate is your home. Do not let the ghosts drive you away."

"Ghosts!" squealed Adam with big eyes. "Can I see one?"

"And what do you know of ghosts?" asked his mother sternly. "Who has been telling you tales?"

Adam shot Julian a guilty glance and then dropped his head. "N-n-no one."

Julian's face wore the exact same guilty expression, and Nell burst out laughing. Shaking her head, she sent them both a look in which exasperation and love were mixed. "I see that I shall have to remind someone of proper stories for tender minds."

Julian cleared his throat and asked hastily, "The twins? Are they waiting for me?" He glanced at Charles. "Wouldn't you like to see my lovely daughters before they go to bed?"

Viewing six-month-old twin infants had never occurred to Charles as something that he would have *liked* to do, but the appeal in Julian's look was plain. Rising to the occasion, he put down his snifter and murmured, "I knew there was some urgent reason that I came to call at just this hour. Lead on."

Not the least fooled, Nell shook her head and said, "That won't be necessary—they're already asleep, and Nanny will scold if you wake them." Holding out a commanding hand for Adam, she added, "Come. Bed for you. And Nanny is going to be very unhappy with you for slipping away like that."

Taking Adam's hand, she smiled at Charles and said, "We've missed you. Will you come to dine on Wednesday next?" Her eyes danced. "Since it is your ardent desire, you may view the twins then."

Charles's lips twitched, but he bowed and murmured, "It will be my pleasure."

Once Nell and Adam had left, aware of the passing time . . .

and the icy ride home, Charles said, "I must be going. I did not mean to linger so long."

"Are you sure that you will not stay for dinner? It would please Nell."

Charles shook his head. "No, I am invited for Wednesday next, remember? I shall see you then."

The ride to Stonegate was every bit as cold and miserable as Charles had imagined, and when the flickering lights of the torches burning on either side of the massive double doors of the imposing mansion came into view, he breathed a sigh of relief. It might be full of ghosts, but at least it offered shelter.

Entering the house, the home of the first Earls of Wyndham before Wyndham Manor had been built several decades later, he was met by his butler, Garthwaite. Shrugging out of his dripping, many-caped greatcoat, Charles waved away the offer of a meal in the dining room—the same dining room, he thought sourly, where Julian had killed Lord Tynedale in a duel that still caused tongues to wag. What a night *that* had been! Asking only that some bread and cheese be sent up to his rooms, he crossed the grand hallway and mounted the stairs. Upstairs, in the suite of rooms that had once belonged to his father and his stepmother, Charles allowed his valet, Bledsoe, to remove his jacket and boots before dismissing him.

One of the first things Charles had done after Sofia's death had been to obliterate all signs of her hand in these rooms. He had left untouched her décor in the rest of the house . . . well, except for that ridiculous silver epergne in the dining room, but he could not bear the idea of sleeping amidst the cold white and silver scheme she had favored for the rooms she had once shared with his father. As Master of Stonegate, it had been only right that Charles inhabit these rooms, and he'd sworn that he would not sleep a night in them until they had been completely renovated. Now, with walls of dark amber silk, velvet draperies and bed hangings in a bronze and gold stripe, and a carpet in shades of hunter green, russet, and gold, the rooms were rich and warm and distinctly male.

Slumped before the fire in his bedchamber, Charles stared at the leaping flames as if he could read his future in the dancing depths. Even Garthwaite's tap on the door and his cautious entrance with a tray of bread, cheese, and some sliced roast beef and fruit that Cook had added to tempt Charles's appetite elicited little interest. Having placed the tray on a low mahogany table near Charles's elbow, only Garthwaite's discreet cough made Charles turn his head and look at him.

"Will there be anything else, sir?"

Ignoring the food, Charles glanced across the room to a bombe chest that held a Baccarat decanter and some snifters. "Decanter full?" he asked.

His homely face pained, Garthwaite said, "Indeed, sir, I filled it myself only an hour ago."

"Then that's all. Good night."

Garthwaite hesitated, and Charles sent him a wry look. "You may have known me since the cradle, Garthwaite, but I would suggest that you not try to bully me tonight into going to bed like a good little boy. I haven't been a good anything for decades—and I'm not about to start changing."

"It's not for me," Garthwaite said austerely, "to question your desire to drink yourself into the grave, but I would remind you that you would be doing precisely what Madame would have expected."

Charles gave an ugly bark of laughter. "Point taken. Go to bed. I shall eat some of the damned food, and I promise I shall not drink myself into a stupor . . . tonight."

Satisfied with his efforts, Garthwaite bowed and departed.

Putting a thick slice of pungent yellow cheese on a chunk of bread, Charles bit into it and forced himself to eat, even going so far as to take an apple and eat it once he finished the bread and cheese. His Spartan meal finished and feeling he had satisfied his butler's expectations, he stood up and crossing to the bombe chest, poured himself a large snifter of brandy. Reseating himself before the fire, he once more simply stared at the fire, his thoughts roaming in no particular direction.

The house was quiet except for the sound of the lashing wind and rain outside and inside, the occasional crack and pop of the fire. Charles should have been relaxed, enjoying the comfort of his own home, but he was not. He had not lied to Julian when he had said that the place was full of ghosts. Not only did the ghosts of Raoul and his stepmother haunt its many passages and rooms, but others wandered there, too.

Staring into the fire, he could almost conjure up the face of his older brother, John, dead for well over a decade, glimpsing briefly in the flickering flames John's easy smile, the steady gaze of the green eyes so like his own. John had been the conscience, the mainstay of the family. Everyone, even Harlan, their father, had looked to John for guidance. Charles lifted a toast to his brother's ghost. You were the best of us, he thought sadly. And Raoul killed you. For a moment, black rage roiled up within him, but he ruthlessly tamped it down. John was dead, and so was Raoul. And thank God, he thought, that Father had not lived to learn that his youngest son had killed his eldest. John's death had been hard enough on Harlan, and his grieving father's only solace had been the knowledge that one day, John's son, Daniel, would inherit Stonegate.

Charles closed his eyes, pain and disillusionment engulfing him. Daniel's reign as Master of Stonegate had been brutally brief. What? A year? Two? Before his death by his own hand. Introduced to Lord Tynedale, a notorious rake and gambler, by Raoul, Daniel, young and inexperienced, had proved to be easy prey for Tynedale. In a matter of months, Daniel had gambled away the fortune he had inherited from his mother and committed suicide. Had Raoul known what would be the outcome of introducing Daniel to Tynedale? Or had it just been the devil's own luck, Charles wondered. He took another swallow of his brandy. Something else they would never know the answer to, he decided wearily.

They were all gone now, Harlan, John, Daniel, Raoul and Sofia, and he was the sole survivor, the last one to carry on the line of this branch of the family. And here he sat, alone in a house full of ghosts and questions, full of recriminations and guilt. How could he have lived all those years with Raoul and never seen the evil that lurked behind the careless charm? Never guessed, even for a moment, that a vicious killer inhabited his younger brother's body. *Half* brother, he reminded himself again, throwing his head back and finishing off the brandy. Whatever the relationship, Raoul had died over two years ago. Or had he?

Putting down the empty snifter, he got up from his position near the fire and wandered into the sitting room that adjoined his bedroom. He lit one of the candle sconces on the wall, and a small pool of light pierced the darkness. Crossing the room, he walked to a large desk, and opening the middle drawer, he reached in and pulled out a slip of paper. In the faint light from the wall sconce, he studied the words on the paper. He sighed. They had not changed. Taking the letter back with him into the bedroom, he laid the letter near the tray of food and after refilling his snifter, settled once more before the fire. He sat there for a while before he picked up the letter and began to read.

The letter was from Viscount Trevillyan. Not really a friend of mine, Charles thought, more of an acquaintance, but Trevillyan had been Raoul's closest friend and Raoul had often visited Trevillyan in Cornwall, sometimes spending weeks on end there. After Raoul's death, Charles had maintained a relationship with Trevillyan, as he had with several of Raoul's other companions, hoping that by knowing them, he could learn more of his half brother—learn if others had glimpsed the demon that lurked behind Raoul's smiling façade.

Trevillyan's letter was a polite reply to one Charles had

written him months ago before he had left for another of his aimless travels through the British countryside. With the war with Napoleon still dragging on, the Continent closed to him, Charles had contented himself with visiting Wales, Scotland, and even crossing the Irish sea to wander Ireland. It hadn't mattered much to him where he went, the main point was to be on the move and *not* be at Stonegate.

Charles skimmed over the weeks-old news of London and Trevillyan's return to his country seat, Lanyon Hall, in Cornwall, near Penzance, for the winter months before the Season began again in the spring. From the complaining tone of his letter, Charles gathered that Trevillyan was not one for the quiet of the Cornish countryside in winter—or at any time, if he read correctly between the lines. But it wasn't Trevillyan's complaints about the lack of society and his utter boredom with the running of his own estates that had caught Charles's eye. It was a short paragraph near the end of the letter that had riveted Charles's attention when he had first read it, and as his gaze skimmed over those words again, a faint sick anticipation stirred in his belly. With mounting dread, he read those words again.

> *At least, thank God, there was a break in the boring routine last week. The whole neighborhood is in an uproar. The body of a woman, horribly mutilated, was discovered by one of our local farmers. No one could talk of anything else. Gossip has it that the body of another woman killed, in a similar manner, was found several months ago, but I have not spoken with anyone who could confirm it, so I suspect it is nonsense. The identity of the young woman found last week is still not known, nor as I write this, have the authorities, a group of complacent old men, who do little more than shake their heads and wring their hands, discovered who murdered her. I doubt they ever will.*

Charles read the words several times, wondering at their significance. Could it be mere coincidence? Or was it possible . . . ? He considered where his thoughts were taking him. Did he really believe that Raoul was alive and continuing his horrific deeds in the wilds of Cornwall?

Was it conceivable that his half brother had miraculously survived his terrible wounds and had somehow made his way to Cornwall? But how would he live? *Where* would he live?

Charles frowned. Money. That was the answer. With no other heirs in the offing, he had inherited the bulk of Sofia's fortune, and still stunned by the events of that night, he had not paid any attention to any other bequests made by her in her will. Was it possible that she had anticipated Raoul's eventual exposure and had guessed that there might come a time when he would have to go into hiding and arranged for him to have funds to draw upon? She had been a coldly clever woman, not unintelligent, and she might very well have anticipated not only that the truth about Raoul's activities would come out, but also for a time when she might not be there to protect him. She would have known that if Raoul was exposed as a vicious murderer and on the run or in hiding, he would not have been able to inherit her fortune, nor have access to his own, so it made sense that she would have made other plans . . . .

Charles set the letter down and took another swallow of brandy. He would write his solicitor tomorrow asking for a full accounting of Sofia's various bequests. His gaze slid to the letter.

Picking it up again, he stared at it for several minutes. A cold smile curved his mouth. I wonder, he mused, if Viscount Trevillyan would like a visitor to help break the boredom of winter in Cornwall?

He glanced around the room. There was nothing for him here except ghosts and memories. He might as well be in Cornwall.

For a moment, doubt assailed him. Was he really going to

trek to Cornwall and impose himself upon a man he barely knew? And poke and pry around in God knew what dark crevices, hoping to flush out a murderer who wore the face of his half brother? His half brother everyone assured him was dead?

He picked up his snifter, swirling the last of the brandy around. Well, what the hell else was he going to do? Stay here and live with ghosts and questions and guilt?

No. He would go to Cornwall and inflict himself upon the unsuspecting Lord Trevillyan.

Charles tossed off the last of the brandy. I am, he decided, committed to a fool's quest. And I'm sure that Julian would think me mad. He grinned. Perhaps my cousin is right—I *am* mad.

Chapter 2

I must have been mad, thought Daphne Beaumont, as she stared in the waning light at the dark, forbidding castle towering before them. Not *precisely* a castle, Daphne amended silently, though to be sure it bore no resemblance to the picturesque cottage they'd been expecting. Imagination is a wonderful thing, Daphne admitted. The building showed clear signs of its roots as an ancient Norman keep, but it was obvious that there had been attempts to soften its original bleak design by additions and alterations. Perhaps in daylight, they might find it delightful, Daphne told herself optimistically.

As the minutes passed and they waited uncertainly, there was no sign of life anywhere, no flicker of light in the tall, narrow windows, no sign of smoke from any of the chimneys, no door flung wide to admit them, nothing. Just this towering mass of stone and timber in front of them that looked grimmer and more forbidding by the moment. So grim and forbidding did the place look that Daphne, not a young woman given to fanciful whims, almost expected a witch or a warlock to swoop down from one of the two towers and put a curse on them. She shuddered. What had she let them all in for?

Flanked on one side by her sixteen-year-old sister, April, and on the other, her seventeen-year-old brother, Adrian, she could feel their disappointment and growing apprehension.

And it's up to me, she admitted glumly, to turn this disaster into a victory . . . of some sort.

At twenty-eight, she was the eldest, older than her siblings by more than decade, and since their mother's death eighteen months ago, their father, an impecunious Captain in a Line Regiment, having died five years previously, the head of the family. As guardian of both her siblings, it had been her decision that they shake the sooty air of London from their heels and move to the country. It would be an adventure, she told them. Though they'd traveled the world over following behind their father, they'd never been to Cornwall, and there was nothing to hold them in London.

The small annuity that had allowed them a few elegances of life had died with their mother, and these last months had been difficult. There had been times that Daphne wondered how they would be able to keep the small suite of rooms they rented in an unfashionable, if respectable, part of London. They had no family, at least none that they knew of, to call upon. They were but a short distance away from being penniless, and having been raised as members of the gentry, they had few skills to fall back on to make their way in the world.

Daphne had known that something had to be done, but what? The woman who had come twice a week to clean and cook had been let go within days of the death of their mother. Fortunately, Adrian had been able to finish his last year at Eton, but his horses had been sold almost immediately after their mother's death, and his fencing lessons had quickly ceased as had April's watercolor and dancing lessons. There would be no more trips to Hatchards Book Shop for the latest gothic novel from Minerva Press, and even Miss Kettle, who had been Adrian and April's nursemaid and then later governess–companion, had been forced to find other employment. Losing Ketty had been a wrench, and the day she had left, there had been many tears shed. Nothing, however, seemed to help stem the tide of disappearing money. No matter how thriftily she shopped, no matter how many luxuries they all gave up, each month there was less money than before in the small trust her maternal grandmother had left Daphne. She had been on the point of seeking employment as a seamstress—a notion that would have given her mother strong hysterics if she'd been alive to hear of it and outraged her siblings—when the letter from the solicitor, Mr. Vinton, had arrived.

It had seemed a godsend, a miracle when they had received word that they, her brother actually, had inherited from some unknown distant cousin in Cornwall, not only a baronetcy and could now style himself Sir Adrian, but more importantly, an estate that provided an income. In tones of disbelief, Adrian had read the letter aloud to his openmouthed sisters. While no specific amount was stated, Mr. Vinton wrote that in addition to the monies from the farms that were part of the estate, there was a five-hundred-acre parkland and some orchards that surrounded the main dwelling, Beaumont Place, as well as several outbuildings.

A wry smile curved her lips. Oh, how the three of them had danced madly around in those bleak little London rooms, laughing and crying at that same time. Adrian would have his horses again and a valet, he declared loftily, a teasing gleam in his blue eyes. And April would have her painting and dancing lessons again, perhaps even a real governess. And Daphne? What would she have? Why she would have peace of mind and freedom from worry over how she would pay for the boots that Adrian kept outgrowing, she had said, laughing at Adrian's chagrined expression. She and April had teased Adrian mightily on his new title, calling him *Sir* Adrian so often and with such emphasis that he had ordered them, as the master of the family, to stop immediately, which had sent them into whoops of laughter.

They had been happy. Drunk with joy. And that euphoria had carried them through the busy days of clearing out the rooms they had lived in for the past four years, selling off most of the furniture, keeping only those things they could not bear to part with. A letter to Miss Kettle had been sent, telling her of their good fortune and begging her to join them in Cornwall.

Mr. Vinton had arranged for a sum of money to be deposited in a London bank to cover the cost of their removal to Cornwall. It had seemed a fortune to them.

Adrian insisted that Daphne act as his banker. "I know it's mine, but I'd lief as not be responsible for it, Daff," he exclaimed, his young face earnest. "How often have you claimed that I'd lose my head if it weren't attached to my neck? You hold it. You're the eldest and wisest of us." He'd grinned. "Even if you are female."

With the money from Mr. Vinton, they'd been able to hire a private coach to deliver them and their few belongings to Beaumont Place, and they had left London full of enthusiasm and excitement. Ready for the adventure. Staring at the bleak structure before them, Daphne wondered if perhaps they weren't in for bit more adventure than they planned.

With darkness falling, the driver had been eager to be gone, and with all their worldly goods hastily piled around their feet, he'd remounted the seat of the coach, urged his horses forward, and disappeared into the gloom of twilight. Leaving us, Daphne thought, stranded.

"Didn't Mr. Vinton write that there were some servants that would have the place prepared and waiting for us?" asked April timidly, stepping even closer to Daphne.

Daphne shook herself. "Yes. Yes. That's exactly what he wrote. The house has sat empty for over two years, but he said that our cousin's housekeeper, Mrs. Hutton, and the butler, Mr. Goodson, would have it made comfortable for us and would be willing to stay on until we settled in. He mentioned a few others and hinted that they all might like to stay on, if it suited us and wages and such could be agreed upon."

To add to their misery, a misty rain began to fall, and as one, they gathered their belongings and hurried up the wide steps to huddle under the covered entrance that had been added at a later date.

"If this is an example of the service my cousin's servants provided him," Adrian said bluntly, "I doubt we'll want them to stay on."

"Perhaps not," Daphne agreed, "but right now, I would be delighted to see at least one of them."

In the shadows under the portico, Daphne could barely make out the knocker on the door, but stepping away from her siblings, she grasped the heavy iron piece and rapped it sharply. An echoing boom rang out, and all three took a hasty step back.

"That should rouse someone," Daphne said brightly, praying that she was right.

To her surprise, someone had heard the knock, and a few moments later, one of the huge wooden doors creaked open. Light spilled out from the candle held high in the hand of a rotund little woman garbed in a gray woolen dress.

"Oh, my," exclaimed the newcomer. "You *are* here. I told Goodson that I thought I'd heard the sound of a vehicle, but he would have none of it." A welcoming smile wreathed her plump features. "Oh, dear, my manners! And us wanting to make a good impression. Please, please come in. I am Mrs. Hutton, the housekeeper."

As one, the trio moved inside the house. Once introductions were given, Mrs. Hutton reached for a black velvet pull rope that hung near one of the doors and gave it a smart yank. She smiled at them and said, "Goodson will be right along, and he can take your things up to your rooms."

It took Goodson only a few moments to appear, but it was time enough for Daphne to take in the impressive entry hall in which they stood. A coved ceiling soared overhead, a sienna-veined marble floor lay beneath their feet, and at one end of the room, a wide staircase with steps made of the same marble flowed grandly upward to the floors above them. Oak wainscoting lined the walls, the upper part of which had been sheathed in a figured fabric of russet and gold.

Out of the gloom at the end of the hall, near the staircase, a tall, gray-haired man in black livery appeared. Bustling forward, he quickly introduced himself as Goodson, their butler, apologizing profusely all the while for not having heard their arrival.

His apologies were accepted, and once the niceties were out of the way, Goodson deftly divested the ladies and Adrian of their outer clothing. "Cook has prepared a meal for you," he said. "We did not know what time you would arrive, and Mrs. Hutton thought that for tonight, you would dine more comfortably in the morning room than in the dining room. But if you wish, the dining room can be prepared for you."

"That won't be necessary," replied Daphne, growing more optimistic by the moment. "The morning room will suit us admirably."

When Goodson had disappeared up the stairs with their things, Mrs. Hutton urged them down the hallway. "Cook only prepared a simple meal—a nice oyster stew, a saddle of veal, some fish, boiled potatoes and coddled cauliflower, and peas in cream. Oh, and a sweet or two to round out the cheese and fruit. If you would like something more substantial . . . ."

Thinking of their frugal meals these past months, it sounded like a feast fit for a king, and the Beaumonts were quick to assure her that Cook had done well.

The morning room showed the same elegant décor as the entry hall, with luxurious draperies and jewel-toned rugs, but it was the blissfully warm fire leaping on the stone hearth and the covered dishes of food spread across the oak buffet nearby that caught their attention.

It was a glorious meal, relief making them almost drunk. They'd arrived at their destination, and after a shaky start, all seemed well. They were safely inside out of the growing storm, Mrs. Hutton and Mr. Goodson seemed a competent, likable pair, and their stomachs were full—Cook definitely knew her job.

Seeing Adrian smother a gigantic yawn and recognizing the glazed look in April's eyes, Daphne rose from the table and requested that they be shown to their rooms.

They trooped along behind Goodson's tall form as he took them upstairs and down the murky hallway. Beaumont Place, Daphne soon realized, was much larger than Mr. Vinton's brief letter had led them to believe. The high ceilings, the long shadowy hallways broken only by the candle that Goodson carried seemed to go on forever, and even his lighting of the candles in the gilt wall sconces near the doors of each bedroom did little to pierce the oppressive gloom. All of the bedrooms they were shown were enormous, and though the colors and fabrics varied slightly, each room was furnished similarly. The massive, old-fashioned furniture, heavy dark draperies, and voluminous bed hangings created a melancholy air that not even the fires crackling on the hearths of the fireplaces in each room or the quickly lit candelabra could banish. Daphne was not looking forward to the moment she would be alone in her very own bedroom. She and April had always shared a room, and for all the times I've wished for privacy, she admitted wryly, for tonight at least, I wouldn't be adverse to sharing a room with April again. A look at April's uneasy features told her that her sister wasn't keen on sleeping alone either. If Adrian's expression was anything to go by, he didn't seem overjoyed, either, to be banished to the master suite at the far end of the long, shadowy hallway.

The tour of their bedrooms completed, there was nothing for them to do but to bid Goodson good night. Left alone, the three looked at each other in the dim light.

"It's rather a large place, isn't it?" said April as she glanced around.

"Much larger than I thought it would be," admitted Daphne.

She grinned at Adrian, her hazel eyes dancing. "I am most impressed by your inheritance, Sir Adrian."

He made a face. "It ain't what I was expecting," he confessed. "I thought it'd be a snug little place that would do us just fine." He glanced up and down the long hallway. "Never expected it would be a bloody castle." He looked very young as he stood in front of her. "Daff, how am I to go on?" he blurted out. "I mean, it's a wonderful thing for us, but it's a bit overwhelming, isn't it?"

Daphne took a deep breath. "Indeed it is, and everything seems very strange to us right now. I'm sure that after a night's sleep, we'll get our bearings and in no time, be wondering how we ever lived in those tiny rooms in London."

"I wish we were there right now," muttered April, casting another nervous glance over her shoulder.

"Well, we're not," Daphne said briskly, putting a brave face on for the younger ones. "We're in our new home where we're going to be very happy. And I, for one, am going to bed."

Not giving either one of her siblings a chance to object, she kissed them each warmly and bid them good night and stepping into her bedroom, shut the door firmly behind her.

Exhaustion swept over her. It had been a long, tiring journey—the days passed in the rumbling coach, the nights spent at the various country inns along the way had not been restful—and Daphne was glad to have reached their destination. Beaumont Place was not what they had expected. It was far larger and grander than any of them had envisioned, but that wasn't necessarily a bad thing, she reminded herself as she dragged out a nightgown from her valise that had been placed on the floor at the end of the bed. Mrs. Hutton had suggested sending along one of the kitchen maids to unpack and act as her maid, but Daphne had declined. She'd never had her own maid and didn't feel the need of one.

It didn't take her long to get ready for bed, and despite the fire, there was a distinct chill in the room. After blowing out the candle on the stand near her bed, she climbed into the big, curtain-hung bed. Slipping beneath the covers, a happy sigh escaped her. Mrs. Hutton had seen to it that the sheets had been warmed, and Daphne nearly purred as the warmth crept along her body.

She had been certain that she would fall asleep the moment her head hit the down-filled pillows, but such was not the case. She was oddly restless, and after tossing and turning for a few moments, she plumped the pillows behind her back and sat up, pulling the quilts and blankets up around her chin. She was, she admitted, a bit uneasy in these unfamiliar surroundings and found herself wishing again for April's company.

The misty rain had become a full-fledged storm, the rain clawing at the windows, the wind howling and shrieking around the house, causing unnatural creaks and groans to rend the air. With only the light of the dying fire to see by, the room seemed even more cavernous and intimidating. Shadows lurked in the corners, the purple damask bed curtains seemed to hover like a great beast over her, and even the heavy furniture suddenly looked ominous and threatening. Daphne shivered, imagining the vague forms of demons dancing in the dim light.

She made a face. What a pea-goose she was! There was nothing to be afraid of, the surroundings were strange, it was true, but there was nothing to fear.

Despite her brave thoughts, a knock on the door made her jump and surprised a small gasp from her. Embarrassed by her reaction, she called out with only the faintest quaver in her voice, "Yes, who is it?"

"April," came the muffled reply from the other side of the door. "May I come in?"

"Of course," Daphne said with relief, lighting the candle beside her bed.

Garbed in a pale pink robe and her nightgown, April hurried into Daphne's bedroom. Her curly blond locks falling over her shoulders, she scampered to Daphne's bedside. "Oh, Daffy, I feel such a ninny, but please, may I sleep with you tonight?" She cast a nervous look around. "Everything is so strange and with the storm . . . ." She turned big, pleading eyes on her older sister. "I know it is foolish of me, but I'm frightened . . . and it would be just for tonight."

Daphne smiled and flipped back the covers of the bed. "Considering the storm and the size of this place, I don't blame you for feeling frightened. Come along, poppet; hop beneath the covers before any more heat leaves."

April shed her robe and a moment later, was snuggled next to Daphne. Her head resting against Daphne's shoulder, she said, "Oh, Daffy, this is so much better. I'm not afraid anymore." She angled her face toward her sister. "Weren't you frightened at all?"

Daphne made a face, honesty compelling her to say, "Perhaps a trifle. It *is* rather a large place, isn't it?"

"Oh, I know. Who would have ever expected us to live in such a grand house? With a butler and a housekeeper, and who knows how many other servants? I'm sure it will take me a week to find my way about. Sir Huxley must have been very wealthy.

"More wealthy than any of us expected," Daphne admitted.

"Well, I'm sorry that he died, but isn't it wonderful that Adrian inherited from him?" She waved an arm about. "Why, our entire place in London would fit into this very room." She giggled. "With space left over for a ballroom, I wouldn't doubt."

"Indeed, it is wonderful," Daphne agreed. Thoughtfully, she added, "It may seem very grand to us, but I believe that Sir Huxley's fortune is comfortable rather than grand—at least that's what Mr. Vinton's letter implied."

"I don't care—it all seems magnificent to me."

A gust of wind slammed against the house, rattling the windows so fiercely that Daphne feared they would shatter. A rap on the door followed immediately, and April started and clutched frantically at Daphne.

"Who can that be?" April cried, her expression terrified.

"I suspect that our caller is none other than our brother," Daphne said.

"Adrian?" squeaked April. "What can he want at this hour?"

"Probably the same thing that you did—company on a stormy night in a strange house."

That was, indeed, what Adrian wanted when he entered the room at Daphne's command. He was wearing a dark blue woolen robe and carrying an armful of pillows and blankets. His expression sheepish, he walked toward the bed. Spying April beside Daphne, he grinned and said, "Oho! I see that I am not the only one who finds this place daunting."

"I think we are all a little overwhelmed by the size of it," Daphne said. Nodding to the blankets and pillows in his arms, she added with a twinkle, "Am I to understand that you intend to camp out in my bedroom tonight?"

He flushed. "I thought I could make a bed on the floor and sleep by the fire . . . if you didn't mind."

Once Adrian had made his bed on the floor to his satisfaction, he wrapped a thick quilt around his body and lay down a few feet from the glowing embers on the hearth. Propping himself up on one elbow, he looked across at Daphne and April. "Now this," he said, "is much better. That vast room of mine is drafty, the fireplace smokes, and with this devilish storm howling about, I'll not deny it—it was downright offputting. I swear, Daffy, I expected any minute to see the ghost of old Sir Huxley rise up out of the shadows and come after me."

April sat up and looked across Daphne at her brother on the floor. "Do you think," she asked in a voice full of ghoulish interest, "that Sir Huxley's ghost haunts the house?"

"There are no such things as ghosts," Daphne said firmly.

"Oh," April replied, her disappointment clear. "Well, if

there were such things as ghosts, I think a ghost would be a fine thing to have, and this place would be perfect for one."

"If you feel that way," taunted her brother, "what are you doing in here? If you wanted to see a ghost, you should have stayed in your own room. Everyone knows," he said, "that ghosts are particularly fond of haunting innocent young maidens . . . *especially* on stormy nights like tonight."

April eyed him with suspicion. She glanced at Daphne. "Is that true?"

Daphne shook her head. "No. And I repeat—there are no such things as ghosts."

Adrian opened his mouth, but Daphne said, "And that's enough about ghosts." Shaking a finger at Adrian, she added, "If you continue, I shall banish you to your own bedroom."

He grinned at her and lay down. Yawning, he said, "G'night. I'll be up at first light and gone back to my room when you awake."

True to his word, when Daphne awoke, Adrian was gone, and when the two ladies arrived in the morning room, they discovered him already there. The oak buffet was again covered with trays and plates of food—kidneys, rashers of bacon, thick slices of country ham, warm crusty rolls, eggs, and fruit. Adrian dug into the food like a starving wolf.

Which was just as well, thought Daphne, watching him return to the sideboard for a third time. At seventeen, he was still slim as a reed, but his shoulders had broadened this past year, and even without his boots, he stood over six feet. She suspected that he was not through growing yet, either. Their father had been a very tall man, and Adrian looked to have inherited his father's height along with the Captain's thick black hair and brilliant blue eyes. Daphne did not consider herself prejudiced, but she rather thought that her brother was going to grow up to be a very handsome man, and now with a respectable fortune behind him, he would have a wide array of eminently suitable young ladies from which to choose his bride.

Her fond gaze fell upon April, who was nibbling on a roll spread with strawberry jam. If Adrian took after their father, April was the image of her mother, possessing the same gorgeous mane of wheat-fair hair, limpid blue eyes, and dainty frame. Daphne had always hoped that April's gentle nature and fair loveliness would enable her to make a decent match, but now with Adrian's unexpected inheritance and his promise to settle a sum on his little sister, her sights had been raised. In due time, April would have a season in London . . . Daphne's cheeks pinkened with delight as she pictured her younger sister snaring a wealthy, perhaps even titled suitor.

That her thoughts were more those of a mother with a son and daughter to settle than those of an older sister with her own future to consider did not enter Daphne's mind. With her father often gone and her mother unable to cope with military life, Daphne had been the mainstay of the family, taking on responsibility for the small household from an early age. Her mother had always been sickly, and when her siblings had arrived, Daphne had effortlessly filled in the breach and taken over the care of the younger ones. There hadn't ever been any question of her having a London season, and even the idea of marriage had only crossed her mind once. When she was eighteen, there had been a young Lieutenant who had been most particular in his attentions, and for a little while, she had dreamed of marriage, a husband and a home on her own. Unfortunately, before they could marry, the Lieutenant had been killed in one of those nameless little skirmishes in India, and that had put paid to Daphne's romantic dreams.

It never occurred to Daphne to resent the fact that her life had been sacrificed for her family—in fact, she would have been quite indignant at that notion and would have scoffed at the use of the word sacrifice. She was perfectly happy in the role she had been given and was content to live out her days as a beloved spinster sister and later, a doting aunt to the many nephews and nieces she was sure would follow. After all, she reminded herself from time to time, she had no fortune, although if Sir Huxley's estate proved large enough, Adrian was determined to settle a sum on her as well as on his younger sister. April's gentle loveliness alone would insure that she made a decent match—at least Daphne had hoped so, but she had long ago faced the reality that she certainly wasn't the beauty that April was. Not for her, the glorious fair hair, dreamy blue eyes, and delicate frame. No, it had been her luck to take after their father, and while there had been a time she had despaired of her height and boyish body, she had years ago accepted the fact that she would never be a beauty. She was a beanpole topped by an unruly mass of black hair, and that was that. Sometimes, though, when she looked in the mirror at her hazel eyes and olive skin, inherited, she was told, from her paternal grandfather, she'd wished, just for a moment, for April's pretty pink and gold coloring. But then some family crisis would distract her, and she'd put aside her foolish longings.

All of her dreams and energies these days were focused on establishing her brother and sister. Adrian's windfall had opened all sorts of new doors, and Daphne was dazzled at the future that awaited them.

Daydreaming of April, a vision in muslin and lace, making her debut at Almack's, Daphne was startled when Adrian asked, "How soon are we to see Vinton? Didn't you say that he would come call?"

"Oh, I completely forgot," Daphne said, pouring herself a second cup of coffee. "Goodson handed me a note as I came down the stairs—if it is convenient, Mr. Vinton will drive out from Penzance and meet with us this afternoon."

After Daphne had sent a servant off with an affirmative answer to Mr. Vinton's note, the three siblings spent the morning following Goodson about as he gave them a tour of the house. It seemed to Daphne that they marched up and down stairs and through endless corridors admiring countless elegant rooms. She agreed with April. It was going to take a while to become familiar with the house. Besides Cook, Goodson, and Mrs. Hutton, there seemed to be a bewildering number of staff—scullery maids, footmen, upstairs maids, gardeners, and stablemen.

By the time of the meeting with Mr. Vinton, Daphne's head was whirling. Excited and nervous, she and Adrian were waiting in the library when Goodson ushered in the solicitor that afternoon at one o'clock.

Mr. Vinton was a middle-aged man with thinning brown hair, ruddy cheeks, and intelligent brown eyes and Daphne liked him on sight. Once the social amenities were complete, seated by the fire, a cup of coffee at his elbow, he set about explaining the full extent of Sir Adrian's inheritance.

The house and servants had given them a clue that Adrian's inheritance was far larger than either had expected, and when Mr. Vinton was done explaining the extent of his wealth, Adrian and Daphne looked at each other stunned. Adrian's fortune was quite, *quite* handsome rather than just merely comfortable, even minus the respectable amount Adrian had decided would be set aside for April and Daphne.

Business taken care of, the conversation became more general, Daphne and Adrian both very curious about their benefactor, Sir Huxley.

"We had never heard of him until my brother received your letter—in fact, we believed we were the last of our family. The relationship must be quite distant," Daphne said as she poured Mr. Vinton another cup of coffee from an elegant silver coffeepot.

Mr. Vinton nodded. "I believe that you shared a great-great-great grandfather with Sir Huxley." He hesitated, then added, "Sir Huxley died over two years ago, and I should tell you that the estate was in the process of being awarded to someone else, another distant relative of yours, a neighbor, in fact. If I hadn't happened to come across a reference to your branch of the family in Sir Huxley's papers . . . ." He cleared his throat and looked uncomfortable. "Viscount Trevillyan, after years of believing that he was the heir, was not best pleased, I can tell you, and when he learned that he was *not* the heir . . . . Most unpleasant."

Adrian frowned. "A viscount? Why would he care about a mere baronetcy?"

"It's true the baronetcy meant nothing to him—his branch of the family was awarded the viscountcy and took the name Trevillyan decades ago for exemplary service to the king," admitted Mr. Vinton, "but the loss of the lands, farms, and income . . . well, that was another story."

"Lord Trevillyan is our neighbor?" Daphne asked.

"Yes—in fact, your land splits his estate into two pieces." Mr. Vinton tugged on his ear. "The majority of the Trevillyan lands lie to the east, but there are several hundred acres that his grandfather acquired that run along part of your west boundary. Lord Trevillyan had been looking forward to consolidating his lands—it has long annoyed him that he has no way of reaching his western property without traveling the long way around the estate. There had been, ah, some sharp words exchanged between Sir Huxley and Trevillyan in the past, especially when Trevillyan's cattle have been driven right through the middle of Sir Huxley's land. Naturally, Trevillyan had been delighted that the problem would be solved when he inherited. And of course, the loss of the fortune . . . ."

"But I am the heir, correct?" asked Adrian anxiously, his bright future disappearing before his eyes.

"Oh, yes, no question of that. Lord Trevillyan's claim was through your great-great grandfather's younger brother. Legend has it that there was some sort of falling out in the family, and your great-great grandfather departed from Beaumont Place, vowing never to return. It was only when I discovered a letter from a common acquaintance of Sir Huxley and your father's, informing Sir Huxley of Captain Beaumont's death, that I learned that there might be other family members with a closer claim to the estate. It took me several months to discover that Captain Beaumont had left behind a family and that you were living in London."

"I suppose this Viscount Trevillyan does not feel very kindly toward my brother," Daphne said.

Mr. Vinton looked even more uncomfortable. "I had hoped that his disappointment would wane in time, but I fear you are correct. He will not be your friend." He fussed with his cup. "There have been some incidents . . . minor infractions . . . and I have been forced to speak to him about it."

Adrian and Daphne mulled this over, looking uneasy. Mr. Vinton smiled kindly at Adrian. "Do not let Lord Trevillyan's displeasure destroy your pleasure. You are a very lucky young man. You have a fine estate and a fortune to enjoy."

Daphne shook off her unease and leaning forward, asked, "Could you please tell us something about the house? It appears very old."

"Yes, that's true. It was originally a Norman keep. Of course, there have been many additions over the years and alterations, but in portions of it, you will still see original stone walls of the early structure." His eyes twinkled. "Like many ancient buildings, it is rumored to have its share of resident ghosts."

Adrian's blue eyes lit up. "Ghosts!" He glanced triumphantly at Daphne. "By Jupiter! I was not so wrong last night."

They conversed for several more minutes before Mr. Vinton took his leave. After Mr. Vinton departed, despite the news that Adrian was the possessor of a fortune beyond their wildest dreams, the shadow of Viscount Trevillyan hung over them. Not even a second visit to the stables to look again at the impressive array of blooded stock, along with various carts, gigs, and coaches that now belonged to Adrian, could banish it.

In the deepening twilight, their cloaks wrapped tightly around them, they walked slowly back toward the house.

"Viscount Trevillyan will not harm us, will he?" asked April, who had learned of the viscount's thwarted plans from Adrian.

"I'm sure he'd like to murder me," Adrian muttered.

Daphne shot him a sharp look. "Lord Trevillyan may be disappointed that he did not inherit, but he is, no doubt, a gentleman—and not given to such bloodthirsty notions. You are being melodramatic."

Adrian hunched a shoulder. "Well, if you find my blood-drenched corpse lying in a ditch, do not say I did not warn you."

By the time they had eaten dinner in the handsome dining room and retired to the front saloon, their natural high spirits had returned—after all, there *was* a fortune at their disposal. They spent an enjoyable evening mulling over the prospect of some new purchases—coats by Stultz and a curly-brimmed hat for Adrian; India muslin gowns and a sable-lined cloak and muff for April; for Daphne, some new gowns to be sure but also a mohair shawl and a fringed silk turban.

It was a merry trio who eventually made their way upstairs to their bedrooms that night. With no storm howling about and already feeling more comfortable in the house, they each sought their rooms with confidence.

Grateful again for the warmed sheets, Daphne nestled under the heavy pile of covers. Feeling less a stranger tonight, she fell deeply asleep.

She woke hours later, freezing with cold—even beneath the bank of blankets. The fire had been reduced to a few orange and yellow embers that blinked on the hearth, and like a living thing, the darkness of the room seemed to press down on her. She pulled the blankets tighter around her to no avail, the cold so intense she shivered violently. Teeth chattering, she sat up, intending to throw the last few pieces of wood on the fire, when she became aware that she was no longer alone in the room. In that same moment, she knew intuitively that it was not April or Adrian who was crooning softly in the darkness beyond the bed. Terror flooded her as she realized that the sound, half sigh, half moan, came from no living being.

Someone, *something* was in the room with her . . . .

Chapter 3

Her heart beating so hard and fast she feared it would leap out of her chest, Daphne exploded from the bed, grabbing for the heavy brass candlestick that sat on the stand near the bed. It wasn't much of weapon, but it was the only object near at hand. She looked toward the source of the sound, and to her horror, amidst the shadows, there was now a wavering white mist in the middle of the room.

In a hard voice at odds with the terror that engulfed her, she said, "Whoever you are, I order you to leave this instant! Now!"

Abruptly, the odd noise stopped, and the mist appeared to recoil on itself at the sound of her voice.

Her hand tightened on the brass candlestick, and Daphne took a step forward. To her surprise, the mist retreated slightly. Her initial terror ebbing and common sense and curiosity coming to the forefront, she took another step, pleased when the mist retreated again. Emboldened by her success she pointed a finger at the mist and said, "Begone! You are not wanted here."

To her astonishment and very great relief, the misty area in front of her vanished. She sensed movement near the far wall, but when she glanced in that direction, her eyes could not pierce the deep darkness that lay between her and whatever had been in her room.

With the presence gone, she was conscious that the bone-freezing cold was also gone. The room was chilly, but it was just the natural chill one would expect and not the numbing iciness that had plagued her only a moment previously.

Which is all well and good, Daphne thought as she scurried to the fire, but what the devil had just happened? Reaction set in, and her entire body trembled, her teeth chattering and her hands shaking so badly, it was several seconds before she could get the candles lit. Only when the room was ablaze with light did her body stop shaking and some of her uneasiness flee. She threw more wood on the fire and pulled on her heavy, dark green woolen robe.

She stayed near the fire, her gaze fixed on the spot on the far wall where she had last seen . . . no, sensed the apparition. It took more courage than she knew she possessed to cross the room and examine that particular section of wall. Holding a candle in one hand, she studied the wall. At first glance, the wall seemed like any other, but as she stared, she noticed in the midst of the Chinese-printed wallpaper, a faint hairline crack . . . a hairline crack, that as her fingers slowly traced it, revealed what might have been the outline of a door . . . . Her heart began to pound, and her breath caught.

Stop it! she ordered herself. There is nothing, absolutely nothing, sinister about this. The house is old, centuries old—perhaps, there was a doorway here at one time—it could have led to another bedroom or a sitting room, and it means nothing. Absolutely nothing. She swallowed. *I hope.*

Sleep was impossible. She sat in a chair by the fire and either stared at the flames or at the section of wall with its faint outline of a doorway. I did not, she told herself repeatedly, see a ghost. I do not believe in ghosts. Whatever I *thought* I saw was caused by the unfamiliarity of the room, tiredness . . . or it was simply my imagination. There are any number of logical reasons for what I thought I saw and heard. There was nothing really in the room with me. I could not have heard that queer warble, or whatever it was, and I could not have seen a ghost—it was a trick of my mind.

And if you believe that so strongly, purred a sly voice in her brain, why won't you get into your bed and go back to sleep?

She took in a deep, shaky breath. Because, she admitted grimly, I do not want to go to sleep and awake to find *it* crooning gibberish next to my bed. I know that it was my imagination . . . . Yes, it must have been my imagination—I am not given to hysterical fancies, she reminded herself stoutly. So it had to have been her imagination. She was over-tired and sleeping in unfamiliar surroundings, surroundings that certainly lent themselves to odd sightings, and her imagination had run rampant—that had to be the explanation. Yet, despite all her rational arguments, Daphne couldn't shake the certainty that she had heard that soft crying in the darkness and that she had seen *something*. She bit her lip. There had been something there, something that had reacted to her voice and actions. She shivered. She wanted what had occurred to be easily explained away, but she couldn't forget the way the thing had recoiled when she stepped toward it, nor how the singsong sound had stopped so abruptly at her command.

She wrapped her robe tighter around her, wishing for daylight. She looked at the ormolu clock ticking on the mantle. 4:00 A.M. Shortly, the servants would be tiptoeing around the house, completing their early morning chores. Soon enough, one would be coming into her room with hot water and a tea tray . . . . She closed her aching eyes, suppressing a yawn. She should crawl into bed so that nothing would seem amiss, not that anything was amiss.

If the servant who crept into the room later that morning with the big pewter tray was surprised to find Miss asleep in a chair by the fire, she gave no sign. She quietly went about her business and in a few minutes, her chores done, slipped from the room, shutting the door behind her.

It was the sound of the shutting door that woke Daphne. She jerked upright with a small, startled shriek, then felt enormously silly when she realized what had woken her.

Daphne wasted little time on her morning ablutions, and half an hour later, she startled Goodson in the morning room where he was just beginning to set up for breakfast.

"Oh, Miss! I did not expect you at this hour," he exclaimed. "It will only take me a moment to finish here, and I shall let Cook know that you are eager for your breakfast. We shall have something for you to eat in no time at all. Will the others be joining you?"

Daphne gave him a wane smile and seating herself in one of the chintz-covered chairs by a window that overlooked the side garden, said, "No, my brother and sister are still fast asleep in their beds. I am the only early riser this morning. A cup of hot tea and some toast will suit me fine."

At this time of year, the garden was not in its finest flush, and Daphne was surprised to see red geraniums and white camellias blooming against the soft green foliage of the boxwood hedge that enclosed this section. Dew kissed the shrubbery, and though the hour was early, the sun was already transforming the dew into diamond dust wherever it touched.

Once he'd seen to her needs, Goodson went back to his regular routine. Sipping the hot brew, Daphne stared out the window. She'd hoped that in the light of day, she'd be able to totally dismiss the odd occurrence of last night, but such was not the case. If anything, the conviction that she had seen something extraordinary in her bedroom last night grew. She sighed, wishing that she had someone older, wiser, and more knowledgeable than herself with whom she could discuss what had happened. Telling Adrian or April was out of the question. Adrian would think it a capital adventure and be raring to sit up every night, hoping for another visitation, and April would be starting and shrieking at every sound. No. She couldn't tell her siblings. Mr. Vinton? She flushed. And have him thinking that Adrian's guardian was a silly, hysterical female? No.

Daphne had never felt so isolated in her life, and until this very moment, she hadn't realized just exactly how very alone she and her two siblings were. They had no one except them-selves to rely upon, and it was up to her to keep the little family safe—which meant she dare not let anyone know what she had seen . . . or thought she'd seen. The last thing she needed was for some busybody to start wondering if she was an addlebrained female and questioning her ability to care for Adrian and April.

And not to be ignored was her brother's sudden elevation to a title and fortune, especially the fortune. Adrian's un-expected and very large fortune created problems all its own. She didn't doubt that there would be others, unscrupulous, greedy others, who would be delighted to have control of it until he reached his majority. If it was suspected, even for a moment, that his guardian, his eldest sister, was seeing things . . . ghosts . . . . She sat up straighter. Well, that wasn't going to happen. As an unmarried woman, her sole guardian-ship of her siblings was unusual enough, and she certainly was not going to give anyone a reason to challenge it.

But I just can't pretend it never happened. I know I saw and heard something. Surely, she thought, there is someone who might be able to help me. Her gaze fell upon Goodson as he moved about the room, fussing first with the table set-tings and then fiddling with the glassware. She took another sip of her tea, considering the butler. She'd gathered that Goodson and Mrs. Hutton, along with most of the servants, had served Sir Huxley for some time—they'd be familiar with the house. They might know stories . . . . She made a face. Gossiping with the servants wouldn't have been her first choice but . . . .

"Were you with Sir Huxley long?" she asked suddenly.

Goodson glanced over his shoulder at her and smiled. "In-deed, yes. I have been in service to the family since I was a youth, and my father and grandfather and beyond all served the Beaumonts. 'Tis the same with Mrs. Hutton and Cook. You'll find that most of our families have a long history of service and loyalty to the family."

"Ah, then you must be very familiar with the house and its history," she said brightly.

"Oh, yes." He shook his head in fond remembrance. "I grew up here, as did several others who now serve you." He smiled. "Since our parents worked here, we were constantly underfoot. When we could escape the eyes of the adults, we spent hours climbing around the battlements, exploring the old passageways and even the dungeons built during Norman times."

"I imagine with a house this old that there are all sorts of stories and legends associated with it," Daphne commented. "Tales of spectral sightings and ghostly shrieks in the night must abound."

Goodson gave her a thoughtful look, and Daphne's fingers tightened on the fragile handle of the cup she held. Had she given herself away? Was Goodson thinking that she was acting peculiar?

"Yes, there are several legends connected to the house," Goodson admitted slowly, his dark eyes still fixed on her face, "but I do not hold with such nonsense." To Daphne's relief, his gaze dropped to the glass he was polishing, and he continued, "It is true that some of the early Beaumonts were, ah, inclined to violence, but that was in a less civilized age. There are, I regret to say, a few distasteful stories . . . or legends, if you will, that have survived to this day." He added disapprovingly, "And *some* people, and ones who ought to know better, I might add, have no business repeating them merely to frighten children and awe impressionable youths."

"Deplorable," Daphne said properly, wondering how she was going to discover the names of those people. Perhaps, Mrs. Hutton . . . .

It was late afternoon before Daphne had a chance to arrange a meeting with Mrs. Hutton. They met in a cozy room near the rear of the house that Daphne had decided would make an excellent office. Seated behind a dainty cherrywood desk, she was ostensibly going over the menus for the next week, but she dealt with them quickly, hardly looking at them.

"We have only been here a few days, but I can see already that the servants of Beaumont Place are well-trained," Daphne said with a smile as she handed the menus back to Mrs. Hutton. "Your staff has done an excellent job of making us comfortable and of seeing to our needs—no mean feat when suddenly saddled with a trio of strangers."

Mrs. Hutton flushed with gratification. "Thank you, Miss! We all hoped that you and your sister and Sir Adrian would be happy here."

"I think that there is no question about that," Daphne replied, thinking of the cramped rooms in London and the nights she'd lain awake worrying about how far she could stretch the pitiful amount of money she had at hand.

"Well, then if that is all, I shall take these to Cook immediately," Mrs. Hutton said, waving the menus in the air. "She is delighted to be actually cooking again . . . Sir Huxley's appetite was so poor those last months that he subsisted on little more than broth and bread, and then, of course, the house sat empty for all that time."

"After Sir Huxley's death, the house was vacated?" Daphne asked, interested.

Mrs. Hutton shook her head. "Not exactly. We periodically aired and dusted, and the gardeners kept the grounds in check, but except for the stable hands who stayed with the horses, no one lived here." Her lips tightened. "Lord Trevillyan told us even before Sir Huxley's burial that we'd be turned off with little more than a recommendation once the estate was his." She sniffed. "He made no bones about it—he already had a fine home of his own and servants aplenty and no need of another house in the area or more staff." She looked outraged. "He was going to abandon the house, just let the place fall into rack and ruin. Shameful, I call it—a fine house like Beaumont Place. Why Sir Huxley would have turned over in his grave."

"As long as they do their job, no one needs to be worried about being turned off," Daphne said mildly. "Sir Adrian has no plans to change anything at this time. He has been very satisfied with the way Beaumont Place is run." And as long as Cook continues to ply him with goose and turkey pie, Daphne thought wryly, he wouldn't care if Beaumont Place came tumbling down around his ears.

"Oh, Miss, that is so good to hear! It has been very difficult for many that used to work here these past few years. Sir Huxley made appropriate bequests for most of us, but without continued employment, it's been hard for some. We were overjoyed when Mr. Vinton told us about the discovery of the new heir."

Not meeting Mrs. Hutton's eyes, Daphne fiddled with a knob on one of the drawers of the desk. "Er, I was wondering," she began, "do you know who I should speak to if I wanted to learn to more about the history of the family and Beaumont Place?" She laughed nervously. "Until we received Mr. Vinton's letter, we didn't even know of its existence or of Sir Huxley. We have much to learn."

Mrs. Hutton beamed at her. "Sir Huxley's mother was an avid historian—I believe that there is a collection of letters and such that she gathered together. They're in the library. Goodson would know exactly where they are kept."

While she was glad, on one hand, to learn of the collection, Daphne's heart sank at the idea of wading through decades, centuries even, of what she was certain would mostly be useless information. The collection would comprise predominately letters between loving parents and their offspring, polite notes from friends and relatives, and perhaps, if she was lucky, to liven the boring process, a spicy missive between lovers. Most likely, she thought glumly, it would take her weeks, months of reading about the daily happenings of the Beaumont family before she came across any reference of spectral doings, if at all.

"I shall certainly look forward to seeing it," Daphne murmured, "but I was wondering if there was anyone who might be able to give me a broad, um, overview of the history of family."

Mrs. Hutton nodded. "Vicar Henley is just the person you should see. Collecting the history of the area and the various families who live here is his hobby."

Daphne nibbled her lower lip, thinking hard. Meeting Vicar Henley would be useful, but somehow, she didn't think that a man of the cloth would spare much time for tales of ghosts and the like.

"I shall certainly talk to him," Daphne said, "but is there no one else who . . . ." She looked away from Mrs. Hutton's birdlike gaze and feeling her cheeks burn, muttered, "Someone who knows some of the less, ah, polite stories of the area."

Mrs. Hutton stared at her. "Has someone been gossiping to you about that unfortunate murdered woman?"

Daphne shook her head, her eyes widening. "What woman?"

Mrs. Hutton's lips pursed. "I'm not one to gossip, but shortly before you arrived here, there was an awful murder— a young woman. No one knows who she was, poor little thing, and it was a pauper's grave for her." With relish, she added, "They say that her body was mangled like a wild beast had attacked it. One of your tenants, Farmer Brierly, found the body, and since his wife is a bosom friend of mine, we naturally discussed it."

"Naturally," said Daphne in a hollow voice, repelled and yet wanting to hear more. "Did they ever discover who killed her?"

Mrs. Hutton shook her head. "No, despite Squire Renwick's best efforts, no one has ever been brought to justice."

Deciding she'd heard enough and that her ghostly visitor was enough for her to deal with right now, Daphne confessed, "Uh, that wasn't exactly what I was after. I was hoping for some, er, stories passed down from generation to generation."

Mrs. Hutton chuckled. "Oh, if it's tales and legends and the like that you're after, then you need to talk to Goodson's sister, Anne Darby—our local witch."

Daphne looked taken aback. "Goodson's sister is a witch?"

Mrs. Hutton nodded, smiling. "Indeed, yes—much to his mortification. She lives in small cottage on the outskirts of Penzance. Her husband died years ago, leaving her with three daughters to raise, and she had no choice but to make her living selling potions and telling fortunes. I don't believe half the stories about her and the dark arts—I grew up with Anne and have always thought that she had a good heart."

Reassured by Mrs. Hutton's assessment, Daphne asked, "And she knows the, er, legends about Beaumont Place?"

"Everyone in these parts knows the legends," Mrs. Hutton said complacently. "We grew up on them, but if you want someone to tell you a tale to make your hair rise off the back of your neck, then Annie's the one to see." She looked vexed. "But you'll have to wait to see her—she's gone to visit her youngest daughter who lives in Polperro, further up the coast. Agnes is expecting her first child and wanted her mother with her. I believe that Anne will be back sometime after the first of the year."

Daphne's spirits plummeted. The first of the year might as well be a decade away as far as she was concerned. It looked as if she was going to have to make do with the vicar and the collection in the library. But then something Mrs. Hutton had said caught her attention. "You said everyone knows the stories. Do you?"

"Well, to be sure, but it's been years since I've paid them any heed." Mrs. Hutton snorted. "The idea of anyone seeing ghostly creatures flitting about or hearing them singing songs in the middle of the night—foolishness, I call it."

"People have claimed to see ghosts in the house?" Daphne asked carelessly, uncertain whether to be glad or upset at that news.

Mrs. Hutton waved a dismissing hand. "There's been some silly housemaids who have claimed to have seen things, and some of the older servants used to tell us children stories of peculiar sightings and sounds. Indeed, even in Sir Huxley's time, there was a young London lady, a nervous sort, I might add, who woke the household, screeching to the skies one night that a ghost was in her room and had touched her face. It was all nonsense, done, I'm sure, to bring attention to her-self—she was visiting with her parents, and there was gossip that Sir Huxley was on the verge of making her an offer. Of course, after that, nothing came of it."

"Of course," Daphne repeated, staring at the gleaming top of the desk. "Well, thank you, Mrs. Hutton. You've been most helpful, and I would appreciate it if you see that none of these, er, stories come to Sir Adrian or my sister's ears. Sir Adrian would think it a May-game but April is quite suscep-tible to just those sorts of tales and I know she would be un-easy." She smiled. "And Sir Adrian would take much delight in teasing her about ghosts and goblins and noises in the night."

"I certainly understand," Mrs. Hutton replied with an an-swering smile. "If that will be all?"

Daphne dismissed her and after Mrs. Hutton had left, sat there and stared at the top of the desk as if the answers she wanted were written there. At least she now knew that Beau-mont Place had a history of ghostly occurrences, she thought wryly, and remembering the scorn in Mrs. Hutton's voice when she'd mentioned the nervous young lady from London, she vowed to keep her mouth shut about anything she *might* have seen.

She glanced out the window, aware that time was fleeing. It was several hours yet before bedtime . . . several hours yet before she had to face another night in that room, and she shivered at the notion of waking to another visitation. She could ask for another room . . . . She grimaced. What reason would she give? It was a perfectly fine room . . . when she had it to herself and wasn't sharing it with a ghost . . . or something. Her jaw set. Besides, she thought, I don't like the idea of being scared away from my very own bedroom.

But she did have some time at her disposal, and so she rang for Goodson and had him show her to the library where the collection of Beaumont memorabilia assembled by Sir Huxley's mother was kept.

The library was an imposing room. Axminster carpets in subdued tones of rose and blue and cream lay upon the gleaming floors, and floor-to-ceiling oak bookcases flanked tall windows with dove gray draperies. The spines of the leather books—blue, green, gold, and red—created a pleasing tapestry wherever the eye fell, and a huge gray-veined marble fireplace dominated one end of the room. Satinwood tables of various sizes and heights had been placed here and there, and chairs and sofas covered in burgundy and sapphire blue velvet were scattered about the room.

Despite its grandeur and size, Daphne felt immediately at home, and she could envision spending many a winter afternoon curled up by the fire reading. The size of the collection dismayed her, however, and staring at shelf upon shelf crammed with the memorabilia of the Beaumont family, lovingly gathered by Sir Huxley's mother, she sighed. It would take her years to go through it.

She glared at the collection for several seconds, and then her shoulders straightened. She might as well get started.

When she joined her siblings for dinner that night, her head was aching, and her eyes burned. Deciphering the intricate script of some of the Beaumonts was a challenge in itself, much less making any sense of what they wrote. After the hours she'd just spent toiling through insipid recitals of parties attended, gowns worn, and the latest *on dit* about people long dead, facing a ghostly presence seemed a welcome respite.

Daphne didn't feel quite so sanguine when she finally closed her bedroom door behind her that night. She lit all the candles in the room and after slipping into her nightgown and putting on her robe, sat by the fire with every intention of remaining on watch the entire night. Despite her resolve, her body betrayed her, and by the time the clock struck midnight, she was asleep in the chair.

She woke just before daylight and after sending a blurry-eyed glance around the room and seeing the guttering candles, decided that no ghosts were coming to call. Throwing her robe on the bed, she crawled beneath the covers and promptly fell asleep.

By the end of the week, there had been no further disturbances, and Daphne decided that perhaps, she had imagined the entire incident. Of course, there were those stories . . . stories that Mrs. Hutton and Goodson dismissed out of hand, and if they didn't give them any heed, then she wouldn't either—for now.

Because she hadn't known where to start in going through the Beaumont papers, she had begun her reading where Sir Huxley's mother had left off some twenty years previously and had been working her way backward. The task hadn't been the ordeal she had assumed it would be and had actually proved enjoyable some of the time, giving her a better insight into the family of which she was a member. But when there were no further disturbances, she wondered at the wisdom of burying herself in the library for hours on end. She had gotten as far as Sir Huxley's grandfather's lifetime and was eager to reach the era when the family had split apart, but there were still some fine days to be enjoyed out of doors, and with no more ghostly visits, she put off further examination. Promising herself that she would return to the letters once winter had fully set in, she set them back on the library shelf.

Daphne and her siblings settled in easily at Beaumont

Place. They quickly adapted to their new life and rarely gave a thought to their former life in London. As the weeks passed, with the exception of Lord Trevillyan, they met the local gentry, several of their neighbors, and all of their various tenants. There was much coming and going between Beaumont Place and Vicar Henley's house, Adrian having struck up a friendship with the two older Henley sons, who were both about his age—Quentin at eighteen, a few months older than Adrian, and Maximillan, just a year younger. April had become fast friends with fifteen-year-old Rebecca Henley, the eldest daughter in the large and sprawling family, and Daphne enjoyed visiting with Mrs. Henley—in her opinion, a most sensible woman. If Mrs. Henley was a sensible woman, Daphne found Vicar Henley, a big, boisterous man, utterly delightful. He had welcomed them warmly into his home and the neighborhood. Sometimes, Daphne felt a trifle guilty at the generosity Vicar Henley had shown since her initial desire to make herself known to the vicar had been to pick his mind about Beaumont Place and any eerie tales he might have heard. She had not expected that a warm relationship would develop between the two families and that she would count the vicar and his wife among her closest friends. When she had hesitantly approached him, the vicar had been eager to relate a few hair-raising stories about Beaumont Place that dated back to the bloody time of the Cromwell's Roundheads and Charles the First. The tales proved to be very exciting and thrilling, but there was nothing in them that Daphne felt shed any light on what she had experienced, although she did perk up when the vicar mentioned legends of hidden staircases and concealed panels . . . . But since the ghost, or whatever, remained silent, she was perfectly happy to push it aside and simply enjoy her new friends and life.

The holidays were a giddy time for the three Beaumonts. For the first time in memory, money was no object, and they spent freely, even a little foolishly, on each other. They entertained their tenants and their families lavishly, as well as their new friends, and threw themselves happily into an orgy of parties and balls and soirees that were held at the various homes in the neighborhood. There were additions to the staff: Adrian's valet was hired, and a pair of lady's maids for Daphne and April.

But best of all had been the arrival of their beloved Ketty on a blustery December night near the end of the year. The moment she had received Daphne's letter, Ketty explained, she had given her notice and made plans to travel to Cornwall. Seeing her small, sturdy frame standing bemused in their elegant entryway brought a lump to Daphne's throat. Still wearing her old brown coat, her ginger-colored hair escaping from beneath the worn felt hat upon her head, and holding her threadbare tan gloves, Miss Ketty stared around her in astonishment.

Miss Ketty's pale blue eyes filled with tears. "The Lord answered my prayers," she said. "I prayed and prayed for my three little birds to be safe and with me again. And look at this wonderful place." She shook her head. "I don't know if I am on my head or my heels!" She glanced at Adrian. "And look at you, *Sir* Adrian, all dressed up like a young lord. Why I could pass you on the street and never recognize my dear little boy. Never in my dreams did I expect such a thing."

"It's no dream, Ketty," exclaimed Adrian with a laugh, and scooping her up, he danced with her in his arms around the entryway. "It's a dashed miracle."

"Now put me down, Sir Adrian. This is no way for a proper young man to act," she scolded, flustered. "Wherever did you learn such manners—certainly not from me!"

Adrian only grinned, but he did set her down. Her feet on the floor again, Miss Ketty looked over at Daphne and April. Her eyes filled with tears again, and she groped for her handkerchief. Her nose buried in it, she cried, "Oh, never did I expect to see my sweet doves again. I worried so about the pair of you, alone in the world, and I was fearful what the future would hold for you."

April ran to her and hugged her. "Dear Ketty, we are so glad that you are here. I have missed you so."

"And I you." Ketty gave a great gusty sigh. "The Lord is good."

"Indeed, He is," Daphne said as she walked up to Ketty and kissed her cheek. Smiling into her worn face, she added, "He brought our own dear, *dear* Miss Ketty back to us."

Miss Kettle's arrival made their transition complete, and by the time late January rolled around, with Miss Ketty firmly settled in the household, scolding and fussing over them, they were comfortable in their new life. Staring out the window of the library one sunny January morning, it seemed to Daphne as if they had always lived at Beaumont Place. The past seemed like a dream, she thought as she sipped a cup of freshly poured tea. No more worries. No more cares.

The day was so fine, in fact, that Daphne gave into Adrian's pleas for a picnic on the beach. In addition to the farms found in the long coombes and valleys that descended from the upper moorland, his estate ran down to the wave-tossed English Channel. The cliff sides leading down to the shore were pocketed with caves and indentations, and they'd already heard stories of smugglers and the like. The beaches were narrow, curving like snakes around the base of the cliffs, their lengths broken here and there by huge rocks and boulders that tumbled into the frothy, turbulent water. It was a wild, dangerous place, yet it held an irresistible appeal.

There was a thin, winding path, more like a goat path, Adrian complained, that led to the beach, but the climb down was worth it. Wearing their oldest clothes, their backs against the rocky cliff, they'd spread a blanket on the ground and enjoyed the feast that Cook had packed for them. As they ate, they'd stared mesmerized by the writhing seas, the bright sunshine making the water gleam and glitter as the waves broke on the shore. Later, they ambled along the rocky beach, exploring and chattering as they went.

They lost all sense of time as their explorations took them further and further along the beach. Coming to a long arm of rocks that stretched out into the water, they clambered over it. Reaching the other side, breathless and laughing, they stopped in surprise at the sight of two men, strangers, standing near the base of the cliffs.

From their clothing, it was obvious that the men were not fishermen or common laborers, and from their expressions, it was equally obvious that they were not pleased to see them. With all the innocence of a friendly puppy, Adrian smiled and walked up to the pair. "Hullo," he said. "I am Sir Adrian Beaumont. May I help you? Are you lost?"

The shorter of the two men raked Adrian with a glance. "No," he said curtly. "But you obviously are. I regret to inform you"—and there was sneer in his voice that made Daphne's hackles rise—"that you are trespassing on my land."

Adrian heard the sneer, too, and his smile faded. "Are you certain?" he asked, determined to be polite. "It is my understanding that all of this is Beaumont land."

"Your understanding is wrong," the man snapped, his dark eyes hard. He pointed to the rocks they had just climbed over. "Beaumont land ends at those rocks. You are on *my* land."

Heedless of propriety, Daphne stepped up beside her brother. "And you are?" she asked bluntly, already having a fair notion of his identity.

He looked her up and down, and Daphne was humiliatingly aware of her old gown and tangled hair. "You must be the sister, the spinster," he said with a dismissive glance.

Daphne's eyes narrowed, and her chin lifted. "Yes, I am his sister, and by your rudeness and arrogance, I must conclude that you are none other than Lord Trevillyan."

"She has you there, Dorian," the other man said, his amusement obvious. Grinning, he added, "Definitely a facer."

Daphne's gaze swung to the taller of the two men. Her nose went up, and she asked haughtily, "And you are?"

He smiled a singularly charming smile. Sweeping off his curly-brimmed hat, he bowed and murmured, "Charles Weston. At your service."

Chapter 4

Daphne's first assessment of Charles Weston was not favorable, and she assumed that he was as rude and arrogant as the viscount—certainly, he was no one that she wanted to know. He was handsome enough in a dark, bold sort of way, but she was not impressed by his easy smile, and those watchful green eyes did nothing to improve her initial opinion of him. But there was something about him . . . something in the wicked curve of that full mouth . . . . A prickle of awareness, some faint stirring of basic female interest in a powerful male, whispered through her. Mentally, she shook herself. Nonsense. She was past all that sort of silliness. Her sole interest these days was the establishment of her brother and sister.

Dismissing Charles Weston with a cool glance, she turned her attention back to the viscount. "We apologize for our mistake," she said stiffly to Lord Trevillyan. "Now that we know the boundary line, you should have no fear that we shall *ever* tread on your property again. Good day."

With a regal nod of her head, she spun around and marched toward the rocks that separated the two properties, April scurrying after her. His young face set, Adrian bowed curtly to the two men and strode after his sisters, his long legs making short work of catching up with them.

Charles watched as they reached the rocks and scrambled

over them, appreciating the way a sudden gust of wind lifted the spinster's skirts, giving him a glimpse of a well-shaped length of calf before she grabbed her dress and clamped it down. Pity—it had been a very nice calf, and he wouldn't have minded seeing more of it . . . and her. In fact, her arrival on the scene gave him hope that his visit to Trevillyan's might not be as dull, dead bodies aside, as it appeared it would be. Only when she disappeared over the mound of boulders did he turn his attention to Lord Trevillyan.

"She was right, you know," Charles said idly. "You were rude and arrogant."

"Oh, what the devil do I care what some upstart old maid thinks?" Trevillyan muttered, his gaze also on the rapidly disappearing trio. "To think that Huxley's fortune went to that boy! A nobody. And that sister of his! Bold as brass. How dare she speak to me in that manner!"

"Well, you weren't very polite to them, were you?"

Trevillyan glared at him. "No, and I don't have to be to a set of mushrooms like that."

Charles shrugged, bored with the subject. He had not been able to keep to his original plan for leaving for Cornwall right after receiving Trevillyan's letter. Julian and Nell had raised a devil of a dust about his sudden plans for departure, and he ended up spending Christmas and Boxing Day with them. He grinned. Quite enjoyably, too, remembering a particularly dashing young widow visiting in the vicinity of Stonegate who had enjoyed his attentions for a few weeks. The holidays behind him, he'd set his sights once more on Cornwall. He'd been Trevillyan's guest for nearly a week now, and he knew all about the Beaumont fortune being snatched out of Trevillyan's hands by some distant cousin no one had ever heard of. When in his cups, which seemed to happen frequently, Trevillyan never tired of repeating how cut up his hopes were and how bloody unfair it was that some social climbing nobody, one who hadn't even known Sir Huxley, had inherited the fortune that should have been his. Since there had been little love lost between Trevillyan and Huxley, Charles rather thought it an amusing little twist of fate that Trevillyan hadn't inherited after all.

Charles turned his eyes to the cliff face they'd been studying before they had been interrupted.

"The last body was found here?" Charles asked, his gaze dropping to a spot Trevillyan had indicated earlier.

"Yes. One of our local smugglers, a fellow by the name of Furness, found her, or what was left of her, a few days before you arrived." Trevillyan frowned. "And I've paid him a dashed fortune to keep his mouth shut. Of course, Squire Renwick had to be told, and our local magistrate, Mr. Houghton. They agreed with me about keeping the business secret. As I wrote you in November, the entire area was in a furor over the previous body, and we thought it best to keep quiet about this one." He sighed. "If it's learned there is another . . . ."

Trevillyan's earlier glee, Charles observed, at the uproar in the neighborhood seemed to have dissipated once a body was found on *his* land. Well, he couldn't blame him for that.

"Hmm. In your letter, you mentioned something about a previous body, an even earlier one, didn't you?"

Trevillyan nodded. "When I first arrived home, I heard some gossip that another woman had been killed—before Farmer Brierly, one of Sir Adrian's tenants, by the way, found the one I wrote you about." He frowned. "I was never able to confirm that one, but if there was another body, then this makes the third in the past five or six months. This sort of violence in our area is unheard of . . . and troublesome."

Charles hadn't learned of this latest body until he'd arrived at Lanyon Hall, Trevillyan's country estate, the previous Wednesday. He'd been impatient to view the site for clues, but today had been the first opportunity for him to inspect the scene.

"Isn't that a cave up there?" he asked, his gaze having stopped at an irregular, yawning hole in the cliff face.

"Yes, it is—one of many. The whole coastline is pockmarked with them," Trevillyan replied. "Part of the allure for smugglers and the like."

"Has anybody examined the interior of the cave?"

Trevillyan shook his head. "No. All I wanted was for the body to be gone and the incident forgotten." When Charles simply looked at him, he muttered, "Squire Renwick and Houghton agreed with me. We didn't want the populace to become hysterical and have pandemonium on our hands. Between us, and well, Furness, we determined that she wasn't a local woman. The Squire, Houghton, and I concluded privately that she was some poor, unfortunate stranger from God knew where and that the sooner she was put underground, the sooner we could put this unpleasant event behind us. The Squire especially felt that the less said about the subject, the better. She was buried that night in the pauper's field."

"And how," Charles asked, having trouble imagining the viscount digging a grave, "did you accomplish that? Wanting as you did to keep it secret?"

"I paid a pair of gravediggers handsomely to do it on the sly," he said. "And the Squire warned them to keep their mouths shut."

"So let me see if I understand you," Charles said. "You, the Squire, the magistrate, this Furness fellow who found her, and the two gravediggers who buried her are all privy to this, er, secret? Is that correct?"

Trevillyan flushed and nodded.

In a silky voice, Charles added, "And now I am added to the list. Are you sure you have not forgotten someone else, such as your valet or butler, perhaps a traveling peddler, who shares this 'secret'? Besides the murderer, of course."

"There's no need to take that tone with me," Trevillyan muttered. "I could do nothing about Furness, and it was my duty to tell the proper authorities! As for the gravediggers, what did you expect us to do—bury her ourselves?"

"I would have," Charles said coolly. "And I wouldn't have

brought in the Squire and the magistrate, especially if I wanted as few people as possible to know about it."

Turning his back on the viscount, Charles scrambled up a sliver of a path that was half hidden by the rocks. It wasn't an arduous climb, and Charles accomplished it easily. The track ended at the cave entrance, and gingerly Charles stepped inside. The cave had little to recommend it. It was dark, dank, and not very big, and within ten feet, ended in a solid rock wall. In the murky light, Charles made a brief examination of the place, but there was no sign that it had ever been used for anything other than perhaps, a handy place to hide some smuggled goods. He hadn't expected any less and quickly rejoined Trevillyan on the beach.

"She wasn't killed there," he said. "I suspect she was simply thrown off the top of the cliff, her killer, no doubt, hoping that the tide would take the body out in the Channel where it might never have been found . . . and if found, any damage could be blamed on the water."

Trevillyan looked at the ceaseless waves and shuddered. "A horrible fate."

"But from what you've told me about the condition of the body, none worse than what she suffered before she died."

Trevillyan couldn't argue with that, and the two men began to walk swiftly toward the main path that they had taken down from the top of the cliff. The day was waning, and there were only a few hours of light left, and they had several miles to ride before dark.

They had just reached the base of the path when a frantic voice rang out behind them.

"Lord Trevillyan! Wait! I beg you! We need your help," Adrian shouted as he ran up to them. "It's my sister, Daphne. She has gotten her foot trapped in the rocks in one of the caves we were exploring. April and I cannot free her."

"I hardly see what you expect me to do about it," Trevillyan complained. "But since I am not without a heart," he said reluctantly, "I shall stop by Beaumont Place on my way

home and inform your servants of your dilemma." He sent
Adrian a chilly smile. "I'm sure that your people can effect a
rescue without my help." And turning his back on Adrian, he
continued on his way.

Adrian's face paled with fury, and he lunged for Trevillyan,
murder in his blue eyes. Charles neatly intercepted the boy and
catching him by the shoulders, said softly, "Have done! It is
your sister we must consider at the moment, not your pride."

His eyes locked on Adrian's, Charles called out, "That's an
excellent plan, Trevillyan. Meanwhile, I shall go with Sir
Adrian and see if I can be of assistance."

Trevillyan spun around so fast he nearly fell over. "Have
you gone mad?" he demanded. "It'll be dark in a few hours."

Ignoring him, Charles quietly asked Adrian, "How far away
is she?"

"A-a-about two miles further down the beach past the
rocks," Adrian stammered.

"Not so far," Charles said, more to himself than anyone
else. Glancing at Trevillyan, he said, "We shall leave it in
your capable hands to see to it that Sir Adrian's people bring
some blankets and hot broth and something that we can
fashion into a sling to carry the young woman back to her
home, if need be. Give them the directions to find us." When
Trevillyan simply gawked at him, Charles added, "Run along
now—we haven't much time before dark." He smiled sweetly
at Trevillyan. "Don't worry about me, my lord. I'm sure that
Sir Adrian will find me a place to sleep tonight. I shall see you
sometime tomorrow at Lanyon Hall."

Not waiting for a reply, with a firm hand on Adrian's
upper arm, Charles goose-stepped him away from Trevillyan
and toward the rocks. When he felt it was safe to loosen his
grip on Adrian's arm, he did so.

"Is she hurt?" Charles asked Adrian as they crested the
ridge of the rocks.

Adrian grimaced. "I don't think she's hurt so much as mad
as fire that she got her foot caught in this silly way."

"Have your temper, your sister?"

"Sometimes," Adrian answered with a smile. "But mostly, Daffy is a great gun, and when she does get angry, there's usually a good reason for it."

"Daffy?" Charles asked, a twinkle in his eyes.

Adrian grinned. "Daphne is her proper name, but April and I have always called her Daff or Daffy."

"And April would be your younger sister?"

Unaware that he was being deliberately distracted and pumped for information, Adrian was happy to oblige him. In the face of Trevillyan's callous attitude, Charles's unexpected offer to help had raised him to hero status in Adrian's eyes, and falling under the spell of Charles's careless charm and encouraging manner, Adrian burbled away as if they were old friends. By the time they reached the entrance to the cave and a distraught April, Charles knew a great deal about the new baronet, his family, and of particular interest to Charles, Sir Adrian's eldest sister, Daphne.

Seeing her brother approach, April left her post at the entrance of the cave and threw herself into his arms. "Oh, Adrian! I am so glad you are back." She cast a fearful glance at the sky. "It is getting dark, and I am so afraid. And poor Daffy! She is in there all by herself." She bit back a sob. "She sent me outside to watch for you. She said she was perfectly comfortable and would not let me stay with her."

"That's because she knows you're afraid of the dark, you pea-goose," said her brother impatiently. "Now buck up! Mr. Weston is here, and he will help us. Lord Trevillyan is on his way to the house, and he will be sending the servants here with blankets and whatnot."

April raised glowing eyes to Charles's face. Her hands clasped together against her bosom, she breathed reverently, "You are our hero, sir. We are most grateful."

Charles smiled at her, aware for the first time of how very lovely she was. This one, he decided, was going to set the *ton* on its ear when she made her debut, and he didn't doubt that she would marry well, mayhap even into the peerage, Adrian having filled Charles in on Daphne's hopes for April.

"Let me see what we are up against," he said easily. "Once I have your sister free, then you may call me a hero." Glancing around, he noted the small fire they had lit earlier. "Why don't you gather up more driftwood for the fire? I'm sure your sister will be chilled when we bring her out, and a cozy fire would be just the thing for her."

"Oh! She has a small fire going in the cave. After Adrian left, she had me bring her some driftwood and a few sticks of burning wood from our fire out here to use to start it," April said. "But we will need more"—she glanced at the sun hanging low in the sky—"especially since it will be dark before anyone gets here. A big fire will help them find us sooner. I shall begin immediately."

"Excellent!" Charles said as he and Adrian ducked under the low overhang of the cave and carefully made their way inside.

The cave was huge, and if it was not for the pinprick of flickering light in the distance, pitch black. The cave floor was strewn with boulders and rocks, and their progress was not swift, but scrambling up a mound of boulders that half blocked the area, they soon reached Daphne.

From his perch atop the rocks, Charles glanced down to where she sat awkwardly on the floor of the cave, her right foot buried to above the ankle by several large rocks. Having heard their approach, she looked up, astonishment on her face when she recognized Charles.

The dwindling firelight caressed her strained features, a smudge darkened one cheek, and her hair fell around her shoulders in a tangled cloud of black silk, and as he stared down at her, Charles had the strangest sensation, as if the earth moved beneath his feet. How very, *very* interesting, Charles thought, intrigued by his reaction to her.

Clearly, she felt nothing similar. Staring up at him, she exclaimed in tones of displeasure, "You! What are you doing here?"

"He's come to help us," said Adrian happily as he joined Charles, and the two of them clambered down the other side of the rockfall. "He sent Lord Trevillyan after the servants." Beaming at his sister, he added, "You'll be free and out of here in no time, Daffy. Mr. Weston will see to it."

The worshipping gaze Adrian sent Mr. Weston made Daphne's lips tighten. Seeing her reaction, Charles grinned, and squatting down near her, he murmured, "April and Adrian have already expressed their sincere gratitude for my help, so I'll just take yours as a given."

She took in a deep breath and putting forth a patently false smile, said, "Why, I thank you, too, sir. We are most grateful for your assistance."

Charles almost laughed in her face. For some reason, he appeared to be the last person she wanted to help her, and he found that very interesting, too.

"How badly are you hurt?" he asked, turning his attention to the matter at hand.

"I'm not hurt at all," she said, grateful for the change of subject. "It is just that my wretched foot is firmly caught. Adrian and April tried to move the rocks, but they were not strong enough. The rocks are tightly wedged together."

"Well, let us see what can be done," Charles said, standing upright.

As she had said, the rocks were wedged together, and nothing that he and Adrian did could make them budge. Taking off his jacket in order to have more freedom of movement, Charles placed it around Daphne's shoulders and returned once more to the fray.

The small fire was dying, and with the setting of the sun, even inside the cave the air was cooler, and Daphne was glad of the extra warmth, even if it came from Mr. Weston's jacket. Her own comfort was the least of her worries, though, and she asked, "Is April all right? She doesn't like the dark, you know. Adrian, perhaps you should go to her and see that all is well."

"Do not worry about April," Charles answered when he stopped to catch his breath, having struggled for several minutes with the stubborn rocks. "She is getting more firewood, and I'm sure that she will build up the fire to keep the dark at bay. She seems a sensible young woman."

"Of course she is," Daphne said sharply. "It is just that I worry about her. She is—"

"I think right now, you should be more worried about yourself," Charles interrupted.

What a rude, overbearing man, Daphne thought, deciding that her first assessment of him had been correct. Even if he was handsome as the devil and even if he was helping her, he was still rude. He had no reason, she decided resentfully, to dismiss her worries about her sister that way.

Charles glanced around, not liking the steep angle of rock nor the fact that several more boulders seemed poised to come tumbling down. If there was another slide . . . His lips thinned. There was, he admitted uneasily, the very real possibility that the cave could be blocked . . . with Daphne in danger of being buried beneath the rubble or at the very least, trapped on the other side. With renewed urgency, he attacked the rocks, keeping a wary eye on the boulders above them.

Feeling a slight give of the main rock pinning Daphne's foot, he had a surge of satisfaction, which quickly died as more stones and small boulders dribbled around them. His eyes met Daphne's, the awareness in those big hazel eyes making him realize that she perceived the danger, too. Beautiful and intelligent, too, he thought, his gaze locked on hers.

They exchanged a speaking glance before she said quietly, "Adrian, my fire is running low and likely to go out if I do not have more fuel. Would you please see if April has gathered enough driftwood to spare some for me?"

Adrian hesitated, looking from one adult to the other, perhaps sensing something was in the wind.

"Your sister's suggestion is wise," Charles said. "We do not have any idea how long it will take us to free her—the light from the fire is helpful as well as keeping her from getting chilled." He flashed him a smile. "And your absence will give me a chance to catch my breath."

Beautiful, intelligent, and brave, Charles decided, wondering idly what Julian would make of her. Not that it mattered.

Adrian set his jaw, and Daphne's heart sank. Oh, dear. He was going to be stubborn.

Before she could speak, Charles said gently, "This is no easy task—it's going be a long night. We do need that driftwood."

Adrian nodded and said, "Very well. I shall not be gone but a moment."

Only when her brother was safely out of earshot did Daphne speak. Her voice steady, despite the anxiety Charles glimpsed in her eyes, she said, "Shouldn't you go with him?"

"What? And leave a damsel in distress?" he demanded, a faint smile playing around his mouth. "Now what sort of hero would that make me?"

"A live one," she said tightly.

Several larger rocks suddenly gave way and bounced and rolled to the ground near them.

"More like a live coward," he said. "A role, I must admit, that does not appeal to me."

"This is no time to jest," Daphne said from between gritted teeth. "You know as well as I do that the rest of those rocks could come down at any time. There is no reason for you to stay."

"And I think there is every reason for me to remain," he said calmly.

"Mr. Weston, you must leave. It is not safe," she argued. "You must save yourself or at least wait until we have more help and can perhaps stabilize the rocks."

Ignoring her, Charles studied the boulders one more time,

and his mouth set in a grim line, he tackled the rocks around her foot again. His heart leapt as there was another shift of the rocks that held her fast, and he yelled at Daphne, "Pull! Pull for all you are worth."

She obeyed him, hope springing through her when her foot moved ever so slightly. Bracing her hands on the cave floor, she pulled and twisted her leg, ignoring the pain that shot through her, her pulse jumping when her foot slid another inch toward freedom. She struggled violently for a moment, but her foot was still trapped. "I cannot free it. I am not strong enough." she uttered in disappointment. "The rocks are looser, but not enough."

There was another shower of rocks and boulders, and dust filled the air, leaving both of them coughing. Charles looked back at her. "Go," she said softly. "Go. Save yourself."

"Like bloody hell," he snarled, and his face grim, he put his shoulder against the rock and pushed with every muscle he possessed. There was a grinding sound, more boulders and rocky debris clattered down around them, but Charles felt the rock move, and he shouted, "Try now!"

Tears of frustration running down her cheeks, Daphne pulled and wiggled and fought with every ounce of her being. Exhaustion and fear took its toll—her ankle was bloody and torn, but she still struggled, the smallest movements giving her the hope to keep trying. But it was no use.

"I cannot," she cried out in desperation. "I'm able to move it a little, but not enough. I am not strong enough."

"Yes, you are," he said harshly. "And by God, you are going to pull yourself free." His shoulder against the boulder, he looked back at her. "We'll do it, Daffy. We'll do it. I'll move this bloody rock, and when I do, you pull, damn it, you pull!"

He set his shoulder against the unyielding surface, pushed until his muscles screamed in agony, but the rock moved, and he heard Daphne's triumphant shout when her foot slid free.

A shower of rocks and boulders crashed down, and Charles barely had enough time to jump away before they struck where he had been standing only a moment before.

Breathing heavily, Charles knelt down beside Daphne, wincing when he saw the state of her mangled ankle in the glowing embers of the fire. She looked up at him. "It looks terrible, I know, but nothing is broken except skin." She hesitated. "Thank you. I am most grateful for your efforts on my behalf."

"Can you stand on it?"

"I think so, although it will probably be a little numb at first."

He helped her to her feet and though she flinched when she applied weight to her foot, with Charles's support under her arm, she was able to stand.

She smiled ruefully. "I won't be going exploring any time soon, I can tell you that."

"You were foolhardy to do so today," Charles said bluntly. "We were lucky. This tale could have had a very different ending." As he stared down into her dirt- and tear-stained face, the knowledge that she could have died today, that he might never have had the opportunity to know her terrified him and infuriated him at the same time, all the more so because he couldn't explain his emotions. His hands closed around her shoulders, and he shook her. "Do you realize how easily you could have died?" he growled. "Those rocks could have given way at any time, and not only you but also your brother and sister could have been trapped in here. No one would have known where you were or where to look for you—did you think of that before you had the shatterbrained notion to go exploring by yourselves?"

Any gratitude she felt for his help evaporated, and Daphne drew herself up proudly. "I am sincerely grateful for your help," she said stiffly, "but that doesn't give you the right to rip at me in this fashion. Today's event was unfortunate, I will concede that fact, but it could have happened to anyone, and I don't take kindly to your criticism."

"At the moment, I don't much give a damn what you think," Charles snapped, still gripped by his unexplained emotions.

"Which is just as well," she shot back, the light of battle in her fine eyes, "since I don't give a jot if I ever see or hear from you again. You are the most overbearing, arrogant man I have ever met."

"That I may be, but at least I don't need a keeper—and you sure as the devil do!"

The sounds of approaching voices made them look in that direction. It was then that Daphne noticed how small the opening was that led to the other side of the cave. All the many slides had added to the jumble of rock and boulders, and where before one could scramble through the opening, it now looked too small even for a child to manage. But she wasn't worried, at least not exactly. It was going to take awhile, but the opening could be widened, and now that help had arrived, they'd be out of here in no time. And the sooner she was away from the detestable Mr. Charles Weston, the better.

Adrian's head and shoulders appeared in the opening, his features anxious. Seeing Daphne standing upright, a huge smile broke across his face. "You're free!" he exclaimed. "Mr. Weston freed you!"

"Yes, he did," Daphne said coolly, not at all happy at being indebted to Mr. Weston. "And now all we need is to widen that breach, and I shall be out of here."

"It will not take us long," Adrian said. "A half dozen of our servants have arrived, and they brought broth, bread and cheese, and blankets, and something to fashion a sling—all sorts of things." Awe in his voice, he added, "Lord Trevillyan is here, too. He said since he knew exactly where we were, that it would be best if he led the servants here. Wasn't that nice of him?"

"Yes, it was," Charles agreed. "I assume the servants brought some pickaxes and what have you to dig us out?"

"Yes, yes, they did. We shall start immediately." He grinned at his sister. "We shall have you out of here in no time, Daffy."

Daphne sincerely hoped so. Her foot ached, and despite Mr. Weston's jacket still draped around her shoulders, she was growing chilled and hungry.

Having a good idea of her condition, Charles stepped away from her and called up to Adrian, "This is going to take a while. Before you start, why don't you pass through some blankets and some of the food." He glanced down at the dying fire and added, "And if there's any extra wood, we'll take that, too. I think your sister would be much more comfortable while we wait."

Adrian agreed, and a few minutes later, a heavy quilt, some blankets, a torch, a half dozen large pieces of driftwood, and a basket of crammed with food was lowered down to Charles. In minutes, the fire was burning merrily. Daphne politely returned Charles his jacket, and she was now wrapped in the heavy quilt and feeling almost toasty. The basket contained a bottle of wine, some bread and cheese, and cold chicken and fruit. A simple meal, but as she took a bite of the chicken, Daphne decided she had never tasted anything so heavenly.

Work began on widening the opening, the clank of the pickax against the boulders and rocks ringing through the cave. Charles had lit the torch, and by its light, they watched the progress. The work continued smoothly, and to Daphne, it looked as if the hole had already doubled in size.

With rescue in sight, feeling in charity with him, she smiled at Charles and said, "We shall, indeed, be out of here in no time."

The words no sooner left her mouth then there was an ominous rumble. In horror, she looked up. The entire roof of the cave seemed to implode as huge rocks, boulders, and a shower of dirt came crashing down on them.

Charles leaped forward and grabbed Daphne, dragging her away from the worst of the falling debris. The air was filled with dust, and they both coughed, choking on the fine particles.

The rumble lasted for only a few seconds, and then there was utter silence. Looking upward in the wavering torchlight, Daphne's heart sank right to her toes. There was no sign of any opening at all. Before them lay a solid wall of rock and boulders. Their escape route had been obliterated.

Her eyes full of dismay, she glanced at Charles. He, too, had been studying the rocky wall before them. Feeling her gaze upon him, he looked at her.

Her voice betraying only the faintest quaver, she said, "It looks as if it will take them a trifle longer than we expected to free us."

"Indeed, I fear you are right," he replied slowly, seeing the path that Fate had set before him. They would be lucky, he suspected, if they were rescued by daylight—which meant he would be spending the night alone with Miss Daphne Beaumont. A member of a proud, noble family, Charles knew what honor would expect of him once they were rescued, and he felt not the slightest alarm or consternation. What he did feel was mingled anticipation and amusement as he pictured the expression on Daphne's face when it dawned on her just what the outcome of this night would be. Somehow, he didn't think she was going to be very happy when she realized that in order to avoid a scandal, Society would demand their marriage to each other. He grinned. And it would be his very great pleasure to change her mind. Ah, but he did love a challenge.

Chapter 5

With little conversation between them, Charles and Daphne had spent a not too uncomfortable night sleeping on the cave floor. Daphne was wrapped chastely in the heavy quilt while he made do with the thinner blankets. The basket of food and the torch had been a godsend. The fire had died just before dawn, but he'd saved the torch for just such an occasion, and so they did not have to sit the remaining hours in pitch-black darkness. And when they woke in the morning, there was still some bread and cheese and a few sips of wine left over from the previous night.

Charles's estimation of the time of their rescue had been optimistic. They spent another increasingly uncomfortable and anxious night before their ordeal was over, and it was late in the afternoon of the second day before Adrian and the others finally broke through the tumbled wall of rock and stone. In those long hours before their rescue, there'd been an odd sense of intimacy between them, the gloomy darkness and their uncertain fate forging a bond that Daphne would have said was impossible twenty-four hours previously. Charles's presence gave her comfort, and his cool indifference to their fate encouraged her to act the same and not give way to the hysteria that sometimes choked her. Ignoring the fact that they were virtual strangers, they made a good effort at pretending that their ordeal was a perfectly normal event. They conversed politely with one another—with a bit of formality on Daphne's part and half hidden amusement on Charles's part. In genteel harmony, they shared the remaining food and avoided any discussion of the grim possibility that they both might die in this cold, clammy cave.

When the first spike of light from the other side shone through, Charles rose to his feet where he had been sitting beside Daphne and said, "Well, now, it looks as if our rescuers have made good." In the dim light, he smiled down at Daphne, who was visibly shivering in the heavy quilt. "And not a moment too soon. Another night in here wouldn't have done you any good."

She made a face. "Nor you," she said as she rose to her feet. "I'm sure you are equally as cold and hungry as I am, and as eager to leave this adventure behind you and pretend it never happened."

Charles studied her face for a moment. "Was it so very bad?"

She sighed. "Not as bad as it would have been if I had been in here by myself." Honesty compelled her to add, "You were very gallant to stay with me, and I thank you for that. You will always have my deep gratitude."

Charles started to tell her what she could do with her gratitude when a shout from above distracted him, and he looked in that direction. Adrian's face appeared in the small area they had cleared.

Seeing Charles and Daphne looking up at him, a huge grin split his face. "By Jove, am I happy to see you! Have patience, and you'll be free of this place in no time."

It took a bit longer because of the instability of the jumbled debris that had kept them prisoners on the other side, but eventually, a hole barely large enough for them to crawl through was achieved.

Exhausted, hungry, smudged, scraped, and scratched, they were eventually freed. Over the past two days, word of their dangerous predicament had spread, and as Daphne was escorted into the weak sunlight, she was astonished to discover that it appeared that anyone of any consequence for miles around had gathered at the scene. The vicar, Squire Renwick, Lord Trevillyan, even Mr. Vinton, as well as thirty or forty other people, many of them Beaumont servants, were milling around outside the cave. A great shout went up when Daphne, followed by Charles, stepped out of the mouth of the cave. April, Ketty, Mrs. Hutton, the vicar's wife, and the squire's wife were part of the crowd, and after tearful hugs and joyous exclamations, they hustled Daphne toward one of several big bonfires that had been lit. To protect her from the stiff wind coming off the Channel, Ketty wrapped her in a heavy sable-lined cloak, and Mrs. Henley pressed a mug of hot soup into her hands. Scolding and fussing, Ketty kept touching Daphne's tangled hair as if to reassure herself that she was actually safe, and April clung to Daphne like a limpet, her small body pressed close to Daphne's side. After giving Daphne a fierce hug, Adrian left her to the care of the women and joined the gentlemen gathered around Mr. Weston.

Daphne's eyes followed his path, and Mrs. Henley smiled and said, "That's a fine young man, your brother—no one worked harder than he did to free you." She tapped the cup in Daphne's hand. "You drink that nice, warm barley broth, and don't worry about a thing."

Dutifully, Daphne sipped the rich liquid. "Thank you. It is so very kind of all of you to come to our aid."

"Everyone was frantic," said the squire's wife, patting her on the arm. "Why, I don't believe that there was anyone in the neighborhood that wasn't touched by your plight." A speculative gleam in her eyes, she added, "It can't have been easy for you trapped with that Mr. Weston. A stranger, isn't he?"

Daphne attempted an explanation, but Mrs. Henley waved it aside. "The main thing is that it ended well," she said. "And Mr. Weston may be a stranger to us, but I have it on good authority that his family and breeding are excellent."

She cast a superior glance at the squire's wife. "His cousin is the Earl of Wyndham, a very *old* and respected name. When we realized that dear Miss Beaumont was going to have to spend the night in that horrible cave with the man, my husband naturally made inquiries of Lord Trevillyan."

Daphne looked astonished. "He is related to an earl?"

"Oh, yes, indeed," Mrs. Henley said complacently. "And apparently the possessor of a handsome estate and I might add, fortune. Which if you ask me, is a very good thing under the circumstances."

Mrs. Henley and Mrs. Renwick exchanged glances, Mrs. Renwick repeating, "Yes, a very good thing."

Oblivious to the exchange, Daphne was looking at Mr. Weston with new eyes. The cousin to an earl? A little spurt of excitement went through her. Oh, wouldn't it be wonderful if there was some way that this chance meeting could be turned into an opportunity for the advancement of Adrian and April into the highest ranks of the *ton*? Instantly, she was ashamed of herself and shook her head. She was every bit as bad as the worst matchmaking mama to be found in London. Mr. Weston had been all that was kind, and he had helped her during a dangerous time, had even risked his own life. It was very bad of her to contemplate, even for a moment, using him, or rather his relationship to the earl, for Adrian and April's advancement, even if her motives were driven by love for her sister and brother.

Still watching him, Daphne noted that Mr. Weston was at a second fire, getting much the same treatment from Lord Trevillyan and the other gentlemen that she had received from the women. Across the distance that separated them, their eyes met. In his rumpled and stained clothing, he looked, she thought, much like a ruffian or a bandit—certainly nothing like the cousin to an earl. The thick black hair falling in tousled waves around his face and his cheeks and chin shadowed by two day's growth of whiskers only added to the image of a lawless man. She studied him a moment, noticing for the first time the hard cut of his jaw and the unyielding shape of his chin. This was not only the polite gentleman who had kept her company these past days, but a dangerous man, too. One she would not care to cross. As she stared, his gaze narrowed, and ignoring the thump her heart gave, she sent him a shy smile before turning away to answer a question from Mrs. Henley.

Like returning heroes, Daphne and Charles were escorted back to Beaumont Place, half the populace from the beach following them home. While Daphne was touched by the concern of her neighbors and friends, she was eager, having repeatedly expressed her great and undying gratitude, to finally leave the hubbub downstairs and escape to her rooms. She felt only a slight pang of guilt at abandoning Adrian and April to the acquaintances that remained, but her siblings were proving to be adept hosts, and now that the excitement was over, everyone would be leaving. Mr. Weston and Lord Trevillyan would spend the night at Beaumont Place, and the last thing she'd done before disappearing up the stairs had been to order rooms prepared for them. Forty-five minutes later, having suffered a long, tearful scolding from Ketty while her bath water had been heated, Daphne gently dismissed Ketty and her maid. Sinking into the warm lavender-scented water, Daphne sighed with bliss, wondering idly if Mr. Weston was enjoying a similar experience. Not lavender, of course, she thought with a faint smile, but some scent that was strong and masculine . . . rather like the man.

Charles would have found a hot bath very much to his liking, but there was business to be attended to first. If Daphne had missed the speaking looks of the ladies and the quiet-voiced conversations of the gentlemen, he had not, and he was not at all surprised when Vicar Henley, accompanied by an uneasy-looking Adrian, asked him to join them in the library for a private word.

Beaumont Place was returning to normalcy, everyone except the Henleys, himself, and Lord Trevillyan having departed. Charles had known it was only a matter of time before he would be asked for just such a meeting. There was no question but that all the local gentry expected he would do the honorable thing by Daphne, and he was quite certain that not a few of the ladies had driven away already planning the nuptials and what they would wear to the affair.

Charles had never thought to marry, and if he had been forced to choose a bride, until the last forty-eight hours, he would have been hard-pressed to name *any* young woman with whom he would be willing to share the rest of his life. His lips quirked. He wasn't certain how it had happened, but he was aware in some elemental way that Daphne Beaumont had changed all that. He was too cynical to believe in love at first sight—lust, perhaps—but he could not deny that there was something about Daphne that made the idea of marriage to her . . . not at all distasteful. A vision of that tall, slim body, the enticing length of leg he had glimpsed when she climbed the rocks flashed through his mind—that and the quick intelligence, the bravery he seen in those lovely hazel-green eyes when she'd realized her danger in the cave and had sent Adrian away. Beautiful, brave, and intelligent. A man could do far worse. He grinned. He seriously doubted that Daffy would feel the same about him—in fact, quite probably the reverse. His grin widened. Ah, there was that challenge again . . . .

Leaving Lord Trevillyan politely conversing with Mrs. Henley, April, and a plump little pigeon of woman who had been introduced as Miss Kettle, Charles followed Henley and Adrian from the saloon.

The door had barely shut behind them in the library before Vicar Henley said, "I'm sure you realize that this is a most unusual circumstance, Mr. Weston, and I find myself in a difficult situation. As you are no doubt aware, Sir Adrian is not of age, and since this involves his guardian and it would not be proper for her to be here at this time, neither he nor she has anyone to act for them. While Miss Beaumont is of age, in a matter as serious as this, the Squire and I thought that it would be best if we gentlemen settled this between ourselves before it goes any further. At Sir Adrian's request, I have stepped into the role as advisor to him. I hope you have no objections."

Charles politely inclined his head. "None."

The vicar cleared his throat. "Uh, no one believes that you acted anything less than a gentleman to Miss Beaumont during your, uh, recent ordeal, but the fact remains that you were trapped alone with her for two nights in that cave." Vicar Henley fiddled with his cravat. "I'm sure you realize the irreparable damage done to Miss Beaumont's reputation and that there is only one way to save her name from being bandied about in a most scandalous way."

Charles glanced at Adrian standing stiffly by the vicar's side, looking as if he wished the floor would open up and swallow him. Charles felt for him. Young Beaumont was a nice lad, and that the boy had developed a case of hero-worship for him had not escaped Charles's notice. Sir Adrian was being pulled two ways, not wanting to offend his hero but determined to salvage his sister's reputation. The young man was in the unenviable position of demanding a stranger, albeit one he seemed to admire, do the honorable thing—whether I want to or not, Charles thought wryly.

Putting Adrian out of his misery, Charles looked at him and said softly, "It would give me great pleasure to make your eldest sister my bride. I can assure you that I will treat her well and that I have the means to see that she is never in want."

Adrian's face lit up. "Oh, thank you, sir! I didn't doubt that a gentleman of your caliber would act any differently, but"—He swallowed and flushed, saying in a rush that would have mortified Daphne, "Thing is—you don't k-k-know us, and Daffy m-m-might not be your cup of t-t-tea."

Charles thought it interesting that Adrian wasn't the least worried about Daphne not liking *him!* Deciding not to enlighten the young man on the difficulties he suspected might arise, Charles smiled at Adrian and said, "I assure you that Daffy is *precisely* my cup of tea."

"Well, now," said the vicar, "with the heavy ground out of the way, I think that we can postpone discussions of settlements and the like until tomorrow. Mr. Vinton, Sir Adrian's man of business, has already stated that he will be happy to handle the business end of things." He looked at Charles. "How do you propose we go on? Will you wish to be married by Special License, or shall I have the banns published? Assuming you wished to be married here?"

Charles could easily obtain a Special License, but he rather thought that in this case, the calling of the banns might be better. He half smiled. The calling of the banns would give him time to convince what he was certain would be a recalcitrant bride of the wisdom of their marriage, and considering Sir Adrian's position in the area, it seemed fitting that they marry here in Cornwall.

"The banns will suffice," Charles replied. "And I believe that Miss Beaumont would prefer to married here." He glanced at Adrian. "Don't you agree?"

Adrian shot him a startled look, clearly unused to making decisions for his eldest sister. "Think you better talk to Daffy," he said.

"I shall do so first thing in the morning." Charles grinned at him. "At the same time I propose to her."

Adrian grinned back at him. "I'll warn you—Daffy's used to having the bit in her teeth and doing as she pleases. Doubt she'll take kindly to a firm hand on the rein."

"That may be, but I'm sure that we shall deal well together."

"Indeed, yes," said the vicar. "Miss Beaumont has always struck me as a sensible young woman. I'm sure that when she considers the honor done to her by Mr. Weston, she will be gratified that a gentleman of his fortune and standing has chosen to marry her." He smiled at Adrian. "Well, young man, Mr. Weston and I have some further business to discuss. Would you mind leaving us?"

"Oh, not at all," Adrian replied, adding artlessly, "Lord Trevillyan has promised to teach me to play billiards."

"Excellent!" said the vicar. "Since you and Lord Trevillyan will be busy, perhaps you would ask my wife to join Mr. Weston and myself." A twinkle in his eyes, he added, "My wife will want to start planning the wedding."

Adrian laughed and promised that he would send in Mrs. Henley.

A few minutes later, a smile on her pleasant features, Mrs. Henley came into the room and taking a seat by the fire, murmured, "I assume that all has been settled?"

Charles tugged on his ear. "Yes, except for informing Miss Beaumont of my intentions."

"Ah, yes. Miss Beaumont has a mind of her own, but she seems all that is proper, and I am sure when the situation is explained to her, that she will be reasonable. After all, she can't want to be looked at askance and shunned by society . . . nor, and probably more important to her, her brother and sister tarnished by this unfortunate affair. The tongues are already wagging."

His eyes shuttered, Charles asked, "Do you think that our marriage will scotch the scandal?"

The vicar rubbed his chin. "In the long run, yes. There is bound to be gossip—I'm sure Squire Renwick's wife is even now penning a letter to her sister who lives near Guildford and that Mrs. Houghton will be writing to her daughter in Ipswich all the delicious details of your, er, escapade." He looked unhappy. "We cannot stop the news from spreading, but the calling of the banns this Sunday and the news that you are to be wed within the month will still any whispers. I think that it will be a nine days' wonder and soon over and done with."

Mrs. Henley sent Charles an encouraging smile. "This cannot be easy for you, the pair of you being strangers, but from what I know of Miss Beaumont, I believe that she shall make you an exemplary wife, one who will not make you regret your marriage."

"I think we should worry," Charles muttered, "whether Miss Beaumont finds marriage to me to her liking."

Vicar beamed at him. "You have nothing to fear on that head. I am positive that when you declare yourself, she will be beside herself with joy."

Having no inkling of the treat in store for her, Daphne woke just after dawn the next morning, feeling much refreshed. It was astonishing, she thought, what a good night's sleep in one's own bed could accomplish, particularly when one was not bothered by spirits . . . or whatever. Humming to herself, she slid from the bed and rang for her maid. Shortly, garbed in a blue kerseymere gown with a dove-colored mohair shawl draped over her shoulders, her hair pulled back into a neat chignon, Daphne entered the morning room. Considering the hour of the morning, she had anticipated that she would find the room deserted, and her step faltered when she spied Charles Weston standing at the window that overlooked the side garden. His back was to her, and she cravenly considered retreating, but he had heard her and swung around to look at her.

He looked, she decided, very different from the ruffian of last night. Exquisitely shaved and barbered, wearing pristine linen, gleaming boots, breeches, and a bottle green coat of superfine, he was the very epitome of a gentleman of means and station.

Walking into the room and approaching the sideboard, where she helped herself to a cup of coffee, Daphne said, "Good morning! I did not expect to find anyone up this early."

Picking up his own cup of coffee that was sitting on the table beside him, Charles said, "I tend to be an early riser." He took a sip of his coffee. "I trust you are recovered from our, er, adventure?"

"Oh, indeed, yes! And I must thank you again for your gallantry." She glanced down at her cup. "It was an unpleasant experience for both of us, but your company made the entire episode less of an ordeal than it would have been." A slight shudder went through her. "I do not think I would have liked to have been buried in that cavern all alone, and your quick thinking by requesting food and fuel for the fire just before we were trapped made it bearable." Her gaze met his. "Thank you. My family and I will always be indebted to you for coming to our aid, and you have our . . . my sincere gratitude."

"Very prettily said," Charles replied, "but I think your gratitude is misplaced—especially when you consider the repercussions of our being locked together alone in that cavern."

Daphne frowned. "Repercussions? What do you mean by that?"

"You don't strike me as a stupid woman—stop and think about it. We were *alone* in that cave for two nights . . . just the two of us with no chaperon . . . ."

"Good heavens! Do not tell me that anyone believes . . . ." Daphne swallowed as a vivid image of Mr. Weston being overcome by passion and violently kissing her flashed through her mind. Her cheeks burned, and looking everywhere but at him, she managed, "I think you refine upon the matter too much. No person of good sense can believe that anything . . . untoward occurred between us. I am not some green miss just out of the school room, and you are not . . . ." She stopped, suddenly aware of how little she knew of Mr. Weston. Perhaps, she thought uneasily, he was a hardened rake with a scandalous reputation, just the sort of scoundrel that in his company, no woman's reputation was safe. Which was ridiculous, she decided. After all, she reminded herself, his cousin was the Earl of Wyndham—surely that counted for something. Mr. Weston had been a perfect gentleman with her during their time together, and while she knew herself to be on the shelf and not a beauty, certainly if he had

been a vile seducer, he would have made some attempt to . . . .
Conscious of her lack of charms, the lowering notion occurred to her that the reason he had been so very polite and
circumspect was because he had not considered her worthy
of his attentions. She shook herself. Now, she was being silly.
She hadn't wanted him to press his attentions on her, had
she? Upset with her thoughts, she said sharply, "The whole
idea is ludicrous."

"Do you think so?" Charles asked with a flick of his brow.
"Certainly, the vicar didn't think so when he discussed the
matter with me last night."

"The v-v-vicar," Daphne stammered, her eyes full of dismay. "Oh, surely not!"

Charles walked up to her and taking her hand in his, said
quietly, "I'm afraid that the answer is yes. You may not have
been aware of it, but even before I spoke to the vicar and
your brother, I had the distinct impression, in view of our, ah,
time together, that the community is breathlessly awaiting
the announcement of our betrothal."

An expression of utter horror crossed Daphne's face, and
Charles didn't know whether to laugh or curse. Not a vain
man, he couldn't help but be aware that the majority of the
opposite sex considered him handsome and that more than
one pair of feminine eyes admired his tall form and address.
Having inherited an impressive fortune upon his stepmother's
death, on the Marriage Mart, he was considered an excellent
catch, and for the past few years, he had been avoiding the
more aggressive of the matchmaking mamas who thronged
to London, hoping to find a husband for their daughters. He
might not have a title or a fortune large enough to make
Golden Ball Hughes blink, but his family was aristocratic—
his cousin was a bloody Earl! And these days, he was wealthy
enough to support a wife, even one who might want to make
a dash amidst the highest ranks of the ton. Stonegate was a
fine estate, one any woman would be proud to call her home.
Charles knew his own worth, and yet this hazel-eyed spinster

of minor lineage and no fortune to speak of was horrified at the idea of marriage to *him!* He wondered if he should be insulted.

"I take it," he said dryly, "that the idea of marriage to me is not to your liking."

Flustered, Daphne didn't know what to say. Any dreams of love or marriage that she may have had, she'd put from her years ago. Her brother and sister's welfare had dominated her life, and all her energies had gone into planning for their futures. She was content in her role as guardian to her younger siblings, and at no time since the death of her young Lieutenant had she ever considered any other alternative. That her circumstances might change had simply not crossed her mind and that someone of Charles Weston's ilk, obviously a man of fashion and prominence, might offer for her, even considering the situation, was beyond her ken.

Falling back on something he'd said a moment ago, she asked, "Adrian? Adrian knows about this?"

Charles nodded. "Indeed. You do not think I would offer for you without your brother's permission, did you?"

"Though only a lowly female, since I *am* his guardian, it does come as a surprise that he is busy arranging my future," she replied testily.

"He didn't have a choice, and it was only proper that he be involved." Charles quirked a brow. "After all, he is the head of your family."

Daphne's eyes flashed with irritation. Of all the nonsensical notions! Her younger brother, *Adrian,* deciding her future, when it was she who for years had made every important decision in their lives. Outrageous! Honesty compelled her to admit, "Yes, I suppose he is, but for all practical purposes, I have acted as the head of our family for some time now." Not looking at him, she added, "And while I appreciate the niceties of the situation, I am not about to be guided in such an important matter by a seventeen-year-old boy!"

"Then perhaps, you'll be guided by vicar and his wife?

Both of them feel that marriage between us is the only way to avoid a lasting scandal." Charles noted the stubborn slant to her mouth, and torn between amusement and a strong urge to shake her, he said, "The vicar and his wife discussed it with me last night. They feel that the only way out of this unfortunate circumstance is that we marry . . . and as soon as possible. Mrs. Henley pointed out that the longer we delay making an announcement of our betrothal, the longer tongues will wag and the more damage there will be to your reputation and standing in the community."

Daphne bit her bottom lip, distressed. That the vicar and his wife, two people who she held in the highest respect, thought it necessary for her to marry Mr. Weston put the situation in a whole different light. She took a nervous step around the room.

Coming to stand in front of him, Daphne looked up into his dark face. For a long moment, she searched those hard features, wondering if she had wandered into a nightmare. Marry this man? This stranger with the cool green eyes and unyielding jaw? She knew little of him—other than that he had risked his life to be with her.

It wasn't a simple situation, she reminded herself miserably. If there was only herself to consider, she might just throw caution to the winds and give in to the demands of society, but there wasn't only herself to think of . . . . If she married him, this man she had known for less than seventy-two hours, not only would her future be in his hands, but indirectly, those of her brother and sister as well. Could she trust him to treat them fairly? Did he realize that in marrying her, not only would he be gaining a wife, but that for a number of years, he would have the care of her two siblings as well? She had to consider their futures, too. And what of Beaumont Place? Did he expect to carry her and Adrian and April off to God knew where and just abandon Adrian's home and estate? What of Ketty and Garthwaite and Mrs. Hutton and all the other servants who looked to her, technically, she reminded herself, to Adrian, for their support and welfare? What of them?

A terrible thought occurred to her, and fear such as she had never known flooded through her. She gasped, and her face went white. Dear God! What if he meant to tear away her from Adrian and April?

Seeing the expression on her face, Charles grasped her shoulders. "What is it, my dear?" he asked, concerned. "I know that this was not what either of us envisioned when I joined you in that cave, but surely, marriage to me can't be so horrifying that the very thought of it makes you look as if you will faint."

Aware of the heat and strength of his hands on her shoulders, Daphne shook her head. "N-n-not exactly," she stammered. "What of my brother and sister? What of them?"

His brows flew together in a quick frown. "What of them?"

Daphne licked her lips. "If we were to marry, you w-w-wouldn't separate us, would you?" Impetuously, she clutched the lapels of his elegant coat. "If you married me, you would have to understand that I have the care of Adrian and April. I must see to their future."

"Even at the cost of your own?" he asked harshly, furious that she thought him such a monster that he would tear her family asunder.

She nodded. "Even at the cost of my own."

"Let me see if I understand you," he said icily. "You would throw my offer away, face scandal and disgrace if I were to say that I will not have your sister and brother in my household?"

Daphne nodded, not understanding the quiet rage she sensed within him.

He shook her. "You little fool! I can survive the gossip that will surround this event, but you cannot. If you don't marry me, not only will your reputation be ruined, but that of your brother and sister as well. Don't you realize that your dreams of a grand match for them will come to naught if you do *not* marry me? Do you think for one moment that any member of the *ton* would wish to align themselves with a member of a family who tolerates and condones the sort of scandal that will follow you?" He gave an ugly laugh. "Perhaps Sir Adrian, with his fortune, might find a bride who would be willing to overlook the reputation you will have, but what of April? I doubt that she'll see any vouchers for Almack's! Or that the offers she'll receive will be honorable."

Daphne closed her eyes in anguish. Of course! She hadn't even considered the impact her refusal to marry him might have on Adrian and April's futures. Good God! The picture he painted was frightful, and with a sinking heart, she realized it was all too true. Her spine stiffened. She would not let *anything* ruin the bright future she planned for her brother and sister, and she would do everything within her power to see that their future was secure. And he was right about something else, too, damn him. Being a man, he could indeed survive the scandal and gossip, but she could not. Her reputation would be in tatters . . . and by association, that of her siblings, or at least April's. There was nothing for it—to protect her brother and sister, she had to marry him.

She took a deep breath and opened her eyes to look at him. Unaware that she still clutched the lapels of his coat, she said earnestly, "If you swear to me that you will never do anything to harm Adrian or April, that you will always treat them kindly and fairly, and that you will do nothing to separate us, I will marry you."

A wintry smile curved his lips. "Not the most gracious acceptance, but thank you. I think."

Her gaze did not waver. "Swear it."

He'd been right about that stubborn chin, Charles thought wryly. He dipped his head. "I swear it. I swear that I shall always treat your brother and sister fairly and kindly and that I will never do anything to separate the three of you." He quirked a brow. "Satisfied?"

Daphne loosed her death grip on his coat and sighed deeply. "Yes . . . you strike me as a man of your word."

"Well, thank God for that!" Charles muttered. "But I am not quite satisfied . . . I think it only fair that I have a taste of what I missed in the cave."

His hands tightened on her shoulders, and Daphne found herself crushed against him. He kissed her with a violence and passion that made her earlier thought of him doing such a thing a pale memory. His mouth was hard and warm and knowing, and locked against his muscled length, his lips and tongue wreaking havoc within her, Daphne could not have escaped from him if she had tried. Assaulted on all sides by new and exciting sensations, she made no protest when his hand moved to hold her head to his liking as he intensified the kiss, his tongue delving deep within her mouth, his other hand cupping her buttocks and pulling her tightly against him. Her senses spun wildly, and with a will of their own, her arms crept around his neck.

Chapter 6

The moment his lips touched hers, Charles knew that he had made a mistake. That Daphne Beaumont appealed to his deepest carnal senses he'd been aware of, but not that she could awaken a mindless demon of desire within him, a demon until this very moment, he had not known existed. The taste of her inflamed him, and he was shaken at how easily both the slight brush of her body against his and the intoxicating sweetness of her kiss aroused him. Blind with need, it was only by the greatest effort that he was finally able to tear his mouth from hers and take a step away from her—and not as he hungered to do, tip her onto the table, and finish what that one brief kiss demanded of him.

As shaken as he was by the kiss, Daphne stared at him, her eyes blind, her thoughts blurred. She touched her lips with her fingers, astonished to find them warm and soft and not flaming cinders. It wasn't as if she'd never been kissed before—her young Lieutenant had stolen a kiss or two, but those kisses had been nothing, *nothing* compared to the kiss of Charles Weston.

If he hadn't been fighting so hard to keep his baser instincts in check, Charles might have been amused by her stunned expression, but as it was, it took all his willpower not to snatch her back into his arms and kiss her again. His breeches were tight where his swollen member rudely pressed against the fabric, his breathing was ragged, and feeling badly rattled, Charles put some distance between them.

To give himself time and to do something, other than throw Daphne on the table and have his way with her, he reached for his coffee, cursing when he saw that his fingers were shaking. He took a deep breath and fought for control. Gaining some mastery over his runaway emotions, he was pleased to see that his hands were now steady. After taking a swallow of his, by now, cold coffee, he said frankly, "At least we shall have no difficulties when it comes to the marriage bed."

Daphne flushed. Her dazed state shattered and her eyes bright with antagonism, she snapped, "It would appear that you are a man of blunt speech."

Admiring her quick recovery, Charles nodded. "I have been known from time to time to speak my mind and not wrap the words in clean linen."

"Well then, I trust that you will not be dismayed when I tell you bluntly that you are one of the rudest men I have ever met."

He smiled, and Daphne suppressed the unexpected urge to smile back at him. "Since we are to be man and wife, I suspect that plain speaking between us will not be a bad thing," Charles murmured. That singularly charming smile widening, he added, "How else will I know when I have offended you if you do not tell me?"

She picked up her cup and took a sip and made a face. Cold coffee—not her favorite—and ignoring him, she walked to the sideboard. After dumping her coffee into the old pewter jug kept there for that purpose, she poured herself a new cup of hot coffee.

Taking a sip, she turned to observe him over the rim of her cup. "And will you be offended when I speak bluntly?"

Repeating her actions with the coffee, he poured himself a fresh cup also. Grinning at her, he said, "I fear, my dear, that from what I have seen of you in the short time I have known you, it would be impossible for me to prevent you from speaking bluntly."

An adorable little smile quirked the corner of her mouth, and Charles was conscious of a strong desire to press his lips to that exact spot. If he'd thought that he could limit himself to just that one kiss, he might have given in to the impulse, but wariness held him back. He very much feared that a fleeting kiss would not satisfy him, and there was no point in shocking the household by making violent love to his betrothed on the breakfast table.

"You are staring, and I wish you would stop this instant," Daphne said with a hitch in her voice. "It is impolite."

"You see?" Charles said. "Already, you are proving the truth of my words."

Deciding that it would do no good to encourage him, Daphne firmly suppressed a smile and concentrated on her coffee. Curiosity got the better of her, though, and after a moment, she asked, "Did Vicar Henley have any advice about how we should go on?"

Charles nodded and brought her current on what had been decided last night.

When he finished speaking, Daphne took a deep breath. She sent him a searching look. "It cannot be easy for you to be suddenly saddled with a wife . . . and a ready-made family."

"Any more than it is easy for you to find yourself betrothed to a man who only a few days ago, you had never met."

Flashing him an uncertain smile, she murmured, "We're both of us in an invidious position, aren't we?"

Charles put down his cup and crossed to stand beside her. Willing himself not to take her into his arms, he said, "It may not be what either of us wanted, but I think we shall deal well together."

Daphne did not appear to have much confidence in his

assessment, but before she could say anything, Adrian, followed by April, came into the room. Expectant expressions on their faces, they looked from Daphne to Charles.

"Have you asked her to marry you, sir?" Adrian asked Charles.

"Well, if I hadn't, you certainly would have let the cat out of the bag," Charles said, his smile taking any sting out of the words. Taking Daphne's hand in his, he lifted it to his lips and after kissing the back of it, added, "Your sister has just done me the great honor of accepting my offer of marriage."

Her hands clasped against her bosom, April sighed dramatically. "Oh, it is so romantic. Daffy, are you not beside yourself with joy?"

Snatching her hand from Charles's grasp, Daphne muttered, "Oh, beside myself, to be sure."

Charles laughed. "Such enthusiasm overwhelms me," he said, his eyes dancing as he glanced at Daphne.

But she would not be drawn, and Daphne spent the next several moments fending off congratulations and excited questions from her brother and sister as they settled around the breakfast table. Adrian and April were thrilled by the outcome, and Daphne was relieved at the easy way in which they accepted Mr. Weston into their ranks. Watching the three of them, she told herself that it was a happy circumstance that her brother and sister liked Mr. Weston, but she wasn't certain that she was entirely comfortable with the way her siblings welcomed him without any apparent reservation. Adrian was clearly bedazzled, gazing worshipfully at him or hanging respectfully on every syllable that fell from Mr. Weston's lips. April clearly felt the same way—her eyes round with admiration, she artlessly peppered Mr. Weston with endless questions, laughing and chatting merrily with him as if she had known him forever, and not only a few days. Not even that, Daphne reminded herself, since Mr. Weston had spent the past two days trapped in a cave with her and not her two siblings.

It occurred to her that she might just feel the tiniest bit

threatened by the effortless way that Mr. Weston seemed to have taken over her family. Her reaction, she told herself, was only natural. After all, she reminded herself, for years, it had been to her that her sister and brother had looked to for guidance. It had been she who had made the decisions concerning their welfare, and now suddenly, there was someone else who would have greater authority over their lives . . . all of their lives. Tamping down a spurt of anxiety, she admitted to herself that perhaps it was not too terrible that Adrian and April were already placing Mr. Weston at the head of the family, ready to defer to him at a moment's notice. Biting her lip, she looked away from the family scene at the table. In a month or less, Mr. Weston *would* be the head of their family.

She glanced back quietly, studying him as he dazzled her brother and sister. Watching him as he drew them out with his warm smile and rapt interest in their opinions, Daphne sensed that beneath the charm and relaxed manner, this was not a man to trifle with. Staring at that hard, dark face, conscious of the powerful body disguised by the fashionable clothes, Daphne shivered. This man, this stranger was going to hold their future in his hands. He'd sworn to keep them together, sworn he would not harm them, but dare she trust him?

Almost as if he had known what she was thinking, their eyes met, and she felt a jolt of some indefinable emotion right down to her toes. Excitement, yes; a physical awareness she had never experienced before, that too; but intertwined was some other elemental drive, and it was that emotion that puzzled and alarmed Daphne. For a long moment, their gazes held, his unreadable, hers wary, then with a faint smile he turned his head away to answer a question from April. Feeling as if she had suddenly been released from a magician's spell, Daphne took a shaky breath. The man had an unsettling effect on her—she could not deny it—nor that if she had not trusted him on some instinctive level, then scandal be hanged, she would not have agreed to marry him.

Lord Trevillyan strolled into the morning room and rais-ing his quizzing glass, surveyed the inhabitants as they sat scattered around the table. Like a collector viewing several fine specimens, his gaze moved from one person to the next.

Letting the quizzing glass fall, he drawled, "I assume that congratulations are in order? That I am to wish you happy?"

Charles nodded. "Indeed you are. Miss Beaumont and I will be married at the end of February. Vicar Henley will pre-side over the services."

"The Vicar certainly wasted no time last evening. It would appear that you have it all settled," Lord Trevillyan said. Bowing in Daphne's direction, he said coolly, "Congratula-tions, Miss Beaumont. You marry into a most illustrious family and should count yourself lucky at this turn of events."

Daphne stiffened at his words, and involuntarily, her gaze flew to Charles.

He threw her a comforting smile before turning his atten-tion on Lord Trevillyan. "It is I who count myself lucky," Charles said smoothly. "It is to *my* great good fortune that Miss Beaumont has agreed to marry me . . . and anyone who believes otherwise is, ah, not wise, don't you agree?"

Trevillyan flushed and looked away. "Er, yes, yes, of course. Never thought anything else."

Trevillyan vanquished, Charles's gaze swept the table, passing lightly over Adrian and April before lingering on Daphne. Amusement crinkling the corners of his eyes, he murmured, "Indeed, I am a blessed and lucky man. Just think—in one fell swoop, I not only gain a beautiful wife, but a fine brother and a lovely sister, as well. Few men are so lucky."

Adrian grinned, April beamed, and even Daphne found herself smiling.

Trevillyan shrugged and walked to the sideboard. Raising the quizzing glass once more, he carefully inspected the ex-panse of food spread out before him.

After pouring himself some coffee and helping himself to a rasher of bacon and coddled eggs, Trevillyan sat down at the table next to Adrian. Taking a bite of bacon, he asked Charles, "So, what is the plan for today? Do you remain here? Or will I have the pleasure of your company at Lanyon Hall? I shall be happy to have you as my guest for as long as need be." He smiled thinly at Daphne. "Of course, I realize that my demands on his time now take second place to yours."

Daphne gave him an equally thin smile. "I assure you that Mr. Weston's time is his own." She glanced at Charles. "He can please himself."

Charles grinned at her. "Carte blanche, eh? I wonder if you will always be so obliging." Observing the sudden flush in Daphne's cheeks and feeling quite satisfied with himself, he said to Trevillyan, "I intend to accompany you back to Lanyon Hall and since you have no objections, remain with you until the wedding." He glanced back at Daphne. "Although I expect that Beaumont Place will find me a frequent visitor."

An hour later, Trevillyan and Charles were on their way to Lanyon Hall. Charles had found it difficult to leave Daphne. He told himself it was because except for the previous night, they had virtually spent the last two days together, but he knew that he was lying. She had fascinated him from the moment he had laid eyes on her, and closer acquaintance had not lessened her appeal. There was something about her, from the unruly mass of black curls on her head right down to the very soles of her dainty feet, that held a compelling allure for him. He smiled. He'd never seen her feet, but he was positive that they would be dainty.

For Charles, women had always fallen into three distinct categories—relatives, servants, or the beguiling members of the demimonde, be they opera singers or others, such as the charming little widow who had entertained him so well this past winter. But with Daphne, he admitted uneasily, everything was different. As his wife, it was true, she would be a relative, yet he could never think of her as he did Nell. His mouth tightened. Or as he had thought of his stepmother. So relative didn't *precisely* apply. He supposed, since she would run his household, she could in the broadest sense be considered a servant, but that didn't fit either. And while she made his loins ache and his body tremble with desire, she was not the type of woman he sought out for those demands. Oh, he wanted her, he couldn't deny that, but there was something beyond mere lust that made her damn near irresistible. Was it simply the challenge? There was that, but he dismissed it. No, there was something else . . . . He considered the intelligence in those lovely hazel eyes, her bravery during their incarceration in the cave, and the enjoyment he'd felt as he'd watched the various expressions flying across her face as she plumbed the nuances of his remarks. He shook his head. It was, he decided wryly, a very good thing that they were to be married because the woman had certainly bewitched him.

"What are you shaking your head about?" demanded Trevillyan. "Regretting your engagement already?"

"No. Simply at the vagaries of Fate," Charles returned lightly. "Just before I came here, Wyndham suggested that I marry. I thought he was mad at the time, but now . . . ." He shrugged. "It doesn't matter. I shall marry Miss Beaumont in a month's time, and that is the end of it."

They rode in silence a few minutes more before Trevillyan said, "What of the other matter? Do you intend to pursue it?"

Charles glanced at him. "The murdered women? Yes, but at the moment, I cannot see my way forward. Beyond the brutality of their deaths and that they were found in this vicinity, there is nothing to tie them together. They are unidentified, so it is impossible to even discover if they knew each other or where they lived." He frowned. "You are not even certain that there was an earlier murder, and we have little but two bodies to go on."

"But you have suspicions," Trevillyan remarked shrewdly. "You know more than you are telling me."

"Do I?" Charles returned with a faint smile.

Trevillyan shot him a narrow-eyed glance. "Raoul always said that you were a fellow who played his cards close to the vest. He used to complain loudly that you never let him know what you were doing or where you were going."

"Did he now?" Charles muttered, hoping his face revealed none of the loathing he felt at the very mention of his brother's name. *Half* brother, he reminded himself again. Only half, thank God!

"You knew him better than I," said Charles a moment later. "You two were friends from Eton and of an age. I'm sure that he told you things that he did not mention to me."

Trevillyan looked thoughtful. "I suppose you are right." He sighed. "I still find it impossible to believe that he is dead, and killed by a madman." He cut his eyes toward Charles. "With your reckless ways, I always expected you to be the one to die before your time—Raoul often expressed that notion himself."

Charles smiled grimly. "I am not surprised. I'm sure that Raoul never forgot that if I died, he would inherit Stonegate."

"Oh, come now," exclaimed Trevillyan, shocked. "Never say that Raoul wanted you dead!"

Charles shrugged. "After Daniel's untimely death, the thought was bound to have occurred to him."

"Well, yes, perhaps it did. It is only natural. Look at the situation between Huxley and myself. I did not want the man dead, but I was aware that it would be to my benefit if he died." Trevillyan scowled. "Or it would have been if that pup, Adrian, had never been born."

"I thought you were getting along with him rather well," Charles commented with a raised brow.

Trevillyan grimaced. "No use being overtly rude, and I was his guest, after all." He glared at Charles. "And none of this would have happened if you had not gone tearing after that sister of his."

Charles laughed and kicked his horse to greater speed.

"Yes, that's true, but do you know, I do not regret it in the least."

Daphne did not *exactly* regret her engagement to Mr. Weston, but she did have concerns, and those concerns were uppermost in her mind when she and Adrian and Mr. Weston met the next afternoon at Mr. Vinton's office in Penzance to discuss settlements. If Mr. Vinton was taken aback at her presence during a meeting that was traditionally held between the males of the families, he gave no sign of it, graciously ushering her and Adrian into his office, where Mr. Weston already awaited them.

Charles's mobile mouth flickered into a smile when Daphne sailed into the room, looking charming he thought, in a mulberry pelisse, light tan gloves, and an amber velvet hat adorned with brilliant peacock feathers. He wasn't surprised that his bride-to-be insisted on being here, and he was skeptical that Daphne would ever sit back and tamely allow her fate to be totally arranged by others. Especially, he amended, by mere men.

She shot him a challenging glance from under her dark lashes but beyond offering him her hand and a polite nod, displayed none of the gratification expected of a young lady who had snared a very eligible gentleman. Charles was uncertain whether to be annoyed or amused by her manner. In the end, amusement won out, and he bit back a smile at the cool profile she presented to him.

Daphne risked another glance at him, her heart thumping madly in her chest when he smiled at her. Embarrassed to be caught looking at him, her gaze dropped, and her cheeks bloomed rosily. She'd been certain that it had been her imagination that had made him so tall and broad, and pure girlish fantasy that had made those harsh features of his so very attractive. But it had not been imagination. He was tall, and his dark blue coat fit those broad shoulders superbly. The nankeen breeches also fit him very well, delineating every sleek

muscle of his thighs with loving detail. She swallowed, remembering what it felt like to have that hard, tough body
pressed against hers, remembering, too, the taste and plunder
of his kiss. A queer ache sprang to life in her belly, and her
fingers curled in her lap as she looked at his mouth. It was
such a nice mouth, she thought, before forcing her gaze to
study the rest of his face.

He wasn't handsome in the traditional sense, she admitted.
His features were too hard, too boldly carved, the chin too
aggressive, the thick black brows too heavy to ever adorn the
statue of a Greek god . . . and yet . . . and yet there was something so intensely male, something so attractive about that
face and body that few women would ever turn away if he
lifted even only one finger to beckon them into his arms . . . .
Daphne shook herself and reminded herself that he was only
a man, not a sorcerer, for heaven's sake! She sat up straighter
and looked down at her hands in her lap, but against her
will, her gaze strayed to that long, mobile mouth again. Memory slid back, and she could recall every moment of his kiss,
every feeling that had swept through her . . . . With an effort,
she tore her eyes away from the distinctly sensual curve of his
bottom lip, and that silly little heart of hers almost leaped
right out of her chest when she discovered that he was looking at her, watching her as she stared at him.

He smiled, and something in those cool green eyes sharpened
that ache in her belly unbearably. Perhaps he *is* a sorcerer, she
thought with a delicious shudder. To her relief, Mr. Vinton
began to speak, and she fixed her attention on what he had to
say.

Adrian had only the vaguest notion of what was expected
of him, but Mr. Vinton was there to advise him and to see
that he made no mistakes in settling his sister's future.
Daphne, on the other hand, had a very good understanding
of the importance of this meeting. It had been because of the
money settled on her mother at the time of her marriage that
the late Mrs. Beaumont had been able to provide for her chil-

dren as well as she had. Daphne wasn't thinking far enough ahead to add children to the mix—she was still reeling from her sudden engagement—but she was determined to safeguard the money that her grandmother had left her. Her lips tightened. And if people thought her vulgar to care so much about money, let them.

Upon her marriage to Mr. Weston, in fact, from the moment of their engagement, Daphne was terrifyingly aware that everything she owned essentially became his, even the clothes on her back. He would determine the dispersal of her money, and under the law, she had no say. She didn't fear, at least not very much, that Mr. Weston would prove miserly, but he was a stranger and who knew how he would act?

As the meeting progressed, she realized that she needn't have harbored any fears that Mr. Weston had designs upon her pittance of a fortune. Not only did he waive any interest in it, but he also insisted that it be part of the monies settled on her. At his words, that insidious fear that had lurked at the back of her mind dissipated, and she smiled shyly at him. She hoped that he didn't think she was a money-grubber, but it had been a difficult struggle since her mother died, and she didn't know how she could have kept the family together without that pitifully small sum her grandmother had left her. To have him take control of it had filled her with the utmost fear, but she relaxed once she knew that it was safe. She gasped and her eyes widened, however, at the small fortune he proposed adding to it.

Charles smiled at her. "What? Not enough?" he asked carelessly. "I can add another ten thousand pounds if you like, and do not forget—we have yet to discuss your pin money." He looked at Adrian and murmured, "What do you think of three thousand pounds a quarter? Do you think that will keep her in clothes and jewels?"

Since she had fed and clothed their entire family on less than three thousand pounds a *year*, Daphne was taken aback. Before she could think, she blurted out, "Isn't that rather excessive? I'm sure that I could make do on less. In fact, I *know* I could."

Mr. Vinton coughed and said kindly, "My dear Miss Beaumont, I am familiar with the extent of Mr. Weston's assets, and there is no reason for you to, er, make do. I assure you that the sum offered by Mr. Weston is not unreasonable. It is a generous amount, and I urge you to accept it."

"Very well," Daphne said meekly, but when she looked at Mr. Weston, her gaze was troubled. It was one thing for him to be an honorable man and offer her marriage, but did he have to be wealthy in the bargain? She bit her lip. The circumstances surrounding their betrothal were causing gossip enough. He was, after all, the cousin to an earl while she was, not to wrap it in clean linen, a little nobody. To learn that he was also wealthy was the crowning blow. People were bound to think that she had staged the whole affair, Daphne thought miserably. Unkind persons would be certain that she was some sort of scheming harpy, willing to do anything to become a rich man's wife.

Charles sensed that something was bothering her, and his eyes narrowed. Surely not because of the money?

As they rose and prepared to depart, he caught Daphne's arm and said to Mr. Vinton and Adrian, "Do you mind if I have a private word with Miss Beaumont?"

"Of course not," replied Mr. Vinton. Smiling at Adrian, he said, "If I can interest you in a cup of tea in the library?"

Adrian, after a curious look at Charles, readily complied, and the two men left the office.

"What is it?" Daphne asked, nervous at being alone with him. Especially considering the train her thoughts had taken only a few minutes previously.

"I believe that's my question," Charles said. "What is wrong? Do you not think the money is sufficient?"

Appalled that he could think her so grasping, Daphne gawked at him. "Oh, no. No. You have been more than generous."

"Then what? And don't prevaricate. Something is troubling you. What?"

Her gaze fell. "I didn't know that you were so wealthy. It . . . it was a shock."

"A pleasant one, I hope," he said mildly.

She glanced up at him. "It is bad enough," she said unhappily, "that you were forced to offer for me and that your cousin is an earl, but now I find that you are quite wealthy." She swallowed and looked miserable. "There is talk enough about our engagement, and now people are bound to think that I deliberately schemed to trap you. I'm sure that some already think that I seduced you."

Charles pulled her into his arms. His lips gently traced the outline of her mouth. "Hmmm, let the fools talk." He kissed her, his mouth warm against hers. Fighting the demon that rode him, he kept the kiss light. Reluctantly lifting his lips from hers, he smiled down at her. "And as for seduction . . . ." His smile became decidedly wicked. "If anyone is going to be doing any seducing, I can assure you, that I shall be doing it. And you, my poppet, will be the one seduced."

He kissed her again, this time, his hunger slipping from his iron grip. He crushed her next to his tall body, molding her slender form against his, making her aware of the powerful muscles and warm flesh concealed beneath his clothing. His lips hard on hers, his tongue took possession of her mouth, demanding a response.

Dizzy with desire, Daphne trembled as his mouth and tongue took their pleasure. Her arms slid around his neck, and she arched against him, reveling in the soft groan that escaped him when her lower body pressed into the swollen length of him.

Heedless of their location, Charles's hands cupped her buttocks, pulling her harder against him. He was drowning in need, the demands of his body driving him nearer and nearer to the edge of no return. In the grip of a powerful desire that gave him no succor, he pushed her up against the wall, his hands fumbling with her clothing, the craving to touch her naked flesh overriding all else.

It was Daphne's startled gasp when his fingers had at last found the heat and center of her that brought him crashing back to earth.

Appalled at how easily he had lost control, his hands dropped, and he abruptly stepped away. Color high on his cheeks, his eyes bright and feverish, he breathed deeply, fighting to regain some mastery over his emotions.

Her eyes dark with turmoil, her mouth swollen and red from his kisses, Daphne stared back at him, never realizing how close she had come to being ravished where she stood.

Charles understood too well the dangers of the moment. A minute more, and he would have freed himself from his breeches and buried himself within her. And by God, if she didn't stop looking at him like that, he might very well finish it, and convention be damned! He put a few more feet between them and ran a shaking hand through his thick hair.

Daphne felt as if she had been struck by lightning—her entire body tingled and throbbed. She was convinced that when she undressed tonight, there would be scorch marks on her skin. I wasn't ready for him to stop, she thought dazedly. I wanted him to continue. And like a common whore in an alley, I would have let him take me. Ashamed at her actions, embarrassment flooded her, and she scuttled toward the door.

"Wait," Charles commanded.

He walked toward her, his eyes narrowing when she shrank against the door. "I have no intention of kissing you again," he said bluntly. He reached out and straightened her hat, which his embrace had knocked askew. Her hat fixed to his liking, like a father with a child, he brushed down her pelisse where it was still ruched up from his frantic search beneath her clothing.

Mutely, she stared up at him, hardly daring to breathe, longing and equally terrified that he would take her into his arms again.

"Well, I think we have settled the question of seduction, don't you?" Charles muttered.

Daphne looked confused, and he cast her a twisted smile. "I have just proven my point. Seduction is my game. Not yours."

Chapter 7

Rejoining the others, Daphne politely refused a cup of tea, and shortly after that, she and Adrian were in his new blue and yellow gig and on their way out of town.

Adrian shot her a puzzled look or two before finally asking, "You upset about something, Daffy?"

She pasted a smile on her lips and glanced at her brother. "No. No. Of course not."

He didn't look convinced. Trying another tack, he said, "I thought the settlement was very generous."

"Yes, yes, it was." She frowned. "Did you have any idea that Mr. Weston was so very wealthy?"

He shook his head, concentrating on guiding his horse, a spirited bay mare known to be a sweet goer, around a heavy farm wagon drawn by two plodding gray draft horses. The open road in front of them, he set the mare at a smart trot and turned his attention back to his sister. "I think it is a jolly good thing for us that he is so warm in the pocket. Imagine if he had been a loose fish without a feather to fly with. We're dashed lucky he was around to save you."

Rattled by how easily she had succumbed to Mr. Weston's lovemaking, Daphne's teeth gritted together. "He did not save me," she said testily. "You did." She looked at the passing countryside, the native oak trees that were well tended, and the long coombes and rich verdant valleys where there was good arable soil. "If he had not insisted on staying with me in that horrible cave, none of this would have happened. It is all his fault."

"But I thought you liked Mr. Weston," Adrian exclaimed, dismayed.

"I like him well enough," Daphne was honest enough to acknowledge, "but you must admit that this whole affair has changed our lives forever."

"Yes, that is so," Adrian agreed. "But I think that once we get used to the idea, that we shall be merry as grigs."

Daphne shot her brother a disagreeable look. How easy it was for him! He wasn't the one being married to a virtual stranger.

She reminded herself again of all the advantages that would befall her brother and sister upon her marriage to Mr. Weston. Mr. Weston's relationship to the earl figured large in those advantages, as did the discovery that her betrothed possessed a fortune that made Adrian's seem almost paltry. Which would be a great benefit to April and Adrian, she conceded, and provided Mr. Weston did not interfere, she could lavish all sorts of gifts on them that had been beyond her means. For a second, she was happily distracted by the thought of the luxurious gowns and gleaming jewels she could buy April and the blooded horses and extravagant accoutrements she could give to Adrian. But that glow quickly faded when she considered the circumstances surrounding her sudden wealth.

Despite the vicar's championship, she knew that her marriage to Mr. Weston was going to be the main topic in many households over the coming weeks. People were definitely going to talk, some of it would be cruel and spiteful—she couldn't pretend otherwise. And they were going to talk and gossip and speculate much more than they would have if Mr. Weston did not have an earl for a cousin and had only possessed a respectable fortune rather than an impressive one. She sighed. As long as none of the gossip spilled onto Adrian or April, she could endure it. She could, and would, endure *anything* for them. Even marriage to Mr. Weston. And just never mind that his kisses aroused feelings and sensations she had never dreamed of and that one look from his cool green eyes made her feel as if her limbs had turned to honey.

Remembering those exciting but most regrettable moments in Mr. Vinton's office when Mr. Weston had taken her into his arms, the taste of him, and the sweet sweep of his hand against the cleft between her legs, her heart raced, and that queer little ache throbbed in her lower regions. She stared grimly ahead. She was not going to dwell on what had happened, or nearly happened, but she was going to take care that she did not put herself in that position again.

Deciding that it did no good to dwell on events over which she had no control, Daphne settled down to enjoy the drive back to Beaumont Place. The day was cool and clear, the steady breeze coming in from the Channel making her glad that her pelisse was nice and warm. The passing countryside didn't have a great deal to excite the senses: the high moorland was desolate except for those areas broken by the rich, narrow valleys. It was also surprisingly green for this time of year and at the moment, free of snow. The Penzance area, she had learned, seldom had snow, and when it did snow, within a few days, it melted away. Barring a few protected areas, the constant, blowing sea winds prevented timber trees from growing to any size, but the air was extremely mild.

A few miles outside of Penzance proper, the road curved around a small hillock, and nestled near its base was a tiny thatch-roofed cottage. Enclosed by a tumbling rock fence, the cottage sat a hundred yards or so off the main road, and a winding footpath led to the front door.

Remembering Mrs. Hutton's description of where Mr. Goodson's sister, Anne Darby, lived, Daphne touched Adrian's arm.

When he glanced at her, she said, "Please stop. I believe that Goodson's sister lives here. Since we are here, I wish to make her acquaintance."

Puzzled but agreeable, Adrian pulled the bay to a halt. Without waiting for his help, Daphne alighted from the gig. Smiling at him, she said, "There is no reason for both of us to descend upon her unannounced, and I know you will not want to keep your horse waiting. Why don't you walk the mare—I shall not be a moment."

It wasn't until she was just a few feet from the wooden door at the front of the cottage that Daphne had second thoughts about the wisdom of her actions. Anne Darby was reputed to be a witch—what business did Sir Adrian's sister have with such a creature? Ghostly business, Daphne decided wryly as she forced herself to cross that short distance.

Her gloved hand was raised to knock when the door swung open. Daphne didn't know what she expected, some wrinkled old crone? But it certainly wasn't the trim little woman who had opened the door.

If Anne Darby and her brother were of an age, Anne looked to be easily a decade younger. Her soft brown hair, neatly tied at the back of the neck, showed scarcely any silver in it, and except for a few laugh lines around her large, lustrous eyes and the corners of her full mouth, there were few signs of the passing years. Her fair complexion looked like that of a woman half her age, and for a moment, Daphne wondered if perhaps it was Anne Darby herself who stood in the doorway of the cottage.

The woman laughed, the dark eyes dancing. "Yes, Miss Beaumont, I am, indeed, Anne Darby, Goodson's sister. I have been expecting you. Please come in."

Taken aback, Daphne hesitated. The woman knew who she was? And she had been expecting her?

Anne opened the door wider and said, "Come, come now. There is nothing to be afraid of. I only put curses on people who annoy me. You are perfectly safe," she grinned at her, "unless you annoy me."

Charmed and mayhap a trifle apprehensive, Daphne allowed herself to be coaxed inside the cottage. Again, she didn't know what she expected, but it wasn't the cozy room in which she stood.

A small stone fireplace was centered on one wall; a worn woolen carpet, the once bright colors faded to a dusty rose and palest green lay upon the floor; and the scent of beeswax, lavender, and some other indefinable scent—heart of toad, tongue of lizard? Daphne wondered—wafted in the air. Blond lace curtains hung at the windows; the furniture was old but obviously cherished. But what caught Daphne's eyes was the table made from a thick slab of oak near the back of the room and the tall cabinet behind it, its shelves filled with gleaming glass bottles of various sizes, bowls, even a marble mortar with a brass pestle. She swallowed. Was that where the witch brewed and concocted her potions?

"Please be seated," Anne said, indicating a settee under one window. "Would you like a cup of tea?"

"Um, no, thank you," Daphne said. "I only mean to stay a moment. My brother awaits me on the road." Curious, she asked, "How did you know who I was? And that I was coming to see you? I didn't know it myself until I saw your cottage."

Anne laughed and seated herself in the small chair across from her. "Nothing very mysterious about it. I came to visit my brother one day last week, and you were pointed out to me. As for the other, Mrs. Hutton mentioned that you had, er, questions about the local legends and that you would be coming to visit one of these days." The dark eyes twinkled. "I've been expecting you for a few days now."

Daphne smiled, liking Goodson's sister. "No crystal ball or black cat?" she asked lightly.

Anne returned the smile and shook her head. "No crystal ball, I'm afraid. I do have a friendly orange tabby, but Samantha is too fat and lazy to be considered a familiar of the devil. I leave that sort of nonsense to the gypsies." Her smile fled, and she studied Daphne. "I cannot tell the future, my dear, but if your heart is heavy and I can help you, I shall."

Daphne flushed. "Am I that obvious?"

"Few people come to see me who are without worries they hope I can make disappear or desires that they want me to help them attain."

Looking anywhere but at that kind, concerned face, Daphne said carefully, "My worries and my desires are my own, but I would like to learn more about the legends surrounding Beaumont Place."

"Vicar Henley is a noted historian in the area," Anne said quietly, her eyes fixed on Daphne's face. "Did you speak with him?"

Daphne sighed. "Yes, I did, but I don't think that his records will tell me what I . . ." She looked helplessly at Anne, unable to think of a way to phrase her request without sounding like a candidate for Bedlam.

Anne's expression sharpened, and she leaned forward. "Why do you think that I would know more than Vicar Henley?"

Wishing she had not started this conversation and that she had not given in to the impulse to stop, Daphne didn't reply. She might have a favorable impression of Anne Darby, but she wasn't about ready to confess to the local witch that she thought a ghost had visited her.

Forcing a smile, Daphne murmured, "Mrs. Hutton said that you would know the, um, less formal versions of the same stories I might find amongst the Vicar's collection." She glanced down at her gloved hands. "Until we learned of Sir Huxley's death and my brother's inheritance, we had no idea that we had any other family." Her eyes met Anne's. "I want to learn the stories and legends about the Beaumont family that have been handed down from generation to generation," she said earnestly, if a bit mendaciously. Her cheeks flaming, she added, "I would be more than willing to pay you something for your time."

Anne sat back and regarded Daphne thoughtfully for several long seconds. Then she shrugged. "I have no objections to telling tales of long ago Beaumonts . . . but are you certain that you want to hear them?" She looked grim. "Some of your ancestors were not very nice people."

"I don't doubt that," Daphne said wryly. "And since yours have served mine from the beginning of time, if Mrs. Hutton and Goodson are to be believed, there must have been a relative or two of yours with a dark past."

Anne nodded and smiled. "Too true, my dear, too true. For every blackhearted Beaumont, I'm sure you'll find an equally blackhearted Goodson lurking somewhere in the background." She cocked a brow. "When did you want to hear some of these tales? Now?"

Knowing that Adrian must be wondering what was taking her so long, Daphne rose to her feet. "Oh, no. I did not mean to intrude upon you this way, but I did want to meet you. Perhaps we can set a time and place to meet again?"

"Of course," Anne said agreeably, standing up. "Since you are the one paying," she said dryly, "my time is yours. What is your pleasure?"

They settled on meeting at two o'clock Friday afternoon, with Daphne preferring to come to Anne's cottage rather than having Anne come to Beaumont Place.

"Just as well," Anne said as she walked with her to the door of the cottage. "My brother will be in a taking if he knows that I am filling your ears with tales and stories he would just as soon pretend he never heard." She shook her head. "Our meetings will not remain secret for long, though, but your coming here will somewhat delay Goodson discovering that we have met." She smiled. "He is sure to ring a peal over me when he learns you are coming here, but it won't be the first time I've upset him, nor the last."

"I don't want to cause trouble between you," Daphne said, concerned.

Anne waved her away. "Don't worry about Goodson and I. I enjoy shaking him out of his complacent pompousness from time to time."

Daphne hurried back along the path where Adrian, looking impatient, was tooling up and down the road. Spying his sister, he pulled the mare to a stop near the edge of the road. "I say, Daffy, it is about time! I was becoming worried, you know," he said when Daphne stopped next to the gig. "What took you so long?"

Giving him an apologetic smile, Daphne scrambled into the vehicle. "I am sorry. Do let us continue on our way."

Grumbling, Adrian urged the mare into motion. After a silent moment, he said, "Are you going to tell me what that was about?"

"It is nothing, really. Mrs. Hutton told me that if I wanted to learn some of the legends and stories about our ancestors, Anne Darby would be the person to see." She smiled at Adrian. "She's reputed to be the local witch, and I was curious about her."

Adrian looked astounded. "A witch? *Our* Goodson's sister?"

"Indeed, yes, but I can assure you, she is nothing like you might imagine. I was pleasantly surprised by her. In fact, I liked her."

Adrian cut his eyes in her direction. "And did she tell you anything of interest? Such as why our thrice-great grandfather left the area vowing never to return?"

Daphne shook her head. "No, there wasn't enough time for much conversation. I merely wanted to meet her." She hesitated. "I am going to see her again on Friday afternoon."

As he rode toward Lanyon Hall that Wednesday afternoon, Daphne's plans to consort with a local witch wouldn't have surprised Charles, but then, little about Daphne surprised him. Stunned him, perhaps. Confounded him? Oh yes, upon occasion. Frustrated him, certainly, but surprise? No.

Paying little attention to the countryside as his horse steadily covered the distance to Lord Trevillyan's country estate, he turned over the meeting at Mr. Vinton's office. He wasted little thought on the settlements—they were a necessary evil and he had no argument with the way things had been set up for Daphne's protection and use—it was those moments alone with Daphne that occupied him.

It was, he admitted, a good thing that he found his bride-to-be so attractive that he could hardly keep his hands off of her, but it also disturbed him. No novice where the opposite sex was concerned, though he tried, Charles could not recall one instance, not even his wild salad days, when he had exhibited such little control over his passion for a woman. He shook his head, amazed that he had somehow managed to keep from seducing Daphne then and there. And that was twice, he thought uneasily, that his command over himself had been shattered. He frowned. All it would have taken was the wrong move on Daphne's part today for him to have done the deed that many people assumed had already taken place. If she had touched him . . . He groaned, his loins tightening, and hot, aching hunger exploded through him at the image in his brain of Daphne's hand on him, caressing, fondling him. Feeling as if he were going to burst his breeches, Charles wrenched his thoughts away from the scene in Mr. Vinton's office.

Cursing under his breath, he kicked his horse into a gallop. Until they were safely married and he could indulge himself, Daphne's undeniable allure was definitely going to test his willpower. Thank God, he thought, he had less than a month to wait, but between now and then . . . A wry smile curved his mouth. Between now and then, he would just have to practice restraint, something he had never been very good at.

Lanyon Hall came into view, and he slowed his horse as he approached the imposing Elizabethan-style manor house. The front of the house was nearly covered with ivy, patches of the gray granite of which it was constructed showing through here and there; the panes of the mullioned windows, framed by the thick green leaves of the ivy, gleamed in the fading sunlight. The stables were another quarter of a mile beyond the house, and Charles rode briskly in that direction.

Leaving his horse in the capable hand of the groom, Charles strolled back toward the house.

Trevillyan had insisted he treat the house as his own, and Charles did so. Crossing the huge foyer with its gray-veined marble floor, he was met by Trevillyan's butler, Eames, a tidy little man of some forty years of age.

"Heard my horse, did you?" Charles said as he smiled and tossed his hat and gloves to the butler.

"Indeed, I did," Eames acknowledged as he caught the items. "There was a letter in the post today for you, Mr. Weston," he added. "I had it delivered to your rooms."

"Thank you," Charles said as he bounded up the broad staircase and quickly walked to his rooms. Entering his suite, he immediately spotted the letter lying in a silver salver on top of a satinwood table near the door.

Recognizing the name of his solicitor, Mr. Gerrard, on the envelope, Charles tore it open. The contents proved disappointing. Mr. Gerrard had followed Charles's instructions and had spoken several times with Mr. Smalley, Sofia Weston's solicitor, but had discovered no record of any transactions that seemed out of the ordinary.

> *Mr. Smalley,* wrote Mr. Gerrard, *was upset by my inquiries, demanding to know if we were accusing him of dishonesty in the handling of Mrs. Weston's estate. I assured him that such was not the case. Mr. Smalley was adamant in stating that he had done nothing dishonest, that he had discharged his duties honestly and honorably, and that he didn't appreciate my questions.*
>
> *I am sorry that I have nothing more to report.*
>
> *May I be of assistance to you in some other manner?*

Charles studied Gerrard's elegant script for several moments. Now what? he wondered. He took a turn around the large sitting room that adjoined his bedchamber. It was possible that Sofia had set up an account under another name separate from her estate. If such an account existed, and it was a big if, Smalley would know of it. Not only know of it, but also where it was and whose name was on it. He frowned. Short of torture, he could think of no way to get the information from Sofia's solicitor. But if there was an account and if money was being systematically withdrawn from it . . .

Crossing to a narrow oak sideboard that held a variety of liquors in crystal decanters, Charles poured himself a small glass of sherry. Taking the sherry with him, he sat down in one of the overstuffed sofas that graced the room and took a sip.

He reread the letter, then laid it on his thigh, staring off into space as he savored the fine sherry and considered his options. If he could discover whether Sofia had, indeed, set up such an account and that someone was using it, that discovery would go a long way to proving that Raoul was alive. And if he discovered this mythical account and found that the money had remained untouched these past three years, that would prove, at least to his mind, that Raoul was truly dead. He knew his half brother well, and Raoul, raised as the spoiled darling of his mother, could not live without money. Charles smiled grimly. And it would never occur to Raoul to *work* to earn his keep.

He sighed and laid his head against the back of the sofa and stared at the ceiling. Unless he departed for London and broke into the offices of Smalley, Slocomb, and Todd and searched Mr. Smalley's files himself, he could think of no way of moving forward as far as the money was concerned. Finding himself actually considering such a course, he jumped up from the sofa and went in search of his host.

Charles found Trevillyan in the library, sitting before the fire, sipping a fragrant rum punch. Since the butler had left a steaming bowl of the punch and some cups, Charles helped himself to a cup before joining his host.

Standing near the fire, one arm resting along the wide marble mantle, Charles took a sip of the punch. "Now that," he said, savoring the warm liquor, "is an excellent way to end the day."

Trevillyan cast him a sly look. "Settlements taken care of?"

Charles nodded. "Yes."

Trevillyan snorted. "I cannot believe that you are going to marry her. Charles Weston married to a little nobody with no fortune, no family, and no particular beauty—it is disgraceful." From the slight slur to his words, it was apparent that this was not Trevillyan's first foray to the punch bowl this afternoon. "If you want my opinion," he mumbled, "since the banns have not yet been called, offer that cub, Sir Adrian, a nice sum and take yourself off to London and forget about the whole affair."

Deciding that it would be rude to throw his drink in his host's face and challenge him to a duel, Charles said in a deceptively mild tone, "I would remind you of two things, my lord. One, unless you'd like me to throttle you where you sit, I think you owe me and my intended an apology, and two, if you ever say such a thing again, I *will* throttle you."

Trevillyan blinked, trying to get his befuddled brain around the fact that he had taken a dreadful misstep. The man who stared across at him bore no resemblance to the pleasant guest who had shared his home these past weeks. Gone was the gentleman with the quick smile and the easy charm, and in his place stood a flint-eyed stranger, one whose grim expression and taut stance warned that Charles meant every word he had just uttered.

"Oh, I say," Trevillyan protested feebly, "I didn't mean anything. I was just, uh, muttering in my cups, you know. Wouldn't offend you for the world, dear fellow."

"And my wife to be?" Charles asked in a silky voice that frightened Trevillyan even more.

"A-a-and, of course, Miss Beaumont. Upon my soul!

Never meant to offer an insult to her . . . or you. Never." Trevillyan looked blearily at his cup. "Bloody punch! Drank too much. Forgive me."

Charles's eyes nailed him to his chair for several terrifying seconds, and then that charming smile appeared, and Charles said amiably, "Certainly. We shall pretend that it never happened."

Feeling as if he had just escaped the claws of a big cat, Trevillyan sent him a sickly smile. "Raoul warned me that you had the devil's own temper, but I never believed him until now. That look in your eye . . . gave me quite a start, I can tell you."

"I thought," Charles said, "that we agreed to pretend the incident never happened."

Not liking the glitter in Charles's eye, Trevillyan muttered, "Right. Never happened."

"So tell me," Charles said politely, "what are our plans for this evening? Do we dine alone, or have you invited a few friends to join us?"

"Thought you'd be dining at Beaumont's," Trevillyan muttered. "Planned to go visit a little ladybird I keep in Penzance."

"By all means, go visit your mistress—do not let me keep you from the fair damsel's side. I can fend for myself. Eames will see to it that I do not starve, and I am quite used to amusing myself."

"Bad host."

Charles grinned at him. "Indeed not. I am a bad guest. Go see your ladybird—in fact, unless we make definite plans to the contrary, assume that your time is your own, and do not worry about me."

"What about the, uh, dead women?"

Charles shrugged. "Unless something else is discovered, I am afraid that we are at a standstill. We don't even know their names, so we have no way of tracing them, either where they came from or who might have had reason to kill them."

"I don't think," Trevillyan observed quietly, "that there was any logical reason to kill them. I did not see the body found by Brierly, but the woman on the beach . . ." He shuddered and added, "It appeared to be the work of a madman."

There was nothing more to be said on the subject. But later that evening, having dined pleasurably on some turtle soup, a saddle of mutton, boiled potato, jellied spring asparagus, and oysters in batter, all washed down with a fine hock, Charles's thoughts returned to the idea of Raoul being alive and plying his grisly hobby.

Declining dessert, taking a glass of hock with him, Charles returned to the library to consider the situation. His long legs stretched out toward the fire, he took the occasional swallow of his hock, his mind busy with the problem of the dead women.

He kept reminding himself that Raoul had been shot twice in the chest and the drop to the bottom of the sluice hole had been a good thirty feet, perhaps more. Could Raoul have survived? His lips thinned. Anything was possible. There had been a great deal of blood, but that didn't mean that his and Julian's bullets had hit anything vital. And while falling down the sluice would have been painful, it might not have been fatal. He scowled. Julian and Nell had no doubts about Raoul's fate. Nell's nightmares, her unholy link to Raoul and the ugly things he did in that dungeon below the Wyndham Dower House, had ended, and that more than anything convinced them that Raoul must be dead.

Nell and Julian might be satisfied, but since Raoul's body had never been found, Charles could not shake the sick feeling that his half brother was still alive. It was illogical, he admitted, and he could come up with no answer that fully explained how Raoul, alone and badly wounded, had managed to vanish into thin air.

Realizing that he was simply covering old ground, Charles turned his attention to the women who had been killed here in Cornwall. From what Trevillyan had related to him, terrible things had been done to both women before they had died. The description of the bodies bore too close a resemblance to what Nell had observed in her nightmares and to Julian's description of the body he and Marcus had seen in the Wyndham woods to be discounted as simple coincidence.

Charles sighed. He couldn't prove that Raoul was alive, or dead, for that matter, but he just couldn't believe that a second monster with Raoul's revolting tastes was roaming the English countryside. But Cornwall with its wild and rocky coasts, its vast lonely stretches, and its denizens comprising a smuggler community and those who traded with them—a secretive community that kept its mouth shut and minded its own business—would appeal to Raoul. For someone who had his own secrets to hide and wanted no curious neighbors, someone who wanted privacy to ply his diabolic trade, Cornwall would be perfect.

Charles took a long swallow of his hock. Right now, he couldn't prove that Raoul was alive. There was one thing he could do, however, and he wondered that he had not thought of it sooner. If Raoul was alive and if he was in the area, he had to be living somewhere.

Nodding to himself, Charles stood up. Of course. Find out what houses or properties had either been sold or leased in the past three years in this area, and he might find Raoul's lair.

Chapter 8

O f course, Adrian told April about Daphne's visit to the witch, a witch who just happened to be Goodson's sister. As they came down the stairs together that evening, Adrian poured the whole tale into April's ear. Since they immediately joined Daphne and Miss Ketty in the dining room and with servants in and out of the room serving the meal, April had no chance to bring up the subject. All through dinner, April stared with awe at her older sister, marveling at Adrian's words. Daffy had visited a witch! And was going back to see her on Friday!

Following their usual routine, the three siblings and Miss Ketty settled comfortably in the small blue salon at the rear of the house. It was a charming room, the walls hung in pale blue silk, the sofas and chairs covered in rich fabrics of a deeper hue, and a blue rug with cream and gold accents overlay the floor. To counter the chill of the evening, the heavy amber velvet drapes were pulled closed, and a fire burned brightly on the grate of the marble fireplace.

April waited only until Goodson had set down the tea tray and departed before she leaned forward and asked excitedly, "Oh, Daffy, may I go with you when you go to visit the witch on Friday? Please?"

Miss Ketty looked up sharply from the piece of tatting she had been working on. "A witch? Don't be ridiculous!"

Sitting across from Miss Ketty, Adrian grinned and said, "It's true. On our way home this afternoon, Daffy visited with a witch and plans to visit her again on Friday. You could have knocked me down with a feather when Daphne said that the witch is our Goodson's sister."

Miss Ketty's lips pursed in disapproving lines. "Miss Daphne! Whatever are you thinking? And it makes no never mind if this, this *creature* is Goodson's sister or not. Consorting with a witch! Why your poor sainted mother would turn over in her grave."

Daphne sent Adrian a speaking glance, but his grin just grew wider. Younger brothers could be so very annoying. "I assure you, dear Ketty," Daphne said quietly, "that Anne Darby is not at all what one would expect a witch to be like. She is very polite, respectable almost, and you would like her."

Miss Ketty snorted. "A witch? I hardly think so! No matter how respectable." She paused, and curiosity evident in her voice, she asked, "Whyever did you want to meet a witch?"

Her cheeks a little flushed, Daphne looked away from Miss Ketty's inquiring gaze. "Mrs. Hutton mentioned her one day," Daphne began carefully, "and said that if I wanted to hear some of the, uh, legends about our Beaumont ancestors, Anne Darby would be the person to talk to."

"Vicar Henley's collection doesn't give you enough information?"

The color in her cheeks deepening, Daphne said, "His collection is very thorough, but it is, er, stuffy reading and not as, um, vivid as the tales I'm sure Anne Darby could tell."

"But a witch, my dear! Are you certain this is wise? The stories she will spin for you are likely to be nothing more than bedtime tales to frighten children."

"What harm can there be in it?"

"You ask? Look at your dear brother and sister—they are all agog to meet this person. This entire conversation is not at all suitable for them."

Daphne shrugged. "I don't see that merely listening to a few stories concerning our ancestors will be so very bad."

Miss Ketty thought for a moment and then asked imprudently, "Have you discussed this notion with Mr. Weston? I wonder what he would say about his fiancée behaving in such a rash manner. I am sure he would not approve."

Daphne stiffened. "This is no concern of Mr. Weston's. I am perfectly capable of making a decision to see Mrs. Darby without getting Mr. Weston's permission. He is to be my husband, not my keeper."

Adrian hooted. "I wouldn't be too sure of that if I were you. Weston doesn't strike me as a fellow who will live comfortably under the cat's paw. Once you are married, I'll wager you'll not find him ignoring his wife's activities, especially when it comes to visiting witches."

"Oh, pooh, who cares what Mr. Weston thinks," April said airily. "Daffy isn't married to him yet, so what she does is her own business." Turning to her sister, she begged, "Please let me come with you—it shall be so exciting." Blue eyes gleaming with laughter, she slanted a glance at her brother and murmured, "Mayhap this witch will give me a potion that will turn Adrian into a toad."

"I ain't afraid of a witch, or her charms and potions, either," Adrian replied loftily, smiling wickedly at his sister. "None of her spells will harm *me!* Now, you are another story—you'll have nightmares for a month." He cocked a brow at Daphne. "Think I better escort you and see this witch for myself."

Miss Ketty looked sternly at Daphne. "You see? Already, they are talking of spells and potions. This is not an appropriate topic for young, untried minds."

Daphne agreed, but there was little she could do about her decision to introduce herself to Mrs. Darby this afternoon. I should have waited, she thought ruefully, and gone to see her alone. Once Adrian knew of the visit, it was a foregone conclusion that April would learn of it. Now that the cat was out of the bag, it was unlikely that either one of them was going to allow her to meet privately with Goodson's sister on Friday afternoon. Giving in to the inevitable, she said, "It may not be the best thing for them, but I'm afraid, since they already know about it, that there is little I can do. Besides, if I do not allow them to come with me, their imaginations will concoct far more lurid events than the tales Goodson's sister is likely to tell."

Ignoring April's squeal of delight and Adrian's shout of laughter, Miss Ketty frowned. "I must protest. You cannot be seriously thinking of taking these two little lambs to visit a witch! Even if she *is* our own worthy Goodson's sister, a fact I find hard to believe. Of course, whatever his sister may be, it is no reflection on Goodson's respectability."

"According to Mrs. Hutton, who grew up with both Goodson and Mrs. Darby, it is, indeed, true," Daphne said.

"Well, I'm glad that's settled," said Adrian, rising to his feet. "What time is our meeting on Friday?"

"We agreed I should come to her cottage at two o'clock."

Adrian bit back a yawn. "I'll have my horse and a carriage waiting for us in plenty of time. Meanwhile, it is bed for me."

"So early?" Daphne exclaimed, suddenly noticing the dark circles under his eyes.

Adrian yawned again. "Been having a devil of a time sleeping lately. Seems that the wind whistles around my corner of the house like a banshee. Sometimes, it so bad that it wakes me up." He hesitated, a faint frown marring his forehead. "The odd thing is that sometimes, above the wind, I'd swear that I hear a child or mayhap a woman crying. It's an infernal racket, I can tell you."

"Oh, you hear it, too?" said April, her eyes big. "I hate it. The first few times the sound woke me, I was terrified. I actually got out of bed and lit candles and searched my rooms for the source, but I found nothing."

Her heart beating in thick, painful strokes, Daphne asked, "Why haven't either one of you said anything to me? If the sound of the . . . wind is so bothersome, your rooms can be changed—the house is certainly big enough."

Adrian gave her a sleepy smile. "What, and give up that magnificent suite of rooms? I hardly think so. I'm no baby to be frightened away by the sound of wind."

"Neither am I," said April stoutly, although there was just the slightest quaver in her voice. "It's only the wind. It can't hurt us."

Daphne forced a smile. "Of course it can't."

Miss Ketty snorted. "And you're going to take them to visit a witch to hear who knows what terrifying tales about the former inhabitants of this house! You mark my words, Miss Daphne, if you persist in this mad plan, you're going to have Miss April waking up every night screaming of ghosts. And it will be your fault."

"Oh, don't scold so, Ketty," Daphne muttered. "I'm certain everything will be fine."

Miss Kettle disagreed, and the next morning, a missive written by her was delivered to Mr. Weston, divulging dear Miss Daphne's stubborn insistence in exposing herself and her siblings to the black magic of a witch. It had not been easy for Miss Kettle to write the note, and she had agonized over sending it. Deciding she had no choice if she was to save Miss Daphne from herself and Miss April and Sir Adrian from a dangerous influence, with a heavy heart, she sent the note on its way. Watching the servant ride away toward Lanyon Hall, she was torn between feeling she had betrayed her darling Miss Daphne and a sincere determination to protect all three of her innocent babes from the deleterious effects of close proximity to a witch.

Charles read Miss Kettle's note, his eyebrows rising at the contents. Daphne was taking her brother and sister to visit a local witch on Friday? A witch who also happened to be Goodson's sister? And he was to stop dear Miss Daphne from this rash action? Miss Daphne was far more likely to separate his head from his shoulders if he dared to interfere, Charles decided without hesitation. If he was unwise enough to meddle in Daphne's plans, she was more likely to become all the more determined to visit with her witch, if for no other reason than to thwart him. He shook his head, a faint smile curving his handsome mouth. It would appear that Miss Kettle had great faith in his abilities to control his bride-to-be. More, it seemed, than he did.

Not certain how he was to handle the situation and bitten by curiosity to know Daphne's reason for wishing to visit a witch, he ordered his horse saddled. Some time later, he was cantering up the driveway that led to Beaumont Place, still unclear of his role in this unfolding farce. As his horse rounded that last wide bend before the house came into view, the sound of thundering hooves coming fast behind him caught his ear. He barely pulled his horse off to the grassy verge before Adrian, astride a big black stallion, and Daphne, riding an equally large and muscular gray gelding, came sweeping into view.

They were racing, with Daphne's gray leading by a nose, but catching sight of him on the side of the road, they instantly pulled up their horses. The gray half reared and fought the bit, making its displeasure clear, and Charles admired Daphne's smooth skill and grace in effortlessly bringing such a powerful animal under control.

She looked stunning this morning. Her skin glowed, roses bloomed in her cheeks, and wearing a dark blue kerseymere habit with black braid and gilt buttons and half boots of black Spanish leather, she was the picture of a lady of fashion. A narrow-brimmed black beaver hat adorned with two scarlet feathers perched at a rakish angle on her head, and her thick black hair, caught up in a bun at the back of her neck, emphasized the delicate bones of her face. With a connoisseur's eye, his gaze traveled appreciatively over the high bosom, the narrow waist, and the shapely thigh delineated by the pull of the fabric as she sat sidesaddle on the restive horse.

Charles had never considered himself a particularly sensual man, but Daphne seemed to arouse a side of himself that he had not been aware of. The mere sight of that blue material lying so snugly against the long line of her thigh sent a pang of lust through him, and the image of that same lovely naked thigh wrapped around his hips flashed through his mind. The image was so real, so vivid he could almost feel the silkiness of her skin, feel the slide of her flesh against his, and he was helpless against the tide of desire that rose within him. He fought against it, cursing his unruly body and wondering grimly if he would survive this exquisite torture until their marriage. The odds, he decided, were decidedly against him as a certain impertinent part of his body made sitting in his saddle dashed uncomfortable.

"Good morning, sir," said Adrian when their horses came abreast of Charles's mount. "It is a fine day to be out and about, isn't it?"

Hoping his jacket hid any signs of his violent arousal, Charles nodded. "A fine day, indeed," he replied. Thinking a wise man would put as much distance as possible between himself and temptation, he considered keeping Adrian between them, but in the end, Daphne's pull was too strong, and consigning his fate to the gods, he urged his horse onto the road beside her cavorting gelding.

He smiled at Daphne. "I woke today," he said, "thinking I might convince you to go riding with me, only to discover, alas, that I am too late."

"Far too late," Daphne replied cheerfully. "Perhaps another day, if I am free."

"Well, no use having wasted your time on a sleeveless errand," Adrian said. "Won't you join us for a late breakfast?"

"Oh, I'm sure that Mr. Weston has other plans," Daphne said quickly.

"As it turns out, I am free and at your disposal." Smiling angelically into her eyes, he murmured, "And as for joining you for breakfast, I shall be delighted."

Daphne shrugged and kicked her horse into a trot, leaving the two gentlemen to follow at a more sedate pace.

"Don't mind Daffy, sir," Adrian said, aware that his sister had hardly acted like a welcoming fiancée. "She don't like being brought to bridle, but she'll come round—you'll see."

Observing with amusement the way his fiancée treated him with polite carelessness as they all gathered around in the morning room for breakfast, Charles doubted that Daphne would ever be a biddable wife. An appreciative smile lurked at the corner of his mouth as she kept her head slightly averted from him and carried on an intense conversation with Miss Ketty about the planting of some new rose bushes in the east garden. Life with Daphne would never be predictable, and he'd wager that the word boredom would never enter his vocabulary once she was his bride.

Another nervous glance from Miss Ketty caught his attention, and when Daphne rose to help herself to a small slice of cold sirloin, he smiled reassuringly at the little governess. He wasn't about to betray her part in his arrival this morning, but that did create a bit of problem for him: to protect Miss Ketty, he had to learn of the proposed trip from someone else. He was turning various gambits over in his mind when April solved his dilemma.

Forgetful that Mr. Weston might not approve of the proposed outing, April smiled at Charles and asked impulsively, "Has Daffy told you that we plan to visit a witch tomorrow?"

Daphne started, and her fork clattered on her plate. Returning quickly to the table, she shot an admonishing glance at her sister. "I'm sure that Mr. Weston is not at all interested in how we amuse ourselves," she said sharply, reseating herself.

"You're wrong there," Charles said, glad that the subject was now out in the open and that Miss Ketty could relax and not fear exposure. "I am *most* interested." Smiling guilelessly, he added, "Do you know, I don't believe that I've had the pleasure of ever meeting a witch."

"Why don't you join us tomorrow? It should be a great romp," said Adrian, deftly jerking his legs aside under the table to avoid the kick he knew Daphne had aimed at him.

"Thank you. I believe I shall," Charles said. "What time shall I be here?"

"The meeting is not here at the house," Daphne said from between gritted teeth. "We are going to Mrs. Darby's house, just outside of Penzance. It is a very small house, and when I made the arrangements, it was understood that I would be her only guest. I do not think that she is going to appreciate having a whole horde descend upon her without warning."

"Then warn her," Charles retorted. "Better yet, send her a note, telling her of the change in plans, and have her come to Beaumont Place. No reason for us to trek to Penzance when there is plenty of room here."

Daphne took a deep breath, thinking Mr. Weston was the most infuriating man she had ever met. And she was to marry him! "There are reasons," she began reasonably, "why meeting Mrs. Darby at her home would be best."

Leaning forward, April said in a confiding tone, "The witch is our Goodson's sister."

Charles's brow rose. "Indeed. All the more reason for her to come here." He smiled lazily at Daphne. "She can have a nice, cozy visit with her brother before she sees us." He looked puzzled. "Er, did someone tell me *why* we are meeting with a witch in the first place?"

"She is to tell us tales and legends about Beaumont Place and our ancestors," offered April brightly. "Daffy said Vicar Henley's papers are too stuffy and that Mrs. Darby's tales will be more vivid."

"I thoroughly disapprove of the entire affair," said

Miss Ketty firmly. "Consorting with witches! It is not at all proper."

"Oh, I quite agree with you," replied Charles sunnily, ingratiating himself further into Miss Ketty's good graces. He smiled at her, one adult to another. "But what are we to do? Miss Daphne has made up her mind, and Sir Adrian and Miss April are looking forward to it. Surely, we should not disappoint them? By having Mrs. Darby here at Beaumont Place, we can keep an eye on things and see that nothing untoward occurs. I think it should be quite safe."

"Goodson does not approve of his sister," Daphne said dryly. "He will not like it when he learns that she is to be here."

"Then we shall just have to let him know that his sister is coming to call tomorrow and allow him to get used to the idea, won't we?" said Charles sweetly.

He watched interestedly as Daphne's fingers tightened dangerously around her cup of coffee.

It was a near thing, but Daphne did not, as she longed to do, hurl her cup at Mr. Weston's head. Instead, she smiled just as sweetly at him and said, "What an excellent idea! And since you are so very busy rearranging everyone's plans, you shall have the pleasure of informing Goodson of the treat in store for him tomorrow."

Rising to her feet, she said, "And now, if you will excuse me, I must go and write a note to Mrs. Darby telling her of the change of plans."

Daphne sailed from the room, leaving Charles to stare after her in comical dismay. "You know, right up until the last minute, I thought I had her neatly boxed in," he observed to no one in particular.

Adrian guffawed. "Think Daffy won that round."

Charles grinned. "Yes, I'll concede that." Glancing around the table at the others he asked, "Is Goodson likely to cut up rough about his sister's visit?"

"Goodson is too well-trained to be anything but the exemplary butler that he is," said Miss Ketty. "While I am sure that he will not be happy about it, I am equally sure that he will act and do everything that is proper."

"There's only one way to find out," Charles muttered, standing up. He took his leave of April and Miss Ketty, and then looking at Adrian, he said, "You'd better come with me. He's your servant, after all."

Adrian threw down his napkin and standing up, said, "That may be, but you're the one who is to tell him." He grinned. "Daffy said so."

"I had not noticed it before, but you are remarkably like your elder sister," Charles complained as the two men left the room.

Faced with the news that Mrs. Darby was coming to call on Daphne tomorrow afternoon, Goodson was not pleased. Watching his increasingly rigid expression, Charles felt for him. It couldn't be pleasant for a man of his position and standing in the household to discover that his new employers knew his relationship to the local witch or that she was coming to call upon them tomorrow.

Flanked by Adrian, when Charles had finished his explanation, Goodson bowed stiffly. "As you wish, sirs," he said with frigid politeness. "I shall see that all is in readiness for Mrs. Darby's visit."

"It ain't so bad," Sir Adrian consoled his butler, "having a witch in the family. By Jupiter, there are times I'd rather have a witch for a sister than April, I can tell you! Be a lot more lively."

There was the faintest twitch to Goodson's mouth. "Thank you, Sir Adrian. I'll try to take your words to heart."

"That's the dandy!"

Having settled events to his liking, Charles was relatively pleased with himself when he finally rode away from Beaumont Place. He'd have liked a private moment with Daphne, but then remembering what happened the last two times he'd been alone with her, he decided regretfully that perhaps it was best that she had remained locked in her rooms. No doubt wishing me to the very devil, he thought with a grin as he kicked his horse into a gallop.

Since he had no definite plans for the day, rather than returning to Lanyon Hall, he turned his horse in the direction of Penzance. His visit with the Beaumonts had been an amusing diversion, but it was time to turn his thoughts to Raoul. Mr. Vinton had struck him as a discreet, respectable, reliable fellow. A local man, too, just the sort who could discover the information he needed without raising questions.

His estimation of Mr. Vinton proved to be correct. Arriving unannounced at the solicitor's place of business, Charles was immediately shown into Mr. Vinton's office.

Smiling, Mr. Vinton rose from behind his desk and extending his hand, said warmly, "Good afternoon, Mr. Weston. I did not expect to see you again so soon. Is there a problem with the settlements?"

Charles assured him that his purpose for calling upon him was for an entirely different matter. Polite but curious, Mr. Vinton indicated a seat by the fire, and once they were seated, Mr. Vinton said, "How may I help you?"

"I wish you to make discreet inquiries for me about properties with some very specific requirements that have been leased or sold during the past, oh, say, three years," Charles said. "I do not want anyone to know that you are making the inquiries for me." Charles leaned forward and staring intently at Mr. Vinton, added, "Our connection must remain secret. No one, and I repeat, no one is to know."

Mr. Vinton looked disturbed. "I must ask, sir, if this has anything to do with the Beaumont family? If it does, I must refuse to act in your behalf."

Charles shook his head. "This has nothing to do with them. It is a private matter of my own."

Mr. Vinton studied him for a long moment. "Very well," Mr. Vinton said eventually. "I will do it, sir. But I warn you, if I discover that you have misled me about the involvement of the Beaumonts, I shall immediately inform Sir Adrian and remove myself from your employ."

Charles rose to his feet, preparing to leave. "I would not, believe me, have it any other way."

On Friday, as he drove his curricle toward Beaumont Place and the meeting with the local witch, Charles thought that the weather was appropriate for just such an encounter. Black-bottomed clouds scudded across a sullen dark sky, and the scent of rain was carried on the breeze that blew in from the sea. Charles suspected that before nightfall, a storm would make landfall. Anticipating nasty weather, he had packed accordingly.

Driving up to the front of the house, he was met by Adrian, who came down the broad steps to meet him. Spying the valise at Charles's feet in the curricle, Adrian exclaimed, "Oh, good, you're staying the night, then? I meant to suggest it yesterday." He glanced back over his shoulder at Goodson, who stood in the doorway. "Mr. Weston will be staying the night. See that rooms are prepared for him and that his valise is unpacked by one of the footmen." He frowned. "Might want to assign one of them to act as his valet."

Goodson bowed. "It shall be done, Sir Adrian."

Charles tossed the reins to the waiting groom and jumped down from the curricle. Shortly, with Adrian at his side, he entered the small blue salon that the family favored for themselves. Daphne was seated on one of the sofas; a small woman with large dark eyes sat beside her, the bronze gown, nearly a decade out of fashion, identifying her as the witch. Miss Ketty, her face set in disapproving lines, the inevitable bag of tatting in her lap, sat nearby in a channel-backed chair. April occupied a matching chair next to Miss Ketty, a small mahogany table between them.

Introductions were made, and Charles revised his thoughts about Anne Darby. He'd ridden to Beaumont Place, not worried exactly, but concerned that inviting a witch into the house might not have been wise. It has seemed, at the time, the easiest way of controlling the situation, but beyond the fact that Anne Darby was reputed to be a practitioner of the black arts and Goodson's sister, a sister whose profession Goodson deplored, he knew nothing about her. For all he knew, Anne Darby could be a cunning fraud, eager to pick Daphne's pocket, or worse, someone who could present a real danger to Daphne and the family. His mouth tightened. *His* family, he'd reminded himself, surprised how protective he felt about the entire Beaumont clan. And so he'd come prepared for trouble, braced even to face Daphne's wrath and turf out her guest if he caught the slightest hint that Anne Darby was not a harmless diversion.

He'd had no clear picture in his mind of what a witch should look like, but this little woman with the serene features and neatly arranged hair, wearing, no doubt, her best gown made him think of a governess rather than a witch. There was amusement and intelligence in the big, dark eyes that met his, and he sensed that there was no malice in her. Which is as well for both of us, he decided wryly. Anne Darby avoided an ignoble exit from the house, and he avoided being in Daphne's bad graces.

There was a tap on the door, and Goodson, followed by a footman, came into the room, both men bearing silver trays filled with refreshments. Observing as the butler went about his duties, Charles wondered at his feelings at having to serve his sister, a sister he disapproved of. What was going on behind those composed features? It was hard to tell, Goodson's face revealing none of the emotions that might be roiling in his breast. Having seen to the needs of the occupants of the room, Goodson bowed and departed, nary by word, expression, or gesture giving any indication that Mrs. Darby was anything other than a guest of his employers.

Charles took a sip from his tankard of warm punch that

Goodson had prepared for the gentlemen, the ladies being served tea or coffee, and waited for the entertainment to begin.

Adrian, after taking a big gulp of his punch, eyed Daphne warily and announced defiantly, "I invited Mr. Weston to stay the night, Daphne. The weather is going to be filthy. Better he stay here tonight. Goodson is seeing to his rooms and sending up one of the footmen to act as his valet."

"That's very nice, dear," she said tranquilly, causing both Adrian and Charles to stare hard at her. She bit back a smile, realizing that she had confounded them. Both men had obviously expected a fight, and her easy acceptance of the situation took the wind right out of their sails. And they'd be shocked, she thought ruefully, to learn that her capitulation had nothing to do with trying to outwit them—she'd already decided that coming to daggers drawing with her brother and her fiancé accomplished little. This was, after all, Adrian's home, and he had a right to invite whoever he wished to stay. As for Mr. Weston . . .

She studied Charles from beneath her lashes, feeling, as always—when she wasn't furious with him, she reminded herself—a flutter in the region of her heart. He was very handsome as he lounged near the fireplace, drinking his punch, laughing at something Adrian said. The dark blue jacket fit his broad shoulders and strong arms to perfection, the buckskin breeches clung to his muscular thighs, and Daphne flushed, remembering the feel of that powerful body crushed against hers, the taste of him on her tongue. He had only to smile at her or fix those cool green eyes on her face for butterflies to dance in her stomach and her knees to melt, and when he touched her, as he had done in Mr. Vinton's office . . . . She swallowed, remembering the liquid heat that had flooded her, the emotions that had risen up inside of her. When he touched her as he had then, she rather thought she went a little mad, the urge to offer herself, to allow him to do with her as he willed, almost overpowering. But it had been he, she reminded herself, her eyes on his long mouth, who had ended their passionate embrace, not she. What was she to make of that? That he found her wanting? Or wanton? She scowled, neither notion pleasing her.

It was the gentle clearing of Mrs. Darby's throat as she sat beside her on the couch that brought Daphne's attention to the matter at hand.

When Daphne glanced at her, Mrs. Darby asked quietly, "Shall I begin?"

Daphne looked at the expectant faces of her siblings and nodded. "Yes, of course. Please do."

Mrs. Darby smiled at her. "I believe I shall begin with the legend of Black Beaumont."

"*Black* Beaumont, eh? He must have been a wicked fellow," remarked Adrian.

"Oh, he was," said Anne Darby, a twinkle in her eyes. "Very. It is whispered that in the days of King John, while good King Richard the Lionheart was away on the Crusades, that he took for his own another man's wife . . ."

Chapter 9

The words barely left Anne Darby's mouth before Miss Ketty, throwing a fulminating look at Daphne, said, "I must protest. I do not believe that Miss April should be listening to such improper nonsense."

"Oh, dear Ketty, never say so," begged April. "I have read the Arthurian Legends. I know all about Sir Lancelot and Queen Guinevere. Surely, this is little different."

"It really isn't," agreed Daphne. "And I think you forget that April will be seventeen in a few months. While to us, she will always be the baby of the family, she is growing up. She is a young lady, and I think it unfair to banish her to the schoolroom." Coaxingly, she added, "It is only a legend, a story. It cannot hurt her to hear it, and if at any time, I think the subject inappropriate, I shall ask Mrs. Darby to cease." Not giving Miss Ketty a chance to reply, Daphne turned to Mrs. Darby and said with a smile, "Won't you please begin?"

As Mrs. Darby spun her tale, Charles watched with amusement as Daphne, April, and Adrian listened spellbound. The Black Beaumont legend was just the sort of thing he'd thought it would be—the young and beautiful wife, Blythe, stolen away from her husband by a dangerous rogue, Black Beaumont. Blythe's *much* older husband, died, of course, of a broken heart within weeks of Beaumont's dastardly deed with Blythe's name on his lips. In reality, Charles suspected that the husband died of old age and that Blythe was more than happy to exchange him for a handsome, virile young warrior of Black Beaumont's ilk. He smiled to himself as Mrs. Darby finished the story with a traditional ending: after her husband's death, Blythe married Beaumont, and they lived happily ever after.

As the story wound down, Charles noticed that Daphne looked disappointed. What had she expected? That Blythe stabbed Beaumont to death and returned forthwith to her husband? His lips quirked. More than likely, that was *exactly* the ending she would have preferred.

Charles was wrong. Daphne had no problem with the story as Mrs. Darby told it, but she was disappointed that the tale of Black Beaumont appeared to have no bearing on the strange visitation she had experienced. She sighed. She knew it was unlikely that she'd be so lucky as to discover the answers she sought so easily, but she was still disappointed.

There was an added urgency to her desire to discover more about the history of the Beaumonts—Adrian and April's admission of the crying wind worried her. It was one thing for her to face a ghostly apparition, another for her brother and sister to be disturbed, even if only by the sounds of the wind. Their confessions lent credence to her growing fear that there was *something* roaming the halls of Beaumont Place. Whatever it might be, good or evil, she thought stoutly, I shall discover what it is and *make it go away.*

The vicar's papers and documents so far had revealed little that was of help to her. Daphne knew that further study of them might tell her what she wanted to know, but instinct told her that she could easily overlook that for which she searched. Ancestors, she admitted glumly, had a way of suppressing or watering down facts so that they did not reflect badly on the family. She sighed. Mrs. Darby's stories might not reveal anything of use, but right now, Goodson's sister was her best source of information.

Forcing a smile, Daphne murmured, "Won't you please tell us another story?"

Between the social niceties and Mrs. Darby's tale, the time had sped by, and dusk was falling. As the light faded, the storm arrived, announcing its presence by the occasional clap of thunder, the low moaning of the wind, and the rain flailing against the windows. Listening to the sounds of the increasing storm, Mrs. Darby said regretfully, "I'd planned to tell you another story, a ghost story, but I'm afraid that the worsening weather makes that impossible. Mayhap another time?"

"Oh, I say," protested Adrian. "Can't have you leaving in filthy weather like this. I insist that you remain here tonight as our guest. Goodson and Mrs. Hutton can fix you up right and tight."

Daphne's pulse leaped at the mention of the word ghost, and she could have kissed Adrian for his invitation to Mrs. Darby. The ghost story might prove to be utter nonsense, but Daphne was desperate to hear it, and when Anne hesitated, she leaned forward and touched her hand. "Please stay. As my brother says, Goodson can take care of everything, and it will be no imposition."

"Yes! You must stay," chimed in April. "It shall be ever so enjoyable." A particularly loud clap of thunder rattled the windows, and April jumped. Turning a laughing face toward Mrs. Darby, she added, "You see—it is going to be a splendid night for ghost stories. Oh, do say that you will stay."

Charles saw the change in Daphne's face when Mrs. Darby mentioned the word ghost. His bride-to-be clearly wanted Mrs. Darby to stay. But why? Mere politeness? A ghoulish streak? He doubted it. But ever helpful, he murmured, "There is no question, Mrs. Darby, of you leaving tonight. The weather is frightful; you must remain as Sir Adrian's guest." He flashed his most charming smile. "Besides, as the young lady has said, it is a splendid night for a ghost story."

Mrs. Darby capitulated. Daphne rang for Goodson and Mrs. Hutton, and they were informed of the change in plans. If Goodson's features congealed into a rigid, immobile mass at the news, Mrs. Hutton was easier to read, a smile breaking over her face at the announcement.

"Goodson shall have another place set for dinner," Mrs. Hutton said. "And I shall tell Cook that there is one more person dining tonight."

"It's not necessary for me to dine with your family," Mrs. Darby said calmly, looking at Adrian. "I appreciate your kindness, Sir Adrian, but I'm not one to get above myself. I think it would be more fitting, and I would be more comfortable, if I dined in the kitchen with staff."

"And considering the hour," said Daphne, eager to gloss over any awkwardness, "I suggest that we allow Mrs. Hutton to show Mrs. Darby to her room and that she rejoin us here after dinner." Turning to Mrs. Darby, she added, "That will give you time to, er, settle in before you once again regale us with another story."

"Settle in?" Charles remarked after the doors had closed behind the two servants and Mrs. Darby. "Don't you mean to tend her brother's wounded sensibilities?"

Daphne smiled. "That more than anything else. Poor Goodson. He is on the horns of a dilemma, isn't he? We shall have to be very kind to him if we are not to be in his black books forever."

Dinner behind them, they were once again gathered in the blue salon, the candelabra had been lit to cast out the gloom, and the fire danced on the hearth. Outside, the wind shrieked around the house, the rain pelted the windows, and the flashing lightning and rumbling thunder created the perfect atmosphere for a ghost story.

The Beaumonts were scattered comfortably around the room, Adrian and April sitting side-by-side on a sofa across from where Daphne again sat beside Mrs. Darby. Charles stood near the fire, his arm resting along the marble mantle facing the room. Mrs. Ketty was in her chair by the fire, her tatting spilling off her lap and onto the floor, her expression that of long-suffering disapproval. She was not the only one unhappy with the situation. The few moments that Goodson was in the room as he placed a large tray of refreshments on a low rosewood table in front of the sofa where Daphne sat were strained. The tension between Goodson and his sister was almost palpable, the air vibrating with condemnation from Goodson, defiance from Mrs. Darby.

Goodson departed, outraged disapproval fairly radiating from him, his bow to her so stiff that Daphne feared he'd have shattered in a thousand pieces if his spine had been any more rigid. She sighed. Tomorrow, she would make amends, she thought as she served the ladies tea and Charles poured himself and Adrian a snifter of brandy.

Daphne took a sip of her tea and glanced at Mrs. Darby. "You mentioned something about a ghost?"

Mrs. Darby set down her cup and saucer and nodded. "Yes, I did." She smiled at April. "I'm afraid there is no happy ending this time. It is a sad, tragic tale."

April's eyes went round, and she clasped her hands under her chin in anticipatory delight. "How lovely. Please begin."

"It was," Mrs. Darby said in a solemn voice, "during the reign of Bloody Mary, and Sir Wesley and his nephew and heir, John, were on opposite sides of the upheaval." Mrs. Darby explained that Sir Wesley had no children of his own and that John was the only child of his younger brother, Edward. Sir Wesley, a secret supporter of Rome, had long awaited the return of the true faith, but Edward, who had died the second year of Mary's reign in 1555, and his son, John, were ardent followers of Henry the VIII's Protestant religion. Edward and Sir Wesley had been bitter enemies—even as boys, they'd fought and argued over the smallest of things. As they matured, the rift grew wider, but it was Edward's marriage to a lovely young heiress that put an end to any hope that the two men would ever be reconciled. Sir Wesley, mad with jealousy and envy, believed that his brother had deliberately seduced and married the only woman he'd ever wanted, thereby depriving him of a family and an heir from his own loins.

Mrs. Darby stopped speaking for a moment to take a sip of her tea, and Adrian muttered, "If that don't beat all! Don't see why Sir Wesley couldn't have married some other gal. If you ask me, it was his own fault he didn't have a son of his own. No reason to blame his brother."

"But perhaps no other woman would do for him," breathed April. "John's mother may have been his one and only true love."

Adrian sent her a look. "Balderdash! You been reading some of those silly books from Minerva Press again?"

"Of course she hasn't!" snapped Miss Ketty. "As if I would allow such a thing."

The guilty look on April's face told a different tale, and not wanting to give Miss Ketty an opening to scold, Daphne said quickly to Mrs. Darby, "Won't you go on?"

Mrs. Darby nodded. "It is said that Sir Wesley's reputation," she began again, "was that of a cold, hard, unfeeling man. His tenants feared him, and he was generally held in low esteem by his neighbors, few caring for his brutal ways. Edward was admired and respected by many, and Sir Wesley hated his brother for that, too. There was no love lost between him and his nephew, either. The chasm was so deep that after Edward's death, Sir Wesley swore that he would stop at nothing to keep John from standing in his shoes."

Despite the cheerily burning fire, Daphne felt a chill and pulled her gaily patterned Chinese silk shawl closer around her shoulders. She glanced around the room, seeing that everyone was intent upon the story that Mrs. Darby was telling. As the seconds passed, the chill intensified, and she noticed that April shivered a little in her thin, spotted muslin gown and that Miss Ketty was rearranging her woolen shawl to cover her arms. Even Charles, a slight frown on his face, reached down to poke at the leaping gold and scarlet flames. A feeling of dread shot through her—the chill was not her imagination, the others could feel it, too. Remembering the icy cold of her bedroom the night she had seen the apparition, Daphne searched the room for the foglike form, but there was nothing. Except, it seemed to her that the candles were not burning as brightly, that a creeping gloom seemed to be stealing into the room.

The storm cast its own eerie spell, the house creaking and rattling from the force of the wind and the brilliant white flashes from the lightning, each flash followed by the angry snarl and rumble of thunder.

After an especially powerful thunderclap, Mrs. Darby frowned and rubbed her arms as if cold before saying, "John, as handsome a young man as you could find, like his father before him, had married an heiress, a lovely young lady, Anne–Marie, only months before Edward's death. And though saddened by his father's death, in the spring of 1556, John had much to be happy about—his beloved Anne–Marie was pregnant, and they were looking forward to the birth of their first child." Mrs. Darby's voice lowered. "It was a bloody time for the Protestants," she said gravely. "With Queen Mary's blessings, the Pope had restored Catholic control over England, and just the previous year, our own brave Bishop Latimer, refusing to recant his Protestant faith, was burned at the stake along with other martyrs who refused to bow to papal Rome." Her gaze moved from one rapt face to another. "It was a terrible time—no Protestant dare openly practice their faith for fear of reprisal. Worse, there were those who used the situation to further their own dastardly aims. Including Sir Wesley. He used his power as Queen Mary's man to seize other lands and fortunes and to retaliate against his neighbors. It is whispered that at Sir Wesley's command, more than one poor soul died screaming in the dungeons beneath this very house and that even his bride, taken in the desperate hope of siring an heir, was not immune to his cruelty."

A wave of cold so powerful it made her teeth chatter swept over Daphne just as April said, "Why is it so cold in here?"

"What is wrong with that fire?" Miss Ketty demanded. "Miss April is right, this room is freezing."

"It is a bit chilly," remarked Adrian. "Must be the storm, the wind forcing itself around the window frames."

"There's nothing wrong with the fire," Charles said. "Look for yourselves. It's burning well, but I'll throw on more wood if you like."

"Please do," said Daphne, though she suspected that no amount of wood was going to make any difference. She watched as Charles piled several more logs on the fire, golden sparks shooting up the chimney. Yet there was no added warmth in the room, and the sensation that something lurked just beyond her sight was overpowering. Whatever was causing the icy cold this time felt vastly different from that night in her bedroom, and she glanced around, afraid of what she might see. That last time, she had been frightened, it was true, but there hadn't been this sense of dread, of terror that rose up in her throat, nearly choking her. The candles dimmed, and she had the uneasy impression that *something* was in the room with them and that it was *not* the sad little ghost that had appeared previously to her.

What the hell was going on? Charles wondered. The room *was* freezing, and he was aware of a feeling of danger, the hair on the back of his neck rising. Daphne's eyes met his, the expression in them making him instantly cross the room to stand beside her.

"What is it?" he asked quietly.

Daphne tried to smile, but her lips wouldn't work and she shook her head.

Anne sent Daphne a searching look and conscious of the cold, the odd dimming of the candles, said slowly, "I grew up hearing stories about this house, and it has long been rumored that parts of Beaumont Place are haunted. Some of the bedrooms . . . even this room, once Sir Wesley's study. There have been . . . sightings . . . things happening for which there is no explanation."

"Now that's enough!" snapped Miss Ketty, thoroughly outraged. "I've held my tongue, but enough is enough. Ghosts! What flummery! There is no such thing as a ghost, and I'll not have Miss April subjected to any more of this nonsense. She'll have nightmares for a week." She snorted. "Sir Wesley sounds quite a nasty fellow and not at all the sort of person I'd like to meet, nor I doubt, that any of us would like to have as a relative. He sounds a perfect scoundrel and deserved whatever fate befell him." Miss Ketty surged to her feet and shaking a finger at Daphne, said, "And as for you, Miss Daphne, look at you—you're shaking and white as a sheet. You mark my words, after tonight, you won't sleep a wink, either."

Charles glanced down at Daphne, his frown increasing when he saw that she was, indeed, shivering and that the color of her skin was pale as new fallen snow. His hand closed round her shoulder, and he asked, "Are you ill, my dear? May I get something? A brandy to warm you?"

Daphne shook her head, her gaze suddenly transfixed. "Look," she whispered, pointing a trembling finger at the fireplace.

As one, the inhabitants of the room stared in the direction of her pointing finger. Where once a cheerful fire burned, there were now only smoldering coals, and a cloud of thick, oily black smoke billowed out of the chimney, spilling into the room. It was a terrifying sight, the smoke moving with a will of its own, shaping and dissolving and then reshaping itself into a vaguely human form. Its attention seemed focused where Daphne and Mrs. Darby sat on the sofa, half formed hands reaching out from the main bulging mass as if it would snatch up one of them.

The effect on the observers was dramatic. With a curse, Charles swept Daphne up from the sofa, shoving her behind him, his big body braced to fight what writhed on the hearth. Mrs. Kettle shrieked and stumbled out of her chair and ran toward the door. April shrank back against the sofa, her eyes huge and terrified. Adrian leaped to his feet, exclaiming, "By Jove! What the devil is *that?*"

As more of it spilled into the room, the sense of an old evil and death hit Daphne like the force of a blow, and she sagged against the sofa, fighting the nausea and terror flooding through her. Charles spared her a glance, but she shook her head, indicating she was not hurt.

Charles's gaze moved to Mrs. Darby. Mrs. Darby appeared unmoved, but the paleness of her face gave her away. She is as frightened as the rest of us, Charles thought grimly.

Mrs. Darby sat there motionless, staring at the ominous, smoky form, at the clawlike fingers that flailed in the air. A small golden object appeared in her hand, and rising to her feet, she confronted the seething, amorphous mass. Holding the object in front of her, she said weakly, "Get thee gone, spirit. There is nothing for you here."

At her words or from the power of whatever she held in her hand, the thing, for there was no other word for it, contracted. Mrs. Darby took another step toward it, the golden object held before her like a shield, and her voice gaining strength, she ordered, "By all that you once held holy, I command you to leave this room."

There was a tense second, and then an odd sighing sound whispered through the air, and as simply as that, the smoke vanished up the chimney. Feeling as if she had been released from some terrible spell, Daphne forced herself to move out from behind Charles. To her profound relief, the fire was once again dancing red and yellow in the fireplace; the room was bright with the light from the many candles; the bone-chilling cold was gone.

Daphne sank down onto the sofa, more shaken than she realized. April and Adrian recovered instantly and thinking it a clever lark, were unfazed by the incident, April saying, "Oh, Mrs. Darby, that was simply wonderful! I have never seen anything as good, not even in London."

"M'sister's right. We've seen several magical shows, but

never anything the equal of that," Adrian said admiringly. "How did you do it? Especially that illusion with the smoke? It was quite the most amazing thing I've ever seen. Why, for one moment there, I thought it would reach out and grab either you or Daphne right up. Capital! Most entertaining."

"Entertaining? I have never heard such utter nonsense in my life!" said Miss Kettle angrily. "It was horrible, and I did not find it the least entertaining." She sent Mrs. Darby a look of pure dislike. "It was shameful! I was terrified, and poor Miss April, why something like this could send her to bed for a week." When Adrian burst out laughing, Miss Kettle shook a finger at him. "There is nothing amusing, young man, about frightening people that way." Gathering her tattered dignity about her, she said, "I am not staying in this room a moment longer to be subjected to any more nasty tricks of that sort." She bent a stern glance on April. "And neither are you, miss. It is past your bedtime. Come along."

April protested, but Miss Kettle would not be deterred, and for reasons of her own, Daphne supported her old nurse. "Ketty is right, April," she said quietly. "It is past your bedtime."

When April would have argued, Adrian stood up and said, "Come along, brat. Miss Ketty is right, the hour is late." Suppressing a yawn, he added, "I'll even go with you." Turning back to the others, he bid them good night, and ushering a complaining April in front of him, Miss Kettle marching right beside her, the three of them left the room.

Quiet fell once the doors shut behind them, the pop and crackle of the fire, the low moaning of the wind the only sounds in the room. Charles picked up his snifter and helped himself to another brandy. He sipped it reflectively for several seconds, his gaze on the fireplace.

Daphne poured herself and Mrs. Darby a fresh cup of hot tea.

"That was quite a performance," Charles said eventually.

"April is right. I have never seen the like, not even in London. Your talents are wasted here in Cornwall."

Mrs. Darby set down her cup of tea. Her eyes fixed on Charles, she said, "That was no performance."

"I agree," said Charles coolly. "I wondered if you were going to try to claim credit for it."

"Credit?" Daphne asked with a shudder. "Why would anyone wish to claim credit for such a horrible thing."

Charles glanced at her, his expression unreadable. "You're very lucky, I think, that your brother and sister and Miss Ketty believe what they saw was nothing more than a splendid piece of theatrics. But I wonder . . . did you know what would happen? Is that why you wanted Mrs. Darby here tonight?"

Daphne shook her head. Wearily, she said, "No. I had no notion that anything so, so . . . spectacular would occur." She looked up at Charles, exclaiming, "You cannot believe that I would have allowed Adrian and April to remain if I'd suspected that anything out of the ordinary would have happened!"

Charles said nothing, his gaze after a long moment moving from Daphne's strained features to Mrs. Darby's face. "Did you expect it?"

Mrs. Darby took a deep breath. "I didn't expect it . . . but I came prepared for it." She looked over at the fireplace almost as if she feared the return of that threatening mass. "I grew up in this house along with my brother, Goodson, and Mrs. Hutton, although she wasn't Hutton in those days, she was just pretty little Betty Brown, and there were always stories about certain rooms being . . . different. It was only natural—Beaumont Place is an old, old house, and people have been born and died within its walls for centuries." She swallowed. "There have been good men and women who lived here . . . and bad men and women. And from time to time, those bad men and women have done wicked, unspeakable things. Many believe that wickedness lingers in some places, as if the very walls, stones, and timbers are indelibly soaked with the ugliness and horrors that have taken place within the confines of the house." She looked uneasily around the room. "I spoke the truth when I said that this room was once Sir Wesley's office. My great grandmother and my grandmother both had the Sight, and neither one of them would ever step foot in this room after dark and never alone, even during daylight." She glanced at Daphne. "The story Mrs. Hutton told you about the young lady from London in Sir Huxley's time is only one of many about haunted rooms in this house."

"Well, nobody told me," said Charles. Pulling up a chair, he sat down. Stretching his long legs out in front of him, he eyed Mrs. Darby. "Suppose you tell it to me, and don't leave anything out."

Mrs. Darby complied, and when she was finished speaking, Charles looked at Daphne. "Was that why you called upon her? To have her verify the story?"

Daphne shrugged, not ready to confess to the far less dramatic apparition in her bedroom. "I told you. I simply wanted to learn more about my ancestors."

"Now why, I wonder," Charles said slowly, "don't I believe you?"

Daphne's chin lifted. "Are you calling me a liar? Having Mrs. Darby relate some of the stories, true or not, seemed a harmless way to have a more, er, rounded picture of the past. Certainly, Adrian and April are far more likely to listen to, er, lively tales about their ancestors than to pore over the crabbed handwriting of some long dead relative. Not everything can be learned from dry, dusty family records, you know."

"And you thought having a particularly unpleasant ghost conjured up would be helpful?" asked Charles incredulously.

"Is that what you saw?" Daphne demanded, her hands clenched into fists in her lap. "A ghost?"

Charles hesitated. He'd never believed, not even for a moment, that Mrs. Darby had been a clever charlatan and that she had merely dazzled them with the skills of a master magician. From the first, he'd known right down to his bones that something else was at work, known that Mrs. Darby had been as taken by surprise by what had appeared on the hearth of the fireplace as the rest of them. But did he believe that he'd come face to face with a ghost tonight? Had that obscene shape really been a ghost? Or had it all been a figment of his imagination? He knew that wasn't true because they'd all seen it, even if Miss Kettle and the youngsters believed it to be an excellent trick. One thing was certain—they'd all seen something tonight that had momentarily scared the hell out of them, myself included, Charles decided sourly. But had it been a ghost? He thought back over the events, the dimming of the candles, the icy cold, the sensation of facing something wicked, that damned shifting shape in front of the fireplace. He sighed. If he hadn't seen a ghost, then he had seen the next best thing.

His eyes met Daphne's. "Yes, I do think I saw a ghost tonight, or at the very least, I was in the presence of evil."

Daphne sank back against the sofa. "I feared I was going mad," she said in a low voice. Her eyes locked painfully on his, she asked, "And the cold? Did you feel that, too?"

Charles nodded. "And the candles failed. I noticed that also."

He glanced at Mrs. Darby. "You said that you didn't expect it, but that you were prepared for it. What did you mean?"

"I didn't plan for what happened to happen," Mrs. Darby said earnestly. "You must believe me. I had no particular stories in mind to tell you when I arrived this afternoon, and I didn't know until I was shown into it that we would be in Sir Wesley's old study. Once we were all situated in the room, though, it seemed fitting that I should tell you the story of Sir

Wesley." She looked across at the fire. "I can't even say that I felt any impending danger—I don't have the Sight like my grandmother and great grandmother, but their feelings about this room made a lasting impression on me." Reluctantly, she admitted, "But perhaps, I did have some sense of warning because when I joined Goodson and the others for dinner, I asked him to lend me the charm he'd inherited from our great grandfather and that he always carried with him." She smiled faintly. "He claimed that it protected him from the spirits. Goodson was furious. Not only that I wanted the charm, but also that I was going to tell the legend of Sir Wesley." She sighed. "My brother so dislikes anything that reflects badly on the family. He would prefer to forget that some of the people who have lived in this house have done terrible things." She made a face. "If I wanted to tell you stories about all the 'good' Beaumonts, he would have no objections. He would even tell a few himself."

"But he did lend you this charm?" Charles persisted.

"Oh, yes," Mrs. Darby said cheerfully. "He didn't want to, but Mrs. Hutton convinced him that there could be no harm in it, and if by chance, an old ghostie came to call, well, wouldn't it be better if I had protection?"

"And it was that charm that you held up to the, um, ghost?" asked Daphne.

"It's not a charm precisely," Mrs. Darby said. "It's a gold crucifix."

"May I see it?" asked Charles.

Mrs. Darby produced the crucifix and handed it to him.

Holding it securely between his fingers, Charles studied the intricately fashioned crucifix, thinking that it was rather small to have wielded such power.

"Do you know its history?"

Mrs. Darby nodded. "As you know, the Goodson family has always served the Beaumont family. One of our ancestors was given that crucifix by the Beaumont he served." She swallowed and stared at the light glinting off the golden crucifix in Charles's hand. "It is said to have been blessed by the Pope himself."

Daphne's hand flew to her throat. "Was it . . . did it belong to . . . ?"

"Until he gave it to my relative on his deathbed," Mrs. Darby said softly, "it belonged to Sir Wesley."

Chapter 10

Daphne had been positive that she'd not sleep a wink that night, but to her surprise, the moment her head touched the pillow, she fell asleep. She woke the next morning to a gray, pouting day, the worst of the storm having blown itself out during the night, but the sky was still leaden, rain falling steadily and the occasional puff of wind whispering around the house, a weak reminder of last night's powerful gusts.

As she bathed and prepared to face the day, Daphne considered the previous night's events. There had not been much conversation, or any point to it, she thought grimly, after Mrs. Darby had identified the crucifix as once being owned by Sir Wesley. Even though she knew what she had seen last night, Daphne had hoped that in the cold morning light, she'd be able to convince herself that she had overreacted, but such was not the case. She might not yet have a clue about the misty little apparition who had awakened her in her bedroom weeks ago, but if she believed anything, she believed that last night, she had seen the ghostly manifestation of Sir Wesley. And only his crucifix, blessed by the Pope, saved us from God knew what evil, she admitted uneasily.

If there was a beneficial aspect to the event, it was that Charles and Mrs. Darby had seen and felt the same things she had. Obviously, she wasn't going mad or imagining things, and until that moment, aware of the relief that swept through her, she hadn't known how heavily that idea had preyed upon her mind. Of course, she reminded herself glumly, she had replaced being mad with being haunted by the disagreeable ghost of Sir Wesley.

And Charles? What did he think? Daphne frowned. He hadn't shied away from the notion that they'd seen a ghost last night. But how would he react if she told him about her little ghost? After Sir Wesley, the crying visitor she'd seen in her bedroom seemed harmless and tame. Might Charles think she had imagined her?

Daphne froze. Now when had she begun to think of that misty shape in her bedroom as her? She didn't know, she only knew that it felt right. She was convinced that whatever had come to visit her that first time had been feminine. Was it, perhaps, the crying that made her think that? Or the smallness of the thing? The lack of a threat? Again, she didn't know, she was only certain that the odd manifestation she'd seen in this room was definitely female.

A sound, half amused, half despairing broke from her, and she dropped her head in her hands. Did she really believe that Beaumont Place was home to not one, but two ghosts? Sir Wesley, and she had no trouble in believing that black, horrible mass they had seen last night had been him . . . or rather, his ghost, and the unhappy, little female spirit who had appeared in her bedroom? And the wailing that Adrian and April had heard, what of that? Was it coming from the female apparition or something else? That it originated from Sir Wesley, she instantly dismissed. He was far more likely to have been the cause of the sobbing than the one doing it. She raised her head, her gaze narrowing. Was it possible? Could there be a connection between her ghost and Sir Wesley?

Realizing that continuing to dwell on the subject would accomplish little, she rose up from her dressing table. After a brief look in the cheval glass to assure herself that she looked normal and not half crazed, she twitched the skirts of her pale pink muslin gown into place and left the room, shutting the door firmly behind her. If only she could shut out ideas about ghosts as easily, she thought wryly, walking down the broad, curving staircase.

She was one of the last to arrive in the morning room, and after helping herself at the sideboard to some country ham and a small bowl of sliced strawberries fresh from their own greenhouses, some toast and coffee, she joined the others at the table.

"How do you think she did it, Daffy?" demanded Adrian the moment she sat down. His blue eyes very bright and alert, he waited for her answer.

"Mirrors, perhaps?" she offered indifferently. Adrian might believe it all a clever trick. Daphne knew differently, but she wasn't about to disabuse her brother of the notion that he'd seen some spectacular sleight of hand.

He considered that possibility for a moment before shaking his head. "No. Someone else would have had to help her." He frowned. "Hmmm, I wonder if this estrangement between Mrs. Darby and Goodson isn't all hum, and they're in it together?"

Daphne nearly choked on her coffee. Looking at Adrian, she asked, "But why would Goodson be willing to help her?"

Adrian appeared to have second thoughts. "I hadn't considered that. There's no reason for Goodson to help her. What about Mrs. Hutton?"

Charles, who had been studying Daphne's face, curious as to why she had been so determined to hear Mrs. Darby's ghost stories in the first place, inquired lightly, "The same question applies, why? In fact, why would any of the servants want to help her?" He smiled. "Have you been such a harsh taskmaster that all the servants are in a league against you, determined to drive you out of Beaumont Place?"

"I think the opposite is true," said Daphne, a glimmer of a smile in her fine eyes. "Adrian is probably the most easygoing master they have ever served. I doubt they would want to replace him."

"Mayhap, it isn't that they don't like us," April said from the opposite side of the table from Daphne, "but that there is a hidden treasure within the house, and they need us to leave so they can look for it."

"I say, April, that's a jolly good idea," exclaimed Adrian, much struck by his sister's reasoning.

"According to Mr. Vinton, the house sat empty for months— they could have searched it to their heart's content," argued Daphne. "Besides, we've been living here for months already, why would they suddenly need us gone?"

Adrian and April looked crestfallen. "I suppose you're right," said Adrian, regret in his voice. "But if Mrs. Darby didn't have help, I wonder how she managed the trick?"

Charles raised his brows. "Why, witchcraft, of course."

Eyes big and round, April said, "Oh, do you really think so? How very exciting! I'd forgotten that Mrs. Darby is a witch. That explains everything."

Adrian didn't look convinced, but Daphne hastily changed the subject, asking if he still intended to take April to the vicar's house this morning to visit with the vicar's daughter, Rebecca. The conversation veered on to more practical matters, and the subject of ghosts and last night's occurrence was dropped.

But not likely forgotten, Daphne thought, as she and Charles waved her siblings good-bye from the front steps a short time later. April was bound to pour out the story to her bosom friend, Rebecca, and she didn't doubt that Adrian wouldn't waste a moment telling the vicar's two sons, Quentin and Maximillan, the whole tale—with much embellishment if she knew her brother. By nightfall, the account, made more colorful and terrifying by each telling, would have spread for miles around. She sighed. She didn't look forward to the next few days and the calls by inquisitive neighbors.

Echoing her thought, Charles said, "I suspect that you're going to have company shortly. And the first to call will be the vicar and his wife, wishing to know the true facts."

Accompanying her back into the house, he asked, "What are you going to tell them?"

Avoiding the blue salon, Daphne walked into the more formal cream and gold parlor at the front of the house. As they entered the room and Charles shut the door behind them, her pulse gave a little jump. She wasn't, she realized, entirely at ease alone with Charles, uneasy about the emotions that churned in her breast, fearful, yet longing, for him to take her into his arms again and kiss her as he had in Mr. Vinton's office. She risked a glance at him, wondering what there was about him that made her act so unnaturally, like a wanton creature with no care but physical pleasure. Growing up in the military, she had met many men in her life, but none affected her as did Mr. Weston. She grimaced. She was simply always too aware of him as *male,* she admitted unhappily, too conscious of those broad shoulders beneath his coat of blue superfine, far, far too aware of his long, muscular legs revealed by the form-fitting breeches he wore. A delicious shudder went through her as she remembered what it felt like to have that lean body crushed against hers. To her horror, her nipples swelled, and a honeyed ache throbbed in the lower regions of her body. Forcing her thoughts away from the dangerous path that they seemed determined to wander, she struggled to concentrate on the matter at hand.

Standing in front of the gold-veined marble fireplace, the warmth of the small fire that burned there casting out the chill of the day, she faced him, hoping he did not guess the turmoil inside of her.

He stopped just a few feet from her and repeated his question. "So? What are you going to tell the vicar and the others?"

"The truth," she said. A challenge in her gaze, she added, "I will tell them that Mrs. Darby put on the most amazing show of magic that we had ever seen. It was quite breathtaking and worthy of anything we had ever seen in London."

"And is Mrs. Darby going to say the same?" Charles asked,

suspicious about Daphne's interest in the occult. What he had seen last night had been astounding, but he still had trouble convincing himself that he had seen a ghost. But while he wasn't entirely easy about it, Charles knew that he had, indeed, seen some sort of ghostly manifestation . . . and he didn't believe in bloody spirits! If he did, he thought grimly, he'd have been haunted these past few years by the ugly shade of his not-so-beloved stepmother and please don't forget, dear half brother Raoul. No, if anyone had had to deal with vengeful spirits, he would have been the lucky fellow. Yet, he'd admit, that he'd seen the ghost of wicked Sir Wesley last night, or something doing a damn good imitation. What troubled him most about the whole peculiar affair, however, was Daphne's involvement in it. She was the one who had contacted Mrs. Darby. Why?

Charles could not shake the feeling that Daphne knew more than she was telling anyone. She might claim listening to ancestral legends was more exciting than dry-as-dust family accounts, but he suspected that she had an express purpose for seeking out Mrs. Darby and for wanting to hear what most people would dismiss as bedtime stories to entertain children. Had she known what would happen? Had she been expecting such a spectacular occurrence? He didn't think so. Unless he missed his guess, she had been surprised as anyone by the apparition, yet he had the feeling that she hadn't been *as* surprised. Whatever his bride-to-be was up to, it was obvious that she wasn't ready to show her hand right now, and he found himself irritated by her reticence. He was going to be her husband, for God's sake! Didn't he have a right to know?

When Daphne remained silent, Charles said with an edge to his voice, "It isn't a difficult question, my dear. Is Mrs. Darby going to say the same thing?"

Daphne shrugged, wishing he'd leave the subject alone. "I don't know. I suppose so. If you remember, it wasn't something we discussed last night. And according to Mrs. Hutton,

Mrs. Darby left at first light, so I didn't have a chance to speak with her this morning."

"What about Goodson or Mrs. Hutton? Did you find out how much they know about what happened?"

"Good heavens, no!"

Charles looked thoughtful. "I'm sure that Adrian and April were not as circumspect as we have been and that several members of the household have heard some version of what happened last night by now, including Goodson and Mrs. Hutton, even if they have not said anything to you." He smiled faintly. "I'll wager a pretty penny that Miss Ketty wasted no time in letting Goodson know about his sister's reprehensible antics and commiserating with him on the cross he has to bear for having such a disreputable relative."

"I fear you are right, and since she is spending the morning with Mrs. Hutton going over which rooms are in need of refurbishing before the guests for our wedding start arriving, I am sure she will talk of little else." She hesitated, her breath catching at the idea that in a few weeks, he would be her husband with command over her body, her very life, in fact. It was terrifying and equally exciting, but she was anxious about every facet of their coming union. She thought she trusted his word not to separate her from April and Adrian or to treat them badly. Certainly, he had done nothing since their betrothal to make her think ill of him. He had been most agreeable, undeniably charming, but he was still an unknown quality, and she knew that cruelty sometimes wore a handsome face . . .

She didn't want to dwell on that fact, and forcing her mind onto the subject at hand, she said, "At least Ketty believes it was a magic show so that is what she will have told Goodson and the others. And Goodson is not likely to disabuse her of that notion. I feel the same is true of Mrs. Hutton, whatever they may think privately."

Charles was only half listening. His attention on Daphne herself and not what she was saying, he thought that she looked very pretty as she stood by the fire. Her gleaming black hair was caught up in a pink and green plaid ribbon, her cheeks delicately flushed, and the high waist of her muslin gown, adorned with a matching plaid ribbon tied in a charming bow just beneath her breasts, drew the eye to her firm little bosom. At least, it drew Charles's eye, and he could not look away. His gaze riveted on those gently curved mounds, and ghosts and other such mundane thoughts vanished from his mind. All he could think of was apples . . . tart, delicious apples. He could taste their sweetness in his mouth, feel their firmness on his tongue, and between his legs, a certain portion of his body sprang to attention.

He wanted, he realized, most desperately to kiss her and feel her slender body molded to his, and he was appalled at the calculated thoughts that shifted swiftly through his brain. Adrian and April were gone for most of the day. Miss Ketty was upstairs busy with Mrs. Hutton. Goodson would not intrude unless someone came to call, and no callers were expected. The likelihood of any interruption was so remote that it didn't bother consideration. They were alone. The door was shut—he'd shut it himself . . . with seduction in mind?

Furious with himself, he tore his gaze away from those tempting little breasts, fighting his baser instincts, but instincts far stronger and a great deal more base and ruthless than he had ever thought possible controlled him. He swore under his breath even as he moved toward her. He knew he was acting like a randy satyr, but he could *not* stop himself from reaching for her and pulling her into his arms. She gave a startled squeak, and then his mouth closed over hers, and except for the crackle of the fire, there was no sound in the room for several seconds.

He kissed her long and hard, his tongue claiming her mouth, his lips warm and urgent against hers. Daphne didn't fight him—she couldn't, her entire body blooming with delight at the first touch of his mouth, the first demanding thrust of his tongue. She opened to him, resistance never crossing her mind, her slim body melting into his, feeling and reveling in his rigid member pressing so insistently, so intimately into her.

Liquid fire flowed through her body, igniting desires over which she had no command. Her head fell back against his arm, allowing him greater access, her fingers caressing his cheek, the thick black hair that grew near his temple. And when his hand closed round her breast, kneading the fullness, teasing the nipple with his fingers, her legs trembled, and at the junction of her thighs, she felt swollen and needy.

Kissing her as if he would die if he did not, Charles pushed down the front of her gown, almost shaking with pleasure when her breasts popped free and his hand and fingers touched bare, naked flesh. The urge to find out if she tasted as sweet as his imagination drove him to drop his mouth to her breasts.

The taste, texture, and scent of her was more intoxicating than anything he could ever remember in his life, and a groan of pure bliss escaped him as his teeth and tongue explored the soft, satiny expanse of her bosom. She smelled like a lavender heaven, the taste of her as sweet and potent as apple brandy. She was perfect. And she was his.

Drunk with desire, Charles swung Daphne up into his arms and carried her to the nearest sofa. He laid her on the sofa and knelt down on the floor next to her, struggling against the urge to rip her clothes from her body and have her laid bare before him like a feast before a starving man.

With huge, shimmering blue-green eyes, Daphne regarded him, trapped so tightly in the scarlet web of passion that she could not deny him anything. His fingers trailed across her naked breasts, and she arched up, feeling as if she had been stroked by fire. And when his mouth descended and he suckled her nipples, her lower body clenched with such a powerful yearning that she cried out, shocked by her body's response.

Lifting his head from the rosy nipple that had mesmerized

him, Charles breathed against her mouth. "Shush, my love. Did I hurt you? I did not mean to."

"No! You didn't hurt me," gasped Daphne, alarmed that he might stop kissing and touching her. "I never . . . I never expected . . ."

But her cry resonated through him and staring down at her on the sofa, recognizing the wonder, the innocence in her face, unwelcome sanity trickled into his brain, awakening him to precisely what he was doing. Reluctantly, he lifted his mouth from hers, his body one long, sensuous ache of unfulfillment. He wanted as he never had wanted anything else before to free himself from his breeches and possess her. He still could. She was willing—he could see it in her eyes, feel it in her kisses. It would take but a moment to shift her, to position her to his liking and pull her down on his bulging shaft and seek relief from the demon of desire that rode him. He would only be anticipating what would be his by a few weeks. So why hesitate? God knew he wanted her so badly he was shaking with it, aching with it, and sweet relief was only seconds, inches away. So why not finish it?

There were those that thought him cold, hard, and calculating, and he would not deny it, but for all his vices, an innate sense of honor ran strongly within Charles. Deflowering her before their marriage in this manner would be the act of a hardened libertine, and while that charge could with truth be hurled at his head, it was not in him to deliberately dishonor Daphne. If she had not cried out, loosening the coil of desire that held them both, if he could have allowed blind, primitive passion to rule him, he would be buried deeply within her at this very moment. But a shred of sanity *had* entered his brain, had made him think about what he was doing. Daphne would be his bride, his wife, and to his astonishment and great disgust, he discovered within himself the need for her to come to him on their wedding night as honor demanded.

Regret like a dagger in his gut, he pulled the bodice of her pink muslin gown back into place and helped her to sit up. "I am sorry," he said baldly, "but I cannot do this."

It was a difficult moment for both of them, Charles doubtful of his control over the beast within him, Daphne mortified and embarrassed at the abrupt ending of their passionate interlude. His apology only added to her distress, but it angered her, too. He was *sorry?* Her hands clenched into fists. She'd like to make him sorry, so sorry he'd never forget it. But she had to know what she had done wrong.

Her face averted, not looking at him as he rose to his feet and took a seat beside her, she asked tightly, "Did I displease you? I think I deserve to know why you are rejecting me."

Charles gave a hollow laugh, and she turned to glare at him, rage glittering in her eyes. He held up a hand as if to ward off a blow, shaking his head as he did so. "Rejecting you?" he asked dryly. "Good God! I am not rejecting you. I am merely stopping myself from acting dishonorably. And displeasing me has nothing to do with what nearly happened here." He shook his head. "You're a blind little fool if you don't realize that I cannot keep my hands off of you, despite my best intentions. All it takes for me to throw honor to the winds is to be alone with you."

She looked at him incredulously. "You stopped because of *honor?*"

"Hmmm, ridiculous, I know," he said with a deprecating smile. "I have trouble believing it myself, and if any of my relatives or friends find out, my reputation will be utterly ruined, but there you have it."

She stared at him, her brain busy considering his words. Part of her admired his stance, part of her wished that he wasn't behaving *quite* so honorably, and part of her was so delighted and relieved by his reply that she could have flung her arms about his neck. She hadn't displeased him. He wanted her. A private little smile crossed her lips. Wanted her so much he couldn't keep his hands off of her.

From beneath her lashes, she sent him a considering glance,

her pulse pounding when she realized that he was watching her.

Their eyes met, and he smiled and shook his head. Lifting up one of her hands, he pressed a kiss to the back of it. "No tricks, my sweet," he warned, something in the depths of those jade green eyes sending a shiver of half excitement, half fright down her spine. "It would not be fair," he added softly, "for you to put too much temptation before me. My hold on honor is thin at best, and I do not think you would be happy if you led me down the path to dishonor."

Her eyes narrowed. "You're making your honor *my* responsibility?"

"Only if you seek to tempt me."

"But that's not fair," she protested, lusciously wicked thoughts of doing just that dancing through her mind, and she wondered if she dared to discover just precisely how thin his hold on honor really was. Talk about temptation! She struggled against the urge to test her own powers of seduction, to see if she could push him over the edge, but she finally decided that he was right about one thing: she would not be happy if she caused him to behave dishonorably. It was totally unfair, but by placing honor on the table, he had put her in the position of having to choose between acting honorably or dishonorably herself. Daphne took the concept of honor, especially *her* honor, every bit as seriously as did Charles, and so with regret, she pushed away any notion of trying to work her wiles on him. Not that she was entirely confident of her own wiles, but it would appear from this morning's interlude, she thought with a small, satisfied smile, that whatever wiles she did possess worked just fine on Charles.

Charles watched the emotions play across her lively features, and he knew the moment she gave up any idea of tempting him further. He was almost sorry that she had chosen the high road, but inordinately pleased on another level. His bride-to-be, it seemed, played honest and fair, and a man couldn't ask for better traits in a friend—or a wife.

Daphne stood up, retied the bow beneath her bosom, and shook out the folds of her gown. Briskly, she said, "Since you're capable of minding your manners when we are in public, I suggest that we not linger here." A teasing glint appeared in her eyes. "Temptation can be so fickle and strike without warning, you know, so the sooner we are in the midst of others, the safer you will be."

Charles smiled wryly and rose from the sofa. "There is truth in what you say," he said lightly.

They had almost reached the door when he said, "I think I shall call upon Mrs. Darby on my way to Lanyon Hall this afternoon."

Daphne stopped and whirled around. "Why would you want to do that?" she asked, unease flickering in her eyes.

"Perhaps because we saw something damned unpleasant last night?" he said bluntly. "Or perhaps because I dislike the notion of Sir Wesley popping out of the fireplace whenever he bloody well pleases?"

Daphne looked startled, and Charles smiled grimly. "Hadn't thought of that, had you, my secretive darling? Have you considered what would happen if Sir Wesley decided to come calling when you're entertaining guests? Can you imagine the expression on the faces of the vicar and his wife? Or the good Squire and Mrs. Renwick? Or, God forbid, Sir Wesley inviting himself to join us when the house is full of guests for our wedding?"

Her face the picture of horror, Daphne swallowed. "I hadn't thought of that."

"Well, I suggest you start thinking about it," he said sharply, unaccountably angry that she would not tell him what was in her mind. How could he help her, he thought bitterly, if the little devil wouldn't tell him what it was she was after. Whatever she was involved in, it was no laughing matter. If the manifestation they'd seen last night was anything to go by, it could be dangerous—she could be in danger.

Fear for her clawed through his chest, and he was furious for being afraid and helpless to do anything about it. He took a deep breath, fighting his anger, his fear, and said more calmly, "If that thing appeared once, it can appear again, and we have no control over when it decides to make an appearance."

"Perhaps we could call upon the local priest and have him do an exorcism or something?" Daphne offered weakly, her eyes big and troubled.

"Ah, excellent plan—let the entire neighborhood know that we have spirits or ghosts or whatever you want to call them floating around Beaumont Place."

Her temper rose, and hands on her hips, she glared at him. "Well, what do you expect me to do?"

"Why don't you try telling me the truth," he said in a silky tone, an unnerving air of watchfulness about him.

"The t-t-truth," she stammered. "What are you talking about? I don't tell lies."

"Mayhap you don't, mayhap you just leave out things . . . such as the real reason you sought out a witch. And invited her into your home to tell stories best related in the nursery to wide-eyed babes."

Her expression stony, Daphne said, "I don't know what you're talking about, and you have no right to question my reasons for doing anything."

An expression crossed his face, something so dark and dangerous in it that Daphne took a step back. Those green eyes hard and remote, he snapped, "I have every right. I am to be your husband."

"But you are not my husband yet," Daphne declared roundly, "and you have no right to poke your arrogant nose into my business. How dare you! This isn't your problem, Mr. Weston. It is mine, and I shall handle it. I don't need you to meddle in my affairs."

A scarlet mist exploded in front of Charles's eyes. His hands caught her upper arms in an iron grip, and he gave her an ungentle shake. "You little fool! I'm not meddling. I'm trying to protect you."

Daphne fought free of his hold, and just as furious as Charles, stunning both of them, she smacked him hard across his cheek. Appalled, they stared at each other, neither one moving.

It was a dicey moment, but as quickly as it had come, Charles's anger fled. "I suppose," he said wryly, rubbing his reddening cheek, "that I deserved that."

Her own rage vanishing as if it had never been, Daphne felt sick. She was not a violent person, and yet, in a twinkling, she had struck a man for no other reason than he wanted to help her. Ashamed, she turned her head aside and said miserably, "I apologize. And you're wrong—you didn't deserve it. You have been nothing but kind since the moment you joined me in that terrible cave, and I have treated you badly."

He loathed seeing her so abject and muttered, "There is no blame. I should not have grabbed you. I started it. You were only defending yourself."

"You're very kind."

"You're wrong there. I am *not* a kind person, at least," he amended, "not usually." Wearily, he added, "Damn it, sweetheart, you're involved in something nasty, something beyond my understanding, and I want to help you." He ran a distracted hand through his hair, his eyes meeting hers. "I don't know what is going on, but something is, and I can't help you if you keep me at a distance."

It might have been because she felt guilty for having slapped him, but she suspected it was because deep down inside, she trusted him and because she was tired of carrying the burden alone that his words unsealed her tongue. Quietly, she asked, "What would you say if I told you that Sir Wesley isn't the only spirit that I've seen within the halls of Beaumont Place?"

Charles stared at her for a long moment. "Bloody hell," he

finally growled, walking to the velvet bell rope in the corner and giving it a sharp yank, "I definitely need a brandy before you say another word." He thought a moment, gave another pull, and announced, "No, not just a brandy, the whole damn bottle!"

Chapter 11

Neither one of them spoke until Goodson had returned with Charles's brandy. His face expressionless, Goodson delivered a tray with a snifter and a Baccarat crystal decanter full of brandy on it. There had been added, at Daphne's request, a pot of tea and some delicate lemon pastries.

Thanking the butler, Charles closed the door firmly behind Goodson and approached the brandy like a man approaching an oasis after being lost for weeks in the desert. He waited until Daphne fixed her tea to her liking and took a seat on the sofa before pouring himself a large amount of brandy in the snifter. He didn't wait to smell the bouquet before taking a large swallow.

The brandy warming his stomach, and feeling somewhat fortified, he looked at Daphne as she daintily sipped her tea and took a nibble of the pastry and said, "Tell me. Everything."

She did, surprised to find that it wasn't as difficult as she had thought it would be. When she finished speaking, Charles's expression was unreadable, but at least he didn't ridicule her and tell her that she had imagined things. Or that she was a candidate for Bedlam.

"This event occurred your first night here?" Charles questioned.

Daphne shook her head. "Not the very first night—I believe

it was the second night." She frowned, thinking back. "Yes. The second night. We'd met with Mr. Vinton for the first time that afternoon, and it was that night that she appeared."

"And you're positive it was female?"

Daphne made a face. "I believe it to be, but since it didn't fully materialize or speak, I was left with the impression that it was female. But the crying, or crooning, definitely sounded female."

Looking thoughtful, Charles took a turn around the room, imbibing freely from his snifter of brandy. "I know that most old places like Beaumont Place have superstitions, stories, legends of ghosts and hauntings and the like connected with them," he said eventually, coming to stop in front of the fireplace. His back to the fire, he faced her and said, "Even Stonegate has a macabre legend about a murdered woman seeking vengeance or some such nonsense attached to it. Wyndham Hall, my cousin's home, is rumored to have the spirit of a knight beheaded by Henry the Seventh . . ." He stopped, considered, and then clarified, "Or at any rate, one of the damn Henrys. He supposedly sulks about, searching for his head." He took a deep swallow of his brandy. "But those," he said, "are just the sort of stories you'd expect about any house of note in the district, especially one that has been inhabited for centuries. I know that my cousin and I, when we were children, always hoped that the headless knight would appear for us, but he never did, and truth to tell, I can't think of one credible person who ever actually claimed to have seen either ghost—the woman or the knight. They're just stories. Legends." He stared down into his empty snifter and deciding that he needed more, er, fortification, poured himself another generous brandy before saying, "But Sir Wesley is something else entirely. We *saw* that thing last night. I am convinced, and no one will change my mind, that it was not just any ghost, but *his* ghost." He took another swallow of brandy. His face somber, he added, "And if I am convinced that I saw the ghost of Sir Wesley, then I have no hesitation in believing that you saw something supernatural in your room."

Daphne sagged with relief. In light of what they'd both seen in the blue salon, she'd been *mostly* confident that he would not laugh at her or think her mad, but there had been that tiny shadow of doubt at the back of her mind. It was incredible enough that Beaumont Place harbored one ghost, but two?

"And, ah, she has never shown herself to you again?" he asked.

Daphne shook her head. "No, never again . . . so far. But don't forget that April and Adrian both have said that they have heard the wind sounding like someone, or something, sobbing. I feel that it must be her because I cannot credit a third such manifestation." Gloomily, she added, "Two is bad enough. But three . . ." She looked at him, her eyes big and anxious. "I fear three would make me not believe my own senses."

He nodded. "I know precisely what you mean, but we should not close our minds to that possibility." He paused, frowning. "I do think," he began slowly, "that however many spiritual beings are at work here, there must be some connection between them. Otherwise, it seems to me unlikely that they both would have chosen recently to make their presence felt. The same would apply to the noises heard by Adrian and April, whether that is the work of a third being or not. I find it hard to conceive that there is not a link between them."

He stared hard at Daphne. "Until you and your brother and sister moved in to Beaumont Place, Sir Wesley and the female apparition, whoever or whatever is crying in the night, appeared to have been content to remain unnoticed."

"Don't forget the lady from London who swore she had seen a ghost when Sir Huxley was a young man."

"Yes, but I suspect we're talking about your little ghost, not Sir Wesley, and the young lady did not live here as do you and your siblings. Don't forget Sir Huxley's lady left almost immediately after she'd claimed to have seen a ghost, or whatever." He looked pensive. "It's notable that except for that one time during Sir Huxley's tenure, there is no gossip or whispers about any peculiar happenings in the house. With all the visitors, servants, and guests who have passed through this house since then, there has been no hint of anything supernatural."

Daphne shook her head. "We can't know that. What about Mrs. Darby's great grandmother and grandmother? They were aware of something odd in the house in certain rooms. As for anybody else . . ." Daphne smiled slightly. "Most people wouldn't dare mention any strangeness they'd observed for fear of looking foolish or worse. I don't believe that having a ghost wandering the halls of his home is something that Sir Huxley would have broadcast throughout the neighborhood." Her expression rueful, she added, "No one would."

"I agree. But you can't keep something like this quiet, either," Charles replied. "Even as we speak, your brother and sister are spreading the word about what occurred last night. Miss Ketty has probably already filled the ears of Goodson and Mrs. Hutton with her version of what she saw. Believe me, the news will spread, and I think that would be true in Sir Huxley's lifetime and even before him. If what we saw was something that occurred even once every decade or so, there would be a reference to it. Just as we know about the young lady from London, if there were other sightings, there would be some mention of them, even if they were dismissed or discreetly discredited. Yet there has been nothing."

Daphne couldn't argue with his logic, though she would have liked to. It made her uneasy to think that for some reason, she and her siblings had provoked or awakened whatever lurked within the walls of Beaumont Place. She shuddered. Was this her fault? Had she inadvertently placed her brother and sister in danger?

Almost as if he read her mind, Charles said slowly, "Something caused these spectral beings to make their presence known." His eyes locked on her face, he muttered, "And I'm very much afraid, my dear, based on what I know so far, that it has to do with *you*. Until you appeared on the scene, all was serene and peaceful. Yet within forty-eight hours of your arrival, your little female apparition appeared."

Her face white, Daphne cried, "Never say so! I have done nothing. And I would never do anything that would put Adrian and April in danger."

His features softened. "I know that, and I don't believe that it is anything that you have done. I think it is your very presence here that has created this situation." Attempting to lighten the atmosphere, he grinned at her and murmured, "Yes, I can understand how the presence of a young, beautiful woman would certainly rouse wicked old Sir Wesley from his ghostly slumber."

Daphne did not think his comment amusing, and jumping up from the sofa, she took an agitated step forward. "Do not jest! Oh, this is a ridiculous conversation. Not one ghost, but two! Possibly three. Listen to us! Discussing ghosts and spirits as if they were real. We both must be mad."

Charles winced. "Ordinarily, I'd agree with you, but we cannot pretend that we did not see something extraordinary last night. I am not given to spiritualism or the like—most of it is pure balderdash—and if I had not seen Sir Wesley's spirit, ghost, whatever you wish to call it, not twenty-four hours previously, I would think anyone who claimed to have observed what we did half mad." He frowned. "Or the victim of an outrageous prank."

Her eyes fixed hopefully on his, she said, "Perhaps that is, indeed, what it was. Adrian and April think it was a grand trick. Mayhap it was. Isn't it possible that we have allowed ourselves to be taken in by a trickster?"

"And your little apparition?" Charles asked quietly. "Did Mrs. Darby arrange that, too?"

"No, of course not! I didn't even know about Mrs. Darby

then." Searching for an explanation as she had so many times in the past, Daphne said, "I was tired. It was a strange bedroom. I imagined the whole thing. I must have!"

"Do you want me to agree with you? Shall I tell you that what you saw in your bedroom was merely the product of your imagination?" he inquired with a sardonic tilt to his brow. "Shall we pretend, even to ourselves, that we were hoodwinked by a clever witch last night? That Mrs. Darby bedazzled us with a sleight of hand that would rival the most famous charlatan in London? That we were duped? Is that what you want?"

Daphne shook her head, her features woeful. "No. If I pretended otherwise, *that* would drive me mad."

Putting down his snifter, he crossed to stand before her. Lifting up her chin with one long finger and staring gravely into her eyes, he said softly, "Whether we like it or not, we are in this together, my sweet, and there is no use either one of us pretending that last night did not happen. *Something* is at work within this house. And unfortunately, it would appear that it is up to us to find out precisely what, and without everyone thinking that we have gone mad as hatters."

Daphne took a deep breath. Smiling tremulously at him, she said, "Thank you for believing me about . . . about . . . her. I have been afraid ever since that night that I was, indeed, going mad, and I feared what would happen to Adrian and April if anyone learned that I thought I was seeing ghosts in my bedroom." Her hand touched his cheek, a butterfly's caress. "You have been so good to us. First, staying with me in the cave, willing to risk death, then offering for me, and now believing that I really do see ghosts. You're a kind man, Charles Weston, and I owe you a debt that I can never repay. You have my utmost gratitude."

Charles swore under his breath and jerking her into his arms, kissed her fiercely. His loins tightened at the taste of her, and feeling the beast within him stir again, he tore his mouth from hers and snapped, "There shall be no talk of debt between us. And the last thing I want from you is *gratitude.*"

Daphne stared at him, puzzled. He was angry, she realized, and he had made gratitude sound like something to be violently detested.

"I d-d-don't understand," she stammered, wondering what she had done to make him so angry.

"No, you don't," he agreed, "and I'm damn well not going to tell you either." He ran a hand through his hair and growled, "And now before I fall into temptation once more, I want to see your bedroom."

Daphne jumped as if stabbed. "My bedroom?" she repeated astonished. "Absolutely not!"

He smiled wryly. "I don't have seduction in mind—I want to see that area where you thought that you saw the outline of a door."

She didn't move, just stared at him as if he had grown two heads.

"What?" he demanded impatiently.

"You can't just go marching into my bedroom," she gasped. "Everyone will think . . . we will never be able to escape the gossip."

Charles muttered something vulgar. Raising his hands in surrender, he said, "Very well, I can't just go marching into your bedroom, but I need to see that wall. And if I can't do it now, what do you suggest? That I sneak into your room after everyone has gone to bed?"

"Good God, no!"

"Then think of a reason for me to examine your bedroom. Now."

For a moment, she couldn't imagine any scenario that wasn't fraught with social peril, then she realized that a perfect excuse lay right before them. Hesitantly, she said, "I do not think that I can show you my room, but I can tell you exactly which wall to look at, and Goodson can accompany you."

Charles looked blank, and she smiled. "Since we are to be married, my current rooms may not be suitable for us to use once we are married. You are merely looking," she explained, "to see if my present room would satisfy you while we are in residence here. It is not the best excuse, but I think it will serve."

"What a clever wench you are," Charles said admiringly. "Tell me quickly precisely where I am to look, and then ring for Goodson."

All went as planned, and while Daphne remained sedately in the front salon, sipping her cooling tea, Charles, accompanied by Goodson, was shown to Miss Daphne's room. Opening the door to Daphne's bedchamber, Goodson said, "Mrs. Hutton and I were discussing just the other day the change in arrangements that will be necessary once you and Miss Daphne are married." Following behind Charles as he entered the big, gloomy room, Goodson added, "This is a fine room for Miss Daphne, but we think that as a married couple, you would both prefer something larger. We wondered if you'd like a bedroom for yourself and a sitting room to share between you?"

Charles made a noncommittal answer, slightly put off by all the purple damask that draped the huge, old-fashioned bed. But then when he imagined Daphne's smooth white silky nakedness against the deepness of the color, he found himself enchanted by it.

Goodson's delicate cough made him jerk his gaze away from the bed, and pretending to examine the room, he wandered about. It was large enough and pleasant enough for them to use whenever they would be in residence at Beaumont Place, but Charles thought that Daphne might prefer more privacy. He smiled. Even if they had separate bedrooms, he doubted she'd sleep many nights alone . . . or clothed, for that matter.

Working his way toward the section of wall that Daphne

had described, he stopped before it and affected much interest in the pattern of the Chinese silk wall covering. "This is quite lovely," he murmured as he studied it closely.

"I believe," Goodson said, "that it was hung when Sir Huxley's mother came here as a bride, sir. I understand that it is all the rage now, with the Prince of Wales loving all things oriental, but Sir Huxley's mother was considered quite ahead of her time."

Charles wished the day were brighter and not so gray, but squint and stare though he did, he could find nothing that resembled a crack or crease in the wall before him. Certainly nothing that looked like a doorway had once existed in this vicinity. Daphne may really have imagined the doorway. He could certainly see no sign of it.

Continuing to study the wall, Charles asked, "Did Sir Huxley's mother institute many changes in the house?"

Goodson smiled. "According to my grandfather, who was the butler then, during the first few years, she always seemed to have some new project in mind."

"Did she make any changes that you know of to this room?"

"As a matter of fact," Goodson said, "she did. That was one of things that Mrs. Hutton and I discussed. This room was originally part of the master's suite until Lady Beaumont had the area where Sir Adrian now sleeps converted into a grander suite, and they moved into them. There was a doorway over here that led to a sitting room with the mistress's bedroom and a dressing room beyond that. It would be an easy task to reopen the entrance and would give you and"— he smiled—"Mrs. Weston an excellent suite of rooms."

Charles was aware of a stab of disappointment. It would seem that there was nothing supernatural about Daphne's outline of a door beneath the wallpaper. His features bland, Charles said simply, "Show me."

Crossing to the other side of the room, Goodson said, "The original door is right here behind this armoire. Lady Beaumont didn't even have it fully closed off. She and Sir Huxley's father thought, should their son marry during their lifetime, that he and his bride would be able to use this suite for themselves."

Charles hid his astonishment. The armoire was on the opposite side of the room, nowhere near where Daphne had claimed to see the outline of a door. Could he have misunderstood her? No. He was positive of his location, and it sure as hell wasn't on the opposite side of the room. "Really," he said as if he found Goodson's words fascinating. "Over here, you say?"

Goodson nodded as Charles strolled over to his side. "You can't see the doorway because of the armoire," Goodson explained, "but with the help of a few sturdy footmen, we can have it moved to a different location." He looked a bit embarrassed. "The rooms haven't been used in decades, sir, and will require some refurbishing, but I assure you that we can have everything ready for you by the wedding. Would you like to see the sitting room and the other bedroom?"

After a considering glance at the huge ancient oak armoire, Charles said, "Of course."

Leaving Daphne's room, Goodson led Charles a short way down the hall. Coming to a large door, he opened it and after taking down one of the candles from the sconces that hung on either side of the door and lighting it, waved Charles inside.

The place smelled musty and unused, but not unpleasant, and with a couple of days of opened windows and a thorough cleaning and airing of the drapes and rugs, that particular problem would be solved, Charles thought as he followed Goodson into the shadowy gloom. Goodson's candle revealed a handsome room with a carved ceiling and several pieces of furniture cloaked in dust covers. Crossing quickly to a tall bank of windows, Goodson threw back the heavy honey-colored velvet drapes in an attempt to dispel some of the shadows. Even with the drapes thrown wide, there still wasn't much light coming in through the dirty windows, but Charles glimpsed an exquisite old rug in shades of amber and green on the floor and realized that the flooring itself was a beautiful walnut parquet. An imposing green marble fireplace dominated the far wall; a gilt-edged mirror hung above the mantle. Nearby, he spied a set of double doors that led, he supposed, to the other bedroom.

He said as much to Goodson, and the butler nodded. "Yes, that is correct, sir. Miss Daphne's room was used by the master, and these rooms were for his wife."

After Goodson opened one of the doors, Charles followed him into another spacious room, the furniture hidden beneath dust covers looming ghostlike in the gloom. Charles didn't waste much time on the bedroom and sitting room. They would suit him well enough.

Walking back into the sitting room, he looked around and finally found the doorway into Daphne's bedroom hidden behind a heavy drape, giving the illusion of another window. Pushing aside the fabric, he grasped the crystal knob and after a bit of a struggle, opened the door. The rear of the armoire in Daphne's room met his gaze.

He took another glance around the sitting room and nodded to Goodson. "Yes, I think this shall do nicely once it has been aired and cleaned."

Goodson beamed at him. "I shall tell Mrs. Hutton, and she will have the maids start on it immediately. Would you like to see the furniture? It is old-fashioned but quite elegant. I'm sure that we can change anything that does not meet with your approval."

"Ah, no," Charles said hastily. "I'm sure that I can trust you and Mrs. Hutton to see that all is as it should be by the day of the wedding."

Charles bid Goodson good day and walked slowly down the broad, sweeping staircase to the lower floor. A moment later, he rejoined Daphne in the salon.

At his entrance, she stood up, questions in her eyes.

Charles shook his head. "I looked," he said, "but I could see no sign of any doorway."

Her face full of disappointment, she said, "Are you certain you looked in the right place?"

He nodded, and after refilling his snifter, he said, "Believe me, I stared at that Chinese wallpaper until I thought my eyes would cross."

Daphne stiffened. "Do you doubt my word?"

Charles shook his head. "No. I just tend to think that in your confusion and terror, perhaps you *thought* you saw the outline of another doorway that night. You examined the wall by the light of a candle, and it's possible that in the uncertain light, you were deceived in what you saw."

"If you think that," she snapped, "then why do you believe I saw the female apparition? Why don't you think I didn't imagine her, too? You didn't see her in my room either, yet you claim to believe me. Why not the doorway?" She shot him a hard glance. "You cannot just believe in part of what I tell you and dismiss the other." Passionately, she added, "I *saw* that outline. I did not imagine it, and it was not because I was frightened and my bloody candle threw shadows! It was there, I tell you!"

Charles realized that Daphne was absolutely correct. He hadn't seen the ghost, yet he believed her about that, and if he believed her about having seen a ghost in her bedroom, why not the doorway?

"I apologize," he said. "And you're right. The doorway is part and parcel of this whole affair, and I was mistaken to dismiss it so lightly." He frowned. "It could be that it was the presence of your little ghost that caused it to appear. It's possible that your doorway is important to her, that there is some relationship between her appearance and the outline." He rubbed his chin. "Did you know that your bedroom was once part of the master's suite of rooms?"

When Daphne shook her head, he continued, "According

to Goodson, it was Sir Huxley's mother who decided to make a new suite of rooms for the master and mistress of the house and moved them down the hall. She was also the one who had the Chinese wallpaper hung. Something else I discovered—that big armoire in your room hides the doorway that leads to the original sitting room and the mistress's bedroom and dressing room. Goodson gave me a tour. He and Mrs. Hutton will be preparing them for us and opening up the doorway between your bedroom and the sitting room." He took a swallow of his brandy. "We shall be quite comfortable whenever we are in residence here."

Daphne reseated herself on the sofa, her thoughts whirling. It gave her a queer feeling to think that she had slept in that room for months now and never once guessed that the old armoire hid a doorway into another set of rooms. In one way, she was pleased. She'd grown comfortable in her bedroom and the knowledge that upon her marriage, she wasn't going to be moving into a different part of the house was comforting. But Charles's words brought something to mind that had been troubling her for a while. How often and how long would he be willing to live at Beaumont Place?

They had never discussed precisely how their time was to be divided between the two estates. Daphne knew that Charles could not simply abandon his own home, Stonegate, in favor of Beaumont Place, but she didn't think it right either that Adrian, until he was of age, be compelled to abandon his own lands and home. Of course, there would be trips to London for the Season, especially once April was brought out, and she was positive that Adrian intended to make a dash in London, but where, she wondered, would they all live when they were not in London?

Uncertainly, she eyed Charles. He had promised that he would not separate her from her brother and sister and she believed him, but where did he plan on them living? Stonegate? Her heart sank. She had grown to love Beaumont Place and the surrounding area, and she wasn't happy at the notion of leaving behind her friends in the neighborhood, such as Vicar Henley and his family. And what about Goodson and Mrs. Hutton? Would they stay here or go to Stonegate? Her heart sank even lower. It had to be assumed that Charles already had his own servants, and so it was unlikely, even if only until Adrian was of age, that he'd hire Goodson and Mrs. Hutton to run Stonegate. She bit her lip, dreading the idea of being a stranger again and having to find her footing in a new house, with new servants, and all that settling into a new place entailed. A new home, she reminded herself, not a place. A home. Stonegate would be her home. And Charles would be her husband.

She looked down at her clasped hands, not willing to speculate too much on all the changes that were happening in her life at the moment. Charles would be her husband, but Adrian and April's needs could not be pushed aside. She understood that her new husband would have his own estates to consider, but what about Adrian's? Did Charles intend to leave Adrian's holdings in the hands of someone like Mr. Vinton and for them all to live at Stonegate with just the fleeting visit now and then to Beaumont Place? He would have the power to do just that.

She glanced at him, studying him beneath her lashes. He was a handsome, powerful male, a man she had known a matter of days, a man she would marry in just over three weeks. What did she really know of him? She knew that he could make her knees melt with a mere look and that he had been kind to Adrian and April and for what it was worth, that he was wealthy and related to an earl. She admitted to herself that she trusted him on some instinctual level, else she never would have agreed to the marriage or told him of the spectral sighting in her room, yet there was so much she did not know about him. Again, she reminded herself that soon enough he would hold her life in the palm of his hand. All of their lives, not just hers. She trusted him . . . but did she trust him enough?

Aware of her covert stare, Charles asked, "What? You're looking at me as if I have suddenly sprouted horns."

Daphne flushed. "I was just, er, wondering—after we are married, how often you think we shall be staying at Beaumont Place?"

"Afraid I might lock you in the dungeon at Stonegate and throw away the key?" he demanded, a bite in his voice.

"That's unfair," she protested. "There are two large estates, two homes involved, with farms and tenants and servants and a myriad of other things. One is yours, and one is Adrian's. We've never discussed what your plans are in regard to either one of them. When we marry, not only is my life in your hands, but until he reaches his majority, Adrian's also. And until she marries, April's as well."

That she did not quite trust him was obvious. That she placed the welfare of her brother and sister above all else was also obvious. That she loved Adrian and April first, last, and always was obvious, too, and he wondered bleakly if the day would ever come that she would allow him a small place in her heart. Would he always come second to her brother and sister? Charles pinched the bridge of his nose. "I suspect that we shall divide our time between the two places and London," he said finally. "If I am needed at Stonegate, then we will be there; if Adrian is needed here, then we shall be here. I have no set plan." He gave her a steady look. "Naturally, once we are married, I shall expect us to spend time at Stonegate. It will be your home and for as long as they wish, the home of your brother and sister, but I imagine we will spend an equal amount of time here. Your brother has an excellent man of business, as do I; between them, I think they will be able to see to things when we cannot be here." He made a face. "Or there."

She still looked wary, and he came to sit beside her on the sofa. Taking her hand in his, he said, "Daphne, I cannot promise you that everything will be as you wish. There may be times that I will demand you put my desires above those of your brother and sister. I may be required to be at Stone-gate for a time, and if I am, then I shall expect you to be there, too. Your brother and sister will always be welcome. We shall certainly spend time here—it is your brother's home. He is young yet, but one day, he must oversee his own estates, and he cannot learn everything he needs to learn living at Stonegate—I understand that. I know that we will be here often, perhaps more than I would like, but I am willing to do it, certainly in these early years. Adrian must learn the ways of his lands, become the true master here, and I will help him in any manner that I can, but I will not lie to you—I will not sacrifice my lands for his." Something implacable entered his face. "Nor will I sacrifice my life for his," he said bluntly, "or allow you to do so."

Daphne met his hard gaze head on. She resented his words, resented his coming power over them, but she knew he was being fairer than most men might have been. Still, it rankled, and her chin lifted. "Very well. Thank you for your candor."

Charles smiled at her. "Candor? My dear, if you knew me better, you'd know that I was being most delicate."

Long after Charles departed for Lanyon Hall, Daphne considered his words. She suspected that beneath that charm-ing demeanor lurked unyielding steel, and she wondered un-easily how far the steel went . . . and how often he displayed the ruthless implacability she sensed within him. Was he hid-ing his true nature? Lulling her into a false feeling of secu-rity?

She wrinkled her nose. No. Charles Weston would do no lulling. He might have chosen his words with care this after-noon, but he had not tried to wrap them in clean linen. It was clear she was marrying a man used to getting his own way and intent on continuing to get his own way, but—and it was this but that soothed some of the fear in her heart—he would be fair in his dealings with them. She could ask no more of him.

It wasn't until she had bid her siblings good night and retired to her rooms that evening that she thought about the
other part of the conversation with Charles. Once she had
dismissed her maid, before she climbed into bed, she walked
over to the big armoire and looked at it. She could see no sign
of the doorway that Charles told her lay behind its bulk.
Shrugging, she walked back to her bed and snuggled under
the covers.

Only when she blew out the candle and the darkness
swooped down on her did she remember something else.
Charles had said that this room had once been part of the
original suite of rooms used by the masters of Beaumont
Place. Her breath caught, and she sat bolt upright in bed.
Good God! She was sleeping in wicked Sir Wesley's bedroom!

Chapter 12

Sleep did not come to Daphne that night. With thoughts of Sir Wesley crowding out common sense she hastily lit a huge candelabrum and kept it handy. Crawling back into bed, she lay stiffly, her gaze on the shadows created by the candlelight that danced around the room, fearful images vaulting through her mind. Heart banging painfully in her chest, she watched all through the very long night for that frightful amorphous form she'd seen in the blue salon to leap out at her from the darkness beyond the candlelight. She would have almost welcomed the sight of the wispy female apparition—that, at least, would have driven Sir Wesley from her mind.

She managed to get through the night, and by morning, she could chide herself for being foolish, but she could not pretend that she would ever be entirely easy in this room again. It was too tainted by the knowledge that Sir Wesley had once roamed through it for her peace of mind. Though she knew it was silly, as she dressed, she kept glancing over her shoulder, worried that she might actually see something forming in the dust motes that drifted in the sunlight that filled the room. Dressed and ready to face the day, she wandered around the room as if seeing it for the first time, wondering what it had looked like in Sir Wesley's time, wondering what ugly deeds may have been plotted or even carried out here at his behest.

Her first instinct was to change her bedroom, but she hesitated. For months, she had slept here without complaint. Refusing to use the room now was sure to cause gossip in the household. There was another reason to remain here—only yesterday, Charles had inspected the rooms that adjoined this one and had declared that they were suitable. While she'd been dressing, she'd heard movement next door and guessed that the servants were already hard at work readying the rooms for their use. She made a face at herself. Unless she wanted more gossip, she was just going to have to endure sleeping here and pray that Sir Wesley didn't decide to pay her a visit . . . or any other ghost.

Some judicious questioning over the next several days revealed that she was, indeed, sleeping in Sir Wesley's former bedroom, his own bed, in fact. Daphne felt ill at that unwelcome bit of news. Mrs. Hutton hurriedly assured her that the feather mattress and the bed hangings were of a more recent date. Only the bed and the big armoire dated from Sir Wesley's time. Daphne wasn't comforted. Just the idea that Sir Wesley, that *thing* from the blue salon, had once slept in the *same* bed left her feeling chilled and uneasy.

No one knew the fortitude it took for her to return to her room each night, the room that was now forever labeled Sir Wesley's in her mind. She kept a candle lit but slept poorly, jerking upright at the slightest sound, be it the pop of the fire or the rattle of the windows on a windy night. But as the nights passed, her fears lessened, and by the time a fortnight had passed, she could sleep almost undisturbed through the night.

Work on the rooms she would share with Charles moved forward. There was a constant bustle next door as drapes were taken down and aired, dust covers were removed to reveal the bronze and green damask fabric on the handsome mahogany and satinwood pieces, and the fireplace grate was cleaned and readied. The windows and mirrors gleamed, the floors and furniture shone with polish, and the scent of apple cider vinegar and beeswax lingered in the air. Moving the armoire completed the work, and once the huge piece was muscled away, Daphne stared at the previously hidden doorway. It gave her a curious feeling to think that Charles would soon be able to walk through that doorway at will, into her room, into her bed . . . .

The descent on Beaumont Place by friends and neighbors curious about what had transpired in the blue salon never materialized, and Daphne was devoutly grateful. She discovered that as soon as it was learned that Anne Darby had been present, all the gossip was simply brushed aside as some very clever theatrics by the local witch.

The wedding was little more than ten days away. Notes of congratulations and presents were pouring in, and the household was in a tizzy preparing for all the guests that would soon be descending upon Beaumont Place. The doors of musty rooms that had not seen the light of day in decades were thrown wide and thoroughly aired and cleaned; Cook demanded more staff and seemed to Daphne determined to concoct meals that would please the palate of a king. There were trips to the dressmaker in Penzance for the ladies of the house, even Miss Kettle breaking down and agreeing to a new gown in puce silk for the wedding.

Though a visit with Anne Darby was high on her list of things to do, there was simply no time. She had managed, however, a word with Vicar Henley during the small dinner party he and his wife hosted for her and Charles a few days later. Seeking a private moment with the vicar, she mentioned Sir Wesley's name, and the vicar had sent her a soothing smile. "My dear," he said, "never worry that some of that old villain's blood runs in your veins. Perish the thought! He may have had a hand in doing away with his nephew, but no one was ever able to prove it." He rubbed his chin reflectively. "From the surviving letters of that time, it was certainly suspected that he killed John—or had him killed. The point for you to remember is that Sir Wesley died without issue." He looked solemn. "It was an ugly time with ugly doings, and I must say, from my research, that it is fortunate for your family that Sir Wesley was not able to get his hands on his nephew's wife and child. I shudder to think what might have happened to them. The moment Anne-Marie's parents heard of John's arrest by his uncle, they swooped down and carried their daughter away to the safety of their own home, well out of Sir Wesley's grasp. It was at her parent's home in Suffolk that Anne-Marie gave birth to John's son, Jonathan. Only after Sir Wesley died did John's widow and his son return to take their rightful position at Beaumont Place." He patted her shoulder and smiled. "You are descended from Sir Jonathan, and from everything I've read, he was an ancestor to be proud of. Put any thoughts of Sir Wesley out of your mind."

Daphne would have asked more, but the squire's wife wandered up just then, and the moment was lost. The vicar's words relieved her, and she was perfectly happy to put Sir Wesley out of her mind . . . provided he did not insist upon popping out of the fireplace at will.

From that moment on, there was never another chance for further investigation into Sir Wesley's dastardly doings, and that suited Daphne just fine—she was far too busy to brood over some long dead distant relative—and thank God for that! Someone, it seemed, always needed her decision or advice, and there were social engagements galore. The coming wedding was the most prominent affair in the area in years, the circumstances surrounding the engagement adding a surprising cachet, and local hostesses competed vigorously for the attendance of the betrothed couple. There were breakfasts, dinner parties, and soirees, one enterprising matron even arranging a horseback ride to Land's End for an alfresco meal served above the crashing surf on the rocks below.

Charles was busy with his own pursuits, and beyond a few short visits to Beaumont Place, he and Daphne only met these days at the various social functions that they attended. Sometimes, he would escort her to the event; other times, as in tonight's outing, they would arrive separately, Daphne traveling with Adrian and April, Charles riding over from Lanyon Hall. This evening's affair had been a small, informal soiree held by the squire and his wife, the fourth such function this week, and as he helped her into Sir Adrian's carriage, Charles murmured, "I never realized how fatiguing being engaged could be." He smiled down at her. "Will you be happy to put this all behind you?"

She smiled back at him, amazed at how swiftly he had become such an integral part of her life. "Indeed, it does seem that we are far more giddy here in the country than even in London."

His lips quirked. "It's amazing what a hint of scandal can do for one's popularity."

Her smile fled. "Do you mind it terribly?" she asked.

"Mind?" He shook his head. "If I did, my dear, I wouldn't be here. I never do things that I do not want to."

A little shiver ran down her spine when she realized that he meant every word. She had only seen his charming side so far, but now and then, she glimpsed the steel beneath the velvet, the glacier behind the warmth, and she knew a little spurt of unease. He was no longer a complete stranger, but she could not pretend that he was not still an unknown quantity to her or one that did not cause her anxious moments.

Adrian and April, having lingered talking to some of the younger guests, joined them, and in the flurry of good-byes, there was no opportunity for further private conversation. With Adrian and April settled inside the Beaumont coach, Charles, who had ridden over with the viscount, gave Daphne a careless wave and rejoined Trevillyan for the ride back to Lanyon Hall.

As far as Charles was concerned, the wedding could not take place soon enough. Not only did he go around in an embarrassing randy state, his nights disturbed by the most explicitly erotic dreams imaginable, but he would also be quite happy to see the last of Lanyon Hall and his host. The viscount was likable enough, not a bad companion, although his bitterness at having lost Sir Huxley's fortune still ate at him, and Charles had grown weary of veiled references to the unfairness of Fate and undeserving cubs who had the devil's own luck. Certainly, the viscount drank too much, being in Charles's opinion, far too fond of the bottle and the gaming table. He did not *dis*like the viscount—Trevillyan was no worse than any one of a dozen young bucks he could name, and he supposed that in Raoul's circle, Trevillyan would have been considered a fine fellow.

Riding toward Lanyon Hall that night, Charles considered the course of his life had he decided not to pay Trevillyan a visit. He smiled wryly in the darkness. He owed the man a debt of gratitude that he could never repay, and an unpleasant chill slid down his back when he considered that if he had not come to visit, he would never have met Daphne. Never mind that Trevillyan discreetly deplored the coming union or was convinced that Charles would come to regret his gallantry. It was a fact: had he not come to visit and had Daphne not catapulted into his life, he would have resumed his reckless, lonely existence, never knowing or guessing at the depth of passion and joy that now consumed him.

Just thinking of returning to Stonegate without Daphne at his side filled him with dread. Dear, darling Daphne, he realized humbly, and Charles was seldom humble, had saved him from a cold, empty fate, and for the first time, he understood what Nell's entrance in Julian's life had meant to him.

Just as Wyndham Manor was no longer the lonely, austere place it had been before Julian had married Nell, so would Stonegate change under Daphne's hand. Like a vibrant spring breeze, her presence would drive out all the old, ugly memories, and Stonegate would once again become the warm, welcoming home he remembered from his childhood. Before my mother died and Father brought home Sofia, he thought tightly. But he would not let the past intrude, would not allow himself to be lost in the black thoughts that so often bedeviled him, and again he thanked God for Daphne's presence in his life. He smiled. Even if she came with a brother and sister and a few ghosts. Adrian and April presented no problems for him—he was very fond of the pair of them and delighted in their youthful exuberance—but the ghosts . . . .

Charles was relieved that the problem of the ghosts appeared to have abated. Which was just as well, he decided, considering the demands and constraints on their time. He had hoped that he and Daphne would have had a chance to discover more about Sir Wesley and the little crying ghost in the intervening days, but events had conspired against them. Though they spoke privately about the unresolved situation, since the ghosts seemed to have become silent for the time being, they were willing to let sleeping dogs lie. Soon enough, he would be living at Beaumont Place, and then he and Daphne would be able to focus on the various manifestations that seemed to haunt the house. A slow grin crossed his face. And he would be able to make love to his wife any time he felt like it, and Sir Wesley be damned! Eager for his wedding day, for what the future might hold and happy for the first time in a long time, Charles kicked his horse into a gallop, wishing that Daphne waited for him at Lanyon Hall.

Arriving at Lanyon Hall, Eames informed Charles that a note had been delivered for him while he had been gone. Handing him the envelope, Eames said, "You were not gone five minutes when it arrived, sir. I did not think it urgent, so I did not send it by one of our servants to Squire Henley's. I hope I did right?"

"Of course you did," broke in Trevillyan, his slurred words revealing that he was well on his way to being foxed. "If it had been important, Weston would have told you to be on the lookout for it." Dismissing his butler, Trevillyan glanced at Charles. "Would you care to join me in another tipple before bed?"

Politely declining the offer, aware that Trevillyan had again imbibed more than enough for one evening, Charles bid his host good night and walked up the stairs to his rooms. Since he'd given his valet the evening off, Charles swiftly stripped off his clothes and hauled on a dark green velvet robe. Pouring himself a snifter of brandy, he seated himself on the sofa and picked up the letter.

Determined to put the lingering question of Raoul's death to rest and to discover what he could about the murdered women before his wedding, Charles had been relentless in his search for answers. Unwilling to wait for Vinton's report, he had spent the intervening time sleuthing on his own. He had been spending afternoons and evenings not given to the social demands to visiting pubs, inns, and downright dens of iniquity in the area, probing carefully and *very* cautiously about any strangers, any newcomers, anything odd in the neighborhood. It didn't help that he was a stranger himself, but it was amazing what a sober man could learn from fellows who had enjoyed one round of ale or gin too many, and Charles had amiably bought many a round to loosen tongues that otherwise might not have wagged. But there was a danger in that, too—twice, he'd barely escaped unscathed from some equally sober gentlemen who had realized that the roughly dressed man sitting in the shadows was also rather openhanded with his blunt and had sought to relieve him of his purse. They had not succeeded and had limped away with a healthy respect for the quiet stranger.

Despite his efforts, Charles had nothing to show for his quest except for a few bruises, a much lighter purse, and an intimate knowledge of every smuggler's haunt along the Cornish coast. He had learned one thing: the common folk were far more anxious about the dead women than the gentry realized. They were frightened for their womenfolk and spoke in low tones about the savage state of the two bodies. There was no mention of a third murdered woman, and Charles wondered if that corpse had ever actually existed. But of the sole thing he searched for, he found no sign. There was never a hint, never a whisper of a stranger, a newcomer in the area, not a word about someone who just might be a killer.

Thinking of his fruitless search, he grimaced, tapping the letter on his wrist. Perhaps Mr. Vinton had been more successful.

To Charles's disgust, Mr. Vinton had discovered nothing helpful. Tossing the letter aside, Charles sat on the sofa, staring at nothing. Except for the two, possibly three, women done savagely to death, he had not found any evidence that pointed to their killer or killers and more importantly, to Raoul being alive and slaughtering innocents. He'd found no money trail, and no one seemed to have noticed or heard of any strangers in the area.

Charles leaned his head back against the sofa and sighed. If only he and Julian had found Raoul's body, then there would not be this gnawing question at the back of his mind. Raoul had been shot twice in the chest, either wound likely fatal, yet it was possible that neither bullet had hit a vital organ. Certainly, Raoul had not been incapacitated enough to prevent him from disappearing down the sluice hole. The underground passageway had revealed no sign of him, and since it emptied into the river, again, it was possible that Raoul had managed to make it to the river and had allowed the current to take him far downstream before it tossed him up on a riverbank. Possible, Charles admitted, but unlikely. The lack of a body could indicate that Raoul did make it to the river and in all probability, drowned or was dead when he hit the water. If his body had been lodged under a rock, it might never be found, or it may even have been swept out to sea. But suppose Raoul had survived the shooting, survived the river, what then? Sofia was dead and unable to help him. So how did he manage to survive? He rubbed his forehead. Was it time for him to admit that Raoul was well and truly dead and that he was merely chasing shadows, seeing things that were not there? Charles took a deep breath. He had done what he could, used what resources he had at his command, and had come up empty-handed. Even though they had found no body, Raoul must be dead. He swallowed some brandy. His half brother was dead, and he would squander no more time or effort trying to prove otherwise.

The gruesome deaths of the two women that had brought him to Cornwall, Charles thought tiredly, had to have been the work of someone else. It was possible that their deaths were not even related to each other and that he had wasted time that could have been more pleasurably employed. The memory of Daphne's soft mouth beneath his leaped to his mind, and his body reacted instantly. Ignoring the impudent organ that sprang to life between his legs, he tossed off the last of his brandy. Walking toward his bed, he decided that it was a good thing he'd been distracted by this Raoul business. If not for that, he'd have been spending every available moment in Daphne's orbit, and he doubted that his resolution to keep his hands off of her would have been kept. Even if he didn't plan to seduce her, he knew himself too well. He would have been unable to resist her allure, and soon enough, he would have sought a secluded moment alone with her, intending to only steal a kiss, but one kiss would lead to another . . . . With her sweet mouth beneath his, his hands would have sought out those soft, tempting curves, and if she did not deny him, and he knew she would not, in a moment, it would be too late . . . .

His body and brain inflamed by the vision of losing himself in Daphne's silken depths, he tossed aside his robe and crawled into bed. He lay there, painfully aware of the aching, throbbing rod that poked up from beneath the covers. Devil take it! And to think that he had ten more days in which to endure this punishment. Pray God the time passed swiftly.

The time did fly, but not as swiftly as Charles would have liked. For Daphne, the days passed far too quickly, the enormity of the changes in her life both exhilarating and frightening.

Beaumont Place buzzed as if preparing for a siege. Extra servants were hired; foodstuffs from Penzance and outlying areas poured into the house in a steady stream; wedding gifts arrived in bewildering numbers, and she wondered if Charles was related to half of England. The household had been in a frenzy of preparation for weeks, but for her, the wedding had been at a distance, her life still her own. Then overnight, the wedding was only two days away, and horses and coaches were driving up to the front of the house disgorging trunks, servants, and utter strangers who would soon be her relatives by marriage. There seemed to be a astonishing number of them, and as Charles made introductions, only a few stood out: Marcus Sherbrook, a cousin who looked remarkably like Charles, and of course, the Earl and Countess of Wyndham. Daphne had been nervous to meet them, anxious about what they must think of this sudden marriage, her lack of social connections and fortune preying heavily on her mind, but the earl's warm smile and the friendly way the countess embraced her beguiled her. If she had thought that Marcus looked like Charles, she was utterly dumbfounded by the resemblance between Charles and the earl. They looked enough alike to be twins, she thought dazedly as she stared at the earl's amazingly familiar features. Then realizing that she was standing and gawking like a village milkmaid, her cheeks bloomed red, her eyes dropped, and she muttered something intelligible.

The countess, her eyes twinkling, hugged Daphne again and said, "Don't be embarrassed. They do resemble each other to a remarkable degree. Unlike you, I was forewarned, and when I met Charles, I was not caught by surprise, but you . . ." She smiled at Daphne. "Charles, the wretch, never mentioned a word, did he?"

Utterly disarmed by the countess's easy manner, Daphne

said, "He is, indeed, a wretch, for he breathed not a word to me. Nor that Mr. Sherbrook also shared the family features."

"Be that as it may, you must admit that I am, by far, the most handsome of the lot," Charles murmured, trying to look modest and failing lamentably.

"Certainly the most arrogant," the earl replied with a laugh. "It is, I'm afraid, his besetting sin." Taking Daphne's hand in his, he said, "We are most pleased to meet you, Miss Beaumont, and to welcome you to our family." He slanted a mocking glance toward Charles. "Having only just met you, already I feel that you will have a leavening effect on that scamp you plan to marry. Believe me, he needs a firm hand."

"Dash it all, Julian, don't be filling her head with that sort of nonsense! I already go in fear that I shall live under the cat's paw. She definitely doesn't need you giving her pointers on how to bring me to heel." He grinned down at Daphne. "She'll manage quite well on her own."

"Well, I certainly mean to try," Daphne murmured.

Nell laughed and clapped her hands together in delight. "Oh, I knew I would like you! You are exactly what Charles needs. I so feared he would fall prey to some sweetly biddable female who would be absolutely no good at all for him. Now tell me, where are Sir Adrian and your sister? Charles's letters have been full of them, and I have been so looking forward to meeting them—they sound an enchanting pair."

Nothing could have endeared Nell to Daphne more than Nell's interest in her siblings. "They are awaiting us in the gold saloon." She smiled. "My brother felt that it would be proper for me to meet you first. Won't you come this way?"

Adrian and April rose nervously to their feet when Julian, Nell, and Marcus, escorted by Daphne and Charles, swept into the room, but once introductions were made, Julian's friendly overtures and Nell's warm interest calmed them, and their nervousness vanished. They comported themselves very well, Daphne thought proudly several moments later, watching Adrian talking earnestly to the earl and Marcus while

April sat on the sofa conversing prettily with the countess. Their manners were impeccable, and who would not be charmed by two such handsome and beautiful young people?

Charles came to stand by her side and whispered in her ear, "Are you scheming already to elicit Nell's help when April makes her debut in London?"

Daphne had the grace to blush. "Not scheming," she admitted with a guilty expression, "but I *was* hoping that if the Countess liked April enough, she might want to introduce her to some of the higher ranking members of the ton." She glanced at Charles, her eyes glowing. "It would be most wonderful for April's advancement in society. Just a word from the Countess could put all of London society at her feet. And if the earl helped him, Adrian would be asked to join the most select clubs for gentlemen in all of London. Under the aegis of the Earl and Countess of Wyndham, their positions in society would be assured."

"And you don't think that I could do as much?" he asked with a lifted brow, astonished to discover that he was a trifle put out that Daphne would look to someone else to launch her sister and brother into the heights of the ton.

"Could you?" Daphne asked innocently. She touched his sleeve. "Oh, Charles! Would you? It would be more than I ever dreamed to have them welcomed into the midst of the *haut ton!* The doors that would open for them! The opportunities!"

Staring down into Daphne's face, her love and pride in her brother and sister blazing in her eyes, Charles wondered bleakly, and not for the first time, if the day would ever come that she would look at him with that same intense loving expression. The lowering thought occurred to him that in Daphne's world, he came a distant third to Adrian and April. He wasn't *exactly* jealous, at least he didn't think so, but he wished that his rivals for her affections were not her brother and sister. A male rival, he would have known precisely how to disable, but he was defenseless against Adrian and April. If they had been a pair of selfish, scheming hellborn babes, he could have, and would have, dealt summarily with them, but what was he to do when pitted against a disarmingly charming youth like Adrian and a beguiling little darling like April? They might not come from a socially powerful and aristocratic family as he did, but their bloodline was certainly respectable, and with Adrian's newly inherited title and wealth, there was nothing to hinder their advancement amongst the rich and powerful. Charles smiled. Who could resist them? They deserved to have all those golden opportunities that Daphne longed for them to have. To his astonishment, he realized that he wanted their advancement into the ranks of the *ton* as much as Daphne did, and he shook his head at how quickly he had entered the ranks of every scheming, matchmaking parent he had ever met.

Charles glanced over to where Julian, Marcus, and Adrian stood talking. "I may not have the cachet of the Earl of Wyndham or the staid respectability of my cousin, Marcus, but there are few doors that are closed to me," he said carelessly, "and as his brother-in-law, I will be more than happy to ease Adrian's path into society." He made a face, honesty making him add, "However, in April's case . . . I think, perhaps, that her social advancement would be best left in yours and Nell's hands." He grinned down at Daphne. "There are a few of the reigning hostesses who might look askance at any female I sought to fire off into society."

"Is your reputation very bad?" Daphne asked uneasily. She was curious about his life prior to coming to Cornwall. She knew of his relationship to the earl, knew that his family was highly esteemed, knew that he was wealthy and owned his own estate, but beyond that, there was a whole blank canvas.

Charles rubbed his chin. "Let me put it this way: a few years ago, mamas with lovely marriageable daughters tended to keep them under lock and key when I was in the vicinity."

He smiled charmingly at her. "But most gentlemen found me more than tolerable."

"Do not let him bamboozle you," said Julian, coming up to join them, Marcus and Adrian trailing behind him. Grinning at Charles, Julian continued, "I tell you, my dear, that he was the worst kind of rake. A handsome, utterly charming ne'er-do-well, a neck-or-nothing rider, and an incredibly lucky gambler."

"Don't forget," chimed in Marcus, "handy with his fives, a devil with a sword, and reckless and wild to a fault."

"All of that," Julian agreed easily, the expression in his gaze hard to define as he stared at Charles, "but also the very man you want at your side should your back be against the wall."

"I shall have absolutely no character left if the pair of you continue to fill her ears with that sort of tittle-tattle," Charles complained. To Daphne, he said, "Do not listen to them. They were always an envious pair. You see before you a changed man. I have sworn off my rakish ways." He lifted her hand to his lips and murmured, "And you, my sweet, have nothing to fear. I shall be an exemplary husband."

"If it kills him," said Marcus sotto voce.

Baron Templeton, his wife and heir, the Honorable Stacy Bannister, arrived shortly, and there was another round of introductions, although Daphne took one look at Lady Templeton and Stacy Bannister and knew them to be related to Charles. Both had the Weston family looks, and it came as no surprise to learn the Lady Templeton was his aunt and Stacy, at twenty-five, his youngest male cousin. She was even more gratified when Stacy took a liking to Adrian, and the stunned look on his face when he met April filled her cup to overflowing.

Dinner that evening was lively, the conversation scintillating, and the food superb. By the time the ladies rose from the table, leaving the gentlemen to their port and wines, she was so filled with optimism for the future for Adrian and April that Daphne's feet hardly touched the floor.

She was still floating, visions of Adrian and April taking London by storm drifting through her head, when she prepared for bed many hours later. Sitting at her dressing table, she swung around and stared at the now opened doorway that led to the sitting room she and Charles would share, and the reality of what was happening filtered through her brain. The day after tomorrow, at eleven o'clock in the morning, she would be married to a man whose name she had not even known a month ago. Her heart gave an uncomfortable lurch. Soon she would be Mrs. Charles Weston, and her fate and those of Adrian and April would be in the hands of a stranger, albeit one whom she had grown to trust and respect. She did not know whether to be ecstatic or terrified. Or both.

Chapter 13

The day of the wedding dawned bright and clear, and for Daphne, the intervening time had passed within the blink of an eye. A formal dinner with all of the local gentry in attendance had been held the previous evening, adding to the madness surrounding the wedding.

Daphne was so busy that she had no time to think about her coming nuptials. Before she knew it, the cumbersome Beaumont family coach was depositing her, Adrian, and April at the broad stone steps of the local church. Flanked by her siblings, she picked up the skirts of her white- and silver-spangled gown, and her heart beating fast, she entered the church.

Her hand trembling on her brother's arm, Daphne slowly walked toward the front of the church where the vicar, Charles, and his groomsman, the Earl of Wyndham, awaited them. She was hardly aware of the dark wooden pews festooned with pink roses and sweetly scented white lilies, hardly aware of the encouraging smile flashed her way by the countess, hardly aware of anything but the austerely handsome man standing so tall and imposing at the front of the church. When their eyes met, her heart, already thudding madly beneath her breast, felt as if it would leap right out of her chest.

Reaching the vicar, Adrian, looking absurdly formal and

very young, took Daphne's hand from his arm and placed it in Charles's. As Charles's hand closed warmly around hers, Daphne was startled at how very right it felt, how very comforting it felt, and her fingers tightened on his. Her gaze searched his dark face, the enormity of what was happening flooding through her. In a matter of moments, she would be the wife of this man, this stranger, yet not at all a stranger. Once the vicar pronounced the words, their lives would be forever linked, and Daphne was astonished by the surge of sheer pleasure that raced through her at that knowledge. Soon, she and her siblings would no longer be just a little trio against the world—when she married Charles, she was marrying into a large and extended family, a family that had welcomed not only her, but her brother and sister as well. She studied him, this man she would marry, conscious of the unraveling of the small knot of uncertainty that had always lingered at the back of her mind. Standing before the vicar, like a bolt from the sky, she realized that she could not imagine marrying anybody else. In that stunning second, she knew three things: she trusted him implicitly, his touch sent her body up in flames, and she was in love with him . . .

Her eyes widened, and she stood there, shocked. Of course she loved him! How could she not? He was honorable and kind and handsome and everything she would have wished for in a husband, his affection for Adrian and April only adding to his appeal. With a blinding flash, it dawned on her that she had been so concerned with Adrian and April's future that she had ignored what her own heart had been telling her for weeks. She loved him! Utterly, completely, and for all time.

Her lips curved in a smile so dazzling that Charles blinked and caught his breath, instinctively moving closer to her. He hadn't a clue what she was thinking; he only knew that he wanted her to keep looking at him with that same sweet expression on her face and that he wanted desperately to kiss her. His eyes locked on her soft mouth, he was actually bend-ing forward when the vicar's voice, speaking the opening words of the marriage ceremony forcibly reminded him of the matter at hand.

Hands held tightly, they repeated their vows, Charles's voice ringing emphatically through the church, Daphne's quieter, more muted. And then it was over—they were married and leaving the church, the others following them out into the pale yellow February sunshine.

Charles and Daphne drove back to Beaumont Place in the smart, well-sprung black and burgundy carriage he'd had delivered by his coachman and groom from Stonegate a few days ago. The coach was pulled by a quartet of gleaming blaze-faced bay horses, each with four flashy white socks, whose spanking trot ate up the distance between the church and Beaumont Place.

Leaning back against the burgundy velvet squabs of the coach as the vehicle swayed and bounced along the road, Daphne stared dazedly out the window. Staggered by the knowledge that she was madly in love with her very new husband, her brain simply could not get over that fact, and coherent speech was beyond her. Blind to the passing scenery, she thought, "I am in love with my husband. *I love Charles Weston!* I love him."

It was only when Charles lifted her hand from the seat and pressed a kiss on the back of it that she started and looked at him.

Charles sent her a quizzical glance, wondering what had prompted that dazzling smile in the church and what precisely was now going on in that pretty little head of hers. He sighed inwardly. Probably some grand scheme involving Adrian or April's debut into society, he thought wryly. Aloud, he merely said, "That went very well, didn't it?"

She nodded, suddenly shy with him. This handsome, charming man was her *husband!*

Kissing her fingers, his eyes fixed on her face, he said, "Hello, wife."

A smile that caused his heart to stop beating before resuming at an alarming pace crossed her face. "Hello, husband," she said softly, her other hand coming up to lightly caress his cheek.

At her touch, the warmth of her hand branding his cheek, Charles swallowed, tongue-tied for perhaps the first time in his life. Christ! She was lovely. And he was bloody fathoms deep in love with her and had been, he suspected, since the moment he'd laid eyes on her. Why else had he risked his life in that blasted cave with her? And saddled himself with a pair of brats? A pair of brats who ranked ahead of him in her affections? He shook his head, unable to concentrate, unable to think of anything but how much he loved her, and how very, *very* much he wanted to make love to her. And if she didn't stop looking at him that way, he was afraid that he'd consummate their marriage right here and now on the coach seat. His loins clenched, the idea of sliding his hand under that white spangled gown and finding all the sweet heat he knew would be there almost overpowering him.

Wrenching his thoughts away from visions of sleek, naked flesh, he stared hard at their clasped hands. Frantically, he searched for a topic of conversation that didn't involve his desire to rip off her clothing and bury himself in her body. Reminding himself of the plans that he had made, plans he had not yet mentioned to his new wife, he snatched at them like a drowning man does a piece of driftwood. The timing was all wrong, he admitted, although he had not yet been able to think of *any* time when she would welcome his news.

Better now when we are alone than at the house, he decided uneasily. She wasn't going to like it no matter when he told her, but it seemed a sensible and necessary plan to him. As he fumbled to break the news to her, he wondered where his arrogance and determination to arrange things to suit himself had gone. A little slice of guilt knifed through him. Well, he had arranged this to suit himself, he admitted, but it was for Daphne's sake as well. And since when, he mused, did he go around nervous about a woman's reaction, even if the woman was his wife. His lips twisted. *Probably since I fell in love with the little witch.* He took a deep breath. *Better get it over with.*

His elegantly arranged cravat feeling as if it would choke him, Charles muttered, "Uh, I've spoken to Julian and Nell, and they have agreed to stay on at Beaumont Place for a trifle . . . while we make a lightning trip to Stonegate. I've arranged for us to leave this afternoon. We will stay the night at an excellent coaching inn I know of outside of Looe and arrive at Stonegate sometime tomorrow afternoon, early evening at the latest."

Daphne sat up, her brow clouding. "Leave Beaumont Place this afternoon? Oh, we cannot! I am not packed. There are guests in the house. And Adrian and April . . ."

"Adrian and April will be fine—Julian and Nell will watch over them. And I took the liberty of having Nell tell your maid to pack your bags. Your maid and my valet are even now on their way to Looe. It is all arranged. We shall be gone little over a week." He waited for the storm to break over his head, but to his relief, she looked more bewildered than angry.

"But why? Surely I can see Stonegate soon enough."

His hand tightened on hers. "Because," he said very deliberately, "I want you to see your new home, meet your new servants, but mostly because I want to make love to you without having to run the gauntlet of knowing eyes every time we step out of our rooms."

Daphne flushed, thinking of sitting down to breakfast tomorrow morning with Adrian, April, the earl, *everyone* in the household knowing . . . Her flush deepened. "Oh. I hadn't thought about that."

I had," said Charles with feeling. "We shall enjoy our wedding breakfast with our family and friends, and then we shall leave for Stonegate."

*   *   *

Charles's plan went off exactly as he had arranged, and Daphne was surprised at how lighthearted she felt as she waved good-bye to her brother and sister and the others as the coach pulled away from Beaumont Place. She'd never been separated from Adrian and April before, and while their well-being was of great concern to her, it occurred to her with a funny little start that miraculously, Charles had become the most important person in the world to her. She looked across at him. Her husband, her soon-to-be lover . . .

They arrived in Looe after dark. But since Charles had sent Bledsoe and her maid, Jane, ahead to prepare things for them, when she entered the suite of rooms that had been procured for the night, Daphne found all in readiness. Her clothes had been unpacked, a bath had been ordered, and Jane said that Mr. Weston had instructed Bledsoe to order a light repast for them.

Daphne was too nervous to think of food, and as she stepped from the copper tub, she glanced at the big bed where she would sleep that night. A shiver of anticipation rippled through her. Charles would come to her, and he would do all those marvelous things to her, and this time, she swallowed, and this time, there would be no stopping. Her nipples peaked, her lower body hummed, and laughing at herself, not certain whether to be glad or appalled at her wantonness, she slipped into a pale pink nightgown of softest cambric, delicate rosebuds embroidered around the neck, sleeves, and hem. She brushed her wild black mane of hair and pinched her cheeks and surveyed herself in the small mirror. She saw a passably attractive woman, not in her first blush, a beanpole with a mop of unruly hair, and wished for just a moment that she possessed April's fair beauty . . . and rounded curves.

When the door between their two rooms opened, Daphne gasped and instinctively clutched the matching pink robe to her small bosom. Dry-mouthed, she stared as Charles walked into the room. Her knees felt weak at the sight of him, his thick black hair damp from his bath, his powerful body cloaked by a robe of heavy silk. She could see sprigs of black hair where the material crossed at his chest, and she knew that he was naked underneath.

She thought the moment would be awkward, but with an expression in his eyes that thrilled her, Charles simply walked up to her, took the robe from her nerveless hand, tossed it on the floor, and pulled her into his arms. He kissed her, his mouth, teeth, and tongue urgent against hers, his hands cupping her hips and pulling her next to his hard warmth.

Daphne moaned, melting into his heat, reveling in the deep thrust of his tongue, the warm slide of his lips on hers. There was no mistaking his arousal, the rigid length of him pushing forcefully against her lower belly. Never breaking stride, never lifting his hungry mouth from hers, he walked her backward toward the bed.

The bed reached, they fell down together onto it, Charles half on her, half on the mattress. It was only then that his mouth lifted from hers, and smiling down into her face, he said huskily, "Hello again, wife. I've missed you."

She touched his cheek, unbearably conscious of his muscled weight pressing her down into the mattress. "We've only been apart for minutes."

"Too long," he said fervently. He brushed a kiss along her jaw. "I need you, Daphne. I want you badly . . ." He kissed her eyelids. "I will try to be gentle . . . know that if I hurt you, it will only be once and that it is passion for your lovely body that drives me."

Daphne's arms went around his neck, and her eyes luminous and full of that same expression that had taken his breath away earlier, she said, "Do with me as you will . . . husband."

Charles groaned, and his mouth came down hard on hers, his hands sliding under her nightgown to caress the silky length of her legs. She welcomed his kiss, his touch, yearning and excitement spiraling up through her as his kiss became more demanding, more urgent, his tongue exploring and tangling with hers, his hands kneading her thighs, stoking the fire that burned within her.

They kissed again and again, each kiss more urgent than the last, each kiss driving them further into the world known only to lovers. Dizzy with desire, her breasts aching and her bones turning to liquid fire, Daphne was hardly aware of Charles shrugging out of his robe. It was only when her caressing fingers touched the warm skin on his shoulders that she realized that he was naked.

She broke the kiss and blinked up into his face. "You're naked," she muttered, "and I am not."

He flashed her a hard, fierce smile. "I'm sure that I can take care of that, sweet."

He shifted slightly, and she gasped when her gown was whipped over her head and her nude body was pulled next to his. Oh, it was heaven! He was warm and hard in her embrace, the springy hairs on his chest brushing seductively against her breasts, his long legs pressing next to hers, and locked between their bodies was that rigid shaft that both excited and terrified her. He moved over her, his rod stoking her, and any fear of the unknown vanished, leaving only excitement spiraling up through her. She moaned as he slowly rubbed against her, and her thighs parted to bring him closer.

Charles shuddered when his body slipped between her legs, and he fought against the urge to join them into one. To have her willing mouth under his, her naked beauty his to take was almost more than he could bear. Repressing the urge to fall upon her like a ravening beast, knowing it was too soon, he wrenched his mouth from hers and compulsively sought her breasts. Ah, God, she was sweet, her nipples tasting like sugared berries on his tongue. He bit down gently, gratified and aroused by the leap her body gave and the way her hand pulled his head closer to her breasts.

Under his seeking lips, Daphne grappled with new sensations, her body twisting beneath him, each pull of his mouth, each long, slow scrape of his teeth against her breasts and nipples sending a hot pulse of desire streaking down to where their bodies surged against each other. Wanting more, eager for more, her hips pushed up against him, the feel of that unyielding length of flesh between their bodies making her mouth go dry and her body hum with wild anticipation. And when he touched her, when his fingers moved through the thatch of curls between her thighs and lazily stroked the soft folds of flesh he found there, she stiffened, delight and anticipation rushing through her. He lingered there, going no further, his light caresses as he pulled and petted that sensitive skin driving her mad. Her fingers dug into his shoulders, and she arched up helplessly, her body demanding more than this teasing exploration. She ached. She needed. She *wanted*.

Charles tried to go slow, wanting this moment to last, but Daphne's generous response was ripping away his good intentions. He felt ready to explode, and the need to bury himself deep within her nearly overrode the restraints he'd placed on himself. He wanted no hurried coupling, but his own hunger, his own desires clouded coherent thought, and his fingers sought her core, one finger sinking into her hot, welcoming depths.

Daphne bit back a scream of delight at the sensation of Charles's finger sliding in and out of where she most ached, where she most yearned for his touch, transforming want into naked demand. Want, need possessed her, and she unashamedly rode his finger, twisting helplessly beneath his hand, and when he inserted a second finger, she shuddered, a fresh wave of pleasure flooding through her. The feeling was so intense, so powerful that her fingers dug into his shoulders and her entire body arched up off the bed, not wanting to be parted from those seductive fingers.

His brain, body, and heart on fire, Charles could no longer control himself, and with a low growl, he replaced his fingers with his rigid member, the swollen head sinking carefully into her. He tried to go slow, tried to prevent himself from thrusting wildly into that sleek, intoxicating heat, but it was beyond him. His mouth caught hers, and he gently bit her lip. His voice thick and almost unrecognizable, against her mouth, he said, "I may hurt you, but know that it will only be this one time . . ." She pushed against him, and he muttered, "I cannot go any slower, Daffy—I want you too much. I swear that after this, it will only get better."

Daphne didn't care. "I believe you," she gasped, "but could you please hurry?"

Choking on a despairing laugh, Charles kissed her deeply and allowed himself to sink fully into her slick depths, the fragile barrier between virgin and woman breached in an instant. His member lodged to the hilt within her, her body soft and warm beneath him, Charles shuddered at the force of the pleasure that roared through him. Daphne was his! His *wife*.

There was pain, Daphne couldn't pretend otherwise, but it was brief and gone in a moment, and the joy, the wonder of being one with Charles instantly banished that small hurt. In dazed delight, she lay there reveling in the solid weight of him pressing down against her, marveling that her body had accepted *all* of him. It was heaven. She wiggled a bit, testing the tight fit, gasping as a sharp pang of pleasure shot up through her when Charles rocked against her.

It was sweet agony trying to remain motionless, trying to give her a moment to adjust, but when she twisted beneath him, Charles could not help himself and began to slide in and out of her, gently at first, then as the demon sprang free, harder, faster, and deeper. His hands fastened on her hips, holding her to his liking, his body thrust into hers, each movement more urgent than the last, each thrust bringing them closer to the edge.

As lost and frantic as Charles, Daphne clung to him, her fingers digging into his back, her hips rising to meet him, the wildness, the passion between them explosive. Low in her body, something coiled, tighter and tighter, forcing a moan from her at the intensity of the sensation. She pushed up frantically against Charles, seeking something, needing, wanting release from this increasing fierce ache where their bodies met and parted. When it came, when that explosion of ecstasy burst through her, she stiffened, a low keening cry bursting from her throat.

Her cry, the clenching and unclenching of her body around him was his defeat, and Charles writhed helplessly in her arms, pumping urgently into her until he, too, found release. He savored each thrust, each throb his body gave as he emptied himself into her before finally surrendering and sliding bonelessly replete to her side.

He kissed her gently. "I shall treasure this night and what we shared for the rest of my life," he said huskily.

Daphne twisted her head to stare up at him. In the candlelight, his features looked harsh and forbidding, the flickering light dancing over his high cheekbones, outlining the stubborn chin and the hard mouth—she thought him the handsomest man she had ever seen.

A soft, mysterious smile curved her lips, and she touched his lips lightly with her fingertips. "It is a memorable night for both of us," she said. An impish gleam in her eyes, she murmured, "The first, I trust, of many."

He groaned, and his mouth fastened urgently on hers. When they were both breathless, he lifted his lips from hers and said thickly, "Oh, yes, you can most assuredly count on that."

Despite an active night wherein Charles had made love to her twice more, they rose before dawn and were pulling away from the coaching inn just as the first faint golden fingers of the sun slid across the sky. It was very late in the afternoon when at last the coach swept through a pair of massive stone gates that had given the house its name. A half mile later, they left the forest-edge road, and the coach swung into the wide circular driveway in front of an impressive three-story stone house with mullioned windows and a hipped gray slate roof. The house appeared very old to Daphne, and of no particular design, and she glanced about eagerly as Charles helped her down from the coach. Three wide steps led up to a stone terrace, and as they walked across it, Charles said, "This will be your home." A cool note in his voice, he added, "The furnishings reflect my stepmother's taste; do not be hesitant to make what changes you like."

Daphne glanced up at him, noting the grim cast to his face. This was the first mention of a stepmother, and it caught her by surprise. "Your stepmother? Does she live here?"

Charles laughed without humor. "No. She has been quite, quite dead almost three years ago."

She would have pursued the topic, but they had reached the entrance of the house, where the dark wooden doors were flung wide and a tall, angular gentleman wearing black livery stood waiting for them. When they reached him, he murmured, "Good afternoon, Master Weston." Turning to Daphne, he bowed low and said, "I am Garthwaite, your butler, Mistress Weston, and I am most happy to be the first of the staff to welcome you to Stonegate."

"Why, thank you," Daphne replied, smiling at him. "That is very kind of you."

"Currying favor with your new mistress already?" Charles murmured, his eyes glinting with amusement as he passed Garthwaite and escorted Daphne into her new home.

Garthwaite's nostrils quivered, but he ignored Charles's comment, merely saying in lofty tones, "It will be a real pleasure to have a woman's hands on the reins of the household once again."

The large foyer that Daphne entered was sumptuous, the walls hung in a dark green figured silk, French mirrors framed in gold leaf adorning one wall and extending up a handsome staircase of green-veined marble before disappearing into the upper reaches of the house. On the opposite wall, an inlaid lyre table had been placed, and above the table was a large portrait of a man and boy, the style of their clothing old-fashioned.

Beyond the portrait was a wide hallway that Daphne assumed gave access to the rest of the house.

Having been helped out of her sapphire blue corded silk pelisse and dispensing with her yellow gloves and hat while Charles made arrangements with Garthwaite for some refreshments to be served in the east salon, Daphne walked over and stared at the portrait. It took only a glance to tell her that the man and boy were Charles's relatives, the resemblance very strong. Was that Charles at the knee of his father? She frowned, struck again by how very little she knew about his family. He had been singularly reticent about his relatives, and she wondered why. Of course, she hadn't made any inquiries either, she thought with a pang of embarrassment. Guiltily, she admitted that other than the earl, Marcus Sherbrook, and Stacey Bannister, she had no idea about his family. His reference to his stepmother just a few moments ago pointed out how much she had to learn about her new husband and the family she had married into.

Charles came up to stand behind her, his hands resting on her shoulders, and she smiled over her shoulder at him. His expression was peculiar, and she asked, "Are you that little boy?"

Charles shook his head. "No. That is my elder brother, John, and his son, Daniel." Bleakly, he added, "They are both dead, John first, and a decade later, Daniel—just four or five years ago."

"Oh! I am so very sorry," she said softly, her heart aching for him. "You must have been devastated," she added, thinking how horrible it would be if she was to lose Adrian or April.

"When John . . . died," he said slowly, "I could not imagine anything worse happening." His face set and his eyes as cold and icy as the North Sea, he said, "I discovered that I was wrong." His thoughts far away, Charles stared for a long minute at the portrait, and then he seemed to shake himself and return his attention to the present. Forcing a smile, he said, "Come! Let us not dwell on tragic events. We are newly married, beginning our lives together, and we will not let the past intrude upon us."

Aware that there was much being left unsaid, Daphne nodded and allowed him to usher her out of the foyer and down a wide hallway, but her thoughts still lingered on what she had just learned. Was the topic of his older brother's death still so raw and painful to him that he could not speak of it? she mused. And what about his nephew, Daniel? His death had been more recent. Was the wound still so tender? What had happened? An illness? Or something else? She suspected the latter. There had been a note in his voice . . . .

"This is the east salon," Charles said, scattering her thoughts. "It is one of the more formal rooms in the house, and as I said earlier, if you wish to make changes, you'll not hear any complaints from me."

Daphne's first impression as she walked into the east salon was that someone had spent a great deal of money and time on it. The color scheme of blue, gold, and cream had been used throughout the large space, and while everything from the gold damask sofas to the gleaming satinwood tables and chairs were in the first stare of fashion, Daphne found the area strangely uninviting. The room was unwelcoming, as if it had been furnished simply for show but with little thought for warmth and comfort. The fire crackling on the hearth of the marble fireplace drew her, and putting her hands out toward its warmth, she said politely, "It is a very nice room."

"And you hate it," Charles said with a laugh. His amusement faded, and he glanced around the room. "Sofia, my stepmother, was very proud of it."

"Oh, I d-d-don't hate it," Daphne stammered. "I'm sure that most people would find it quite delightful."

Charles lifted her chin with one careless finger. "But you don't?"

Her cheeks reddened, and she muttered, "I don't dislike; it is just not the w-w-way I would have furnished it."

He brushed a kiss across her lips. "Then we must change that, mustn't we? It is your home now, sweet, and it should reflect the things that you like, not my stepmother."

Only a simpleton would not have surmised that there had been some conflict between Charles and his stepmother, and Daphne was no simpleton. That he had never mentioned Sofia's existence until they arrived at Stonegate was telling, but more so was the note in his voice when he spoke of his stepmother. From his manner, she'd hazard a guess that there had been no love lost between him and his stepmother and that being here in this house brought whatever feelings he had for his stepmother to the surface. They had only been here a few moments, but already, Daphne sensed a change in him. Something both troubled and angered him. She could hear it in his voice, see it in the hard curve of his mouth. His brother, his nephew, and his stepmother were all dead in less than fifteen years. Was it just those tragedies that disturbed him? Her gaze searched his, but his cool green eyes gave nothing away.

Deciding to have it out in the open, she asked carefully, "You truly didn't like your stepmother, did you?"

"Not like her? My dear, you have no idea," he drawled. "I loathed her." He looked around the room again. "And the sooner all sign of her is obliterated from this house, the happier I shall be."

Daphne was shocked by the naked hatred in his voice. "Oh, Charles! Surely she was not that bad."

A mirthless smile curved his lips. "Believe me, she was blacker than you can imagine." Daphne's troubled expression made him attempt an explanation. "This was my home," he said slowly, "and I loved it, but when my father married Sofia, everything changed. She was very wealthy, and my father . . . my father needed her fortune. She was the interloper, a rich one at that, and she made John and I feel as if we were intruders, not even worthy of being dust beneath her feet." He gave a harsh laugh. "She was clever, I'll grant you that— always very careful to appear a fond and doting stepmother in front of everyone, including my father, but behind his back . . ." His mouth thinned. "Once my father died, her dislike was blatant, and until her death, I never spent more time here than was necessary."

"But once your brother, John, and his son, Daniel, died and there was just the two of you, didn't the situation grow better?" Daphne asked, deeply troubled. "After all, except for your cousins, all you had was each other."

Charles pulled at his ear. "Ah, I forgot," he said carefully. "I haven't mentioned Sofia's son, my half brother, Raoul, have I?"

Chapter 14

Daphne stared at him a long moment before asking sweetly, "Are there any *other* relatives that you have forgotten? Or shall I forever be opening my door to yet another member of your family that you failed to mention to me?"

Charles grinned. "Technically, you wouldn't be opening the door—that's Garthwaite's job."

Daphne ignored that sally, and hands on her hips, she said, "I would remind you that I have just become a member of this family. With the exception of your relationship to the earl, something I learned from others, and being introduced to your cousins and others that attended our wedding, you have been singularly secretive about the closest members of your family. I must tell you that I find secretiveness to be a most unattractive trait, especially when it concerns family members."

"The family is rather complicated," he said warily, "especially when you factor in the old earl, my paternal grandfather."

"At the moment, I'm not interested in your grandfather," she snapped. "It's bad enough I know nothing of your family, and I didn't even learn of John and Daniel's existence, or their deaths for that matter, until just a few moments ago. Since you and your stepmother were not fond of each other and she has been dead for a few years, I can understand, partly, your avoidance of talking about her. But now I discover that you have another brother! Where is he? How old is he? And when do I meet him?" Her gaze narrowed. "Or are you about to tell me that he, too, has met a tragic end?"

"Half brother," Charles corrected automatically, avoiding answering her last question. The expression on her face warned him that he was about to discover that his sweet wife had a temper and that if he wished to stay in her good graces, he had several tricky minutes in front of him. Dash it all! This wasn't how he'd envisioned their first moments at Stonegate. Certainly, at some point, he'd planned to tell her about Raoul, not everything, but enough to satisfy any curiosity she might have about him, but this wasn't that point. It had been wrong, he realized, not to have told her some facts about the family that she was marrying into, but in all fairness, events had moved rather rapidly. He thought back over the past weeks, trying to imagine a time when it would have been appropriate to murmur into her ear, "By the way, did I mention that I had an older brother, John, who was murdered nearly fifteen years ago? Or that John's son committed suicide, oh, about four years ago, and almost three years ago, my stepmother, a woman I loathed, was killed by a madman . . . the same madman who just happened to kill my half brother at the same time?" Not even to Daphne, or at least not yet, would he confess the truth of that terrible night. Telling her about Raoul and what had happened in that dungeon below the Dower House was not something he viewed with pleasure.

As the minutes passed and Charles remained silent, Daphne sighed. "Aren't you going to answer me?" she asked quietly. "Is there some reason that you don't want to talk about Raoul?"

"There are several reasons," he admitted, "but the main one is that I didn't intend to bore you with family tragedies your first hour in your new home."

She studied him for moment, reminding herself again of

the brief time that they had known each other. They had known each other a month, and though trust and respect had grown quickly between them and she loved him, she reminded herself with a touch of wonder, they didn't know each other very well . . . yet. She sensed that he was not deliberately hiding things from her, but that he had not yet decided how to present something that she suspected would be unpleasant. Guilt smote her. They had only been at Stonegate a matter of minutes, and she was already interrogating him like a shrew. Deciding that perhaps this was a topic that could be postponed, she finally said, "You will tell me later?" A faint smile curving her mouth, she added, "Even about the Old Earl?"

Charles laughed. "Especially about the Old Earl."

Once Garthwaite had served them tea, a brief tour of the house was next. It was a big, handsome house, and Daphne had to pinch herself several times to make certain she was not dreaming as she was shown by Garthwaite into room after room, each one more spacious and elegant than the previous one. This magnificent place was now her *home*. With Charles at her side, she would spend the rest of her days in this house. Their children would be born here, and a tingle went through her at the idea of the wide hallways and empty rooms ringing with the sounds of children running and laughing through the house. She glanced occasionally at Charles, who trailed behind her, wondering what was going through his mind. His expression was hard to define. There was pride in his home—she could see it in his eyes—but there was also something guarded in his expression, as if he was protecting himself and dare not let his true feelings show. Had his stepmother tainted his love of the place? Or were there other reasons? Perhaps something connected to his father? His half brother? She sighed. There was so much to learn about his family, and it certainly did not help that her husband was disinclined to talk about them. Curiosity ate at her, and she wondered at the series of unfortunate events that seemed to have plagued the family. Obviously, his mother was dead. But what of his father? Charles had never once made any reference to him. She made a face. Until she walked through the front door of Stonegate, he'd not mentioned any of the others either, so that omission should come as no surprise. But she wondered how long ago Charles's father had died. It could not have been recent for surely if it had been, he would have said *something*. A terrible thought occurred to her. Was his father's death in the same period of time that had so cruelly taken John, Daniel, Sofia and . . . Raoul from him? A shudder rolled through her. Had she married into a family that was cursed? Telling herself not to be a goose, she pushed those thoughts away and concentrated on being delighted and awed by her new home.

Time flew, and soon enough, Daphne was being shown to her rooms to change for dinner. Having seen throughout the house the style and taste that Charles's stepmother preferred, she had expected her bedroom to be as cold and rigidly formal as the rest of the house, and she had been prepared to dislike it on sight. Instead, she was charmed to be shown into a suite of rooms that revealed a very different hand at work. The amber silk walls and cream ceilings imparted warmth to the big rooms, and while the bed hangings and draperies of gold-striped bronze and the carpets in tones of hunter green, russet, and cream were somewhat masculine, she was quite happy with her new rooms.

Jane had already ordered a bath prepared in the attached dressing room, and Daphne was soon sinking into the warm carnation-scented waters. The water felt decadent against her skin, and the memory of Charles's urgent mouth against her breasts sent a shaft of longing through her. Her cheeks pinkened. The things they had done last night! Heat that had nothing to do with the water temperature flooded through her, and she gasped as her nipples hardened and an insistent ache bloomed between her legs. Her mind was flooded with memories of Charles kissing her, tasting her, making love to her, and by the time she stepped from the tub, her whole body was tingling, yearning for his touch. Uncertain whether to be alarmed or amused by her reactions, she quickly dried herself and slipped into a blue dressing gown.

Her black hair waving wildly around her shoulders, Daphne wandered into the bedroom. She stopped short at the appearance of a small table laden with various covered dishes near her bed; a bouquet of white lilies and yellow rosebuds had been set in the middle, and two chairs had been drawn up next to the table. Candlelight bathed the room in a soft glow, and the perfume of the lilies drifted in the air.

The door that connected their rooms pushed open, and Charles strode in. He was wearing a black robe, the lapels heavily embroidered in gold and crimson thread, and a thrill traced through her at the knowledge that like her, he was naked beneath the fabric. Spying her, he grinned and said, "Excellent! You haven't dressed for dinner yet." His eyes slid down her slender form. "Although," he murmured with a glint in his eyes, "I wouldn't have minded undressing you . . ."

Trying to ignore the way a pulse throbbed low in her body at his words, she waved a hand in the direction of the table. "Is this your doing?"

"Indeed, it is. It has been a very long day, and I thought for tonight that you might prefer simpler fare and to postpone the grandeur of the dining room for another day." He smiled. "One in which you are not longing for your bed."

She smiled back him. "Oh. Am I longing for my bed?"

He walked up to her and pulled her into his arms. His mouth teased hers, his teeth nibbling at the corners of her lips. "If you are not, my sweet," he said huskily, "I certainly am."

Daphne melted into his arms, her mouth opening to him, savoring the taste and thrust of his tongue. His hand on her bottom, pushing her up against his hard shaft, made her moan, and her fingers tangled in his hair, pulling his head closer to her.

Dinner was quite late.

They eventually feasted on turbot with lobster, lamb cutlets, peas and asparagus, plover's eggs in aspic jelly and meringues à la crème, among other dishes and then once again, retired to bed. It was only when they were lying side by side, breath, pulse, brain, and body slowly returning to some degree of normality after another bout of lovemaking, that the subject of Charles's family came up again.

With Daphne cradled next to him, her head nestled on his shoulder, Charles stared at the silken canopy over head. Fate was a peculiar thing, he decided ruefully. It seemed incredible that he had left Stonegate hardly two months ago intent upon discovering if Raoul was alive and slaughtering innocents again and had returned a married man. A married man, he admitted, a bit astonished, who was madly, wildly in love with his wife. He turned his head and dropped a fleeting kiss on Daphne's forehead. It almost didn't matter that she didn't love him, that Adrian and April were her first concerns. As long as she allowed him to be part of her world, he was content. He frowned. Actually, he allowed, that was a dashed bloody lie. He knew that he would never be satisfied until Daphne loved him . . . as he loved her.

Charles was pleased and not a little surprised at the promising start of their life together, but then he didn't know why he should be. He supposed that there might have been a way to escape the parson's mousetrap once they had been rescued from the sea cave, but by then, he was so thoroughly in her thrall that even finding an honorable way out of marrying her had held no appeal to him. With a start, he realized that he'd *wanted* to marry her. Even back then. It had been a gamble, perhaps the biggest in his life, but then, he acknowledged cynically, he was ever the gambler.

He pressed another kiss to Daphne's forehead. Yes, he was a gambler and look what it had gained him. The only woman he could ever imagine sharing his life with, the only woman he could ever imagine bearing his children. Something clenched within him, the idea of children, the awareness that last night or even tonight, he could have planted a child in her womb, filling him with a curious mixture of panic and joy.

The thought that one day he might be a father had never crossed his mind. Would he be a good father? he wondered uneasily. He'd adored his own father; John had been a good father to Daniel, and Julian was an exemplary father. Perhaps there was hope for him.

Raoul's contorted features jumped into his head, and a kernel of fear lodged deep within him. He'd always believed that Raoul's sheer evilness had come from Sofia, but what if he was wrong? What if part of the malignancy that had driven Raoul to inflict such horrific acts on innocents had been inherited from his own side of the family? What if he carried that same evil seed? And passed it on to his own child? A shudder roiled through him.

Daphne felt the movement of his body, and she angled her face toward his. "What is it? Are you cold?"

Charles shook his head. "No," he said flatly.

A note in his voice alerted her, and rising up on one hand, she looked into his grim features. "What is it? Have I done something to displease you?"

"Good God, no!" he exclaimed. He smiled crookedly. "I was thinking of family . . . and the family that we may have one day."

She frowned. "And this makes you uncomfortable?"

"No. It's just that . . . ." His voice trailed off, and his eyes searched hers. Dare he tell her the truth? Was this the moment? He swallowed. She had a right to know. But what if she turned from him in revulsion and disgust?

The expression on his face alarmed her. She touched his cheek. "Charles, what is it? Surely it is not so terrible that you cannot tell me." She smiled slightly. "After all, we have faced Sir Wesley together—what could be worse than confronting a vile old ghost?"

His gaze roved over her features, and he traced the shape

of her mouth with one long finger. "There is so much that you don't know."

"But you're going to tell me, aren't you?" she said softly.

Charles nodded slowly, his mind made up. "Some of the Westons have not been very, uh, virtuous," he muttered. And that, he thought disgustedly, doesn't even begin to cover it, not when you consider the Old Earl and his legion of by-blows scattered throughout the British Isles and . . . Raoul. Daphne looked expectantly at him, and avoiding the hard ground, he added reluctantly, "I loved my father, but after my mother died, he became . . . a drunkard and a gambler. He brought us to the brink of ruin, and if it hadn't been for his marriage to Sofia, we might have lost Stonegate." Deliberately, he said, "Theirs was no love match. He married her for her money because if he hadn't, Stonegate would have fallen in rack and ruin about our ears. Sofia's fortune is the only reason that Stonegate exists as you see it today."

"That doesn't sound so very bad." She gave him an encouraging smile. "Impoverished gentlemen have been marrying heiresses since the beginning of time."

He was avoiding the crux of the matter, and he knew it. He sighed, wondering when he had turned into a coward. But he knew the answer to that—when he had fallen in love with Daphne. He could not bear the idea of her recoiling from him in horror and revulsion. And she is very likely to do just that, he thought wretchedly, when I tell her about Raoul. What woman wouldn't?

Her face full of concern, she touched his cheek again. "Charles, what is it?" she asked quietly. "What is so very bad that you feel you dare not speak of it?" She smiled faintly. "I may not find it so very bad, you know."

"You will," he stated unequivocally.

Fear knotted in her stomach. Whatever Charles was keeping from her, it was obvious that it was more, and a great deal worse, than a drunken, spendthrift father. Taking a deep breath, she said, "Then perhaps you better tell me about it."

He looked away from her a moment. They stood at the edge of a chasm, and he wished they'd had more time together before it had yawned before them. Once he told her, would she shrink away from him in panic and aversion? Would she shun him? Order him from her bed? Yet unless he spoke, the secret of Raoul would lie between them like a black, ugly festering wound, destroying any chance he had of winning her, any chance of them finding lasting happiness. His jaw clenched. He must tell her . . . and live with the consequences. God help him.

His face set, he pulled her down next to him. When she was comfortably nestled beside him, he said bleakly, "Let me tell you of Raoul . . . ."

And so he told her. Everything. Nell's nightmares. The dungeon beneath the Dower House. The multitude of woman who had died shrieking beneath Raoul's knife. John's murder by Raoul and Sofia, and Sofia's death by his own hand. His reason for being in Cornwall. Everything.

When he was finished and Daphne lay stiffly and silently at his side, his heart sank. Would she now look at him in terror and repugnance, knowing he had shot and killed his stepmother? Knowing that at least some of the same blood that ran in Raoul's veins ran in his? What would he do if she turned from him in disgust? How could he live?

That such creatures as Raoul and Sofia existed appalled Daphne. Despite the challenges she'd faced, she'd led a normal, unassuming existence, one in which murderous relatives and wanton slaughter did not exist. She'd been prepared to hear of some philandering rake or an adulterous spouse, perhaps even an illegitimate birth lurking in the midst of Charles's family, but nothing like the horrific tale he had just related.

The inexplicable mental link between Nell and Raoul was difficult for her to grasp, but the ghostly events at Beaumont Place helped her understand and accept that there were things for which no rational explanation existed. John's murder repelled her, and her heart ached for Charles. Knowing how she felt about Adrian and April, she couldn't conceive the motives, emotions that had driven Raoul to commit such a dastardly act. That Raoul murdered for his own pleasure disgusted and horrified her, and it was utterly obscene, she thought, that Sofia had known and protected him. There was no question in her mind that Sofia had deserved to die. As for Raoul . . . She shivered. To think he might still be alive and living near Beaumont Place.

She jerked upright. Wide-eyed with terror, she blurted, "We must warn the others! What if he was to snatch April? I could never forgive myself if something happened to her."

Charles took comfort that she had not leaped from the bed making the sign to ward off evil at him. Carefully, he said, "April is safe. He only stalks those of the lower classes, choosing as his victims women whose disappearance will not make much of a stir."

"Which doesn't make it any better, does it?" she said gently. Looking at him, seeing the rigid way he held himself, her heart ached for him. It had not been easy for him to speak of such intimate horrors. How he must have suffered knowing that his brother . . . . She paused, and her mouth tightened. His *half* brother had been a monster. And now, having confessed his terrible secret, he looked as if he were braced for a beating. Love and understanding stirred in her breast.

"Oh, my poor dear Charles! How ghastly for you," she cried. Flinging her arms around him, she hugged him tightly. "You must have suffered so very much, knowing that Raoul had killed your good John and helped cause Daniel's death. I cannot imagine how you stayed sane." Raining soft little kisses along his jaw, she murmured, "Sofia deserved to die. She was a wicked woman, but she cannot harm anyone again—she is dead, punished for her wickedness. I hope that as she burns in hell—as surely she must—she knows that you are Master of Stonegate and that her fortune is yours to do as you please. And if as you believe Raoul is alive, we will find him and stop him."

A fierce light leaped to his eye, and his heart began to beat again in thick, rapid strokes. Jerking her onto his chest, he found her mouth and he kissed her again and again, love surging through him. Sweet, adorable Daphne! She had not rejected him. She was not repulsed by him.

Daphne responded frankly to his kisses, wanting to draw away the hurt, the pain she knew he had suffered. Still suffered, for it was clear that guilt and remorse ate at him. He made love to her with a tenderness that woke a desire so powerful she shook and trembled from the force of it. His touch was so gentle, filled with such passionate homage that she was half mad with longing, and she writhed on the bed, begging him to take her, pleading for him to end the sweet agony he had aroused. With a smothered groan, he joined them together, his swollen member sliding in and out of her slick warmth in increasingly frantic thrusts. In those last moments, there was a feral madness between them, gentleness gone, hands, mouths, and bodies seeking, demanding succor until breathless and gasping, their bodies convulsed and ecstasy flooded through them.

When he could speak again, Charles bent over and brushing back the waves of black hair that cascaded across her forehead, kissed her tenderly. "Do you know," he said softly, "I am very glad that you went exploring in that cave. I do not like to think what my life would be without you."

Daphne's heart lurched at his words. She loved him, and unless she was reading more into his words than he meant, it appeared that he might very well love her. It wasn't a declaration of love, but it was close and she treasured his words, holding them close to her heart.

Her smile luminous, she caressed his lips with her fingers. "Hmmm, I am very fond of that particular cave myself. One day, we should visit it again."

His eyes darkened, and his fingers brushed against her nipple. "If we do, my dear, be prepared to be ravished. Quite thoroughly, in fact."

Tingling from his touch, Daphne smiled and said, "I shall try to brace myself."

Charles and Daphne spent three days at Stonegate. They wandered over the house and estate, Charles pointing out the various rooms, items, and areas of interest. They drifted through a dreamscape, lost in each other, falling deeper and deeper in love, aware and yet not aware of their surroundings, of the servants watching them with smiling approval. There were sweetly intimate breakfasts in the morning room; on one day, a gay alfresco meal enjoyed in the garden; and scrumptious meals served in the dining room. Nights were spent in wild, passionate lovemaking, but there were those dark moments that they spoke of Sofia and Raoul. Seeing the pain and guilt in his eyes whenever their names were mentioned, Daphne swore to herself that she would make him happy, make him forget that terrible past, but she knew that her husband's heart would always bear the scars inflicted by Sofia and Raoul.

"Do you really believe that Raoul is alive?" Daphne asked him that last evening at Stonegate as Charles inspected the contents of the family safe in the room used by his father as an office. The safe was concealed behind a bookcase that easily swung out from the wall—if one knew where to find the catch that released it.

Daphne was seated on a silver and white sofa near the fire, and Charles glanced over his shoulder at her as he took out a large jewelry box constructed of ebony and satinwood elegantly decorated with seed pearls and gilt. "Hmm, I don't know. Those dead women make me believe that he could be, but I have not been able to find anything tangible that encourages me to think I am right." He looked thoughtful. "Raoul would need money, and while I'm convinced that Sofia was farsighted enough to make certain he would never want should his true nature be discovered and he was forced to flee, I can find no trail of it. Most telling of all, Nell no longer dreams of him."

Daphne suppressed a little shiver. "It must have been horrid for her to see him actually killing those poor women."

Charles nodded. "It was, but Nell is a strong woman." He grinned. "She'd have to be to be married to my cousin." He sat down beside her, the box on his lap. "But let us not speak of them. Let me show you all the pretty trinkets that are yours to wear as you see fit."

Opening the lid of the jewelry box, Daphne gasped at the array of diamonds, emeralds, and rubies and other precious stones that gleamed in the candlelight. "Oh! There are so many lovely pieces."

"Yes, and as my wife, they are all yours." He touched one or two pieces. "Some of them are very old, but each generation has added to them, and I shall be no different—I have every intention of showering you with jewels upon occasion." His eyes caressed her. "In the meantime, I think that this emerald necklace and earrings, given to my great-great grandmother by her husband, would look very fine on you." A sensual smile curved his mouth. "Of course, you would be wearing nothing else."

"Of course," she agreed with a becoming flush.

They spent an agreeable several minutes examining the various pieces, but as time passed, Charles frowned. Seeing it, Daphne asked, "What is it?"

"My stepmother," he said slowly, "loved jewels. She was always buying them . . . I remember several of them—a sapphire pendant, a diamond and pearl necklace with matching earrings, and many other pieces. They are not here."

"Do you think she put them somewhere else? Left them with her banker in London? Or with a jeweler to be cleaned, and they have not been returned?"

He shook his head. "No. Her solicitor, as well as her banker, turned everything over to me when the estate was settled." He walked over to a massive mahogany desk and after opening several drawers, found what he was looking for. He thumbed through a sheaf of papers, and plucking out one, he came back to sit beside her on the sofa. "This is a list of all Sofia's personal belongings. You'll notice that there is no mention of *any* jewelry. And I know her one extravagance was jewels. I may have forgotten some pieces of jewelry she owned, but not all of them. So where are they?" He glanced down at the glittering array of jewelry in the box in Daphne's lap. "What's missing would easily be worth a small fortune . . . and Raoul would need a fortune."

"Jewels," Daphne said slowly, "would be easy to hide and transport with no one being the wiser . . . . She could have given him various jewels to conceal in places that he could easily reach should the worst happen."

"They would be better than money safely set aside in a bank," Charles added, following her train of thought. "A small cache here and there would insure that he had plenty of money." Scowling, he studied the jewels. "It appears that she was intelligent enough not to take family heirlooms, but I see no sign of the many jewels that she bought over the last twenty or so years. The missing items represent a fortune— and that's just counting the ones I remember. There could have been many I never saw or do not recall. Certainly, they would be fortune enough for Raoul to live where and as he pleased."

His expression thoughtful, Charles shut the lid to the jewelry box with a snap. He stood up and placed it in the safe. After pushing the bookcase into position, he returned to sit beside Daphne.

"If he is alive, I think we have discovered how he has been living these past three years," he said grimly. "He had a hunting box in Leicestershire, a suite of rooms both in Brighton and London, a small yacht and a house that he kept at Poole. He could have stashed jewels in any one or all of those places."

"You inherited his estate as well as his mother's—wouldn't there have been a record of properties owned by him?"

"I'm sure that there was, but I never paid any attention to it. Why should I? I believed him to be dead, and quite frankly, in the months following Sofia's death and presumably his, I just wanted to be as far away from Stonegate and anything connected with the pair of them as I could be. Gerrard, my solicitor in London, handled everything, and from time to time, he would send me letters informing me of his progress in the settlement of the estate." Charles stared at the fire, his expression remote. "At that time, I didn't give a damn about any of it."

"Did you sell the yacht or the hunting box or anything?"

He shook his head. "For all I know or care, the yacht has sunk to the bottom of the Channel. Gerrard takes care of everything not connected to Stonegate."

"Well, I suggest that you write Mr. Gerrard and find out what properties Raoul did own," Daphne said practically. "It is probably far too late to do any good, for I'm sure that as soon as he was able, Raoul would have moved swiftly to gather his, er, inheritance—assuming he survived."

Charles nodded. "And if we find any jewels . . ."

She beamed at him. "Then it will prove that he is dead and those poor women in Cornwall met their fate at someone else's hand."

"It appears that we shall be extending our trip to include a brief excursion to Brighton, with a stop at Poole along the way before we return to Cornwall." He slanted her a glance. "Unless, of course, you wish to return to your brother and sister? I can join you as soon as I have searched the house at Poole and his rooms in Brighton. I would not keep you from Adrian and April longer than necessary."

There was something in his voice that made her look sharply at him. She sensed there was more behind his question than polite consideration. Did he not want her with him? Was he, she wondered sickly, bored with her and regretting their marriage? Even as that thought crossed her mind, she impatiently dismissed it. No, it wasn't that he was bored with her or their marriage; it was something else. A mistress? Again she realized how little they knew of each other. For all she knew, her husband had half a dozen mistresses scattered across the British Isles. And, she thought gloomily, he wouldn't be the first husband to seek his pleasures outside of the marriage bed. Yet she doubted Charles was a philanderer, but it was possible, because they had married so quickly, that he had not made a final settlement with his mistress . . . if he had a mistress. Her only recourse, she decided, was, until she knew what was in his mind, to tread warily. Cautiously, she asked, "Do you wish for me to return to Beaumont Place without you?"

"I want you to do what will make you happiest," he replied with equal caution.

Now what was she to make of that? Disliking the situation and not willing to fence indefinitely with him, she stood up and shook out the folds of her spotted muslin gown. "If you think that I am going to let you have all the adventure and go off on this, this scavenger hunt by yourself, you can think again," she said bluntly. "I shall go with you to Poole and Brighton." She gave him a level look. "I am your wife, and my place is by your side."

Her spine rigid, she marched from the room, leaving Charles to stare after her in mingled despair and delight. She was coming with him! he thought, elated. Even if, he acknowledged gloomily, she had neatly sidestepped his offer to return to her brother and sister. Had she done so because she cared for him and wanted to be with him? Or because, he wondered with a razor-sharp stab of pain, it was her duty?

Chapter 15

Though Charles came to her bed that night and their love-making was as passionate as ever, Daphne was conscious of a faint restraint between them. They pretended otherwise, but it was there, hovering in the air between them like an unwelcome wraith. She wrinkled her nose. Not a fair comparison when held up to Sir Wesley and the little ghost in her bedroom at Beaumont Place.

Having bid good-bye to the staff, it occurred to her, as Charles assisted her into the carriage early that next morning, that she seemed to be surrounded by ghosts in one form or another. Not only the ones at Beaumont Place, but also the shades of Charles's brother, Raoul, and his stepmother, Sofia.

She cast a glance over at Charles, wondering what he was thinking as he stared out of the window of the coach. Why, she asked herself for the tenth time this morning, had he made the offer for her to return to Cornwall? Didn't he want her with him? Was he already regretting the bonds of matrimony? Or had his suggestion been nothing more than simple consideration? Whatever the reason, she suspected that it had been more than just consideration—there had been a note in his voice, something in his stance that made her think that there was a deeper meaning behind his words. But what? And why would he send her away? She could think of dozens of reasons, some even logical, why he wouldn't want her to accompany him, but none of them lessened the hurt that lodged like a thorn in her heart.

"I'm sorry," Charles said, breaking into her thoughts, "to drag you along on what I am sure is a fool's errand."

She smiled uncertainly at him. "I think of it as an adventure. Our first adventure together."

He picked up her hand lying on the seat between them and pressed a kiss to the back of it. "The first, I hope, of many," he said huskily.

Giddy with love for him, Daphne smiled widely at him. It didn't matter why he had offered to send her back to Cornwall, what mattered was that she loved him and they were together. "Undoubtedly, we shall have many adventures in our lives together," she replied. Her smile wobbled just a trifle. "Some more enjoyable than others."

His eyes caressed her face, and he kissed her hand again. "Much more enjoyable—I swear it to you."

Her spirits buoyed by his words, she leaned back against the velvet squabs and settled down for the journey to Poole.

After the long hours in the coach and nights spent in cramped country inns, Daphne was glad when they reached Poole. It was midmorning when they approached the seaport, and Charles ordered the coachman to drive directly to Raoul's property, just at the edge of town. The property proved to be more extensive than Charles had been led to believe by either Raoul or Sofia. From the main road, amidst the trees and shrubs, he barely glimpsed the rooftop of a house. A narrow, overgrown driveway angled between the trees, and as the coach left the main road, driving toward the house in the distance, it was then that it occurred to Charles that the place might be locked and that he had no key. To his relief, nestled in a bend of the road, was a small cottage that housed a caretaker, Mr. Jacques Robinet. Mr. Robinet was a small, elderly gentleman, hard of hearing if the left-hand cupping his ear was anything to go by. Looking frail enough to be blown over by a strong wind, Mr. Robinet explained, in a heavy French accent that made his speech nearly incomprehensible, that he had worked for Miss Sofia's family in France and had accompanied her family to England. Anxiety creeping into his voice and his dark eyes darting nervously to Charles's face, he admitted that he lived rent-free in the cottage in return for keeping an eye on the place. It was obvious that Mr. Robinet was at once awed to finally be meeting the new owner and clearly worried that he might be forced to move.

Charles put the old man's fears to rest, telling him only that they had stopped by on a whim to inspect the house but that he had no intentions of making any changes; Mr. Robinet's position was secure. Mr. Robinet was clearly relieved as he placed the heavy brass key into Charles's hand.

"*Merci,* Monsieur Weston," Mr. Robinet said in a quavering voice. "*Moi,* I will serve you as I did Monsieur Raoul and Madame Sofia. You will see. *Merci beaucoup.*"

Charles nodded and said, "I'm sure that you will, and I will rest easier knowing that you are here to watch over the place."

"That was very kind of you," Daphne said once the coach had pulled away from Mr. Robinet.

"What else could I do?" Charles muttered. "I wasn't about to throw the old fellow out of his home."

The two-storied Georgian-style house was set in the middle of a tidy little garden, and as they mounted the steps, Daphne said, "It is a good thing that you did not have Mr. Gerrard sell the place, isn't it?"

Charles shrugged. "I should have ordered him to do so once the estate was settled, but it simply didn't matter to me at the time. I told him to continue to pay the bills and that at some point, I would go over things with him and decide which expenses to eliminate. There are probably any number of expenses laid at Raoul's door that I am still paying for these days." At her scandalized look, he laughed. "Extravagant, I know, but as you said, rather a good thing, since no one has lived in the house since Raoul."

Charles and Daphne spent several frustrating hours poking about the stale, dusty space, looking specifically for any likely hiding places for a cache of jewels. They found two, one behind a bookcase in a small library downstairs and another on the second floor underneath a loose board near the bed in what had obviously been Raoul's bedroom. One held several indiscreet letters written by the wife of a noted leader of the *ton*, the other an iron key. Charles promptly burnt the letters in the fireplace, but the iron key puzzled him. It wasn't to the house, so what was it used for? And why did Raoul have it in a hidden place?

From the second floor of the house, Charles noticed a small building at the far end of the garden. In the summer, unless one knew what to look for, the stone building would have been hidden by the rampant climbing rose vine that covered it, but this time of year, with the leaves of the rose just unfurling, Charles could make out its size and shape. He looked from the building to the iron key in his hand, premonition coursing through him.

He needed to search that stone building, but he hesitated to leave Daphne alone in Raoul's house. He knew that the odds of Raoul being alive were slim to none, but he wasn't taking any chances that Raoul would suddenly nip out of the woodwork and spirit her away. When he suggested that she might want to wait in the coach for him while he explored the building in the garden, the look she sent him told him better than words that she was not going to cooperate. She would go with him.

The garden was extensive, and in another month or two would have been breathtaking, but neither one of them was aware of anything but their destination. After his third false start down one of the many winding paths, Charles said grimly, "It is a good thing I spied the place from Raoul's bedroom window, else I'd never have guessed that it existed."

"It's possible," Daphne said, her hand nervously tightening on his arm, "that he planned it that way."

"I'm sure he did," Charles replied curtly, his eyes cold and hard.

After traversing a frustrating array of curves and loops along the way, the building abruptly appeared before them. The path ended in a tiny clearing, the squat, windowless stone building blocking further exploration. The moment they stepped into the clearing, they both stopped as if they had slammed into a wall of steel.

Daphne had never thought herself particularly imaginative, but staring at that ugly little building, she was conscious of an air of evil. Instinctively, she took a step backward.

Freeing his arm from her hand, Charles said in a voice she didn't recognize, "Stay here."

Daphne took one look at his face and froze. This tall, black-haired man beside her was an utter stranger—it was as if the Charles Weston she had known and married had never existed. This stranger frightened her, his face was harsh and set in grim lines, but it was his eyes . . . She swallowed. His eyes were as empty and cold as the North Sea, and she shivered again, taking a step away from him. She did not recognize this man, and he frightened her.

Oblivious to anything but the building in front of him, the iron key held tightly in his hand, Charles walked over to the thick-timbered door in the middle of the building. He knew that the key would fit, and he knew what he would find beyond that door. He looked at Daphne. "Do not," he snapped, "follow me."

Turning back to the door, he slid the key in the big, black lock and gave it a savage twist. The lock gave way, and he pushed open the door and walked inside.

Charles didn't need to explore the interior to know that Raoul had used this place, as well as the dungeon beneath the Dower House in Devonshire, for his vicious amusements. Women had died here. Died in agony, screaming for help that never appeared. And Raoul, his own brother, had been the monster who had slaughtered them . . . for pleasure. Bile rose in Charles's throat, and loathing and horror washed over him.

The only source of light came from the doorway, but guessing what would be there, Charles reached along the wall for the candle and flint that had been placed on a narrow ledge. Lighting the candle, he stepped into the room, carefully shutting the door behind him and dropping the iron bar that locked it from the inside. He wanted no one to see this room, least of all Daphne.

It was not a dungeon, but the room, though on a much smaller scale, was terrifyingly similar. A tiny cell was in one corner, and iron manacles hung from the wall; a stone slab served the same purpose as the one in the dungeon beneath the Dower House, the dark splatter of stains on its surface silent testimony to the horrifying fate of Raoul's helpless, nameless victims.

Moving stiffly like a man whose limbs were frozen, Charles forced himself to explore the area. His greatest fear was not realized; he found no bodies. Raoul, he decided, must have disposed of the remains of his victims under cover of darkness. Most likely, by throwing them into the sea, he thought sickly, forcing himself to look more closely at the room and its meager contents. He didn't expect to find anything useful, and he did not. His search complete, he unbolted the door and fairly shot out of the building, gulping in great breaths of air, trying to cleanse the odor of death from him, trying to push away the horror of that small room.

He locked the door and strode over to where Daphne waited for him. Daphne took one look at his pale, tortured face and flung herself into his arms, wrapping herself around him as if the touch of her body could draw all the pain and poison away from him. Her lips pressing desperate little kisses along his neck and jaw, she said, "Do not think of it. Put it from you." Cupping his face in her hands, she made him look at her. "He was a monster. You are not. You are nothing like him, and you bear no blame or guilt. His deeds are his own . . . and that of his loathsome mother."

Charles gave her a twisted smile. "I know the truth of what you say, but I cannot . . ."

Daphne shook him. "You must. You must not let his sins become your sins." She shook him again, harder. "He was the evil one, not you." She clutched him close. "Never you."

Charles crushed her next to him and buried his head against her neck. For silent moments, they stayed locked together, Charles feeling the horror, the ugliness drift from him as he drank in the sweet scent of her perfume, the soft warmth of her body. Daphne would allow no devils to ride him, and she would always lead him into the sunlight and drive away the darkness. She might not love him, kindness might prompt her actions, but she was his salvation, and he loved her more than life itself. His lips found hers, and he kissed her deeply, reveling in her instant response, reveling in the joy that she brought him.

Lifting his lips from hers, he tried for a light note. "Thank you. Not many brides would be so accepting of a fiend like Raoul in the family tree." He ran a caressing finger over her mouth. "I am sure this is not quite how you expected to spend your first few days of marriage."

She smiled tremulously. "Does it matter? If Fate is kind, we shall have many, many years together, years which we shall look back on with joy. So what are a few days of, um, unpleasantness over the course of a lifetime?"

"Unpleasant is one way of putting it," he said dryly, urging her away from this cursed spot and toward the front of the house.

Daphne spared a last glance at the building. "What are you going to do with it?"

"Burn it from the inside out and let it fall into itself," he said grimly.

*   *   *

"Despite that ghastly little building, we didn't really find anything helpful at the house," Daphne said a few minutes later as the coach bounced down the driveway toward the main road. Thoughtfully she added, "But that doesn't prove anything either."

"I would have been more encouraged if we *had* found some jewels," Charles replied sourly.

"Because it would prove that Sofia did give them to him and he didn't return for them?"

He nodded. "At least we would have something to show for our efforts and confirmation of our suspicions. And if we had found some jewels, it would indicate that he did die because he didn't come back for them. As it is, we're still stumbling around in the dark." He looked at her, noting the weariness in her eyes. "I shouldn't have brought you along," he said abruptly. "I should have insisted that you return to Cornwall."

"And have everyone gossiping that we had quarreled so soon?" Daphne muttered, looking at her gloved hands in her lap.

His eyes narrowed. "Is that why you came with me? To keep others from gossiping about us?"

"Does it matter why I came with you?" she asked, lifting her gaze to his face. "Isn't it sufficient that I am by your side?"

No! By God, he thought fiercely, staring blindly out the window at the gathering dusk, her presence was *not* sufficient. Her reasons for being here beside him mattered enormously. It mattered so much it was eating him alive, tearing him apart, and he wondered again why she had remained with him and not returned to Cornwall. He wanted her presence here with him to be because there was no other place on earth she'd rather be and not, he admitted with an acrid taste in his throat, because she wished to avoid wagging tongues or it was her damned *duty*. He smiled bitterly to himself. It wasn't enough that she loved her siblings above all else, but it appeared that she also loved duty and the avoidance of gossip with an equal fervor. Which left him where in her affections? Somewhere dangling at the bottom?

His thoughts too painful to bear, he said, "Of course your mere presence is all I could ask for."

Daphne frowned. Since that evening in the library at Stonegate when he had proposed she return to Cornwall, there was frequently an odd undercurrent between them. We're fencing with each other, she decided dolefully, but I don't know why. I don't even know its cause. And if I don't know why or what, how can I fix it?

Her gaze fixed on his profile, she asked quietly, "What is wrong between us? Something is . . . I can feel it. I know that our marriage was not what either of us wanted, but I thought . . . I thought that we were dealing very well together." The threat of tears clogging her throat, she blurted out, "Have I done something to offend you?"

Her words ripped into him like a lion's claw. How could he blame her for putting Adrian and April before him? She had years and years of memories with her brother and sister, and she'd known him what? A month? Less? It wasn't her fault that he had fallen madly in love with her almost on sight. Nor was it her fault that she did not love him as he loved her . . . yet, he amended vehemently. She *would* love him! But not, he realized, if he allowed his own despair and jealousy to fester between them.

"Oh, my darling," Charles said thickly, "you could never offend me." Pulling her onto his lap, he added, "And there is nothing wrong between us." With her head nestled against his chest, he pulled off the charming green bonnet that matched her velvet pelisse and tossed it on the seat. Brushing a kiss against the soft, fragrant black curls that tickled his chin, he murmured, "This . . . thing with Raoul has made me like a wounded bear. I am sorry that I allowed it to come between us." He tipped up her chin and smiled down into her face. "When I scowl and snap or seem preoccupied, never believe that it is because of something that you have done."

His handsome apology didn't quite address the problem because it wasn't his scowling and snapping that had disrupted the harmony between them, but Daphne was happy enough to allow the subject to drop. Besides, it was wonderful to be in his arms and have him looking at her with such a warm light in his eyes. He must care for her. She knew that they had liking and respect between them. A faint blush stained her cheeks. And desire, of that there seemed aplenty, she admitted, feeling her blush deepen. But would those things be enough for them to make a happy life together? She desperately wanted him to love her, and she knew that if she could not make him love her as much as she loved him, inevitable heartbreak lay down the road.

Wrenching her thoughts away from the path they had taken, she smiled back up at him. Striving for a light note, she murmured, "Does this mean that no matter what I do, such as fritter away all of my pin money long before the next quarter's payment, you will never frown when the tradesmen come dunning you at your door?"

He laughed. "No, you little minx, I don't mean that at all. I mean that if I am angry or upset with you, you will know *precisely* the reason why."

Content for the moment, Daphne settled comfortably against him, listening to the strong beat of his heart beneath her ear. Hopefully, one day, she thought drowsily, and not too far distant, that heart will beat for me . . . .

Since there were still a few hours of daylight left, they decided to see what they could discover about Raoul's yacht, supposedly berthed in the harbor in town. The harbor at Poole was a busy place, but this time of the day, there was not the hustle and bustle there would have been a few hours earlier. Still, there were plenty of people wandering about, and it only took a few inquiries from passers-by to find the slip where Raoul's yacht, *The Dark Hunter,* was moored. Charles had always thought the name of Raoul's yacht was fanciful, but now he found the name repugnant.

Having boarded the yacht, Charles and Daphne set about looking for any place that Raoul could have safely hidden some of Sofia's jewels. While the yacht was small, it was also compact, with dozens of places to search, and Charles despaired of finding anything useful. No one was more surprised than he when after a several minutes exploration, he discovered a small niche hidden in the headboard of Raoul's bed. He fumbled for a second but managed to retrieve a small leather bag stuffed deep in the niche.

His eyes met Daphne's as he pulled the bag free. It wasn't empty—he could feel the weight in his hand. With trembling fingers, he opened the bag and dumped the contents onto the dark blue wool blanket on the bed. A diamond necklace, a pearl-encrusted sapphire brooch, and a pair of matching earrings glittered and gleamed against the background of the coverlet.

"So now we know," Daphne said shakily. "Sofia did plan ahead."

Charles nodded slowly. "But why," he wondered aloud, "did he hide them on the yacht and not at the house?"

A terrifying thought occurred to her. "Perhaps he did," she said.

Charles stiffened, easily following her train of thought. "He came to the house and took the jewels hidden in it," he said slowly, "but not these. Why not?"

There was a shout from outside, and someone cursed.

"Of course," Charles said as enlightenment dawned. "The house is secluded, surrounded by forest and garden, guarded only by a half deaf, crippled old man. Simple enough for Raoul to slip into the house, take what he needed, and disappear. But the harbor where his yacht is moored is an entirely different story."

"I suspect that someone is always around the docks. Boats and ships arriving at all different times of the day and night," Daphne said. "There would be sailors returning to their ships after a night in town, guards patrolling to stop theft, captains, merchants inspecting their cargo. Once he left the safety of the buildings around the docks, he would have found it far more difficult to reach the yacht unseen."

Charles nodded. "I agree." He glanced at the jewels. "We have proof now that Raoul stashed away some of his mother's jewels. But we still don't know whether he came back to the house and took what he had hidden there or if his yacht was the only place, at least in this area, that he used as a hiding place."

Plucking up the jewels, Charles slipped them back into the leather bag. Concealing the bag within his coat, he took Daphne's arm and said, "We can decide nothing here. We shall find an inn and consider our next course of action."

Daphne found it interesting that he did not order the coachman to drive in the direction of Brighton or London, both places where Raoul was known to have lodgings, but instead chose the opposite direction, the direction from whence they had come. Looking at him in the gloom of the interior of the coach, she asked, "Aren't we going to continue the search? You said that he had rooms in Brighton and London."

He reached over and took her hand in his. "Finding the jewels on his yacht changes everything. Along with the bodies of those women in Cornwall, they are another sign that Raoul could very well be alive." He looked away, his jaw working. "It was foolhardy to bring you with me, especially considering the possibility that we might have, at any moment, been confronted by a monster." He shook his head as if to clear it. "When we found the jewels, I realized that I have been looking for Raoul with no real expectation of finding him, and that was reckless and dangerous. I placed you in peril today, and I shall not again," he said grimly. When she would have protested, he looked back at her and put a finger against her lips. "Listen to me, Daphne! If you were with me, half my attention would be on you, and Raoul would take advantage of that. Good God! What if we had found him today? I am not even armed. I must have been mad to take you with me."

Though Daphne argued until she wanted to scream and drum her heels in frustration, Charles was adamant. She would play no further part in determining whether Raoul was alive or dead. They were returning to Cornwall.

"And I suppose," she said acidly, "once there, that you intend to immediately abandon me at Beaumont Place while you go haring off all over the countryside looking for more of your stepmother's jewels."

He shook his head. "Not immediately. First, I must hear from Gerrard and have a full list of all the places that Raoul could have secreted them away." Despite her resistance, he pulled her into his arms and kissed her fully.

Daphne fought gamely against the hot rush of pleasure and desire that flooded her as his mouth teased hers, but in the end, even angry with him, she could not resist. The stiffness left her body, and her arms crept around his neck. She kissed him back, her lips warm and seductive against his.

"You are an utter beast," she said when they finally broke apart. "And I shall never forgive you."

He smiled angelically at her, and she suppressed the urge to box his ears. Men!

Their return to Beaumont Place was greeted by great delight, and if anyone noticed that there was slight air of tension between the pair, no one commented. Although Nell, having closely observed the newlyweds during dinner, said to Julian as they slid into bed that evening, "I think Daphne is irritated with Charles."

Julian laughed. "The lady has my sympathies. I have frequently been irritated with Charles." Laughter fading, he asked, "Something serious, do you think?"

She shook her head. "No, they're clearly enamoured of one another. Daphne's eyes light up when he enters the room, and she is constantly searching for him when he is gone. She loves him."

"And Charles?" Julian asked with a lifted brow.

"Oh, he's absolutely mad about her. The expression on his face when he looks at her and thinks himself unobserved . . ." She sighed dramatically. "Ah, if you looked at me that way, milord . . . ."

Julian's eyes darkened, and he pulled her into his arms. Dropping soft kisses across her face, he muttered, "I do all the time, you little devil. I am besotted by you."

Nell giggled and snuggled close to his big body. "It's nice, isn't it? Being married and in love?"

Julian moved suggestively against her. "Very."

Married less than two weeks, Daphne and Charles might not have the easy relationship that Julian and Nell had forged in the past three years, but there was a bond between them, and Daphne had great hopes that someday, Charles would love her. She knew the state of her own heart and marveled at how effortlessly she had fallen so deeply in love with him. Like a ripe plum falling from a tree, she thought half amused, half annoyed.

Seated at her dressing table, brushing her thick, curly black hair, she caught a glimpse of him in the mirror as he lounged in the doorway between her bedroom and their shared sitting room. He was watching her, and the expression in those jade green eyes made her pulse race and heat pool low in her belly. He was wearing a dark green velvet robe, and she knew that he was naked beneath the fabric . . . as was she under her lavender silk dressing gown. With a hand that trembled, she put down the silver-inlaid brush and swinging around on the tufted satin stool, faced him.

He pushed away from the doorway and crossing to her, murmured, "Don't stop because of me. I like watching you."

"But I was only brushing my hair," she said.

"Hmm, and very seductively, too, I might add," he said as he came to stand beside her and picked up the brush. "Let me show you," he said huskily. Gently, he turned her back toward the mirror and slowly began to brush her hair.

Having Charles brush her hair was entirely different than when she did it herself. There was something about the way the bristles slid through the long strands, the look in his eyes, and the heat that radiated from his big body into hers that made her acutely aware of her own body. She didn't know how he did it, but in a matter of moments, those long, slow, seductive strokes through her hair had her nipples hard and tingling, and she was moving restlessly on the satin stool, trying to ease the honeyed ache building between her legs.

Their eyes met in the mirror, and her breath caught at the naked hunger in his. He dropped the brush and spun her around. His hands on her shoulders, he pulled her to him and kissed her. His lips were warm, his tongue deeply probing, and Daphne shuddered in his arms as desire swept through her.

Picking her up in his arms, he carried her to the bed. A moment later, they were naked on the bed, and mouths fused, limbs entwined, they sought and found the scarlet summit.

Her breathing gradually returning to normal, the sweet aftershocks of passion still rippling through her, Daphne sighed dreamily, snuggling against his muscled length. The marriage bed, she decided, had much to recommend it.

He glanced down, a lazy, satisfied smile curving his mobile mouth. "Was that a happy or sad sigh?"

She pinched his side. "And what if I said sad?"

His eyes darkened. "Then I would have to do this . . . ."

His hand slid down her hip and slipped between her thighs, and she gasped when he touched her intimately, his finger parting her and sinking slowly into her silken depths. His expression intent, he rubbed his thumb gently over the small nub hidden in the tight curls between her legs and whispered, "And this, too." The sensations were overwhelming, and she stiffened and cried out as her body clenched suddenly around his fingers and jolts of pleasure exploded through her.

"Hmmm, that sounded happy to me," he breathed against her ear.

"Very," she managed when the world came sliding back into focus.

Daphne didn't know how long she had been asleep. She only knew that she woke with a start, so cold that her teeth were chattering. Despite the heavy quilts and the warmth of Charles's body pressed against her back, she couldn't stop shivering. A glance at the fire showed that it was still burning, the yellow and orange flames leaping and dancing in the fireplace, yet the cold was intense.

A sound, the faintest sigh from the shadows beyond the bed had her heart banging in her chest. With dread, her head slowly turned in that direction, and there it was . . . that misty, amorphous shape she had seen previously.

The little ghost was back.

Chapter 16

Daphne nearly shrieked aloud when a hand clamped around her wrist, but almost instantly, she realized that it was Charles who held her so firmly. His touch both warned her to silence and comforted her at the same time. She was not alone this time. She could feel his big body, tense and watchful behind her.

"How long," he whispered, "has it been here?"

"Moments . . . I think," she answered, barely moving her lips, her eyes locked on the shifting mist before them.

The ghost, for there was no other word for it as far as Daphne was concerned, seemed to realize that they were talking about it. While the form was not recognizably human, there was something human about it, and as she stared at it, Daphne could almost imagine a head cocked as if listening to what they were saying.

For long minutes, nothing happened. Daphne and Charles remained frozen in their original positions, the fog-colored misty shape hovering beyond the bed. Not as terrified as she had been the first time the apparition had appeared and with Charles's solid warmth at her back, Daphne studied the form, trying to imprint in her brain as many facts about it as she could.

The feeling that it was female was very strong, yet Daphne couldn't have explained why she felt that way. Partly it was the size, she decided, the delicacy of the shape. Certainly, it bore no resemblance to the powerful apparition they'd seen in the blue salon. Nor was there the sensation of violence and evil about it. There was, she admitted, just *something* female about it. The ghost was silent, and there was no sound in the room except for her's and Charles's quiet breathing and the pop and crackle of the fire. As the minutes crawled by, the vague shape just floated in the air, changing only slightly as she and Charles stared at it, the edges seeming to ripple and the occasional misty tendril waving slowly in the darkness.

"So how long do we remain in this standoff staring at each other?" Charles muttered in her ear.

"I don't know. Last time, I told it to go away, and it did."

Charles half sat up, and the shape shrank back slightly. "Go away," Charles ordered.

The ghost hung there for several seconds, neither moving forward or backward, and Daphne had the feeling that it was watching them, studying them as they studied it. Yet she had no perception of menace—there was nothing threatening about it—and she realized that she wasn't afraid of it.

Feeling emboldened, Daphne sat up, Charles following her, his arm curling around her shoulders.

At their actions, the apparition suddenly blossomed, nearly doubling its size, and Daphne was conscious of a sudden sensation of fear and anxiety coming from the ghost. Their movements had obviously disturbed it in some fashion.

Daphne leaned forward. "What is it?" she cried. "What do you want?"

The form floated nearer, and instinctively, Charles's arm tightened protectively around Daphne, and he pulled her close to him, locking her body against him.

The ghost stopped only inches from the bed, clearly agitated, the color darkening, the amorphous shape surging in all directions. Despite the changes, Daphne still wasn't frightened, at least not *very* frightened. If she had been alone, her feelings might have been different, but knowing Charles was with her gave her some comfort.

"I don't know about you," Charles said grimly, "but I've had about enough of this." Throwing the blankets aside, heedless of his nakedness, he swung his legs over the side of the bed.

His movements were clearly challenging, and Daphne gasped when the shape flew to confront him. No longer were just fear and anxiety rolling off the ghost, but fury and hatred now mingled with the other emotions Daphne had felt flowing from it. It feared and hated whatever Charles represented to it, and it was going on the attack.

"No!" Daphne screamed, flinging herself in front of Charles as if she would protect him with her own body. "You shall not hurt him."

The mood in the room changed instantly. The ugly emotions that had been swirling in the air were gone, the agitated movements of the ghost vanishing with them. No longer billowing up in dark, angry colors, before their eyes, the apparition shrank back to its original size, turning once more into a small misty shape that floated gently in the air before them.

Daphne had the impression of puzzlement as the thing hovered there. The seconds ticked by, and then there was a soft sighing sound and the shape drifted away, a faint white glow the only sign of its passing. Upon reaching the wall with the Chinese wallpaper, the ghost appeared to hesitate, and then just like the last time, it was gone.

Charles leaped from the bed and lighting a candle, rushed over to the area where he had last seen the apparition. Holding the candle high, he searched the wall for what he was certain was a hidden spring to open a secret door. He found nothing.

Having taken the time to find and put on her dressing gown, Daphne came up beside him and handed him his robe. "If we're going to go hunting for ghosts," she said, only half teasing, "I suggest you put something on."

Handing her the candle, he shrugged into his robe. When his robe was on and firmly belted at the waist, he took the candle back and continued his search for the mechanism that would reveal the concealed door. "Where," he asked, "was it that you saw that crack in the wall?"

She stepped beside him and pointed to a section of wall. Upon closer inspection, in the wavering light of the candle, they both spied the outline of a door. Charles ran his hand along the seams, but he felt nothing but the glassy smoothness of the wallpaper. No lumps or bumps, holes or fissures. Nothing.

"There has to be a latch, a handle, something," he growled in frustration. "That damn thing didn't simply walk through the bloody wall."

"I think she did," Daphne said slowly. "Or rather, she walked through a doorway that used to exist."

Charles looked at her sharply. "What makes you say she?"

"Don't you agree?"

He sighed. "Yes, I agree. I can't tell you how or why, but there is the distinct impression of femininity about the thing."

"Ghost," Daphne said firmly. "It was a ghost, and we both saw her."

Charles couldn't argue with her. They had both, he admitted, seen a ghost, a female ghost, tonight. And spoken to it, he thought wryly, remembering his feeble, "go away."

Daphne clutched his arm and pointing at the wall behind him, gasped, "Look! It's disappeared."

Charles swung back, and search though he did, there was no longer any sign of the doorway to be found on the wall.

"That's exactly what happened the last time," Daphne said. "It was there, and then when I looked again, it was gone. I thought I was losing my mind."

Taking her by the arm, Charles led her back to the bed. "You're not losing your mind, and neither am I. That blasted thing was here tonight, and there was a definite outline of a doorway on that wall." He glared at the wall in question. "And first thing tomorrow morning, we're going to find it."

It wasn't first thing in the morning—they had guests in the house and had to present reasonably normal behavior. They met everyone for breakfast in the morning room and since the day was fine, accompanied Adrian, April, Julian, Nell, and Marcus, who had also remained at Beaumont Place, for a ride. Marcus and Adrian rode astride, the ladies and Julian rode in a small open carriage driven by Charles. Though they chafed at the delay, the morning passed most agreeably for Charles and Daphne, and Daphne was glad of the opportunity to get to know Nell and her husband and Marcus better. It was apparent that Nell and April had become easy with each other, and from the comfortable manner that Adrian had around both the earl and Marcus, it was equally apparent that Adrian was no longer quite in as much awe of his lordship as he had been. Daphne was delighted. For April and Adrian to count such notables as the Earl and Countess of Wyndham as not only connections by marriage, but also dear acquaintances could only be to the good. And for them to be able to call steady, imperturbable Marcus Sherbrook friend would only add to their stature amongst the *ton*. Her dearly held dream of her brother and sister taking London by storm actually looked likely to come true.

Daphne would have liked Charles's relatives under any circumstances for they were warm and charming people, not at all toplofty or high in the instep, but their openhanded generosity and kindness to her siblings endeared them to her. Nell's mention of the possibility of hosting a ball for April next year at the Wyndham residence in London, as well as procuring vouchers for Almack's, made Daphne's heart swell with profound gratitude. When Marcus said something about introducing Adrian to Manton's Shooting Gallery in London this spring and Julian had followed by asking Charles if he could have the pleasure of putting Adrian's name up for membership at White's, Daphne nearly burst into tears of happiness. Thanks to Charles's family, her brother and sister's futures were assured. If she hadn't already been head over heels in love with her husband, the kindness of his relatives to her siblings would have snared her heart. Aside from Nell, Julian, and Marcus's easy acceptance of her and her siblings into the family, she found them utterly delightful, and by the time the drive ended, she and Nell were chatting away like old friends. Giving Charles a brilliant smile as he helped her down from the coach, she could only marvel at her luck—not only did she have a handsome husband she adored, but she had also married into a singularly agreeable family. She was so lucky! Her nose wrinkled. Well, she *was* lucky, even if she did have a ghost visiting in her bedroom and a deranged, dangerous brother-in-law possibly lurking about.

Her smile and the look she gave him rocked Charles back on his heels. There had been something in her smile, something in the warmth in her gaze that made his heart thud in his chest. Could it be? Was she coming to love him?

Unable to lose the moment, the second they were inside the house, he whisked her away into a small room just off the dining room. His hands about her waist, he held her gently against him and asked softly, "You have a glow about you. Is there a special reason for it? Might I hope that I have something to do with it?"

Daphne flung her arms about his neck and hugged him. "Oh, dear, dear Charles, indeed you do!" She leaned back and looking up into his face, said, "Your cousins, they are so very kind! I feared, considering the circumstances of our marriage, that they would disapprove and treat us with disdain for our lowly station, but they have welcomed us into your family without hesitation and have shown us nothing but affection and goodwill. Nell's suggestion of a ball for April is more than I dreamed of. And Marcus and Julian's offer to help Adrian . . ." Tears of happiness choked her voice. When she had command of herself, unaware of the blow she had just given her husband, she said, "Everything is just wonderful, isn't it?"

"Wonderful," Charles repeated dully, inwardly cursing himself for being a fool. Of course it was April and Adrian's needs that came first with her. How could he have so stupidly forgotten? Hiding his chagrin, he ushered her back to join the others.

After a light repast at midday, the ladies sought out the front saloon where Daphne and Nell, in perfect charity with each other, continued their discussion of plans for April's introduction to the *ton* next year. The gentlemen, left to their own devices, split up, Adrian taking Marcus to the barn to continue a discussion of the merits of the various horses owned by Sir Huxley and Julian retiring to his rooms to answer some pressing letters engendered by his extended stay at Beaumont Place, leaving Charles to set off in pursuit of his own scheme. Having seen to the needs of his guests, Charles headed to the library where he intended to do some digging in the Beaumont family's history.

Reaching the library, Charles rang for Goodson, and as soon as the butler appeared, Charles asked, "What can you tell me about the room that Mrs. Weston uses as her bedchamber?"

Goodson shrugged, saying, "Why only that until Sir Huxley's parents' time, it had been used by the masters of the house, along with the sitting room and the room that you now use."

"Do you ever remember hearing of another room as having been part of the original suite? Perhaps a small dressing room adjacent to Mrs. Weston's bedchamber?"

Goodson frowned. "No, I can't recall anything of the kind. I can ask Mrs. Hutton, but I doubt she would know more than I do. Is there a problem?"

Charles shook his head. "No. I am just curious about the house. Do you know if any construction plans connected to

Beaumont Place exist? Especially of renovations that may have occurred?"

"Lady Agatha assembled a collection of the family papers. Miss, er, Mrs. Weston had begun going through them shortly after she arrived here. Perhaps there is something within them?"

"Where are they kept?"

Goodson walked over to a section of the library and pointed out several shelves. "To my knowledge, this is the complete collection. After she died, no one continued her work, so nothing has been added for the last thirty years or so, but beyond that, you'll discover the collection is quite impressive."

Dismissing the butler, Charles studied the shelves. A quick review revealed, as Daphne had discovered earlier, that Lady Agatha had been very thorough in her collecting, but more importantly for Charles, items were arranged by year, which gave him a place to start. Though he and Daphne hadn't discussed it at length, they were both convinced that the little ghost in the bedroom and Sir Wesley's apparition were somehow connected.

"It is just too mind-boggling to consider that we have two entities with no commonality between them and that they both just happened to reappear about the same time," Daphne had said last night just before they had fallen asleep.

At least, Charles thought as he started carefully leafing through a sheaf of papers from the 1550s, Lady Agatha was a good chronicler and had done a decent job of filing everything by date. He didn't know precisely what he was looking for, but since he and Daphne agreed that Sir Wesley seemed to be the key, they needed to concentrate on his lifetime, hoping there was something in Lady Agatha's collection that would explain the visitations.

He found nothing that caught his eye as he quickly scanned the various documents and papers, and he suspected that as was often the case, earlier ancestors had destroyed most things that would have revealed unsavory facts about the family. He was elated when he discovered a pair of letters written by Sir Wesley's elder sister, a nun in some obscure order who had returned to England when Mary I had taken the throne and reinstated Catholicism. The letters were written to Sir Wesley's younger spinster sister, Edith, who resided with her brother. The letters, written in a firm, crisp hand, were interesting on two counts: one, Charles hadn't known of the existence of the two sisters, and two, from the letters, he learned that Sir Wesley had married. Charles could have probably learned the same information from the various church records, but the letters saved time. He grinned. And were much more entertaining than a dry recitation of marriages, births, and deaths. Sister Margaret may have been a nun, but she dished up a fine broth of scandal, Charles thought, amused at her tart tone and patent disapproval of her brother.

Though he had only Sister Margaret's reply to letters written by Edith, he could deduce quite a bit. Sir Wesley's bride had been a mere child, although probably not thought of as such in that age, Charles admitted to himself as he read. Lady Katherine had been fourteen when her father, if he read between the lines correctly, had been compelled to marry his daughter to Sir Wesley, a man approaching sixty. Sister Margaret sermonized at some length about Sir Wesley's shortcomings and his nearly insane desire to keep his brother's offspring from inheriting Beaumont Place and everything that went with it.

In the first letter, Charles learned of John's death and gathered, again reading between the lines, that Sister Margaret strongly suspected that Sir Wesley had been behind that young man's untimely passing. In the second letter, written several months afterward, Charles discovered that John's child, a son named Jonathan, had been born. But Sir Wesley was undaunted—Katherine was heavy with child, and Sir

Wesley was ecstatic, convinced the child would be the son, the heir he desperately wanted and needed to keep Jonathan from inheriting.

Charles put the letters down and stared off into space. Since Daphne and her brother and sister were descended from Jonathan's line, young Katherine must not have given Sir Wesley a son. Or Sir Wesley's son died without issue. Some sort of record probably existed in the collection that would be helpful, but this afternoon, he wasn't about to plod through decades of Beaumont memorabilia hoping that he would uncover more revealing information. Discovering the two letters had been a stroke of luck, and while it was possible that he might find more items relating to Sir Wesley, he decided that he had wasted enough time for now.

He considered the situation as he left the library, looking for his wife. Sister Margaret's letters had been enlightening and entertaining, he thought with a grin, but they hadn't given him any information about the existence of another room connected to Daphne's bedroom. And since he'd found no reference anywhere to any extra room, there was, he concluded, only one thing to do: tear the bloody wall down, and see what lay beyond.

He met Daphne coming down the hall in search of him. The ladies had dispersed, Nell retiring to her bedroom to nap, and April staying in the music room with Miss Ketty to practice chords on the piano, leaving Daphne to please herself.

Together, they retired to their rooms, and Charles quickly related what he had learned from Sister Margaret's letters.

At the first mention of Katherine's name, Daphne stiffened. "Oh, Charles. The little ghost. It must be Katherine."

"We don't know that," he said quietly. "I tend to think it might be, having read of Sir Wesley's treatment of her, but it is possible that your little ghost is some other unfortunate woman."

Daphne brushed aside his argument. "Believe what you want. I *know* it is Katherine," she insisted stubbornly.

Leaving aside the identity of their nocturnal visitor, they conferred about their next move, and Charles was relieved that Daphne was of the same mind about tearing the wall down. "I just hope that Adrian doesn't take exception to us demolishing a wall in his house," Daphne said.

Charles grinned. "I suspect that if we discussed it with him, your brother would be first in line to see what may be behind that wall."

Daphne didn't disagree, but she was still a bit apprehensive. Not so much about any damage they might cause as with coming up with a logical reason for their actions. Keeping their activities a secret was out of the question. Goodson was startled at their request, but he swiftly fulfilled it, even going so far as to carry the sledgehammer into Daphne's room himself, a stout footman depositing the pickax and crowbar near the wall where Charles directed. Goodson may not have asked any questions—he was too well-trained for that—but Daphne was quite certain that he and Mrs. Hutton had their heads together in the kitchen speculating about what they were doing in the bedroom. She didn't blame them. With Goodson and Mrs. Hutton atwitter at their odd request, it wouldn't take long for word to spread to the rest of the household. She wouldn't be at all surprised if Adrian, followed by a wide-eyed April, didn't come bursting into the room at any moment.

Having dismissed Goodson and James, the footman, Charles stripped out of his fashionable bottle green jacket and tore off his expertly arranged cravat. Sledgehammer in hand, with Daphne at his heels clutching the crowbar, he approached the section of wall.

He glanced over his shoulder at Daphne. "You're certain? Once I strike the first blow, there's no turning back."

Daphne grinned at him, and her eyes alight with excitement, she said, "Just do it! There is no telling what we may find on the other side of that wall."

It was messy, dusty work, Charles's sledgehammer smashing through the Chinese wallpaper to the surface to which it had been attached. They soon discovered that a thin coat of plaster had been applied to lath work and that the lath had been put up right over an old oak-paneled wall. They also discovered that there were at least three other patterns of wallpaper that had been hung prior to the current Chinese wallpaper. It was obvious that prior to the coat of lath and plaster and the first hanging of wallpaper, the entire room had once been paneled in a fine English oak.

They had no intention of tearing down every scrap of wallpaper and plaster and lath, so they concentrated their efforts in the one area where they'd seen the outline of a door. When they had cleared about a six-foot width, the rubble of plaster and lath and scraps of torn wallpaper at his feet, Charles studied the wooden wall before him. Small pieces of plaster and lath clung here and there, and the exposed wall showed the nicks and gouges made by their tools. A fine white powder coated the entire area, including their faces and hair.

Cautiously, Charles began to explore the section they had uncovered, his fingers searching for a seam, a break in the apparently solid expanse. Several minutes passed, and then his breath caught when he found an almost undetectable unevenness in one section of the wall. "This has to be a secret door," he said softly. "And the mechanism to open it has to be nearby."

"But there's nothing . . ." Daphne began, only to gasp and say, "Look there, to your left, that narrow row of carvings."

Charles walked over to stare at the line of carvings. From floor to ceiling, there was a row of expertly carved, evenly spaced rosettes attached to the oak paneling. He suspected that if they cleared more of the wall, they'd find more rows of rosettes placed at various intervals about the room.

"So which one is it?" Daphne asked, coming to stand beside him. "One of them must be a lever that opens the door."

"I agree," he said, reaching out to tweak the rosette directly in front of him. Nothing happened. He looked at Daphne and shrugged. "And on to the next one."

The third one, about waist high, that Charles gripped seemed to give just the tiniest bit. "Oho," he said. "I may have found our lever."

After not being used for so many decades, centuries perhaps, the rosette proved stubborn, but no more stubborn than Charles and Daphne. They struggled with it for several minutes, and then putting all his strength into it, Charles gave the rosette a vicious twist, and with a creak and a groan, the oak panel slowly, inch by inch, parted to reveal a gaping black doorway.

Her heart pumping like a battle drum, Daphne stared at the opening. It was clearly a secret doorway and it was obviously very old, going back to Sir Wesley's time and beyond. She didn't know whether to be pleased or dismayed by their discovery.

She and Charles looked at each other, then back at the doorway.

Utter darkness met their gaze, and dank unpleasant air flowed into the room. Charles lit a candle, and walking over to the doorway, Daphne crowding behind him, he thrust it into the black opening.

"By Jove," he exclaimed, "there's a staircase back here."

"Oh, let me see!"

Taking the candle from Charles, Daphne stuck her head through the doorway and stared amazed at the winding staircase that met her gaze. "A secret staircase," she breathed. *"That's* what she was trying to show us."

"I wouldn't go that far," Charles warned. "But let's explore what we've discovered."

Daphne gulped. "You mean go down those steps? Now?"

He grinned. "Didn't I promise you adventure, my love?"

"Oh, but Charles . . . what if something happens to us? No one will know where to look," she protested, not delighted with the idea of wandering down a secret staircase that had been hidden for who knew how long and led who knew where.

"When we don't show up for dinner, someone will come looking for us. They'll see our handiwork and assume that we followed the steps. They'll find us soon enough."

"Probably lying at the bottom of that wretched staircase with our necks broken," she declared gloomily.

"Afraid?" he taunted.

Daphne's chin came up, and her eyes flashed. "Of course not," she said loftily. "I was merely trying to act like an adult and not go haring off like an irresponsible child."

He shrugged. "Then stay here—I'll do the exploring."

"Over my dead body," Daphne muttered, following closely behind him as he stepped onto the first stair.

The staircase was very steep and twisty; cobwebs draped the passage. Like the steps beneath their feet, the walls on either side of them were of thick stone, and in some places, Charles had to duck his head, the height barely reaching six feet. The stairs snaked both up and down, and after a brief argument, it was decided that they would explore the upper reaches first. As they stumbled and fumbled their way upward, they speculated that the staircase had probably been built when the place had been a Norman keep. Certainly, the staircase was very old and had been unused for decades.

To their astonishment, they had not climbed very far when the staircase divided, one part continued upward, the second angling down and back into the house itself. The stonework was different where it divided, and the section that wormed its way into the house, to their untrained eye, appeared to have been constructed at a later date.

"By heaven, this is splendid!" Charles exclaimed, his eyes glittering with excitement. "I'll wager there are all sorts of hidden passages throughout the house. If we look, I'm certain we'll find that there are other rooms that open onto these staircases." A note of envy in his voice, he added, "Stonegate and Wyndham Manor have nothing like this. What Julian, Marcus, and I wouldn't have given to have discovered something like this when we were boys. It's bloody wonderful."

"Oh, wonderful indeed," Daphne murmured dryly.

"The original staircase was probably built for the troops to move about the keep undetected during siege or battle," Charles said, ignoring her less than enthusiastic reply. He waved the candle about, studying the walls. "I would guess that at a later date, when the keep no longer housed troops, this staircase was unused and forgotten . . . until some enterprising ancestor of yours decided to turn it into a way to move about the house in secret and added the newer section. Why, I imagine that you can access several different rooms from here."

In the wavering light of the candle, he grinned at her. "Of course, finding which rooms have doorways onto the staircase might be a challenge."

"Adrian is going to be over the moon with delight," she admitted. "I have no doubt that he will waste little time in exploring the staircase and finding every hidden doorway, popping out of the walls and scaring us all to death in no time. Especially," she added in hollow tones, "April."

Charles laughed, his teeth flashing whitely in the darkness. "No doubt," he agreed.

Deciding not to stray from the original staircase, they left behind the offshoots and continued their upward climb.

Daphne was glad that Charles was in the lead—he got to brush aside the worst of the cobwebs. Once she stopped and stared back in the direction they had come, and a shiver went through her at the oppressive darkness that pressed close behind her.

As they climbed, the blackness receded gradually, replaced by a gray gloom that brightened with every step they took.

Shortly, they stepped out into the spotty sunlight, surprised to find that dirty-skirted clouds were scudding across the sky, sure signs that a storm might be in the offing. The staircase ended near one of the towers, and they found themselves standing on one of the old crumbling battlements, part of the original Norman keep. Signs of the original fortifications were still visible, but it was an unsafe place. Rubble littered the space, and the few remaining stone crenellations looked as if they could topple over at any moment. Warily, they approached one of the crenellations and looked down. Daphne swayed at the sight of the sheer drop of eighty feet or more that met her gaze. Putting out her hand to steady herself against the low stone wall, she gasped when a section gave way, and with a terrifying rumble, several large pieces fell to the ground far below.

Even before the first stone crumbled beneath her hand, Charles's arm was about her waist, jerking her back from the ragged gap that suddenly appeared. She had been in no danger of falling, but she was grateful for his quick action.

Smiling up at him, she said, "Thank you."

Staring down into her dirty face, a smudge darkening one cheek, traces of plaster dust and God knew what else scattered across her features, Charles's heart clenched, an upwelling of love for her so strong flowing through him, he could barely contain it. Her neat chignon with which she had started the day was half undone, and tendrils of cobwebbed hair waved wildly about her cheeks, but even with her grimy face and soiled gown, Charles thought she was the loveliest thing he had ever seen. He adored her. And she thought him, he reminded himself grimly, merely useful in accomplishing her desire to see Adrian and April established amongst the highest reaches of the *ton*.

As the moments spun out, Daphne's smile faltered. "What is it?" she asked softly. "What makes you look so?"

He forced a crooked smile. "Nothing of importance," he said. Setting her away from him, he turned back toward the staircase and remarked over his shoulder, "I was only think-ing that few brides would be so indulgent and understanding as you have been. I am, indeed, a fortunate man."

Puzzled and deeply troubled, Daphne followed him as he began the downward descent. His words should have reas-sured her, but they did not. How could they when he made the word fortunate sound like a curse?

Chapter 17

Charles and Daphne wasted no time in returning to their rooms. Guided by the dancing light of the candle, they carefully made their way down the winding steps. The steep descent made haste impractical, but soon enough, they were stepping off the hidden staircase and through the doorway in the wall of Daphne's bedroom.

Looking around at the destruction they had wrought, the pile of broken and splintered laths and the chunks of plaster with bits and pieces of wallpaper still clinging to them, Daphne muttered, "You know that there is no way that we can keep this secret. Even if we could dispose of all signs of our, um, handiwork, there would still be that exposed oak wall. Worse, I'm sure that by now, Goodson will have divulged all to Mrs. Hutton. I wouldn't be surprised if within five minutes of Goodson's talking to Mrs. Hutton, the entire staff knew that we were up to something most unusual." She made a face. "Since Goodson and Mrs. Hutton are such bosom friends with Ketty, it is inevitable that she will learn of today's doings, and if Ketty knows . . ."

Idly moving a piece of plaster with his boot, Charles nodded. "If Ketty knows, then Adrian and April will soon hear of it." His gaze met hers. "So how much do we tell and when?"

"I don't know," she admitted, walking over to the secret

doorway. Trying to slide the door shut, she said, "It's all a bit impossible to take in, and as for what the others are going to think . . ." She shook her head, repeating, "It's impossible." Despite her yanking and pulling on it, the door would not move, but with Charles's help, they were able to finally muscle it back into place. Daphne glared at the scarred and pockmarked oak paneling. "I thought shutting the door would make me feel better," she complained, "but it doesn't."

"Perhaps after a bath and dinner, it won't seem so *very* impossible," Charles replied with a smile.

She twisted around to look at him. "You're enjoying this, aren't you?"

Charles shrugged. "Well, it is rather an adventure, isn't it? I'll wager a fair sum that you're going to be hard-pressed to keep Adrian from exploring the moment he hears of it."

Daphne cocked her head at him. "And your cousins and Nell? What are they going to think?"

Charles grinned. "Oh, Marcus and Julian will be right on Adrian's heels . . . with Nell following close behind."

"They won't think it strange? Especially if we mention the reason *why* we were prompted to take a sledgehammer and crowbar to a perfectly good wall?"

"Julian, Marcus, and Nell would probably take a ghost in stride, considering the previous events. Adrian would consider it a great lark." He looked thoughtful. "Although I don't believe that April is as fragile as you think, she and Miss Ketty might present problems."

"Miss Ketty will definitely be a problem, and I disagree with you about April. Hearing that a ghost really is floating about the house would not be best for her state of mind." Daphne frowned. "I suppose we could keep quiet about the ghost—make up some story for our decision to inspect this particular area behind the wallpaper."

Charles looked interested. "Perhaps. What do you propose? That one of us noticed the outline of the door, and overcome with curiosity, we set to work?"

"Something like that. However, it does seem that our actions were a bit extreme for idle curiosity."

"I agree. Adrian, April, and Ketty would probably swallow the story, but I doubt my cousins would."

"But would they question you? Or would they accept it, even suspecting we weren't quite telling the truth?"

Charles stared at the newly exposed oak paneling. "I think," he said slowly, "if we lay the blame on you, we can skim by." When Daphne just stared at him, he added quickly, "Stop and think, Daffy. My family doesn't know you very well yet. How do they know what queer ideas you might get in that pretty little head of yours? They are much more likely to believe that you were the one who discerned the vague outline of a doorway behind the wallpaper. Which is," he pointed out with a grin, "the truth." Warming to his theme, he continued, "Once you had seen the outline, nothing would stop you until you saw for yourself whether or not a doorway actually existed. Julian and the others will assume that I, being newly married and indulgent of my bride, merely humored you when you suggested, er, removing the wallpaper. Of course, no one," he said virtuously, "was more shocked by what we found than I was." His grin widened. "They might think it odd or peculiar of you to decide to wreck a perfectly good wall in pursuit of something you thought you saw, but they would probably shrug it off. But if I am the one . . . well, they would immediately know that I was running a rig of some sort."

Daphne wanted to argue, but there was much truth in what Charles said. She hated having his relatives think that she was so shatterbrained that on little more than a whim, she attacked her bedroom wall with sledgehammer and crowbar. But then, she reminded herself, they *had* found a secret door and staircase, so her whim had not been without merit.

Feeling a trifle better about it, she nodded. "Very well. We shall tell them that I was convinced that I had spied the outline of a doorway behind the wallpaper and that you, um, humored me and helped me make our discovery."

They both turned to stare at the debris scattered across the floor of Daphne's bedroom. "We shall have to tell the same tale to the servants," Charles said.

Daphne sighed. "I know." She wrinkled her nose. "I shall *so* enjoy being thought a perfect pea-goose by one and all."

"You're fair and far off with that thinking! Your intuition led to the discovery of a secret staircase, and that, my dear, will have everyone believing that you are too clever by half."

Daphne shrugged and looked down at her ruined gown. "I don't want to be thought of as clever, right now; all I want is a bath and a change of clothes."

It was fortunate that both Daphne's and Charles's dressing rooms could be gained by the servants' stairs and that by closing the door between Daphne's bedchamber and the dressing room, all signs of their handiwork were out of sight. Having rung for baths for each of them, they parted, Charles entering his own private dressing room while Daphne rummaged through her armoire for a change of clothes.

Mindful of what lay on the other side of the door, once the hot water had been carried upstairs from the kitchen and poured into the big copper tub, Daphne dismissed her maid, telling her she would ring for her when, or if, she needed her attention. The bath was heavenly, and aware for the first time of aching muscles, she lingered in the warm water. She had washed her hair and skewered the dripping mass on top of her head with a large carved wooden pin. Her skin was all pink and rosy from a thorough scrubbing, and nearly boneless with relaxation, she lay her head back against the rim of the copper tub, closed her eyes, and sighed extravagantly.

"My sentiments precisely," drawled Charles as he stepped through the door between her dressing room and her bedroom.

Daphne sat up with a shriek. "You startled me," she confessed, guessing from his damp hair and the robe he wore that he had already bathed. Staring at the silky black hair that sprouted in the deep V neckline of the robe, she also guessed that he was naked under the garment. Their eyes met, and the expression in his green gaze made her pulse leap and a tickle of desire kick through her.

Crossing to the satin dressing stool, he picked up a heavy white towel. With a decidedly carnal curve to his full mouth, he murmured, "I apologize, but I fear, my dear, that I intend to do far worse to you than startle you."

In one swift movement, he pulled her from the tub and gathered the towel around her naked body. Clamping her next to him, his mouth found hers, and he kissed her with a heat and hunger that sent lightning sizzling through Daphne. Breathless and dazzled by his kiss, when he swung her up into his arms and carried her into her bedroom, after it must be noted, shutting the door to the dressing room firmly behind him, she offered no resistance. A purely masculine smile on his face, he said, "Oh, yes, I shall certainly do much more than startle you. Much, *much* more." And dropping her onto the bed, he jerked the towel away and tossed it on the floor.

Their lovemaking had always taken place at night in the concealing darkness and beneath a decent covering of sheets. Daphne was suddenly very aware that despite the lateness of the day and increasing clouds, intermittent sunlight still shone into the room . . . and she was lying totally naked and exposed before her husband's roving gaze. Overcome with shyness, she flushed and sought to cover herself, but Charles gently swatted away her hands and said softly, "No, no, sweet, though our marriage is only a few weeks old, we have gone far beyond mere modesty."

That wasn't precisely true, Daphne thought half hysterically—they might know each other's body *in the dark* but not in daylight! And with, she decided resentfully, one of them still clothed.

Burning with embarrassment, miserably aware of her own nakedness, she muttered, "That's easy for you to say—you're still clothed."

"Easily rectified."

He stripped off his robe, and it joined the towel on the floor by the bed.

Staring at all the muscled male beauty before her, Daphne forgot her own nakedness. He had made love to her numerous times, she had touched and fondled that splendid body to her heart's content, but she had never actually seen him completely naked. She could not have looked away if her life depended upon it. He was beautiful, she thought giddily, her eyes traveling across the broad shoulders, wide chest, and down to the hard, flat belly. She gasped when her gaze found the thick, bulging rod springing up from the mat of black hair between his strong thighs. Oh, my. Wasn't *that* simply magnificent!

"If you don't stop eating me with your eyes, I am afraid that you will ruin my plans for a feast."

Her eyes bright with budding desire, Daphne jerked her admiring gaze upward to meet his eyes. "Y-y-your feast?"

"Hmmm, yes," he murmured as he sank down onto the bed beside her. "You. You look . . . luscious."

Even with him lying equally naked beside her, Daphne was miserably conscious of the spill of sunlight into the room, of the fact that he could *see* her, and every flaw of her less than perfect body. She was aware of her too small breasts and boyish hips, parts of her that were always decently hidden by clothing or blankets or darkness. It was one thing to be bold and brazen in bed in the dark, but another to be lying here without wearing a stitch of clothes with the sun still in the sky! She wiggled around, trying to conceal her nakedness by dragging up a small portion of the coverlet, but Charles would have none of it.

Flipping back the coverlet, he ran a caressing hand over

her shoulder and arm. "Still shy of me?" he asked softly, the expression in his eyes making her feel as if she was sinking into a pool of mulled wine.

"It seems so strange to be, uh, undressed during the day," she offered uncertainly. "There is so much . . . light."

"All the better to view the lovely sight before me," he crooned, cupping one breast. "Just like this round little dumpling."

His hand on her breast was heavenly, spirals of pleasure radiating outward wherever he touched. She licked her lip. "It, they aren't very big."

"No," he agreed gently, "not big, just perfect." Fondling her bosom, he added, "You see how they fit my hand. Perfectly." He kissed her, his mouth warm and coaxing. When his head lifted, Daphne moaned in protest, needing, wanting more. His eyes darkened as they met hers. "And you are mine, all mine."

Charles's gaze dropped to her breasts, the nipples tight and rosy. Flicking a finger over one sweet nipple, he said, "I find I am in the mood for strawberries." He bent and lightly closed his teeth over her nipple, and Daphne arched, delight streaking from her head to her toes. "No, not strawberries," he said against her breast, "raspberries. Small, ripe, and all mine."

He tasted the other nipple, his hands beginning a long, slow glide down her body. Fire and desire thrummed in his veins as he tasted and bit and suckled her breasts. Her skin was soft and smooth, like the finest silk, and he wanted to stroke reverently and grab with primitive abandon at the same time. He wanted her. Wanted to taste and sample every tempting inch of her in every imaginable way. Wanted her beneath him. On top of him. Locked around him. Wanted her beyond life itself.

Daphne gave herself up to the moment, conscious of the delicious weakness in her limbs, conscious of the glowing warmth flooding her. Every tug of his mouth on her nipples sent a wave of longing through her, every touch of his hands aroused an ache that begged to be soothed. She pushed her hips up against his groin, purring with pleasure when his swollen member lodged against her cleft. Flinging one leg over him, she rubbed along the thick length of him, her breathing uneven and rapid when he rubbed back, increasing her desire.

Her hands explored at will, down his back, over his taut buttocks, even dipping daringly lower to caress and cup the tight sack between his thighs, and Charles thought he would explode when she touched him there. His plan for a long, slow seduction nearly went by the wayside in that moment, but with a groan, he moved away from her, his body slipping lower, his mouth sliding across her belly, downward, seeking the heart and heat of her.

When he buried his mouth in the curls between her thighs, when his tongue probed and his teeth scraped gently against the delicate flesh he found there, Daphne stiffened, astonished and just a little alarmed at what he was doing. Her first instinct was to stop him from such a lascivious, surely depraved act, but then his tongue swirled over a particularly sensitive spot, and hot, wanton pleasure washed through her, leaving only stunned acceptance in its wake. Stopping him was beyond her, the new emotions, sensations so intense she could only writhe beneath his wicked, knowing mouth and his able, clever fingers that he used so well. When ecstasy took her, she went willingly, spinning wildly into the velvet abyss.

But Charles was not done with her yet. As she floated slowly back to earth, he was there, caressing her, nibbling once more at her breasts, his hand gently moving through the curls at the V where her thighs met. Small shocks of pleasure still rippled through her, but then as they ebbed and Charles continued to taste and explore her, heat built beneath his hand, and the magic began again.

His mouth caught hers, his kiss hot and urgent, and when he parted her thighs and lowered himself between them, she was eager for him. Daphne's arms tightened around him, and like a flick of flame, her tongue met and slid along the length of his, stoking the simmering fire that leaped higher and higher between them.

Charles possessed her in one frantic thrust, sliding deep within her, his hands on her hips holding her, positioning her beneath him as he plunged again and again into her. The soft sounds she made, the clench and clasp of her molten heat around him each time he sank into her was exquisite torture, the urge to drive harder, deeper, and faster warring with the longing to make this moment where they rocked on the edge of completion last forever. He fought to hold this moment, fought to meet her pumping hips, but his body demanded succor. Daphne's low keening cry was his undoing, and he could not stop the rush, could not stop his seed from bursting from him. With something between a growl and a moan, he rode the wave, taking Daphne with him as the world vanished and they drowned in pleasure.

For a long time, they remained locked together, too satiated and replete to move. Eventually, Charles slid from between her thighs and lay beside her. Daphne turned her head to stare at him. Wonderingly, she touched his dark face. "I think," she said slowly, "that we were just very wanton."

He smiled. "Do you? Did you like being wanton?"

Dreamily, she said, "I think that I could become quite accustomed to it."

He nuzzled her neck. "Then perhaps we shall do this often."

Some time later, Charles descended the stairs and made his way once more to the library. He rang for Goodson, and when the butler arrived, he said, "Would you please inform my cousins and the countess that I wish to speak with them here as soon as possible? Also, bring a tray of refreshments for us."

Goodson bowed and said, "I shall see to it immediately."

While he waited, Charles lit the kindling on the hearth and once that was crackling nicely, threw on several applewood logs. With the snap of the fire in the background, he returned to the Beaumont family papers, idly turning this page and that, not certain what exactly he was looking for amongst the documents. A confession to all his wrongdoings written in Sir Wesley's own hand would be nice, he thought. Or at least another mention of Katherine. And the fate of the child she carried. He didn't disagree with Daphne's belief that their little ghost was Sir Wesley's child bride; he had the same sense that it could be no one else.

The sound of the opening of the door jerked his head in that direction, and he smiled as Marcus walked into the room.

Bearing a strong resemblance to both Julian and Charles, although not as striking as the resemblance between the other two cousins, Marcus had always been the quieter, the steadier, and least reckless of the three. The one cousin, Charles thought smiling, most likely to advise them to proceed carefully and not rush into scandal and danger. For all the good it did, Charles admitted to himself.

His expression wary, Marcus walked toward him, saying, "I mistrust that look in your eye. I sincerely hope that you are not about to spring something unpleasant on me."

Before Charles could reply, Goodson appeared with a tray and the requested refreshments. He was still serving Charles and Marcus when Julian and Nell entered.

There was polite chatter as Goodson went about his duties, supplying everyone with a mug of the spicy punch, the scent of cinnamon and cloves mingling pleasantly with the faint hint of the burning applewood in the room. His services no longer needed, Charles dismissed him. He followed the butler to the door and once it had closed behind Goodson, Charles very deliberately locked the door.

Marcus, standing with one hand resting on the mantle of

the marble fireplace, cocked an eyebrow at Charles's action. "Secrets, cousin?" he asked.

Julian, seated on the damask sofa next to Nell, glanced at Charles as he joined them by the fire. The expression on Charles's face chilled him, and he demanded, "What is it? Why have you gathered us here?"

Without preamble, Charles told them all. He explained the reasons for his trip to Cornwall, confessing his own inability to find any trace of Raoul to support his feelings and ending with the discoveries that he and Daphne had made.

"Daphne knows of Raoul?" Marcus asked sharply. "You told her about him and then dragged your bride of only days along with you while you searched for proof that he is still alive?"

Charles sipped his punch. "Yes, I did—and my bride would have it no other way. I did attempt to send her back here, but she would have none of it." A faint smile flitted across his face. "Daphne is rather, er, intrepid and not to be swayed when the mood takes her."

Her eyes dark with anxiety, Nell leaned forward. "Do you really believe that Raoul is alive? And somewhere in this area living off the jewels that his mother secreted away for him?"

"I do," Charles said flatly. "And my reasoning is thus: we never found his body, and we should have. There have been at least two women, if not three, ripped to pieces in the manner that Raoul preferred. And many of Sofia's jewels are missing, jewels that I know she owned, jewels that I saw with my eyes. Do I know the extent of her private jewel collection? No, of course not—the woman bought jewelry like a starving jackal attacks a week-dead carcass. But I know of several pieces that are missing, and it makes sense that she gave them to Raoul to hide or even hid them for him. We found no jewels at the house in Poole, but we did discover a cache hidden on his yacht." Charles's mouth tightened. "Whether any will be found in his Brighton or London rooms or at his hunting lodge or any of the other places he would have had access to remains to be seen."

"But Nell never dreams of him anymore," declared Julian impatiently. "Surely that counts for something."

"Perhaps," Charles said, "for some reason the link between them has been broken. Nell may no longer be beset by nightmares but doesn't mean that Raoul is not alive."

"This is ridiculous!" snapped Marcus. "Just because we didn't find his body doesn't mean that he is alive. He was shot in the chest, *twice,* I might add, and he fell, what? Twenty or thirty feet down the sluice hole. It's true the cavern below led to the river, but I hardly think he could have survived the river in the condition he was in. *If,* and it is a big if, he survived your bullets and the fall, he would have drowned once he reached the river. He's dead."

Julian agreed with Marcus, but it was Nell who said slowly, "All of that is true, but suppose he kept a small rowboat there?" She swallowed. "And used it to escape?"

Julian studied her pale features. "It is possible, but . . ."

"Not only possible, but highly likely," Charles said. His gaze traveling from one intent face to the other, he said, "I am convinced that he and Sofia, most probably Sofia, planned ahead for the day that Raoul's monstrous behavior would be exposed." He glared at Marcus. "The jewels *are* missing. And Daphne and I *did* find a cache of jewels on his yacht. And do not forget that bodies of women have been found here in an area that he frequented often and was familiar with." He looked down at his gleaming boots. "I am convinced," he said harshly, "that Sofia gave him much, if not all, of her personal jewelry and instructed him to hide it in places he could reach should the worst happen. Nell's idea that he might have had a small boat ready with who knows what sort of supplies in it makes perfect sense. What is to say that he didn't have another hiding place nearby? A place we didn't know about that he could escape to initially, regroup, and then move on and . . . disappear." His mouth grim, he added, "Raoul wouldn't have thought of it on his own, but Sofia bloody well would have."

Marcus took a long drink of his punch. Julian stared at the fire. Nell's eyes were fixed on her lap, where her fingers were so tightly clasped the knuckles shone white, like bleached bones. Taking a sip of his own punch, Charles waited, knowing that each was considering the situation.

Julian spoke first. His voice heavy, he said, "Very well. It is possible."

In a small voice, Nell added, "I think it is more than possible. I think it is true."

Marcus sighed. "I don't know if it is true or not, but I'll concede that it is not beyond the realm of possibility." He looked across at Charles. "So what do we do now?"

"Find him," Charles said.

"And where do you suggest we begin?" asked Marcus in exasperation. "You've already admitted that you've found no trace of him here. How do you expect us to do any better?"

Charles smiled tauntingly. "You've always thought that you were wiser than me—here is your chance to prove it."

It was a dicey moment, and Charles wondered idly if Marcus might actually attack him, but his cousin apparently throttled back any murderous tendencies he felt and laughed instead. "Damn you," Marcus burst out, appreciative amusement gleaming in his eyes, "I suppose I shall just have to do that."

Julian rose from the sofa. A hint of a smile around his mouth, he murmured, "I have always said that Charles's audacity is the only thing that makes him bearable. It is so pleasing to be proven right. Again."

Someone tried the door to the library. "Charles? Are you in there?" asked Daphne from the other side.

Charles opened the door and ushered her inside, locking the door again. From the friendly expression on her face, no one would have guessed her inner turmoil as she walked up to the trio at the other end of the room and greeted them. As she took a seat in a chair near the fire, however, the covert glance she cast them was wary.

Nell sent her a warm smile and said, "Do not be alarmed. He has told us about the jewels and his belief that Raoul is still alive. We believe him."

Relief crossed Daphne's face. "Oh, I am so glad. I feared that you might think him, us, quite mad."

Julian smiled at her. "If you are mad, then we are, too. Your husband has convinced us of the possibility that Raoul may, indeed, still be alive."

"Only the possibility?" Daphne asked.

Marcus nodded. "Charles is thoroughly convinced that Raoul is alive, and it seems that you are, too. Until there is proof to the contrary, we are willing to help in any way that we can."

It wasn't quite the enthusiastic endorsement that Daphne could have wished for, but it sufficed.

For several minutes, the conversation centered on Raoul and how they were to proceed. They were all in agreement that they must investigate cautiously and in secret.

Conscious of the passing time and of the fact that any second, Adrian or April might come looking for her, Daphne said, "We can discuss this later, but at the moment, I am worried that one of my siblings may come looking for me." She rose to her feet, and twitching out the folds of the skirts of her pale mauve gown, she added wryly, "My brother is young, but he is not unintelligent. Should he discover us here behind a locked door, he would know instantly that something was afoot."

Charles nodded and walking over to the door, unlocked it and threw it open. "Do you think this will disarm him?" he asked lightly.

"No doubt," Daphne replied, walking toward him.

She was just stepping past Charles when Adrian appeared in the doorway. "Here you are!" her brother exclaimed. "Been looking all over for you." He glanced beyond her and seeing the others, smiled and said, "Oh, hullo. Didn't realize that everyone was in here."

"We were just leaving," Daphne said quickly. "Uh, the countess wished to see the library, and I have been showing her the room."

"And a very pretty room it is," said Nell, rising to her feet, smiling at Adrian. "You are fortunate to have such an extensive collection of wonderful books."

Adrian grinned. "Wasted on me, I'm afraid. Not much for reading."

"No," said Charles, a teasing gleam in his eyes. "You are much more likely to be found hanging around the stables mooning over some showy hack I wouldn't allow one of my tenants to own, much less own it myself."

"Unfair!" declared Adrian, not at all put out by Charles's words. His face alight with laughter, he looked at Marcus and urged, "You tell him, Mr. Sherbrook. You saw my stock. You said you liked it."

Marcus smiled and clapping Adrian on the shoulder, said, "Pay him no mind. My cousin has always had a very high opinion of his own opinion, even when no one else agrees with him."

Julian laughed. "A hit! I congratulate you, Marcus. Seldom does one slip beneath Charles's guard."

Smiling, Charles waved Daphne and Nell toward the door. "Do you know," he said sotto voce, "I have just remembered one of the reasons I enjoy the company of beautiful women: they *so* appreciate me."

Laughing, the group left the library and as one, headed for the front salon. Walking into the room, they discovered that April and Miss Ketty were there before them.

A flurry of greetings was exchanged, and everyone scattered around the room, the gentlemen standing, the ladies seated. The conversation ebbed and flowed, and then Daphne made the mistake of saying to her brother, "Earlier, you said you were looking for me. Why?"

He pulled on his ear, looking uncomfortable, but blurted out, "Wanted to know why in the devil you needed a crowbar and sledgehammer brought up to your rooms this afternoon. You doing some remodeling?"

Chapter 18

Daphne's heart sank. She'd hoped to postpone any explanation about the secret staircase until at least after dinner, but Adrian's question begged an immediate answer. To her further dismay, a quick glance around the room revealed that everyone was looking at her in varying degrees of astonishment.

"What utter nonsense!" exclaimed Miss Ketty. "Wherever did you get it in your head that Miss Daphne wanted a sledgehammer brought to her rooms. Ridiculous!"

Adrian flushed, but his chin took on a decidedly stubborn cast that Daphne knew too well. "If you must know," he said stiffly, "it was my valet, Bertram. He told me that he heard it from Mrs. Hutton herself. And *she* heard it from Goodson."

"Never say that you have been gossiping with the servants!" Miss Ketty gasped. "Surely I have taught you better. Your poor mother would turn over in her grave if she could hear you now."

"Oh, don't scold him, Ketty," Daphne begged, hoping to put off a tearful tirade. She slapped a smile on her face and said, "It is true. I did request those tools be brought to my rooms this afternoon."

Goggle-eyed, April asked, "But why? Whatever did you need them for?"

Daphne threw Charles a harassed look, and he shrugged. The cat was half out of the bag already, and there was no way they could stuff it back. Like Daphne, he had hoped that the news of the discovery of the secret staircase could be delayed. Twenty-four hours would have done nicely, he thought wistfully. He would have definitely preferred that the news of its discovery not follow so closely on the heels of his conversation with his relatives about Raoul. Nell, Julian, and Marcus were still reeling from *that* facer, and it would have been better if they'd had a little time to digest what he'd told them before being confronted by the flimsy story he and Daphne were going to tell. He brightened when it occurred to him that perhaps, preoccupied with the news about Raoul, they wouldn't look too closely at Daphne's reasons for attacking her bedroom wall.

Charles smiled at April and said, "Your sister was convinced that she could discern the outline of a doorway hidden behind all the wallpaper in one of the walls in her bedroom. This afternoon, she showed the area to me, and while the outline was very faint, it did look as if there could be a doorway underneath the wallpaper. So we, um, proceeded to find out if our supposition was correct."

Apparently not at all concerned with any damage done to his house, with ghoulish interest, Adrian demanded, "And did you find anything?"

Charles laughed. "We did. We discovered that there *was* a door behind the wallpaper and plaster. It had been covered over a couple of centuries ago, perhaps in the 1600s or even earlier." Charles's amused gaze traveled over the spellbound occupants of the room. "My clever wife has a very good eye."

"You uncovered a secret doorway in Daffy's bedroom?" April squeaked.

Charles bowed. "Not only was there a door behind the wallpaper, but it also opened onto a staircase. A very old staircase—it could date, to our untrained eye, back to when Beaumont Place was first built."

"By Jove!" exclaimed Adrian, his blue eyes incandescent with excitement. "A secret staircase. Wait until my friends hear of this!" Looking very young, he added with naïve pride, "I'll wager that the vicarage has nothing like this. I must see it!"

"Yes, I'm sure you must," Daphne agreed, "but it might be better if we waited until after we ate to go exploring."

Brushing aside any interest in food, this from a young man with an appetite like a famished wolf, Adrian argued for immediate exploration of the staircase; April, her expression one of apprehension and eagerness, sided with her brother, and for several moments, Daphne had her hands full. Ignoring Miss Ketty's gloomy predictions of the fate of those unwise enough to go wandering up and down nasty secret staircases, Daphne concentrated on convincing Adrian and April to wait until later to explore.

While Daphne dealt with her siblings, Julian strolled up to Charles, and for his ears alone, he murmured, "First, Raoul and now this. For a newly married man, you have been very busy."

Charles slid him a limpid look. "You know how easily I become bored if I am not always doing something."

Julian grimaced. Sometimes, there was just no dealing with his cousin. Nodding his head in Daphne's direction, he asked, "Did she really just happen to notice the outline, or is there more to the tale?"

"Daphne is very observant," Charles said circumspectly. He disliked keeping Julian in the dark, but explaining about the little ghost, Katherine, as Daphne insisted calling her, was more than he was willing to divulge at the moment. No reason to complicate the situation, he told himself virtuously.

Julian's eyes narrowed. "You're hiding something."

"Prove it," Charles retorted.

Julian snorted. "I can't, and you bloody well know it." He

sent his cousin an unfriendly look. "I just remembered how infuriating you can be."

"But you love me anyway," murmured Charles.

"Enough!" Julian said, and shaking his head half in disgust, half in amusement, he wandered back to where Nell sat on one of several sofas in the room. Marcus stood behind her.

Nell glanced up at Julian when he approached. "What were you and Charles talking about?"

His eyes on Charles, Julian replied, "What he knows that he's not telling us."

Marcus looked startled. "You think that he is keeping something from us?"

"Hmmm, yes, I do, but whether it is important or not remains to be seen. With Charles, one never knows if he's keeping quiet for his own amusement or if there is a good reason for it." Thoughtfully, Julian added, "Usually, there is a good reason."

"Julian . . . this secret staircase worries me," Nell admitted. "What if it has something to do with Raoul?"

Julian looked at her. "If the staircase had anything to do with Raoul, Charles would have said something. He might be infuriating, but he would never do anything to put you or his wife or anyone else in danger."

"Not knowingly," Nell said. "I mislike it. It seems too much of a coincidence—his telling us about Raoul, and then we learn that he and Daphne have discovered a secret door and staircase."

"But it must be a coincidence. I know of no other logical explanation," argued Marcus. "The door was closed up centuries ago. There can be no connection between Raoul and a long hidden door and staircase in this place." His eyes on Daphne, he concluded, "I'll confess that it is fantastic that she just happened to notice the outline behind several generations of wallpaper, but stranger things have happened. It might very well just be a coincidence."

"Coincidence or not," said Julian, "I am very interested in seeing this staircase."

Goodson knocked on the door and upon entering, announced that dinner was served.

Daphne rose to her feet. "Thank you, Goodson." After Goodson departed, she sent Adrian a stern glance and said coolly, "We will continue this discussion after dinner. Until then, not one word from you about it."

Adrian nodded sulkily, but since his nature was sunny, by the time they were seated in the dining room and enjoying the first course of turtle soup and baked salmon, among other offerings, he was once again his congenial self. Daphne suppressed a smile. He may have given way to her, but she was not fooled—the instant they left the dining room, he would demand to see her discovery.

The storm hinted at earlier in the day arrived, and even inside the stout walls of Beaumont Place, the rain and howling wind could be heard. Thunder rolled overhead, and lightning crackled.

There had been no question of the gentlemen lingering long in the dining room over their port. The ladies had barely settled themselves comfortably around the front salon and Daphne had just handed out tea when Adrian and the others joined them.

As if their earlier argument had never been interrupted, Adrian strode over to stand in front of his sister. His blue eyes blazing with excitement, he demanded, "*Now* may we please see the staircase?"

"Oh, yes, please, Daffy," chimed in April, setting down her cup. "Please! It is a thrilling discovery, and it is unfair of you to keep it all to yourself."

Daphne hesitated. She knew that they would see the staircase soon enough, but she wondered if tonight was the best time. The storm worried her, reminding her too vividly of the night that Sir Wesley had made his appearance. She cast a wary glance at the fire burning cheerfully on the hearth and was glad that they were here in this room, well away from the blue salon.

Putting aside memories of Sir Wesley, the storm created a new set of worries for her. The staircase was in a section of the most ancient part of the house—who knew how safe it would be—and the idea of her brother and sister merrily tripping up and down that staircase with a storm clawing and shrieking outside alarmed her. Rain could have leaked through the roof, making those narrow steps slick and lethal. What if the wind tore open a weakened portion of the outside wall? Or lightning struck?

A terrific clap of thunder exploded overhead, making Daphne jump. Setting down her cup and saucer, she said, "Don't you think it would be better to wait until tomorrow after the storm has passed before we do any exploring? It could be dangerous for us to be wandering up and down that old staircase until we know it is safe. Charles and I only examined one small portion of the upper reaches, and that only briefly—there could be all manner of danger. I think we should wait."

Adrian and April would have none of that, both of them pleading like children denied an extravagant treat. Daphne gamely held to her position, Miss Ketty coming down firmly on her side, to no avail. Adrian and April were united—they wanted to see the secret doorway and stairs tonight.

Charles put an end to it by saying, "Your sister is right about the lot of us traipsing about the staircase—it could be dangerous, and the storm makes it more so." Chuckling at Adrian's mutinous expression, Charles added, "However, I see no reason why we gentlemen cannot take a brief look around tonight. I, for one, want a better look." He glanced across to Julian and Marcus. "Don't you?"

Adrian's happy shout drowned out Daphne's cry of protest.

It would seem, she thought furiously, that her husband was as much an adventure-mad boy as her brother. Julian and Marcus's prompt acceptance made it clear that the vice ran in the family.

"And what of us?" Daphne demanded. "Are we merely to sit here and drink tea and wait while you go exploring? Perhaps risking your life and limb?"

"Remain here, absolutely not!" Charles grinned at her. "I thought that we could all adjoin to your bedchamber, and while we gentlemen are, er, risking life and limb, you ladies can study the doorway you so cleverly discovered."

Daphne, Nell, and April objected vigorously, but the gentlemen won the argument, and soon enough, they were gathered in Daphne's bedchamber, staring at the destruction she and Charles had wrought. There was a moment of stunned silence at the sight of all the litter heaped and scattered across the room and the scarred oak wall with its row of rosettes.

Adrian ambled over to the wall and stared at it. One hand resting on a rosette, he glanced back at Daphne. "Which one opens the door?"

Reluctantly, Daphne replied, "The second one down from where your hand is now."

Adrian's hand dropped, and he gave the rosette a hard twist. He jumped back, and there was a collective gasp when with a low, grating rumble, the door slid open.

"By heaven!" exclaimed Julian. "There really is a secret door."

"You didn't believe us?" Charles asked with a lifted brow.

"I believed you," said Julian, "I just didn't . . ." His face alight with the same excitement that was on Adrian's face, he added with boyish enthusiasm, "This is wonderful! There is no telling what we may find."

Once the gentlemen had each taken a candle, with Charles in the lead, they entered the staircase. "Be careful," Charles said as he began the descent. "The steps are narrow, and some may be crumbling."

The ladies crowded around the doorway, watching as the men disappeared into the darkness. Only when the male voices grew faint and the flickering lights of the candles vanished did they step back from the door.

Having seen the staircase, the suffocating darkness of it and the faint damp sheen on the rough stone steps, April admitted, "I think that it is a good thing that the gentlemen are exploring it first."

"No doubt," Daphne answered crossly, "but it seems palpably unfair that we have to sit here and drink tea while they have all the adventure."

"You wouldn't think it much of an adventure," said Miss Ketty bluntly, "if you fell and broke your neck. Foolishness is what I call it."

Since she hadn't been all that eager to explore the staircase when they had first discovered it, Daphne couldn't argue with Miss Ketty's comments. Her old nurse was right—it wouldn't be much of an adventure if one of them got hurt. Which was the crux of the matter for Daphne: she was anxious for Charles. What if *he* fell and broke his neck?

Nell looked down the staircase for several seconds longer. Except for the candlelight from Daphne's bedroom that spilled through the doorway, the blackness was complete. It was like looking into a black, bottomless pit, she concluded with a flutter in her stomach. Almost, she thought fearfully, like staring into the pitiless depths of Raoul's black eyes . . . .

Shivering, Nell stepped away from the doorway. She did not consider herself a coward, and heaven knew if Julian needed her, she would charge down the steps in an instant and no thought of danger to herself would slow her, but she echoed April's words, "It probably *is* best that the gentlemen see that it is safe first."

The gentlemen were having a grand time. The sounds of the storm could be heard even within the confines of the staircase, and as they descended lower, they discovered hair-line cracks in the walls that allowed rain to seep inside.

"This is bloody dangerous," Marcus said as they passed one particularly noticeable fissure. "A section of the wall could come crashing down at any moment."

"Doubt it," said Charles cheerfully from his position in the lead. "These are thick and stout walls, and they have stood for centuries. I'm sure they'll stand long enough for us to explore."

Adrian, following directly behind Charles, said defensively, "Of course they will! Beaumont Place is well-built." As they negotiated another twist in the staircase, he asked, "Where do you think this leads? What do you think we'll find?"

"Most likely, it will lead to the outside," Julian replied from his position at the rear. "But it could lead us to another passage or a room where the troops were garrisoned."

"Or a dungeon," Charles said, remembering another time, another staircase.

"Or a dungeon," Julian agreed grimly, beset by the same memories. This staircase was more ancient, but it was eerily similar.

Lifting his candle to inspect the upper reaches of the stair-case, Marcus said, "I say! Look up there! Along the outer wall. See that narrow ledge beneath those boarded up spaces? I'll wager if the boards were taken down, you'd find archer slits."

After finding a few more identical areas along the wall, they agreed that Marcus was right.

Staring thoughtfully at the heavy slabs of wood that covered the archer slits, Charles said, "If those timbers were removed, the sun could reach inside and light the place, which makes sense. I wondered why there was no outside light at all."

"It would also allow fresh air," said Julian.

Frowning, Adrian asked, "But how did the archers get up there? And why build their stands so high above the stairs?"

"No doubt they used ladders to get up there," answered Marcus. "Once the archers were in place, the ladders could be placed against the wall out of the way, still allowing the stairs to be used for troops and supplies when they were under attack."

Adrian sighed ecstatically. "This is bloody marvelous! I cannot wait to climb up there and see for myself."

Gingerly, they traversed the stairs. Charles became aware almost immediately that the lower they went, the colder it became. Fighting off the chill he felt even beneath his fine wool jacket, he reminded himself it was simply the natural airflow and *not* something connected with the supernatural. He was being imaginative, he decided wryly, but he couldn't pretend that he wasn't also uneasy.

The staircase made a sharp turn, and rounding the corner, they discovered a landing. The landing was large enough for all four men to stand comfortably on it, and pausing in their explorations, they stopped to examine the area. A close look at the inner wall brought a frown to Charles's face.

Running his hands over the stonework, he said, "I'll wager that there was an opening here once." His fingers lingered on the iron remnants of a wall sconce. A quick glance revealed another one less than six feet away. "These must have been on either side of a door or hallway. My guess is that there was once a chamber here."

As if a door to the Arctic had blown open, Charles was assailed by bone-biting cold that took his breath away. Imaginative or not, the icy sensation was unnatural and too familiar for his liking, and the back of his neck prickled. Cautiously, he glanced around, relieved not to find a ghostly presence hovering behind him. And which one, he wondered grimly, would it be? Sir Wesley? Or Katherine?

"Christ!" Julian said, breaking into his thoughts. "Is it just me, or is anyone else freezing? It feels like the middle of a December snowstorm in here."

"I agree," said Marcus. Puzzled, he looked around. "It wasn't that way a moment ago."

"No, it wasn't," remarked Adrian. He looked at Charles. "Reminds me of Mrs. Darby's trick that night. Remember how cold the room got?"

"I don't think this is a trick," Charles said levelly. And how in the bloody hell am I going to explain that it might very well be a ghost?

"Perhaps a section of the wall has fallen," offered Marcus. "That would explain this blast of icy air."

"Perhaps," Charles agreed, knowing that it hadn't. I should have asked Goodson for his crucifix, he thought bitterly, because no conventional weapon will stop Sir Wesley.

Shrugging off the cold, Marcus came to stand beside Charles and studied the wall that had first caught his attention. After a long moment, he said, "Do you know, I believe you're right about a chamber having once been here. The stone *is* different. Even the masonry work is different."

Julian, too, having apparently accepted the cold as normal, held his candle nearer for a better look. Nodding, he said, "It appears to have been done at a later date. There were always renovations being done to these old places. This could have been where they kept the weapons or a guardroom. It's possible, in the early days, when the keep was smaller, it might even have been the lord's antechamber or bedroom. Who knows?"

His blue eyes glittering with suppressed excitement, Adrian said, "By Jove! I wish we had brought a sledgehammer with us. There is no telling what we might find behind that wall." A reverent note in his voice, he breathed, "There could be a secret treasure room . . . ."

Deciding he had no choice but to act as oblivious to the iciness of the passage as the others, Charles tamped down his unease and clapped Adrian on the shoulder. Forcing a smile, he said, "Or simply an empty space with nothing but mice droppings in it."

Adrian grinned ruefully. "You are probably right, but I want to know what is on the other side."

"Your house," Charles said. "You can do what you want with it."

"If Daphne lets me," Adrian muttered.

"I think your sister will be as curious as you."

Adrian's face brightened. "Yes. And since *she's* already destroyed one wall in my house, what is one more?"

The flames of the candles danced wildly as another gust of glacial air swirled around them, and startled, Julian glanced over his shoulder, demanding of no one in particular, "What the bloody hell was that?"

"Probably just the air currents coming up from below," Marcus said dismissively, turning back to look at the wall.

Charles considered disabusing him of that notion, but deciding an explanation, especially the explanation he would give, would most likely gain him a pair of manacles in Bedlam, he kept his mouth shut. Anxiety built up inside him, though, a sense of impending danger climbing through him. The wall needed to be examined—he didn't deny it or that it was more than probable a room lay behind it. He just wished he had Goodson's crucifix in his vest pocket. His mouth tightened. He didn't, and his only choice at the moment was to get everyone the hell out of here.

Abruptly, he said, "I think we have seen enough for tonight. I'm sure the ladies are wondering what is taking us so long."

"But we haven't even reached the bottom yet!" protested Adrian.

Julian sent Charles a curious glance. "I'm sure that a few minutes more won't make a difference."

"And I'd like to take a better look at this wall before we move on," said Marcus.

Defeated, Charles shrugged his shoulders. Perhaps he was overreacting. Maybe the cold was normal. Maybe he was imagining things . . . or not.

The wall fascinated Marcus and Julian, and with Adrian crowding behind them, they continued to poke and prod at it. Clenching his jaw to keep his teeth from chattering, Charles looked carefully around the landing, but to his relief, no ghostly manifestations met his gaze. Yet.

"I do believe that there is something behind this section of wall," Julian said at last, stepping back from the wall. He smiled at Adrian. "Whether it may be a treasure room or not remains to be seen."

"We will find out tomorrow," vowed Adrian excitedly. "It is my house, and I want to know what is behind that wall. First thing in the morning, we shall return, tear open some of those archer slits for better light, and then break through this wall and see what is behind it."

Without warning, a powerful blast of icy air slammed into them, and the candles winked out. Charles sensed a malevolent force surging in the blackness just before he was thrown against the wall. In the darkness, Adrian cried out, and there was the terrifying sound of a body plunging down the stairs.

Cursing, with shaking fingers, Charles relit his candle. Blood leaked into his eye, and he swiped it away, realizing that he had cut his head when he hit the stone wall. Uncaring of the blood that trickled down one side of his face, he looked anxiously around the landing. One lightning glance showed that Adrian was missing. Dreading what he would find, he held his candle up and looked down the twisting staircase. No corpse met his gaze, but he could picture Adrian's body tumbling end over end . . . . His heart pumping in hard, painful bursts, he rushed down the stairs.

The steps seemed endless, and Charles pushed back the panic that churned in his chest. Dear God, did this staircase ever end? A groan came from the darkness ahead of him, and aware that it would do Adrian no good if in his haste, he trampled him, Charles slowed his progress. "Adrian," he called out. "I am coming to you."

Edging cautiously around a curve, Charles found Adrian crumpled on another landing much smaller than the one above. The boy's body was partially wedged against the stone wall, and when Charles stepped onto the landing, Adrian moaned again and half-sitting up, cradled his arm next to his body.

Kneeling down beside him, Charles asked softly, "How bad is it?"

The face Adrian turned to him made Charles suck in his breath in dismay. Blood flowed freely from nasty cuts on his temple and forehead, there was a wide scrape along one cheek, and his lower lip was busted. Other bruises were already popping out, but the main thing was that he was alive.

Flashing a wan smile, Adrian mumbled, "I think my arm is broken . . . and I may have hurt my ankle."

Julian and Marcus arrived on Charles's heels, and the three men quickly ascertained, aside from the broken arm, a banged up ankle, and a multitude of cuts and bruises, that Adrian was unharmed. He would be sore for several days and most likely, limping for a while, and the arm would take weeks to mend, but he had been lucky. He was alive.

Charles ripped off his cravat and fashioned a sling for Adrian's arm. They could do nothing about the blood until they returned to the main part of the house.

Adrian was oh, so gently helped to his feet. He was unsteady, and it was obvious that while nothing else was broken, his entire body had taken a beating, and his ankle was painful. With Charles on one side of him, Marcus in the lead, and Julian following behind, the four slowly made their way up the stairs. The return journey seemed forever, Adrian leaning more heavily on Charles with every step they took.

After a few moments, Adrian said in a very young voice, "Daffy is going to be mad as fire. She wanted us to wait."

Charles smiled. "Your sister will be so happy that I am not returning your corpse to her that I don't think you have anything to fear." He gave a mock shudder. "It is my fate you should worry over—I was the one who overrode her wishes."

Adrian gave a weak chuckle. "That's true. But you have nothing to fear—you'll talk her 'round in time. Everyone knows that she adores you. You can see it on her face when she looks at you."

Feeling as if he'd been poleaxed, Charles stopped so suddenly he nearly jerked Adrian off his feet. Adrian's startled yelp brought him quickly to his senses, and apologizing profusely, he made his feet move one in front of the other. The remainder of the trek passed by Charles in a daze. Adrian thought Daphne adored him? How could that be? Did she? Dizzying delight swelled in his chest. Was it possible? Daphne loved him?

Marcus passed through the doorway into Daphne's bedchamber first. It had been decided that he should warn the women before they saw Charles and Adrian's bloodied faces. At the sight of Marcus, the ladies, who had been scattered around the room conversing desultorily, leaped to their feet.

"Did you find something exciting?" asked Nell, smiling.

"Er, no," Marcus said. "There was an accident."

Nell's smile vanished. "Julian?" she asked in breathless accents.

Marcus shook his head, his eyes flitting to Daphne.

Daphne's heart stuttered in her breast, and feeling as if she might faint, she demanded, "Charles? Where is he? Take me to him!" She took a deep breath and asked fearfully, "Is he alive?"

"Oh, it is nothing so serious as that! I didn't mean to alarm you. Everyone is fine," Marcus said hastily. "Well, not exactly fine," he corrected, wondering why he had to be the one to spread the bad news. "Adrian took the worst of it— his arm is broken, and his ankle is hurt."

Adrian and Charles staggered through the doorway, and at the sight of Charles's blood-streaked face, Daphne cried out,

"Oh, Charles! My love! What has happened to you?" Oblivious to anything but Charles's tall form, she rushed across the room to him.

Clutching his arm, she stared into his face. "If anything had happened to you . . ." She fought back the emotion that clogged her throat. He was safe, and that was all mattered.

"It is only a cut on my eyebrow," Charles said, his eyes locked on her. "Adrian is in far worse shape."

"Is he?" she asked distractedly, barely sparing a glance at her brother who was being tenderly lowered onto a chair by Julian and Marcus; April and Miss Ketty hovered around him.

"Your poor face," she said, her gaze returning to him.

Charles touched his eyebrow and winced. "I've had worst wounds." He grinned. "And it was worth it. Daphne, that staircase is fascinating! We discovered ledges where archers stood and the slits they used to fire down on the enemy. Best of all, we think we've found a hidden chamber!"

Exultation flooding him, Charles stared tenderly at her. He didn't want to talk about his wounds or even the damned staircase and what they had found. What he wanted was to sweep her up into his arms and spirit her away from the others to a private place. A place where they could explore all the interesting possibilities raised by Adrian's comments. It hadn't escaped his attention either that she wasn't paying the least heed to her brother. All her attention and concern was for *him!* The compulsion to drag her into his embrace and declare himself was nearly overwhelming, and all he could do, he admitted disgustedly, was stand here babbling about the damned staircase, grinning like an idiot.

Her alarm fading with every passing second, Daphne was aware of a rising indignation. He might have been killed. He had scared her to death. And he had enjoyed every minute of it, she decided, seeing his grin and the gleam in his eye. The wretched cur.

The trickle of blood from his cut caught her eye, and her heart clenched. "Is your cut very painful?" she asked.

"Yes," he replied, looking forward to her sweet ministrations.

Her eyes narrowed. "Good!" she said tartly. "I *told* you to wait until tomorrow!"

Chapter 19

It was impossible to keep the discovery a secret. The staircase existed, and the exploration of it would require the services of some stout footmen. Besides, Goodson's help had been needed in procuring the necessary items to clean and bind Adrian and Charles's wounds. Once the situation had been explained to the butler and he had been given permission to tell the rest of the staff, Daphne knew that by daylight, the news would have spread far beyond Beaumont Place.

Excitement blazed through the house at the news, and when Goodson had ordered the removal of the debris from Daphne's bedroom, there'd nearly been a riot amongst the servants, each one eager to see the secret doorway. Quelling the bedlam with a mere look, Goodson made his choices, and two footmen had hauled off the heavier trash, and a trio of maids had swept and mopped. Shortly, except for the newly exposed wall, all signs of the destruction wrought by Charles and Daphne had been removed.

The severity of the storm made it impossible to fetch a physician to set Adrian's arm, but fortunately, Charles's valet, Bertram, had once been a batman for a colonel in the army and was quite proficient at dealing with cases like Adrian's. Adrian's arm had been skillfully set, his ankle wrapped for support, his cuts and bruises seen to, and he had been sent to bed with a judicious dose of laudanum. Charles's split eye-brow was seen to, not by his doting wife as he had hoped but by the ever efficient Bertram. April and Miss Ketty also re-tired for the night.

Now with April, Adrian, and Miss Ketty soundly asleep in their beds, the others gathered in the library. The gentlemen were drinking brandy from crystal snifters, and the ladies were sipping negus that Goodson had prepared for them.

Settling down into the welcoming comfort of the bur-gundy velvet sofa in front of the fire, Daphne gently inhaled the pleasing scent of lemon and nutmeg that wafted up from her negus and took a sip. Heaven.

The two ladies were seated side by side on the sofa; the gentlemen were scattered about the room. Julian was seated in a chair near the sofa, his long legs stretched out toward the warmth of the blaze on the hearth. His brandy snifter resting on the gray-veined marble mantle, Charles stood at one side of the fireplace, Marcus at the other. There was little doubt that they were all thinking about the events of the night. And what had been said and *not* said, Daphne admitted uneasily, recalling the scene before Adrian had grumpily sought out his bed.

Adrian's insistence that he had not fallen but had been *pushed* down the steps had been brushed aside as heated imagination by April and Miss Ketty.

"Pushed you!" exclaimed Miss Ketty. "Why, I never heard anything so foolish in my life. Why would one of these fine gentlemen push you down those stairs?"

"I didn't say that one of them pushed me," Adrian replied stubbornly. "I said that it *felt* like someone pushed me."

"Oh, *felt* like," repeated April, rolling her eyes. "You just don't want to admit that you stumbled over your own feet."

"I did not!"

"Did too!"

"That's enough," said Daphne, entering the fray. Smiling at Adrian, she added, "It doesn't matter. You're very lucky that all you broke was your arm." Her smile wavered. "You could have broken your neck, you know."

Adrian hunched his good shoulder. "I know, but I tell you—"

"What you're going to tell me, young man, is that you are going to drink this draught right now and go to bed," interrupted Miss Ketty, thrusting the laudanum under his nose. "And with no further argument." Since his arm was aching and he knew that tone in Miss Ketty's voice, Adrian gave in and retired.

None of the five adults now gathered in the library had questioned Adrian's assertion that he had been pushed, but Daphne suspected that no one had dismissed it out of hand, either. She glanced at Charles, curious as to what he was thinking. So far she'd not had a moment to speak privately with him, and she sensed that he had much to tell to her.

"Odd doings tonight," Marcus said abruptly, breaking into her thoughts.

Staring at the flames bobbing on the hearth, Julian said, "Most odd."

Daphne put down her half finished negus, and looking at Charles, she asked quietly, "In the dark, is it possible that one of you bumped into Adrian and accidentally caused him to fall down the stairs?"

Charles shook his head. "No. None of us touched him, even accidentally."

"It was no accident," Julian said slowly.

Charles glanced at him sharply.

Julian met his gaze unflinchingly and said, "There is something very peculiar going on in this house, and I think it is time that you and your wife told us the truth." He looked at Daphne. "You just *happened* to spy the outline of a doorway that led to the staircase?"

Daphne flushed, her gaze flying to Charles's. For a long second, their eyes held, and then Charles sighed and looking at Julian, said, "Nothing slips by you, does it?"

"You forget that I've known you a long time. I know when you're hiding something from me," Julian answered, his keen gaze fixed on Charles's face.

"Charles, what is it?" said Nell. "Is it about Raoul?"

"You might as well tell us," said Marcus. He frowned. "I agree with Julian: Adrian's fall was no accident. If you know something, you need to tell us."

"It has nothing to do with Raoul," Charles muttered, almost wishing that it did. His relatives would be far more likely to accept the notion that Raoul had pushed Adrian down the steps, he thought acidly, than the idea that a ghost had done it.

"Then for God's sake, what is it?" demanded Marcus impatiently.

"Surely you know that you can trust us," said Julian.

Charles threw Daphne a hounded look. She knew he would hold them at bay forever if need be, but it was unfair to ask him to do so.

"It is something rather fantastic," Daphne said in a low voice. "Most people would say even, um, unbelievable." She swallowed. "Some people might think that we are mad . . . or highly imaginative."

Julian and Nell's eyes met. Turning to look at Daphne, Nell covered Daphne's hand with one of hers and said, "We are not unfamiliar with, ah, the unbelievable. And the highly imaginative can be instructive."

"My wife is correct," added Julian. "Three years ago, we faced our own fantastic events, and I discovered that there is much in this world that I do not understand, that I cannot explain. Tell us."

Daphne looked at Charles, and he smiled encouragingly to her. "They are related to me, my love; you'll find them not *un*intelligent."

Julian's lips twitched, and Marcus snorted. Nell smiled encouragingly at Daphne and repeated Julian's command. "Tell us."

And so Daphne and Charles told them about Katherine and Sir Wesley. All of it. When they finished speaking, there was a long, thoughtful silence.

Marcus sipped his brandy. Julian stared at the fire. Nell held Daphne's hand.

"Ghosts," Marcus said after several nerve-racking moments.

"Katherine and Sir Wesley," murmured Nell, staring off into space.

"Well, why in the devil not?" said Julian. "That makes as much sense as anything else that has happened so far." Sending Charles a searching glance, he asked, "And you believe that it was Sir Wesley we felt on that landing? And that he shoved Adrian down the steps?"

Charles nodded. "I do. Remember, I have felt his presence before, and it is not a sensation one is likely to forget."

"But why?" Daphne cried. "Why did he attack a mere boy, of all people?"

"Because Adrian wants to open the chamber," Charles said calmly.

Daphne's eyes widened. "Of course! Sir Wesley doesn't want us to find out what is in there!"

"But what could be so terrible that this, this ghost doesn't want us to discover even now?" demanded Marcus. He shook his head. Looked at his brandy. Shut his eyes and murmured, "I cannot believe I asked that question. First, Nell and her nightmares, and now, ghosts!" Plaintively, he asked, "Does anyone but me long for the day when the only things unexplainable were Parliament and the weather?"

"But think how boring that is," teased Charles.

"I *like* boring," complained Marcus. "I like my life calm, ordered, *normal.*"

"Pity," said Julian, watching Marcus with affectionate amusement. "In another few years, if you don't change your ways, you'll be a member of that cadre of crusty old men one finds in the reading rooms at White's or Waiter's."

"The ones," added Charles, "that are always harrumphing and complaining about the ill-mannered young of today."

Marcus looked offended. "Well, thank you very much for that! Just because I am more sober in my habits than either one of you, there's no reason to be insulting." He glanced from one smiling cousin to the other. His gaze narrowed. "And I suppose that you two paragons of wisdom have a solution to save me from myself."

"Indeed," said Charles, grinning.

"You need a wife," said Julian, his eyes dancing.

"One who will turn your well-ordered life on its heels," added Charles with a wicked gleam in his eyes.

Marcus looked at Nell and Daphne for help, but they just smiled at him. "A wife," he said in tones of horror. "I'd rather settle for ghosts!"

Daphne found it remarkable that they accepted the notion of ghosts so easily, and she said so.

Julian grimaced. "If this conversation had taken place three years ago, I would have most likely assumed the pair of you were candidates for an asylum or that my cousin had married a woman of a highly excitable, imaginative nature, but we are not unfamiliar with the, ah, unexplainable." He sighed. "I could wish it otherwise, but I cannot pretend that there is much in this world that is beyond my understanding."

Nell nodded. "He had a difficult time believing that there was a mental connection between Raoul and I and that in my nightmares, I could actually see Raoul's monstrous deeds. I cannot explain it myself. But he came to believe me and accepted, with no little reluctance, I might add, that I dreamed of real events as they were happening." She smiled faintly. "After that, ghosts are quite simple."

Daphne glanced at Marcus, a question in her eyes. "And you? Do you believe?"

Marcus hunched a shoulder. "I don't want to, but it's either believe or assume that my entire family has turned into a pack of lunatics." He gave her a crooked smile. "I'm not saying I'm totally convinced that it was a ghost tonight in the passageway, but I am saying that I shall at least *consider* the idea of ghosts."

It wasn't quite the wholehearted endorsement Daphne would have liked, but at least Marcus hadn't just simply dismissed the notion as utter nonsense.

Nell agreed enthusiastically with Daphne that the little ghost had to be Katherine and that it could only have been Sir Wesley's malevolent spirit that had pushed Adrian down the stairs. Julian endorsed Nell's opinion, but Marcus resisted somewhat, and it took the four others some time before they finally convinced him to accept the reality of Katherine and Sir Wesley. Once Marcus's skepticism had been put aside, a plan of action was decided upon. Tomorrow, while the ladies perused the collection of family papers for any mention of Katherine or Sir Wesley, the gentlemen would see to the opening of the old arrow slits in order to let more light into the staircase. With that accomplished, they could then tackle the destruction of the wall on the landing. Everyone expected to find a chamber of some sort behind the wall.

"I think, too," Charles said as they prepared to retreat to their bedrooms for what remained of the night, "that we shall search for another entrance to the staircase. I cannot believe that it is a completely internal passageway, and I'll wager that there is door that opens to the outside. We just have to find it."

Daphne was uneasy about using her bedroom until the newly discovered secret door could be securely locked. Bad enough she had a ghost visiting her at night, but the thought of that doorway's existence and of something *else* opening it and coming into her bedroom while she slept was more than she could bear. She snatched up her gown and dressing robe from the bed and retreated to her dressing room to change. Having slipped into a primrose yellow robe and a white lawn gown embroidered with tiny yellow daisies, she steeled herself to go back into her bedroom. She stiffened her spine and walked out of the dressing room. Her gaze went immediately to the newly exposed oak wall. No one looking at it would ever suspect that there was a doorway hidden there. Even knowing where it was, she could not discern the outline of the door, and she wondered how she had even glimpsed it beneath all the various coats of wallpaper and plaster and lath.

Her breath caught. She hadn't glimpsed it. Katherine had shown it to her. Katherine had wanted her to find it.

She was staring so intently at the wall that she didn't hear Charles enter the room, and his hand on her shoulder was the first warning she had of his presence.

Nearly leaping out of her skin when he touched her, she shrieked and whirled around. "Oh, Charles!" she exclaimed when she saw who it was. "It is only you."

"I'm sorry," he said. "I didn't mean to frighten you." He grinned. "Who did you think I was? Sir Wesley?"

"I didn't think. You just startled me." She glanced back at the scarred wall. "Do you think we could sleep in your bedroom tonight? I am uneasy about that door."

Charles was uneasy about that door, too, specifically the staircase behind it. Until they knew more about it and where it meandered, he'd already concluded that it would be wisest if they chose other rooms for their use.

Sweeping her up into his arms, he dropped a kiss on the tip of her nose and said, "My sentiments exactly," and carried her off to his bedroom.

Shutting the door to his bedroom with his shoulder, he tossed Daphne onto his bed and locked the door. The door safely locked, he swung around, and arms akimbo, he looked at the enticing sight she made sprawled across his bed, her hair undone from its tidy knot at the back of her head framing her face in a riot of curls. The yellow robe was half open, and he glimpsed the faint gleam of her skin beneath the almost sheer fabric of her gown. Slim as a willow, sweet as a sugared plum, she lay smiling at him, those mysterious half green, half blue eyes soft and warm.

"Hmmm, yes, this is much better," he said, coming to join her on the bed. He pulled her against him and kissed her soundly on the lips. "Yes. Much, *much* better," he murmured several moments later when he finally lifted his mouth from hers to stare down into her flushed features.

He'd been longing all evening for privacy with his wife, just the two of them, and he savored the moment. Intently, he studied her face. Could Adrian be right? Did Daphne love him? Her reaction when he and Adrian had appeared before her, both of them streaked with blood, had been most gratifying. It had been to him that she had rushed, her beautiful eyes full of anxiety, not her brother. And it had been his wounds that had been the focus of her concern, not Adrian's far more serious ones. Charles tried to feel guilty for being pleased, tried to be ashamed at his elation at the way she had brushed aside Adrian's condition to worry over his, but it was beyond him. The joy of finding himself first in her thoughts was far too powerful for any guilt to mar his delight.

Daphne had put *him* first, not her brother, and for Charles, that was monumental as until her advent in his life, he hadn't even known that he wanted to be first in someone's heart. He loved Daphne with all of his being, and he longed, nay, hungered for her to feel the same about him. Adrian's words rang in his ears. Could it be true? Dare he believe?

Daphne squirmed under his steady regard. "What is it?" she asked finally. "Do I have a spot on my nose? Why are you staring so?"

"Can't I stare at my lovely wife?" he asked softly, his heart so full of love he thought it would burst. Yet vulnerable as he had never been in his life, he hesitated to speak of his love. What if Adrian was wrong? What if he had misinterpreted her anxiety for him? Charles tried to master his chaotic emotions. I should tell her how I feel, he told himself raggedly. I should boldly speak aloud my love and not dither like a schoolboy. But he could not, and hitherto always confident and sure of himself, he discovered that he was shy and uncertain . . . for perhaps the first time in his life. Avoiding the subject uppermost in his brain, he dropped his head and lightly bit her bottom lip. "Are you still angry with me for not waiting to explore the passage?"

Gently, her fingers caressed the cut on his eyebrow. "I wasn't angry so much as terrified." She closed her eyes, remembering the stark terror she had felt when Marcus had said that there had been an accident. Meeting his gaze, she said, "You could have been killed . . ." Her throat closed up, and tears seeped into her eyes. Her voice thick, she finally got out, "I would have died if something had happened to you. You are everything to me."

Her words undid him, and unable to hold back his emotions any longer, he muttered, "Oh, Daphne! I adore you!" Raining kisses across her cheeks and nose, he said huskily, "You are the most glorious thing that has ever happened to me, and I shall thank God every day for the rest of my life that you took into that pretty little head of yours to explore that sea cave."

Stunned, Daphne stared up at him. She'd hoped for this. Yearned with all her heart for this. Yet now that the moment was upon her, she could hardly take it in. "You love me?" she asked wonderingly.

He shook his head, a tender smile curving his mouth. "No. You haven't been listening, my sweet. Love you? Absolutely not. I *adore* you!"

Joy bloomed within her, and she threw her arms around his neck. "Oh, Charles, I love you, too! So very much." She laughed and added, "No. Not love. I *adore* you."

Charles couldn't describe his happiness at that moment. This incredibly precious woman loved him. Him! Charles Weston. And no one else. *Him!*

He buried his face in her wild black hair. "Daffy, sweet, darling, adorable Daffy, I *do* love you. I lost my heart almost from the moment I laid eyes on you."

"That soon?" she asked.

He raised his head and looked into her eyes. "That soon," he said. "I remember watching you climb over those rocks and thinking . . ." He grinned. "Thinking most indecent thoughts."

"That wasn't love," she argued, though her eyes were laughing at him.

"Yes, it was," he protested. "If it wasn't love, why else did I stay with you in the sea cave?"

Guilt smote her. "Oh, Charles, I disliked you at first. I didn't fall in love with you until our wedding day."

"It doesn't matter," he said with quiet joy. "All that matters is that you love me and I love you."

Daphne's fingers traced his hard features, lingering on his mouth. "Mmm, it's nice, isn't it? Being in love. Being in love with your spouse."

"Very nice," he murmured. Flicking open her robe, he cupped one breast, anticipation rippling through him when he discovered her nipple already hard and swollen. "And I intend to show you precisely how very nice it is." And did.

It had been well after three o'clock in the morning when the five parted to seek their beds, and it was a bleary-eyed group who met in the morning room just after noon the next day. After several cups of strong coffee and a substantial meal, they were revived somewhat and ready to set their plans in motion.

With April accompanying them, Daphne and Nell adjoined to the library and the shelves upon shelves of Beaumont family papers. Telling April only that they were looking for references to Sir Wesley and his wife, Katherine, each lady took a stack of pages and sat down to read.

The gentlemen, followed by a half dozen husky servants gathered from the fields, set out to remove the boards from the arrow slits. Despite his broken arm and bruised ankle, and hobbling along with a cane, Adrian insisted upon coming with them.

As they left the house, Charles took Goodson aside and requested that a chair be sent around to the south side of the house. "That young cub will be glad of it before long," Charles murmured as he turned to rush off and join the others.

The day was raw and unpleasant, a cutting wind blowing in from the Channel, but there was no rain, and the sun was attempting to make appearance.

Knowing the general location and what they were looking for, it didn't take long to find the outside wall of the staircase. Stepping back from the curving, towering walls of what had once been part of the outer edge of the original Norman keep, Charles easily spied the indentations in the stone façade. Ladders would not suffice to reach them, and while the servants were hastily constructing scaffolding, he and the others, followed by a limping Adrian, searched for an entrance.

In Sir Huxley's time, the gardens on this side of the house had been seldom used and, thus, had been had been allowed to run rampant. From the trees dotting the landscape, one could guess that the grounds had been extensive, but the shrubs, grasses, and bushes were so overgrown that the area looked more like a wilderness than part of a formal garden. A jungle of green pressed next to the stone walls of the house.

Spreading out, Charles, Julian, and Marcus worked around the wall, peering through the tangle of greenery, hoping to find a door. Time passed with no discovery.

Meanwhile, Goodson arrived with the chair Charles had requested for Adrian. Adrian looked mortified, but he was glad of Charles's thoughtfulness and gave up the battle of pretending his ankle was just fine. Sitting down on the chair, he sighed with relief.

From his position, Adrian had a good view of the action. He observed the servants hard at work constructing the scaf-

folding for a while and then switched his gaze to the efforts
to find an entrance into the staircase. Tired of doing that and
wishing he had stayed inside, he glanced around at the
ragged gardens, deciding he would have to talk to the head
gardener about bringing them back to snuff. Eventually, his
attention came back to the house. He studied the curving
wall for a time, then watched the others as they pried away
vines or pulled back the various pieces of concealing shrubbery. Bored, he considered the section of wall in front of him,
the surface nearly obscured by a thick row of several overgrown lilac bushes.

He had been staring at a dark patch in the stone surface of
the wall for quite some time when he froze, realizing what he
was looking at. Rising from his chair, he hobbled toward the
wall. "Over here!" he cried excitedly. "I think I've found
something."

Adrian had found the entrance for which the others had
searched so diligently, for there behind the lilac bushes was a
massive door. The ancient heavy-timbered door was an-
chored to the stone wall with huge black iron hinges. Darkened by age, the lumber was nearly as black as the hinges,
and concealed behind the lilac bushes it was nearly invisible.

"If we hadn't been specifically looking for it," Charles
mused, "we could have walked past it a hundred times and
never noticed it." Clapping Adrian on the shoulder, he said,
"Splendid work! And to think I tried to convince you to stay
inside."

Adrian flushed. "You would have found it eventually," he
said fairly.

"But not as soon," said Julian, smiling kindly at him.
"And you were the one who discovered it."

A closer examination revealed that behind the row of
lilacs, there was a narrow pathway, the branches not extending all the way to the wall itself. Charles's mouth thinned as
he studied that tight space between the wall and the lilacs. It
was no natural occurrence—the lilac branches had been sys-

tematically broken off, creating a tunnel-like path. A secluded path, he thought with an unpleasant trickle running down his spine, just wide enough for a man to walk through . . . Scowling, he ran his hand over the splintered ends of one of the branches, noting the signs of healed wood. The break wasn't new, at least not recent—it could have been done months or years previously, but not, he thought tightly, centuries ago.

"What are you waiting for?" demanded Adrian, his eyes bright with excitement. "Aren't you going to open the door?"

"Of course," Charles said slowly, "just as soon as I am armed."

Adrian's eyes nearly popped out of his head. "Armed?" he squeaked in a voice that would have embarrassed him any other time. "Whatever for?"

"Because this path is man-made. That leads me to believe that someone has already discovered our doorway and has been using it for some time." He sent Adrian a dry look. "I don't relish coming upon our, um, uninvited guest defenseless."

Julian and Marcus looked over the pathway themselves, and their expressions were grim when they stepped away from the lilacs. The three men exchanged hard glances. Charles knew that the same thoughts were in his cousins' minds. Raoul. He didn't know what they would find behind the ancient wooden door, but instinct told him that this was precisely the sort of lair that would appeal to Raoul.

"I agree with Charles," Julian said. "We should be armed."

"By Jupiter!" breathed Adrian, oblivious to the air of tension in the three older men. "Do you think that the smugglers are using my house?"

Adrian appeared more thrilled than alarmed by the notion of smugglers commandeering a section of the house, and Charles felt some of his fear dissipate. Of course, that was the most likely explanation for the pathway behind the lilacs. Smugglers. The house wasn't that far from the Channel.

They had not yet explored the full length of the secret staircase. It was possible there was enough room in the lower reaches of the house for the smugglers to hide their goods before transporting them out of Cornwall. This entrance could be well-known to locals and used since time immemorial. It was a logical conclusion. Yet he could not shake the feeling that Adrian was wrong. There were too many sea caves in which the smugglers could stash their goods. Why the devil would they cart them way up here?

Forcing a smile, Charles said to Adrian, "You could be right, but before I go through that doorway, I want a weapon in my hand."

Charles had hoped that the news of their find would not filter through to the ladies. At least, not until he and Julian and Marcus were armed and had made an initial exploration into whatever lay behind that door. Unfortunately, he had forgotten to tell Adrian to keep his mouth shut and while he and the other two men were busy arming themselves, Adrian had limped into the library and excitedly divulged all to the women.

Convincing the ladies to remain inside until the gentlemen had seen for themselves whatever might be behind the door had been out of the question.

"The last time you went exploring," Daphne had said fiercely, "you could have been killed. I'm not staying here, wringing my hands, waiting for news of your death. I'm coming with you! And short of locking me in my room, you cannot stop me."

When Charles, Julian, and Marcus returned to the door Adrian had discovered, they were armed, each carried a lantern, and they were followed by a contingent of curious onlookers.

The weather had changed dramatically since Adrian had discovered the doorway. Gray, sullen clouds scudded overhead, and the wind, already biting, had picked up; then, the first leading edge of rain began to fall. Another storm was blowing in from sea. Thunder boomed, and in the distance, jagged lightning tore across the horizon.

Faced by the force of the storm, almost as one, Adrian, April, Miss Ketty, and the servants retreated to the shelter of the house, leaving only Charles, Julian, Marcus, Nell, and Daphne to continue the exploration.

A brief skirmish between Charles and Daphne confirmed her determination to follow him.

Glaring at his beloved, who glared right back, Charles growled, "This could be dangerous."

"All the more reason for me to come with you," snapped Daphne.

Cursing under his breath, Charles ducked behind the lilacs, followed in a single line by the others. Silently, they crept along the narrow pathway.

The door in front of him, Charles paused. He studied it a long second and then putting down his lantern, his pistol held at the ready, his fingers closed around the thick iron handle at one side of the massive door. He lifted the handle, the ease and silence with which it moved telling him that someone had oiled it well. His pulse pounding, he pushed on the door. And like the lid to Pandora's box, it opened.

Chapter 20

Utter blackness met Charles's gaze. As Julian handed him his lantern, Charles muttered, "I hope that Adrian is right and that we are on the brink of discovering a smuggler's den and not . . . ." His lips thinned. "And not something else," he finished tautly.

"You no more than I," said Julian softly. Their gazes locked. "If it should prove to be . . . something else, can you do it?"

Charles smiled icily. "Oh, I can do it. I *must* do it."

There was one last attempt by the gentlemen to convince Daphne and Nell to wait inside with the others. Huddled next to the house, enduring the slapping branches of the lilac bushes, getting wetter and more frustrated with every passing second, the three men wasted valuable time in a fruitless argument with Daphne and Nell about the inadvisability of their presence during this initial search. Both women stood firm; there was no swaying them.

Her chin held at a pugnacious angle, Daphne said, "We either come with you . . . or we follow you. It is your choice. We are *not* going to be sent away like naughty schoolgirls."

Feeling hard-pressed not to strangle his beloved, Charles snarled, "Very well, come with us. But for God's sake, stay out of the way."

After lighting the lanterns and seeing that everyone was

armed, including the two women, the group gathered itself to plunge into the unknown. Charles hesitated, irritated and worried about the presence of Daphne and Nell. Staring at the pistol in his wife's hand, Charles flashed her a harassed glance. "Nell knows how to shoot—Julian was her instructor—but are you certain you know how to use that?"

Daphne nodded. "Do not forget, I grew up in the military; my father taught me to shoot when I was ten years old." She smiled faintly. "I am not a marksman, but I promise you I won't shoot myself."

"Bloody well take care that you don't shoot one of *us!*" he snapped and turned his back on her.

His expression grim, holding the lantern before him, Charles stepped out of the now pouring rain and through the doorway. The others followed him.

Leaving the door open, glad of the faint light from outside and the fresh air the opened doorway provided, they glanced around the room lit with the fitful glow of the lanterns. Everyone was convinced that this was part of the original structure. Smoke-stained stone walls met their gazes. Signs of ancient torches still hung in the crude iron sconces that lined the room; a few pieces of old weaponry and broken furniture were scattered across the floor. The rectangular room was not huge, but it could have easily held several armed fighting men and their weapons. Even with the air blowing in from outside, there was a musty, unpleasant odor, and cobwebs heavy with the debris of centuries draped the corners and decorated every nook and cranny.

The door that provided them access was in the middle of the outside wall, and they did not venture far, bunching together just inside the room, but out of the rain and wind. Motioning for them to wait, Charles took several steps away from the group. His lantern light fell upon an arched opening at the far end of the room. Further exploration revealed a staircase that angled upward. After a moment's study, he said over his shoulder, "I suspect that this is the same staircase we were on last night. We may not know all its twists and turns, but we know ultimately where it leads."

Leaving the staircase for the moment, he swung back to rejoin them when Daphne gasped, "Charles! Look! Look at the floor."

A thick layer of dust lay on the stone floor, but what held everyone's attention were the three distinct trails of footprints that crisscrossed the room. The first trail led from the doorway where they were gathered to the opposite end of the room where they saw another doorway. A second set of prints ran from the staircase and across the middle of the room and then mingled and disappeared into the first. The final trail had been the one Charles had taken directly from the doorway to the staircase, his damp footprints clear to see in the midst of the pathway that had already been there before he had walked across the room.

Feeling the hair rise on the nape of his neck, Charles stared at those footprints. The pathways were well-marked, but whether one person or several had made the tracks in the dust could not be determined. No ghost had made those trails, he thought tensely. But someone had. Someone who already knew of this forgotten area of Beaumont Place. Someone who had been aware of it and had been using it for some time . . .

It was Nell who said what was on everyone's mind. "It is Raoul," she said in accents of horror. "I know it. I can feel him."

Julian looked at her sharply. "You said you had no more nightmares."

"It's true I haven't dreamed of him, and I don't know how to explain what I am feeling now," Nell said honestly, her sea green eyes wide and frightened. "I just know, as surely as he came to me in nightmares all those years, that Raoul made those footprints."

"If that is true, then there is no question of you and Daphne continuing with us," Julian said.

"Julian's right," said Charles, coming to stand in front of Daphne. "We cannot hunt him if we are worried about you. You need to go back into the house with the others and wait for us there."

Daphne shook her head. "How do you know we would be safe?" she asked, her gaze steady on Charles. "If it is Raoul, he is already familiar with this section of the house. Who knows what else he may have discovered? What other ways into the house he might have found? While you are searching for him down here, he could be slipping into the house and doing the very thing you fear."

Her words were irrefutable, and biting back a curse, Charles stared rigidly at the dark outline made by the doorway at the other end of the room. It was unlikely that there were other hidden or secret ways into the house, but dare he take the chance?

His eyes met Julian's. "She has a point," Julian said reluctantly.

"And we would be five against one," chimed in Nell.

Charles and Julian looked at Marcus. Marcus hunched a shoulder. "Don't ask me to decide—they're your wives."

Charles's gaze dropped to the trail of footprints. He hoisted his lantern for a better look, his eyes following the path clearly defined on the dusty floor. He knew in his gut where those footprints would lead, and he wondered that he hadn't realized the truth sooner. He'd wasted all that time and effort searching for Raoul's hiding place, and it had been right beneath his nose all the time. Beaumont Place.

When Raoul had disappeared down the sluice hole in the dungeon beneath the Dower House, Sir Huxley had been a dying old man, cared for by servants in a rambling, isolated old house. There were no close neighbors. No meddling family to contend with. There was only this very old house, a house, the then-heir had often stated, he would abandon and allow to fall into rack and ruin. Raoul would have known all that—Trevillyan had never made any secret of it. And if

Raoul had known of the secret entrance before Sir Huxley had died . . .

It made perfect sense. His brother had always been secretive, inquisitive, and if he had been considering Beaumont Place before Sir Huxley's death, he would have made it his business to know everything about the house and its history. Charles speculated that on his latter trips to Cornwall, Raoul had accompanied Trevillyan on visits to Sir Huxley . . . and had no doubt run tame through the house. It was almost certain Raoul would have made some secret forays, unknown and unnoticed by anyone else, to explore the place and grounds. The awareness that it had once been a Norman keep made it only logical that there would have been dungeons, old fortifications. The boarded up arrow slits were plain to see along this side of the original outer wall of the keep; deducing that there was a staircase or at least a walkway would have been the next step. And if there was a staircase or walkway, it most likely would have a way to access it from the outside. It was true that the door through which they had entered had been concealed behind the lilacs, but as soon as they'd started looking for it, it had been easily found.

Knowing that Raoul had been gravely wounded after he'd dived down the sluice hole at the Dower House and disappeared, it was difficult to estimate how long it had taken him to heal and make his way to Cornwall, but Charles didn't doubt that he had. Somehow, somewhere, Raoul had survived . . . and when strong enough, had gone to earth in Cornwall.

Adrian's house, while not ideal, fit Raoul's needs, and like a malignant shadow, Raoul had slipped into Beaumont Place and made himself at home in the lower reaches of the house. Charles snorted. No wonder he had been unable to find any hint of his brother's presence in Cornwall. He felt a rush of gratitude for the little ghost, Katherine. If she hadn't appeared to Daphne . . . if she hadn't led the way to the secret doorway in Daphne's room, at this very moment, they'd be inside, happily gathered around the fire, drinking punch, unaware that beneath the house . . . .

Charles shook himself. Glancing back at the others, he asked Daphne, "You are determined to come with us?"

She nodded, her fine eyes resolute as they met his.

Giving in to the inevitable, he sighed and muttered, "Everyone stay together. No wandering off to explore. At the slightest hint of something not quite right, say so. We can take no chances. We are entering Raoul's domain. Remember always that he will not hesitate to kill any one of us." His mouth tightened. "All of us if he could."

Silently, they fell in behind Charles as he headed toward the shadowy doorway at the other end of the room. Charles led the way, then Julian, Nell, and Daphne, with Marcus in the rear.

The heavy door at the far end of the room opened to reveal a wide hall. They passed two rooms, one on either side of the hall, the doors half rotten and hanging at drunken angles.

"Quarters, perhaps?" Julian murmured after they quickly examined the rooms.

"They could have been used for something like that," Charles said. "Ammunition. Food. Who knows?"

Approaching a set of narrow stairs, Charles hesitated at the top, staring down at the black void before him. The scent of mold and decay and something else, something that made his jaw clench and his fingers tighten on his pistol, wafted up to his nostrils.

He glanced back over his shoulder. "He may be down there or he may not, but you must be vigilant. Your lives depend upon it."

It was a short series of steps, ending in an antechamber that showed signs of being used as living quarters. No attempt had been made to clean the room, the cobwebs, the dirt, and dust from countless years plain to see in the corners and scattered across the stone floor. Unable to help herself,

Daphne lifted one corner of her skirts higher to avoid coming in contact with the filth in the room.

In the sconces hanging on the walls, they could see the stubs of tallow candles; a single wooden bed had been pushed against one wall, the thin straw mattress covered by a tangle of quilts. Next to the bed was a small table; a half burnt candle in a brass holder sat in the middle of it. An old armoire had been placed on the far wall. An inspection of the contents revealed a meager wardrobe, but of good quality and workmanship. A doorway lay on the other side of the room; on that same wall, there was a cupboard upon which sat a pottery bowl and pitcher, a dirty pewter plate, and some utensils. Nearby, two chairs sat beneath a scarred wooden table. The tabletop was littered with breadcrumbs, the unidentifiable remains of food, and half empty bottles of brandy and port.

His lip curling in distaste, Charles considered the area, wondering how his fastidious brother with his love of fine food, wine, clothes, and horses could have come to this. Could he have been wrong about Sofia's jewels? Had Raoul escaped with only the clothes on his back, and had he been living a hand-to-mouth existence all this time? He shook his head. Surely, Sofia's jewels would have fetched more than enough for Raoul to live in comfort and not in this squalor? Or could they be wrong? Were these belongings and the footprints those of a vagrant squatter?

Charles gingerly poked again through the few pieces of clothing in the armoire. There was a clank as something suddenly tumbled to the floor from the pocket of the many-caped greatcoat he had been examining and landed near his foot. Using his white linen handkerchief, he picked up the object and held it in the light of his lantern. His breath caught as he recognized it—a diamond-encrusted emerald choker he had often seen worn by Sofia.

Julian came to stand beside him, staring at the glittering jewels in Charles's hand. His voice hard, Julian said, "If we needed further proof that Raoul is alive and has been using this place, that pretty little bauble gives it to us. It is a distinctive piece, and I remember seeing it many times around your stepmother's neck."

They spent more time searching through the room and its paltry contents but found nothing else of note. Keeping the choker wrapped in his handkerchief, Charles handed it to Daphne, and she stuffed it in the deep pocket of her dark blue cashmere gown for safekeeping. The weight of it was a reminder of Raoul's presence and Sofia's perfidy.

Approaching the door on the opposite side of the room, Charles pulled it open. Another flight of steps met his gaze, and the scent of blood, of death, of evil flowed into the antechamber like London sewage from a storm-swollen gutter. Filled with fury and fear at what he might next find, he sped silently down the crooked staircase.

The stairs stopped in a large room. Glancing around at the heavy manacles that draped the smoke-stained walls, no one needed the sight of the four cells to know that they were standing in the dungeons of Beaumont Place. A huge fireplace lay at one end of the long room; an assortment of instruments whose ugly purpose needed no explanation lay carelessly on the blackened hearth. A bundle of faggots stood against one side of the fireplace.

There was no sluice hole in this dungeon, nor was there the bloodstained slab upon which so many women had died screaming for succor. There were, however, the remains of an old rack, the evidence of new repair bright against the old wood and metal. More disturbing were signs that some of the bloodstains on the stone floor around the rack could not have been there for centuries. Charles knelt down for a closer look. They were not fresh, but they were not very old, either. Rising to his feet, he glanced at Julian and Marcus and nodded curtly. They had found the Monster's lair.

There was little conversation between them as they moved stoically around the dungeon. It was difficult to discern what might have been moldering there for centuries and what might be from more recent times. One of the cells appeared to have had an occupant at some time within the last year or so—there were fewer cobwebs, and the dust on the floor had been greatly disturbed. But it was the condition of the manacles that suggested they had been used not too long ago. The edges of the metal gleamed brightly as if someone had twisted and fought to escape from their hold, the few scraps of bloodstained cloth caught on the chains looking too new to be very old. The pieces were stiff and brown with dried blood, but the three men agreed that it was unlikely they were relics from centuries ago.

The dungeon was a horrid place, reeking of death and evil. Looking around him, Charles wondered if Sir Wesley's nephew, John, had died here. Perhaps even Katherine, the very young wife? Who knew how many lives had been lost here in Sir Wesley's time, and even before him?

Daphne came to stand beside him. Putting her hand on his arm, she said, "I cannot bear to be here any longer. Is there a reason for us to remain?"

He glanced at her and giving her a twisted smile, said, "Not quite the adventure you thought it would be?"

She shook her head. "I didn't expect an adventure; I just didn't want to remain behind worrying and wondering what was happening with you." She looked around. "This is a beastly place, isn't it?"

Charles shrugged. "Not all dungeons have as bloody a history as this one, if what we know of Sir Wesley is true. Not to excuse him, but it was a savage time, a cruel age. Remember King Henry had two of his wives beheaded and waited ahorse for news of Boleyn's death before rushing off to marry Jane Seymour. And don't forget that his father probably murdered the princes in the Tower, and not Richard, as the Tudors would have us believe." He smiled without humor. "Our ancestors were not as civilized as we are today."

Her eyes on the rack, she said in a low tone, "Some of us

have not left that age behind, not the cruelty or the savagery." Unable to tear her gaze away from the rack, imagining the terror, the pain of Raoul's helpless victim, horror washed over her, and needing the air and the light, she said, "Please, let us go."

Charles wanted nothing more than to rush Daphne up the stairs and out of this wretched place, but they must have some sort of plan before they left. His thoughts raced. The women could not be allowed to return outside alone while he and his cousins remained behind to set a trap. Not knowing Raoul's whereabouts made it far too dangerous—sending the women away could be sending them straight into Raoul's arms. Charles wasn't afraid to face his half brother on his own, but he knew he'd have the devil's own time convincing the others to leave him here alone. The notion of he and Julian remaining while sending Marcus to see the women safely into the house didn't sit well, either. Even if Marcus agreed, and he doubted his cousin would, he wasn't willing to send Daphne and Nell back with only one man to protect them. In the end, there was only one plan: the three men must escort Daphne and Nell to safety, and then he and his cousins would return to deal with Raoul.

Most worrisome was the possibility that Raoul would come back and discover he'd had visitors. They had not tried to hide their presence. And when his half brother discovered that the emerald choker was missing . . .

Charles didn't want Raoul to bolt. If Raoul escaped from here, who knew how long it would take to run him down again? How many women might die in the interval? His half brother had sought refuge here, and they had a chance of ending this nightmare here and now, but only if they moved swiftly and caught him by surprise.

They had discovered Raoul's hiding place, but the advantage still lay with his half brother. Raoul had had months, years to explore this area. The dungeon seemed a dead-end, but what if it wasn't? What if there were more secret doorways? Hidden passageways? Raoul could be watching them this very moment.

A sense of urgency came over Charles, and he motioned to the others that they should leave. Almost whispering, he said, "We go out the same way we came in. I'll lead, then Julian, Nell, Daphne, Marcus."

There was no argument. Leading the way, Charles sprinted up the stairs, Julian followed, and then Nell. Nell had taken a half dozen steps before something—a sound? instinct?—made her pause and glance back at the empty passage. Daphne should have been directly behind her . . . Nell froze; hearing only the thundering of her blood, she stared back at the faint outline of the doorway to the dungeon. There was no one there. Not Daphne. Not Marcus.

"*Julian!* Charles!" she shrieked. "To me!"

Julian was at her side in a moment, Charles right behind him.

In trembling accents, she said, "Daphne and Marcus . . . ."

Charles's gaze flew to the bottom of the stairs, where he willed his wife's sweet form to appear. It did not. Pushing roughly past Julian and Nell on the narrow stairs, knowing there was no time for finesse, he bounded down the stairs and into the dungeon.

Marcus lay on the floor, a crimson pool of blood encircling his head, his pistol hanging limply in one hand, his lantern nearby. Beside him lay a second pistol. Charles blanched, realizing that he was staring at Daphne's pistol.

Julian and Nell tumbled into the room, Nell crying out when she saw Marcus. Sinking to the floor beside him, she tenderly cradled his head in her lap. Gently, her fingers traced out the wound at the back of his head. Looking up at the two men, she said, "He is alive, but it is an ugly wound."

Charles glanced frantically around the room. There was no sign of Daphne. "A secret door," he muttered, struggling against the primal fear that threatened to overpower him. Raoul had Daphne. Think of her, he ordered himself. Think of Daphne. You must find her. "There has to be another bloody secret door," he shouted and sprang across the room, staring wildly at the nearest wall.

At first, he could find nothing, his search too frenzied to be of any use. He fought to gain mastery of himself, knowing that he would do Daphne no good by giving way to the wild terror that flooded him. Shoving his pistol into the waistband of his breeches, he took a deep breath and despite the urge for speed, made himself study the wall, forced his fingers to move slowly and thoroughly over the seemingly impenetrable stone surface. A moment later, he found what he searched for so desperately, a small stone slightly out of alignment from the others in the wall.

With fingers that visibly shook, he touched the stone, the air whooshing from his lungs when the section of wall in front of him slid noiselessly aside, revealing a narrow opening.

"By heaven!" exclaimed Julian, leaving Nell to tend Marcus and coming to stand beside Charles. "You were right. There *is* another secret doorway."

His voice harsh, Charles said, "There may be more such doorways . . . and Raoul will know them all. I do not." Charles grabbed his pistol and threw Julian a look in which fury and terror were mingled. "I am sorry to leave you with Marcus . . . I-I-I hope he recovers, but I must go."

His expression bleak, Julian nodded. "Go! And bring her back safely."

"I will," Charles swore fiercely as he stepped once more into the unknown.

Raoul's attack had been so silent, swift, and savage that the first inkling Daphne had of his presence was when a powerful arm closed around her waist and the sharp blade of a knife dug into her throat. "One sound," hissed a voice in her ear, "and I will slit your pretty little throat even as we stand here." He jabbed the knife against her skin. "Understand? Nod if you do."

Daphne nodded, the sour taste of horror rising in the back of her throat. Raoul swung her away from the stairs, and she glimpsed Marcus lying motionless on the floor, blood oozing from the back of his head. Fright skittered through her chest. Was he dead? Please, dear God, no!

Raoul jabbed her again, and she felt blood seeping down her neck and disappearing into the neck of her gown. "Put down the pistol," he said. "Quietly, if you don't wish to join him."

She hesitated, wondering if she could stall for time, knowing that any second, Nell would notice she was not behind her. A deeper jab of the knife made up her mind for her, and she promptly followed his orders, setting her pistol beside Marcus.

Raoul was a strong man, and she was whisked effortlessly across the room and through an opening in the wall, yet for all his strength, she was aware that there was a shuffling motion to his movements. He pushed something with his shoulder, and the wall slid shut, plunging them into pitch-black darkness.

Daphne fought back a moan as the suffocating blackness pressed against her. She was terrified, unable to think, numbed by the horror of the attack on Marcus and the knowledge that she was in the power of a madman.

"Hurry! Hurry!" he muttered, pulling her up several steps. "Your beloved will be looking for you at any moment." She thought he laughed. "And we don't want dear Charles to find you, do we?" This time, she heard the laughter in his muffled tone. "At least not right away."

Raoul continued to half drag, half carry her up the stairs, the knife pressed against her throat. Gripped by incomprehensible terror, it was made worse by the slow slide of her own blood down her neck. Had he cut her deep enough to kill her? Was she already bleeding to death?

They climbed awkwardly up a few more stairs before Daphne lost her footing and fell, the knife slicing deeper when she stumbled to her knees. Only Raoul's arm around her waist kept her from tumbling down the stairs.

Cursing, Raoul dragged her upright. "Clumsy bitch," he snarled.

His words snapped her out her numbing terror. A ball of fury sprang to life within her. How dare this monster murder Marcus and abduct her! Destroy her life with Charles? How dare he! A bite to her voice, she said, "If you would take the knife away and allow me to walk on my own, I'm sure we'd make better time. Even an imbecile would realize that I am right."

There was a startled silence and then a laugh. "My brother seems to have married himself to a shrew," he said.

The knife was removed, and the arm fell away from her waist. His hand captured her wrist in a brutal grasp, and he said, "Perhaps you're right. We shall try it your way, Madame."

"You're never going to get away with this," Daphne said, holding on to her courage. "Charles will find us."

"But will he find us soon enough to save you, my pet? That's what you should be asking yourself."

"Charles will find me," she said defiantly, and she knew it was true. Charles *would* find her. Hopefully, alive, she thought with a thrill of fright.

"Oh, I intend for him to find you all right, but not perhaps, as soon as you would like," Raoul said easily. "Come along now; we cannot dawdle."

"He'll find us," Daphne repeated, as much to convince herself as him.

"I doubt it," Raoul said, dragging her along behind him. "Your ancestors must have been a sly, secretive lot. The old house is riddled with hidden passageways, and I know them all. Charles does not. And here, my pet, is our first turnoff."

Daphne couldn't guess how Raoul knew where to turn, but the next second, she was jerked in a different direction.

They had left the original staircase, but how, Daphne wondered desperately, could she mark the change? How to guide Charles? An idea occurred to her, and she dropped to her knees as if she had fallen, groping frantically for the emerald and diamond choker. Just as Raoul viciously jerked her to her feet, she managed to free the choker from her pocket and leave it on the stairs to mark their turning. Pray God, Charles noticed it.

The wetness at the neck of her gown gave her another idea, and with her free hand, she dabbed at the damp material. She clawed along the stone wall, hoping she was leaving a blood trail.

Climbing a few more steps, Daphne became aware of a change in the air. Suddenly, it was freezing, and a different kind of terror took hold of her. She knew that bone-numbing feeling. Recognized it. Sir Wesley? Or Katherine?

The iciness must have puzzled Raoul because he stopped and tested the air like an animal scenting danger. "That's bloody odd," he muttered as much to himself as Daphne. "We'll be warm soon enough, but first, there's a few twists and turns we need to take to throw off good old Charles."

In the darkness, Raoul counted the steps to the first offshoot he planned to take. Reaching it, a wall of air so intensely cold that it drove him backward prevented him from climbing in that direction. Frowning, he attempted it again, but the cold was a palpable barrier and blocked any movement up that turnoff. Perplexed but not alarmed, Raoul gave up and continued climbing. There were other offshoots ahead that would serve him as well, but to his growing bafflement, each time he sought to change course, he slammed into that impenetrable glacial barrier.

They came to a junction, the staircase from the dungeon merging with another set of stairs. All of his planned diversions cut off, a trickle of unease ran down his spine as he realized that he was being driven slowly but surely to the battlements. Baffled, he wondered about the source of the odd, bone-penetrating chill. A subterranean opening he hadn't discovered? Confident the cold would disappear as mysteriously as it had appeared, Raoul bit back a curse and yanked Daphne ever upward, heading in the only direction that lay open to him.

Daphne felt the change in course. Her neck had stopped bleeding, and uncertain if the blood streaks she'd made had even been visible against the stone walls, seeking a way to leave Charles a clue, she remembered his handkerchief in the pocket of her gown. Surreptitiously, she took it from her pocket and three steps up, dropped the square of white linen on the stairs. Oh, please dear God, she prayed, let Charles see it. And find me.

As they climbed higher, faint gray light crept down the staircase, and Raoul knew they would soon be outside on the battlements. They could take refuge from the storm, he decided, in the old tower. It wasn't the way he had planned it, but if Charles did happen to find them . . . An ugly feral gleam leaped to his eye. He might have to forego the hours of pleasure he'd planned with Daphne, although he doubted she'd find them pleasurable, but if he had to gut her before Charles's very eyes, there'd be great enjoyment in that. And then he'd kill Charles. He thought a moment. Perhaps not. Raoul giggled. Yes. He would let Charles live, knowing that for the rest of his life, Charles would suffer with his wife's final agonizing moments seared in his brain.

Chapter 21

When his lantern light picked up the glitter of the emerald and diamond choker, Charles's step faltered. Relief roared through him as he stared transfixed by those gleaming jewels. His clever darling had found a way to guide him, to give him a sign that she was still alive. Or had been when she had dropped the choker, whispered a sly voice in his brain. Pushing the voice aside, believing that somewhere ahead of him, Daphne was alive and trying to help him find her, with renewed determination, he surged up the stairs.

The lantern was a calculated risk, knowing that the light would give Raoul warning of his approach, but he saw no help for it. He could only hope that he'd spot any ambush Raoul might lay for him.

Spotting that first faint streak of blood on the wall, his heart nearly stopped as rage mingled with an aching terror. He never questioned that it was Daphne's blood, and he stared a long time at that thin crimson line, gruesome images filling his brain. Wrenching his thoughts away from the horrors that she might be enduring, Charles climbed swiftly, the occasional faint smear of scarlet guiding his steps.

He came upon the first offshoot and flashed his light up the flight of stairs. Certain Daphne would have left him a sign, he examined both the offshoot and the staircase upon which he was standing. A smear of blood on the wall of the staircase he had been climbing gave him his direction, and he rushed upward.

Rapidly, he followed Daphne's few and ever fainter marks on the walls. The staircase abruptly ended at an intersection with another wider set of stairs. Stepping onto the new stairs, he stopped and looked around him. The area looked familiar, and with a start, he realized that he was standing on the stairs that he and Daphne had first discovered. Was it only yesterday? He looked back at the offshoot he had just left and remembered that they had passed just such a turnoff on their way to the battlements. He studied the stairs for a moment. So which direction did he go? Up to the battlements or down to the ground floor?

Spotting his handkerchief lying just a few steps above where he had stopped, he sent up a prayer of thankfulness. Once again, his courageous, sweet wife had shown her resourcefulness. He bounded up the steps, racing toward the battlements. Reaching the top, he hesitated. If Raoul was waiting for him, once he stepped out onto the battlements, having both his hands full of lantern and pistol could prove disadvantageous. Reluctantly, he set the lantern down and prepared to face what lay ahead.

In the gray murkiness filtering down the steps, Daphne recognized her location. It also gave her the first glimpse of her captor. Seeing his twisted leg as he pulled her up the final steps, she understood at last the uneven gait. His left leg had been broken and set improperly, and had healed badly.

Dragging her out onto the battlements and into the drizzly rain, Raoul's gaze darted about nervously. He was uneasy and wary. Not frightened yet, but on edge, sensing that there was some other force at work in bringing him to this spot.

He would speculate later about the cause, but right now, he needed to get out of the storm and prepare for Charles's arrival because Charles was surely coming after him. His eyes fell on the old stone tower, and his grip on Daphne's arm tightened as he moved forward.

Daphne dug in her heels and clawed at the wrist that held her prisoner. A knife blade flashed in front of her eyes, and Raoul muttered, "I can kill you now as easily as later. Give me any trouble, and you'll die before you draw another breath." He ran the knife gently down the side of her throat. "And you don't want that, do you? No, you want to live and hope that Charles will come, don't you?" He smiled. "You women—you're all the same. And you'll do anything for one more breath, anything at all to live one second longer." He pulled her close and brushed his lips along her cheek. "I've never taken a woman of my own class before, but I suspect you'll be no different from all the others, sweet. Once I have you naked and writhing under my knife, you'll beg and plead just like they did."

He was, she realized sickly, truly a monster. Yet except for those empty eyes, he didn't look a monster. As tall as her husband and with the same build and the same coloring, except for the black eyes, she recognized his resemblance to Charles, although it was not marked. With his looks, position, and fortune, she wondered why he had chosen to maim and kill.

"Why?" she asked suddenly. "Why do you do it?"

He smiled and said softly, "Because I like to."

Chilled when Raoul gave her wrist a tug, hating herself for it, Daphne followed him across the battlement.

The first band of rain had blown through, and though the wind and rain had slackened slightly, the far horizon was black with the main part of the storm. Above them, the sky was gray and dreary, a few dark-skirted clouds racing overhead.

Conscious of Raoul's uneven gait as he limped toward the old stone tower, she asked, "Were you always crippled?"

He stopped and threw her a vicious look. "No. I have my dear brother and cousin to thank for that!" He laughed bitterly. "I broke my leg getting away from them and damn near died from their bullets."

"How did you get away?"

"Thinking to turn me up sweet with your interest?" Raoul inquired nastily.

Daphne shrugged. "Everyone thought you were dead, but obviously, you're not. You escaped somehow; I merely wondered how you did it."

She didn't think he'd answer her, but then he said, "Mother always feared my, er, hobby would be discovered and that I would have to flee, so at her insistence, I kept a small boat at the mouth of the cavern beneath the dungeon. It was stocked with everything I might need." He grimaced. "Of course, I never thought I'd need it or that I would be badly wounded when I did. I managed to reach it and push it into the current before I climbed in and collapsed. The river did the rest, taking me far away from Charles and Julian's orbit."

"But how did you survive so grievously wounded? Surely someone tended your wounds?" Daphne asked. She was genuinely curious, but she was also aware that if she could keep him here talking, Charles's chances of catching up with them increased.

"You ask too many questions," he said and turning away, dragged her after him.

"I do," Daphne admitted, scuffing her feet and walking as slow as she dared. "But since you plan on killing me anyway, why not tell me?"

He stopped and looked back at her again. "If for no other reason than to shut your mouth, I'll tell you. My boat eventually washed up near an old peddler's campsite, and he and his daughter, thinking I was the victim of a highwayman, tenderly nursed me for months." He smiled, and something in that smile caused Daphne to move as far away as his grasp on her wrist would allow. "And when I was healed, I killed them both, took their cart and horse, and traveled to Cornwall. To your house."

Revulsion on her face, she muttered, "With a side trip or two to pick up the jewels your mother hid for you."

"Oh, you and Charles discovered that, did you? Clever of you." His hand tightened brutally on her wrist. "Come along now. I'm tired of talking."

Jerking her after him, he set off again.

Daphne resisted as much as she dared, wondering as she did so of her fate. Would she ever see another sunrise? See Charles's beloved face again? See Adrian and April again? Or would she die beneath a madman's knife?

Her eyes filled with tears, and she fought back a sob. She didn't want to die. She wanted to live. She wanted Charles. And with gut-wrenching certainty, she knew she'd never see him again if Raoul took her into that tower. Of their own accord, her feet ceased moving.

Raoul shot her an impatient look. "If you don't stop annoying me . . ."

Daphne's jaw clenched, and her eyes bright with determination, she snapped, "You're going to kill me anyway. Why should I make it easy for you?"

Astonishing both of them, she launched herself at him. Her free hand balled into a respectable fist, she hit him in the nose with everything she had. Her fist landed with a satisfying thud, the force of her blow rocking Raoul backward. His nose broke, and blood splattered everywhere. He roared in pain, and his hold on her wrist slackened; she twitched from his grasp and sprang free.

Blood streaming from his nose, Raoul lunged forward, but Daphne scooted out of his reach.

"Bitch!" he shouted, stalking her across the battlement.

"Monster!" Daphne taunted, the wind tearing at her hair, sending it flying like a black cloud around her face. She didn't feel brave, but she knew that if she was going to die, she'd rather go down like a roaring lion than a bleating lamb.

Her only escape was down the staircase, and she edged in that direction.

Raoul knew exactly what she was up to and moved to block her. There wasn't much room to maneuver, and his crippled leg denied him speed and agility, but he had the knife, which gave him an advantage. Across the small space that separated them, they confronted one another, Daphne with the tower at her back, Raoul scuttling opposite her, the entrance to the stairs at the side of them.

Daphne gauged the distance, calculating her chances of making it to the door and down the stairs before Raoul reached her. Even with his damaged leg, he was a formidable opponent, and she knew she would have only one chance. And if she failed . . . The taste of fear in her mouth, she dashed toward the door, but even with his crablike gait, Raoul moved with astonishing speed and cut her off.

With the door to his back, he grinned at her. "Naughty, naughty," he mocked. "Do you really think I'm going to let you slip through my fingers?"

Daphne scrambled backward, putting as much distance between them as she could in the limited space. Fighting back the terror that rose within her, she made a feint to the left, but Raoul only laughed and did not move from his position.

"You may try all the tricks you want, but as long as I hold the door, you're not going anywhere," he said, his teeth baring in a parody of a smile.

Daphne eyed him, considering another wild attack. If she knocked him down the stairs . . . . She bit her lip. If she knocked him down the stairs, unless she was lucky enough for him to hit his head or break his neck in the fall, it wouldn't accomplish much. But if he broke an arm or a leg . . . She studied him, the alert stance, the knife held ready. Surprise had worked for her last time, but he was prepared now, and she abandoned the idea.

Raoul scurried forward, and she hastened back, keeping her distance. Despair and desperation her only companions, she struggled not to allow them to overcome her. Did she really believe she could best Raoul? Charles's face popped up in her mind, and her sagging spirits lifted. Give in? No, by God! All she had to do was stay alive until Charles arrived. And he *would* arrive. Pray God in time.

The wind picked up, howling around the tower; the skies became grayer and more threatening, and the drizzle turned to rain. Chilled by the wind and the rain and her wet clothing, Daphne was hardly aware of the iciness creeping into her bones as she frantically tried to find a way to escape.

She leaped back as Raoul scuttled toward her, the savage swipe of his knife narrowly missing her. Advancing, feinting, retreating, and scrambling violently, she and Raoul performed a macabre dance. All I have to do, Daphne reminded herself again and again as she avoided Raoul's knife, is stay alive until Charles can find me.

The chattering of her teeth gave her the first sign that the cold seeping into her very core was not only from the storm. Even as understanding formed in her mind, the air thickened, and a heavy mist swelled up between her and Raoul.

Raoul halted, staring puzzled at the floating, amorphous mass in front of him. He was conscious of the biting cold but more importantly, of the passing time. Charles's imminent arrival worried him more than the freezing cold and the odd mist before him. He knew his brother. Charles would not rest until he found them. No more time could be wasted on Charles's bloody inconvenient wife.

Gripping his knife, Raoul lunged at Daphne and to his astonishment, was slammed to the floor as he met an impenetrable wall of ice. He stumbled to his feet, staring at the shifting, shapeless matter as it writhed and swirled in front of him. Unnerved, he made to go around it, but it flowed with him, step for step.

What the devil was this thing? Where had it come from? The first faint quiver of fear slid through him when he realized that it had been this, this *thing* that had driven him here to the battlements. Unsettled, forgetting Daphne for the moment, he scuttled back, thinking to disappear down the stairs, but the gyrating mass flowed effortlessly behind him, preventing his escape. Worse, contorting into unimaginable shapes, the thing drove him away from the door toward the parapet. Aware that he was in the presence of something beyond his ken, Raoul watched in horror as the thickening haze grew larger and darker.

Daphne stared through the rain at Raoul's frantic efforts to escape from the relentless pursuit of that ever twisting, ever swirling vaporous energy. No matter how he sought to elude it, it followed, pressing against him, forcing him back against the parapet.

The apparition had to be Katherine, she thought vaguely. Katherine protecting me. Helping me.

Tearing her gaze away, she half ran, half stumbled toward the staircase. Only five steps separated her from it when Charles stepped out onto the battlements, a pistol in his hand. With a strangled cry, she flew into his startled embrace.

One arm locked around her, the other holding the pistol steady, he hardly dared to believe the miracle that had brought her back to him. *"Daphne!"* he cried brokenly, oblivious to the shrieking wind and rain, the numbing cold as he crushed her slim body against him. Alert for danger, he still risked a glance down into her pale, strained features. "Oh, my love, I never thought to see you again."

"You came! I knew you would," she sobbed, clinging to him, kissing his cheek, his chin, anywhere her lips could reach. "I told him you would come for me."

He stiffened, his gaze sweeping the storm-ravaged battlement. Through the rain and mist, he glimpsed Raoul near the parapet. Putting Daphne safely behind him, he stepped forward, but Daphne's hand on his arm halted him.

"Don't go," she whispered. "Don't go out there."

Charles started to argue, but the reason for the bone-biting cold and the peculiar murky haze in the midst of a raging storm suddenly dawned on him. "The ghost?" he asked in a low tone.

Daphne nodded, her eyes on Raoul. "Katherine saved me. *She* forced Raoul here."

Charles didn't question her. His arm tightened around her waist, and he turned to look in the same direction.

There was little to see, Raoul's body often obscured by the roiling, heavy mist in front of him. His arms waved madly as he punched and stabbed again and again into that writhing mass, all to no avail.

Across the space that divided them, Charles saw a look of abject terror fill his brother's face as the cloudy mass towered menacingly above him. Raoul took a half step back, his knee hitting the broken edge of the parapet. The ancient stonework crumbled, and with a scream that Charles would hear until his dying day, Raoul disappeared, plunging off the battlement.

Charles and Daphne watched mesmerized, as the mist, as if it had accomplished what it meant to do, shrank and vanished.

His face set and grim, with Daphne at his side, Charles walked to the section of parapet that Raoul had gone over. Looking down, he saw his brother's body lying still and unmoving amidst the fallen rubble. For a long time, Charles stared at Raoul's twisted form far below him. He wanted to feel sorrow, remorse at his brother's death, but he could not. Too many women had died because of him, and if Raoul had had his way, Daphne would have died by his hand. It's over, he thought numbly. It's finally over. The Monster is dead.

They kept Raoul's identity a secret. Except for the five that had been privy to Raoul's true nature, the poor man who had died so tragically in the fall from the battlements of Beaumont Place had been an itinerant peddler. Why he had been hiding in the bowels of the house and why he had attacked Daphne and Marcus remained a mystery. Amid curiosity and speculation, the peddler was buried in the pauper's field, ironically to Charles, next to the body of the unidentified woman found on the beach. There was no marker on the grave, but Charles knew he would never forget its location. Like Raoul's last scream, it would remain with him forever.

Julian and Nell, accompanied by a now-healed Marcus, had departed the morning after the burial. The two gentlemen would have liked to stay and help explore the hidden staircase, but Nell was longing for her children.

With the departure of guests, life at Beaumont Place returned almost to normal. Almost. The staircase with all its myriad junctions had yet to be fully explored, and then there was that hidden chamber . . . or so Adrian was convinced.

Three days after the peddler was buried, Adrian insisted that the wall be taken down. The old arrow slits had been opened, and lanterns and torches had been scattered up and down the staircase. Between the natural light and that provided by the torches and lanterns, the staircase, while still gloomy, was no longer shrouded in impenetrable darkness.

That sunny morning, while Adrian happily gathered up his workmen and prepared for the assault on the wall, Charles went in search of Goodson. Finding the butler polishing silver in the pantry, Charles studied him for a moment.

Becoming aware of Charles, Goodson looked up, startled. "Did you ring, sir? I'm sorry, but I didn't hear it."

"No, I didn't ring," Charles said. Pulling on his ear, he added, "Um, this is a bit awkward, but I wonder if I might borrow that crucifix of yours."

Goodson stiffened, an expression of grave disapproval crossing his face. "Sir, never tell me that you have fallen prey to my sister's outrageous tales!"

"You've never noticed anything odd about this old house? Never once felt a chill where there should be no chill?" Charles asked quietly, his gaze steady on Goodson. "Never heard the wind sounding like the faint sobbing of a woman? Never, ever caught a glimpse of something out of the corner of your eye, but when you looked, nothing was there?"

For a moment, their gazes held, then Goodson sighed. "I will get it for you."

And that, thought Charles, was that. Goodson might not admit it, but the butler wasn't above believing in ghosts, either.

Armed with the crucifix, Charles was almost sanguine as he joined the two servants and Adrian on the landing.

Daphne and April stood on the stairs a few steps above the landing, their expressions expectant. Excited anticipation was in the air as the hefty stable boy lifted the sledgehammer and struck a mighty blow, his companion following after with a powerful swing of the pickax.

Stone chips flew as the two servants worked in rhythm with each other. The work went fast, and Charles had actually begun to believe that Sir Wesley might not make an appearance when the now familiar bone-etching chill hit him.

His eyes met Daphne's. She felt it, too. Everyone did, the two servants stopping their work as if they'd been frozen where they stood.

Adrian looked around, puzzled. "It's dashed cold in here all of sudden, isn't it?"

"Hmmm, yes, I believe it is," Charles drawled, wondering from which direction Sir Wesley would strike. He gazed down the stairs, almost relieved to see a faint dark shape forming in the shadows. No one else had seen it yet. "These old houses," he said idly, "well, they have odd humors, don't they?" His fingers closed around the crucifix, and he took a step to the edge of the landing, placing himself directly in the path of the rising menace. Eyes locked on it, he murmured, "Shall we continue? The sooner we discover what is behind that wall, the sooner we can warm ourselves by the fire." Nodding to the servants, he said, "Continue, please."

At his words, the blackness billowed up from the bottom of the staircase. Like a thick, black fog, it loomed over them, the cold rage emanating from the mass nearly knocking

Charles down. But he remained on his feet and whipping out the crucifix, he held it aloft and said, "Go and never return. You cannot stop us, and we *will* find what you have hidden. May God forgive you for what you have done."

To his very great relief and no little astonishment, his incantation worked. Or perhaps it was the crucifix, Charles thought slowly. It didn't matter. What mattered was that as suddenly as it had appeared, the iciness was gone, and the black, roiling mass melted away.

There was a moment of stunned silence, then Adrian demanded, "What the devil was that? What did you do?"

Putting the crucifix away, Charles looked back at him. A faint flush on his cheeks, he muttered, "Ah, I have been taking lessons from Mrs. Darby. I did that rather well, didn't I?"

"Rather too well," remarked his wife dryly. "You nearly frightened the rest of us to death."

He smiled at her. "You have my word I shall never do it again."

"Oh, but it was a splendid trick," Adrian said, his eyes narrowed and suspicious. "I want you to teach it to me."

"Absolutely not!" said Daphne firmly. Smiling at him, she added, "Shall we find out what is behind that wall?"

Distracted, Adrian promptly forgot about learning any magic tricks and urged his workmen on.

The wall proved to be surprisingly easy to break through—a half dozen more blows, and a small hole appeared. Several minutes later, they had demolished a section large enough for everyone to scramble through. With Adrian leading the way, they entered an antechamber and pushing open the heavy wood door at the end of it, a room was discovered. A room untouched for hundreds of years.

Concealed deep within the walls of Beaumont place where neither water, nor light, nor heat, not even the bitter cold of a December night had penetrated for centuries, the room revealed its secrets. There were signs of decay and age, but overall, the room and its contents were almost perfectly preserved.

It was a sealed tomb, Daphne thought as her gaze moved around the tapestry-hung walls. A splendid rug lay on the stone floor. Bed hangings of gold and cream silk draped the huge bed. Faggots were neatly stacked next to the hearth of a huge gold-veined marble fireplace.

Filled with dread, her steps lagging, Daphne approached the bed. A small woman, her once young skin mottled and dried with age, her long golden hair streaming out behind her, lay curled in the center of the bed. In her arms, Daphne saw that she held an infant. The woman's cheek lay tenderly on that misshapen head, the babe cradled protectively in the woman's arms. Around the two bodies, there was an ugly array of rusty brown stains, and at first, Daphne assumed they had come from the birthing of the child. Her breath caught as her gaze rested on the bodice of the woman's once white linen gown—the same rusty stains were there, too. Only then did she notice the dagger, its blade dark with what could only be blood, resting on the edge of the bed.

So much was clear to Daphne as she stood staring at the pitiful remains. She understood now why the little ghost had appeared to her, revealing that first night the outline of the door that opened onto the concealed staircase. Katherine had wanted to be found. She had wanted justice for herself and her babe. And she came to my aid, Daphne realized, to stop Raoul from murdering me as Sir Wesley had murdered her. Everything made sense, especially Sir Wesley's attempt to keep them from discovering this room. Even from beyond the grave, he'd not wanted his evil deeds to be found out.

Daphne's fingers lightly touched the cold, stiff shoulder of the woman on the bed. But you foiled him, didn't you, Katherine? she thought.

If the death of the peddler had caused a stir, the discovery of the bodies of the woman and her child in the concealed room at Beaumont Place was ten times worse. Everyone from

Lord Trevillyan down to the lowliest scullery maid in the neighborhood had questions, and speculation was rife.

Before the burial two days later, a close examination of the bodies by the local physician determined that the infant had been female and had died from a crushed skull. The woman had died either by her own hand or had been murdered. She had been, in the physician's opinion, stabbed in the chest, but he would not speculate further.

It was obvious from the room and its contents that the woman had been of high birth, and it was assumed she was a member of the Beaumont family. The two bodies were quietly interred in a place of honor in the family graveyard. For the present, a marble angel holding a laughing infant in its arms marked the grave; a name and date would be inscribed once their identity was established.

It was difficult for Daphne not to blurt out the truth, but then explaining how she knew would have created all sorts of problems. However, knowing that the bodies were those of Katherine and her newborn, Daphne was able to gently guide the search where she wanted it.

The room itself proved the richest source of information. Calling on the expertise of a scholar from London well-known for the study of ancient artifact, from the items and furnishings, he had dated the room to the mid-1500s. Within a decade or two, he reminded them with a wry smile before departing for London.

Once they started searching in that time frame, the clues were everywhere, especially since Daphne, ably assisted by Charles, made certain to point everyone in that direction. From the church records, the date of Sir Wesley's marriage to Katherine Lehman on October 2nd, 1557, was found. Records of Sir Wesley's death in early 1559 were also found. It was telling that there was no record of Katherine's death. After her marriage to Sir Wesley, she vanished from all the public records that they could find.

The Lehman family in Cornwall had died out sometime in

the 1700s, but in his collection, the vicar had most of the Lehman family papers and, to Daphne's great joy, several letters from Katherine to her mother. Those letters were a treasure trove of information, but they made for unhappy reading as the details of Katherine's wretched marriage to Sir Wesley were revealed. Katherine's fear of her husband, her loneliness and longing to be with her family came through in every line she had written. In one letter, Daphne discovered the reason Katherine had been banished to the room off the secret staircase. Heavy with child, terrified of her fate and that of her child should she deliver a girl instead of the son her husband so desperately wanted, she had tried to flee to her father's home. Betrayed by a servant, Sir Wesley and his men had caught her within five miles of Beaumont Place and dragged her back. He had ordered her placed under guard and safely locked away until she gave birth to his heir.

There was only one letter after that, dated November of 1558.

> *Mother,* Katherine had written in her heart-breakingly childish hand, *I long most desperately to see you and feel your gentle arms around me. My time is near, and oh, the joy that would be mine if I could only be at home with you and Father and my dear little brothers. I miss everyone. Kiss them all for me and tell them I love them.*
>
> *It is lonely here in this prison he has made for me, and I yearn only for the day I shall hold my baby in my arms. I am frightened of the future. I cannot bear to think what will happen should the child be a girl. A son is all he can speak of, and I fear his rage and terrible temper if I do not bear an heir. Pray for me.*

Prayers, Daphne thought grimly as she set the letter aside, hadn't been enough to save Katherine from Sir Wesley's wrath. As surely as if she had seen it with her own eyes, she was convinced that in a blind rage, Sir Wesley had smashed the skull of his newborn daughter and then stabbed his wife. She knew it. She just couldn't prove it. No one could.

It wasn't a great deal to go upon, but from what evidence they had found, even the vicar concluded that the woman and baby were most likely Katherine and her newborn daughter.

And so it was on a fine afternoon in late June, Daphne and the others gathered at the gravesite as the inscription was chiseled into the marble base of the statue marking Katherine's grave. His work done, the craftsman gathered his tools, doffed his cap, and left for Penzance.

The rest of the family wandered off, leaving Daphne and Charles alone at the gravesite.

Seeing his wife's woeful expression, Charles slid his arm around her waist and murmured, "It happened a long time ago, my love. You had nothing to do with it."

Daphne sniffed and wiped at her eyes. "I know all that—it is just so sad. She was so young. Just a child herself. She didn't deserve to be murdered by a wretched old man who was furious with her because *he* hadn't been able to sire a son. I hope he rots in hell. None of it was her fault." She looked up at Charles. "We owe her so much. She saved me from Raoul. She couldn't save herself, but she saved me."

Charles nodded. "She was brave and resourceful, rather like you."

"Oh, Charles!"

"Oh, Daphne!" he teased. His gaze rested on the marble angel. "She gave us our future; we shall not squander it."

"No. We shan't." Daphne hugged him. "We are so lucky. We have each other, and we have love." And come next January, she thought dreamily, we shall have a child. Her hand crept to touch her still flat stomach. A girl. And I will name her . . . Katherine.

GREAT BOOKS, GREAT SAVINGS!

When You Visit Our Website:
www.kensingtonbooks.com
You Can Save Money Off The Retail Price
Of Any Book You Purchase!

- All Your Favorite Kensington Authors
- New Releases & Timeless Classics
- Overnight Shipping Available
- eBooks Available For Many Titles
- All Major Credit Cards Accepted

Visit Us Today To Start Saving!
www.kensingtonbooks.com

All Orders Are Subject To Availability.
Shipping and Handling Charges Apply.
Offers and Prices Subject To Change Without Notice.

LP413   157